THE
MADAGASKAR
PLAN

THE
MADAGASKAR
PLAN

A Novel

Guy Saville

HENRY HOLT AND COMPANY   NEW YORK

Henry Holt and Company, LLC
Publishers since 1866
175 Fifth Avenue
New York, New York 10010
www.henryholt.com

Henry Holt® and ® are registered trademarks of Henry Holt and Company, LLC.

Distributed in Canada by Raincoast Book Distribution Limited

Library of Congress Cataloging-in-Publication Data

Saville, Guy, 1973–
The Madagaskar plan : a novel / Guy Saville.—First edition.
    pages ; cm
ISBN 978-0-8050-9595-1 (hardback)—ISBN 978-0-8050-9596-8 (electronic copy)
1. World War, 1939–1945—Fiction.   2. Madagascar—Fiction.   I. Title.
PR6119.A953M33 2015
823'.92—dc23
2014041147

Henry Holt books are available for special promotions and premiums.
For details contact: Director, Special Markets.

Published in the United Kingdom in 2015 by Hodder & Stoughton

First Edition 2015

Designed by Meryl Sussman Levavi

Printed in the United States of America

10 9 8 7 6 5 4 3 2 1

Once again
to
my own Cole

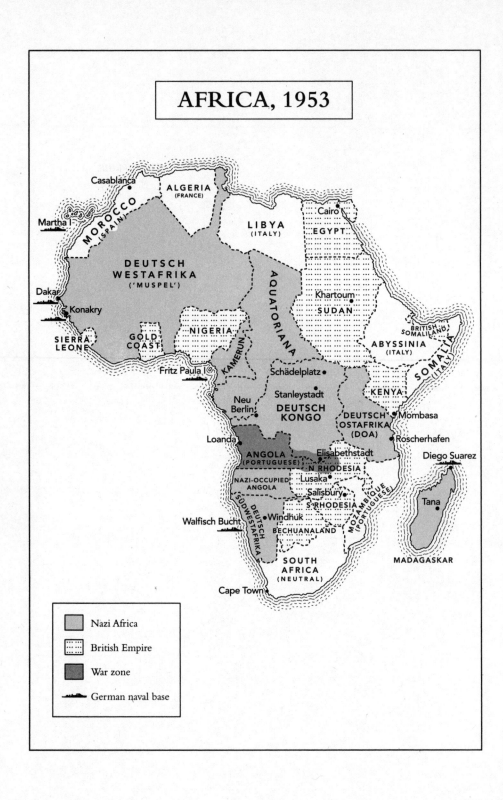

AFRICA, 1953

Casablanca

ALGERIA
(FRANCE)

Martha I.

MOROCCO
(SPAIN)

LIBYA
(ITALY)

Cairo

EGYPT

DEUTSCH
WESTAFRIKA
('MUSPEL')

Khartoum

SUDAN

Dakar

Konakry

NIGERIA

GOLD
COAST

SIERRA
LEONE

AQUATORIANA

BRITISH
SOMALILAND

ABYSSINIA
(ITALY)

SOMALIA
(ITALY)

Fritz Paula I.

KAMERUN

Schädelplatz

Neu
Berlin

Stanleystadt

DEUTSCH
KONGO

KENYA

DEUTSCH
OSTAFRIKA
(DOA)

Mombasa

Loanda

Roscherhafen

Elisabethstadt

Diego Suarez

ANGOLA
(PORTUGUESE)

N RHODESIA

NAZI-OCCUPIED
ANGOLA

Lusaka

Tana

Salisbury

DEUTSCH
SÜDWESTAFRIKA

S RHODESIA

MOZAMBIQUE
(PORTUGUESE)

Walfisch Bucht

Windhuk

BECHUANALAND

MADAGASKAR

SOUTH
AFRICA
(NEUTRAL)

Cape Town

	Nazi Africa
	British Empire
	War zone
	German naval base

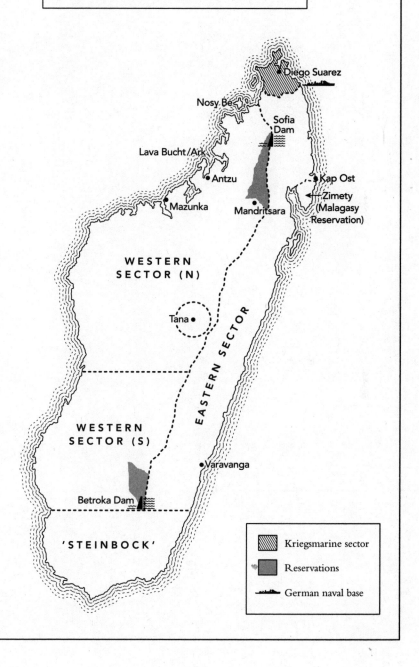

MADAGASKAR, 1953

Diego Suarez

Nosy Be

Sofia
Dam

Lava Bucht/Ark

Antzu

Kap Ost

Mazunka

Zimety
(Malagasy
Reservation)

Mandritsara

**WESTERN
SECTOR (N)**

EASTERN SECTOR

Tana

**WESTERN
SECTOR (S)**

Varavanga

Betroka Dam

'STEINBOCK'

▨	Kriegsmarine sector
▧	Reservations
⚓	German naval base

I hope the concept of the Jews
will be completely extinguished
through the possibility of a large
emigration to Africa or some
other colony.

—HEINRICH HIMMLER
Memorandum to Adolf Hitler,
25 May 1940

+ + +

Despite the Führer's ideological
misgivings, it is my belief that
this weapon can deliver us the
final victory in Africa.

—WALTER HOCHBURG
Top-secret communiqué to Germania,
22 March 1953

Those with a detailed knowledge of northern Madagascar will notice that I have taken certain liberties with the geography—this has been for the sake of the narrative. For the same reason, I have simplified the tussling array of organizations, departments, and individuals that the Nazis would have employed to run their "Madagaskar Plan." I hope experts in both fields will indulge this license.

THE
MADAGASKAR
PLAN

The World, 1940–52

FOR A FEW hours in May 1940, it was hoped that British forces at Dunkirk might escape. Then Hitler gave the order to destroy them.

The disaster that followed saw thousands of British troops killed and a quarter of a million taken prisoner. Prime Minister Churchill resigned. He was succeeded by Lord Halifax, who judged the public mood of dread and sued for peace. In October that year, Britain and Germany came to terms, signing a nonaggression pact and creating the Council of New Europe. The occupied countries—France, Belgium, the Netherlands, Denmark, and Norway—were granted autonomy under right-wing governments and took their place alongside Italy, Spain, and Portugal. Although weakened, Britain's empire continued to span the globe.

With his western borders secure, Hitler launched a surprise invasion of Russia in 1941; two years later the Soviet Union was no more. The Reich now extended from the Rhine to the Ural Mountains; its capital was renamed Germania. Those around the Führer began calling for the reacquisition of the colonies Germany had lost after the Versailles Treaty. "On the day when we've solidly organized Europe," Hitler told an expectant SS audience in response, "we shall look toward Africa."

The armies of the Reich marched to the equator, conquering a vast swath of land from the Sahara to the Belgian Congo. As this new territory edged nearer the borders of the British Empire, Hitler and Halifax agreed on further peace accords guaranteeing the two countries' mutual neutrality. The culmination was the Casablanca Conference of 1943, during which the continent was divided—Churchill said "cleaved"—between the two powers. Britain would retain its interests in East Africa; Germany would take the west. Other negotiations granted Mussolini a small Italian empire, while Portugal kept its colonies of Angola and Mozambique.

Throughout these upheavals the United States remained staunchly isolationist.

Germany's African empire was divided into six provinces. Gradually civilian and military administrations were replaced by SS governors, answerable to Himmler but semi-autonomous and with almost unlimited power. The most ambitious was the governor of Kongo, Walter Hochburg. The builder of gleaming new cities and an African autobahn network, Hochburg ruthlessly exploited the continent's natural resources to "stiffen the sinews of Europe." He was also responsible for the wholesale deportation of the black population to the Sahara and a fate few dared to question.

Despite a decade of peace and prosperity, Hochburg remained restless: he wanted the swastika to fly over all of Africa. In 1952, he attacked Portuguese Angola and began preparing to invade British Northern Rhodesia. The Colonial Office in London, along with elements in Germania who feared Hochburg's growing power, decided to move against him. They arranged a botched assassination attempt to provoke Hochburg into invading Rhodesia prematurely, forcing him to fight on two fronts and overextend himself. Defeat would mean the end of his ambitions.

On 21 September 1952, even as the German army was bogged down in Angola, Hochburg ordered his panzers into Rhodesia. He assured Hitler of a swift victory . . .

THERE HAD BEEN no news since the morning they parted. No telegrams, no letters, no breathless messengers arriving with the dawn. Not a word from Burton in five weeks and a day, only radio reports that she didn't want to hear: war in Kongo and thousands slaughtered. She had struggled not to count every single hour.

Madeleine Cranley lay on her side, sheets wrapped around her, and tried to sleep. Her long dark hair spilled over the pillow. Inside she sensed the fluttering of the child she was carrying. She was five months now, the baby due in February. Whenever she ate with her husband she made a display of gorging herself, hoping the extra weight would disguise her belly. Her throat was constantly stuck with unwanted food: cakes and puddings and gravy churned with acid. Her jaw ached from grinding.

In the hallway the clock chimed the half hour, then two o'clock. Madeleine flickered in and out of consciousness; at some point she reached over and switched off the light.

The tension in her face began to slacken, warmth enveloped her . . . and as dreams offered their respite, she heard distant footsteps. She imagined they were Burton's. He had gone to Africa to kill the SS governor of Kongo, his heart unshakable with revenge; she'd pleaded with him not to. Now he was back . . . sliding into bed like he did on their rare nights together, his body cold and welcome, smelling of musk and wood smoke. Before she relented to his arms, she wanted him to know how furious she was with him, how he had driven her almost insane with worry. He whispered an apology—but she no longer needed it; to have him home was enough. They were going to spend the future together.

A guttering breath escaped her: Burton would never come here.

Her mind roamed over the other possibilities of the household. She didn't recognize the familiar pad of the servants, and it couldn't be her husband; he was away tonight on business. Nor did the footsteps belong to her daughter, Alice. They were too clodding, too cumbersome.

There was a stranger in the house.

Madeleine turned on the lamp and strained to hear. The house creaked quietly. Had she imagined the footsteps? For years after she'd arrived in Britain as a refugee, the sound of boots on hollow stairs had fractured her dreams.

She thought she'd heard them come from the floor above, pass her door, and go down the main staircase. Thick soles muffled by carpet.

Madeleine untangled herself from the bedsheets and, mind still fuzzy, went to the landing. The light was on, though the house should have been in darkness. She climbed the staircase, aware of the unwieldy weight of her stomach. There were two levels above her: at the very top the servants' quarters, below that the floor where guests stayed and Alice's room.

She opened the door as silently as possible, in case she'd been dreaming all along. Her lungs tightened. Alice's bedside lamp was on, illuminating the tumble of her daughter's room—but the bed was empty. Madeleine slid her hand beneath the covers: the mattress was baby warm.

"Elli?" It was her pet name for Alice. "Elli?" For some reason, she was whispering.

There was a connecting door to the playroom. Madeleine opened it: nothing but darkness and the glint of rocking-horse eyes. Fog pressed against the window. Back in the bedroom, she checked the wardrobe. Sometimes Alice would stow away beneath piles of blankets and teddy bears. It, too, was empty. She thought of the time Elli had gone missing on Burton's farm. *Don't worry,* he'd said, *we'll find her.* His tone was so confident, so settling.

Madeleine returned to the floor below and hung over the balustrade. "Elli?" she called.

The housekeeper, Mrs. Anderson, appeared: black dress, hair in a tight black bun. She possessed a servility that made Madeleine tense, aware that as the mistress of the house she was more foreign than the Polish gardener.

"Have you seen Elli?"

Mrs. Anderson let a rare smile shrink her lips. "Alice"—she enunciated the syllables—"is with us downstairs."

"What's she doing?"

"Nothing you need concern yourself with, Mrs. Cranley."

"It's the middle of the night! My daughter should be in bed."

"As should you."

"What did you say?"

Another smile tautened Mrs. Anderson's face; then she was gone.

Madeleine strode to her room to fetch dressing gown and slippers; she wanted her toes covered before confronting the housekeeper. She pushed through the door and stopped short. Her arms clutched her belly.

On the bed was a suitcase. The battered suitcase she had fled Vienna with fourteen years earlier, after the *Anschluss*, when the Nazis took over the country.

"I thought I told you to throw this away. Yet Mrs. Anderson informs me it's been hidden in the cellar since you moved in."

It was her husband, Jared.

He was a senior civil servant at the Colonial Office and dressed in his uniform of charcoal-black pinstriped suit and waistcoat; the smell of the night lingered on the cloth: autumnal, damp, penetrating. Brilliantine darkened his blond hair. His eyes looked rheumy, as if he had recently wept. He was packing the case.

Madeleine said, "I thought you were away tonight."

"I had some good news: rushed back to share it with you."

"Is that why Elli's downstairs?"

"You really mustn't call her that. It sounds too German. People talk enough as it is."

Jared continued to pack. There seemed no logic to the items he chose: summer dresses, wool stockings, her favorite cardigan. He reached for a silk camisole, scrunching it in his fist. "I don't remember buying this. It looks cheap."

Madeleine recognized it as a gift from Burton. Heat prickled her cheeks. In the past month there had been plenty of such innocent provocations. At breakfast Jared had taken to reading aloud headlines from the *Times*—"NAZIS BEATEN BACK TO KONGO BORDER"; "SIEGE OF ELISABETHSTADT BEGINS"—and asking what she felt about so many soldiers being butchered in Africa. But he couldn't know. How could he sit there eating toast, sipping his tea, with the knowledge that across the table his wife was pregnant with another man's child? Exhaustion was making her paranoid.

She made her voice as sweet and light as possible: "Are we going somewhere?"

He ignored the question and buried the camisole deep in the case. Unsure what to do, Madeleine waited in silence for her husband to finish, hands continuing to protect her abdomen, her bare feet growing cold. Finally he threw in some bottles of perfume, snapped the lid shut, and lifted the suitcase to test its weight.

"We don't want it too heavy." He looked her in the eye. "Not in your condition."

Madeleine felt the press of her bladder. She forced a laugh. "What condition?"

Jared let the case drop and crossed the room until he was looming over her. She wanted to take a step back—but refused.

He reached for her pajama top. She'd bought three new pairs recently, all a size too big, with Empire lines to hide her waist. He teased the ends, then began to undo the buttons. His movements might have been seductive if not for the rawness of his eyes. His smooth, manicured hands encircled her stomach, only a thin barrier of skin separating his splayed fingers from her baby.

Madeleine couldn't help herself: she retreated.

In response he leaned forward as if to kiss her ear and whispered something. It was so soft, Madeleine could hardly catch it.

It sounded like *I know*.

                                                                              ✦ ✦ ✦

From somewhere the bitter tang of cigarettes. Madeleine took another step back and found herself against the door. The fingers ensnaring her belly pressed harder, till the pressure rose into her rib cage. The baby kicked.

"Jared, please, you're hurting me."

He spoke again: this time a declaration. His face was like cold wax, the nonchalance of the previous weeks gone. "I know about you and your lover—"

A rushing in her ears, simultaneously high-pitched and deafening, a low rumble. She needed to sit down.

"—the farm. The little life you were planning together. I've known since the spring."

Madeleine shook her head.

"Everything I gave you," he continued, "and this is how you repay me."

For a long time she'd known this moment would come and had rehearsed her response. She wanted to rebuke him for the way he had shrunk her world even as it expanded to ball-gown dinners and hotel suites in the capitals of Europe. The way he told her not to eat as though she were a navvy, or his disapproval if she smiled too graciously at a doorman. *Every-*

one should know their place, Madeleine. How she had spent years playing the part of a wife—gladly at first, sincerely—without believing his role as a husband. Madeleine felt no urge to justify, she just wanted to explain. Burton wasn't the cause of their estrangement; he simply offered her the life she wanted. But now, seeing Jared's eyes ringed with tears, the remorse welled in her.

"It was never like that." More than once, the guilt had made her spurn Burton. She reached for her husband, grazing the dark fabric of his jacket. "I'm sorry, Jared. I . . ."

He snatched his hand away, showed his back. His shoulders gave a slight judder. For a long moment, neither of them spoke. Madeleine thought she heard someone behind the door, listening in on them; that hint of cigarettes again.

"I shall give you a choice," said her husband. "You can either leave tonight or"—he swallowed, his throat clicking as if the next words were rancid—"or I'll forgive you everything. We can continue as before. A termination would be best, but if that's too much I'm prepared to raise the child as my own. No one need ever know."

Madeleine found herself dumb.

"Well?"

"Jared, I . . . I . . ."

"Choose." When she didn't reply, he repeated himself; this time she heard something creep into his tone. Contempt, brutality.

She stepped forward and reached for the case. "I need to get dressed."

"You'd really choose him over all this?" He motioned to the room. Madeleine followed his hand, held open like an emperor's: the Spink & Edgar bed, linen from Peter Reed, wardrobes choked with this season's fashions, drawers that hid the diamond rings and pearls she'd never cared for. She thought of the drafty, bare rooms of the farmhouse and how comfortable she was there.

"I'm sorry, Jared. I love him."

"Did you ever love me?"

"I can't remember anymore."

He removed the case from her grip, set it down. "There's one other thing. Before you make your decision—"

"It's too late for that."

From his jacket he produced an envelope and placed it in her hands. "I told you I rushed home. I've been expecting this for weeks, and couldn't wait to share it."

The seal had been broken. There was a cover letter and a dozen typed pages of names.

"I don't understand," said Madeleine.

It was a communiqué from the Admiralty about a British warship in the Gulf of Kamerun. HMS *Ibis*. Sunk, presumed torpedoed by the Kriegsmarine, the German navy. The *Ibis:* it meant nothing to her, and yet there was a stirring in Madeleine's gut that wasn't the baby. Thirty men had been pulled alive from the water. All other hands were lost.

She looked up at Jared.

"The second sheet," he said. "A list of the deceased."

Madeleine turned to the page, scanned the names. It was at the bottom: Burton Cole.

Suddenly the whole world was sliding to one side, as if she were on the stricken ship herself. The papers tumbled from her hand, floating across Cranley's shoes. She struggled to breathe, each lungful shallow yet needing all her effort.

"Everything went wrong in Kongo," said her husband, the tiniest shard of delight audible in his words. "He had to flee—to Angola. And then a ship back home. Or so your lover thought."

"Kongo." She could barely speak. "How do you know about Kongo?"

"Who do you think sent him there? Planned his reunion with Hochburg?"

"You?"

"Cole was the perfect tool for the job, though kept unawares about the Colonial Office. He snared Hochburg in our trap of invading Rhodesia and, once he'd served his purpose, was left to die."

She was shaking, almost doubled over, seeing the man who had been her husband for the first time. It was like that one occasion he had lashed out. A single blow to the stomach that put her on her knees; she couldn't even remember what she'd done. Afterward Jared apologized for his lapse in control, swore it wouldn't happen again as he filled the house with enough lilies to make her nauseous. She never told Burton about it.

"It should make your decision easier." His tone was businesslike, the civil servant briefing his minister. "I presume you'll be staying. I'm sure we can put this silly little affair behind us—"

She leapt at him, clawing his face. Her nails came away red.

Cranley shoved her back. Madeleine stumbled and fell; the baby bounced sickeningly inside her, like a stone.

Her husband stepped forward, treading on the lists of drowned sailors.

His fingers bunched into a fist. She caught the glint of his wedding ring: it would break her front teeth.

"All the scorn I endured for you," he said. "Jared Cranley, the man who could have had *any* woman he desired, yet married a Jewish domestic. Did it for love." He reached for his handkerchief, let out a snort. "I've heard it said that I'm the most romantic man in London."

With a sob, Madeleine stood up, grabbed the case, and opened the door. She'd find Alice, flee to the farm.

"This is Mr. Lyall," said Cranley.

A man with a squashed nose and thick beard barred her way. He was dressed in a black suit that looked as if it had been slept in. The stench of cigarettes around him was enough to make her wince.

She tried to pass, but he blocked her path. Tried again, this time swinging the case at him. The clasp came loose, showering the room in clothes. Madeleine shoved past—then was on the floor, the small of her back stinging. She had no strength to stand up; she was crumbling inside with grief.

Lyall brandished a truncheon. He prodded it against her mouth.

"You always had a beautiful smile," said Cranley. He looked at the garments strewn around the room. "Forget the case," he said to Lyall. "I just want her gone."

As Madeleine was yanked to her feet, she heard her pajamas rip. "What about Alice?" she asked.

"She'll have everything she needs: a beautiful home, a doting father. I know Mrs. Anderson will make an excellent governess."

"Promise?"

"You might be a Jewish whore, but Alice is still my daughter." He dabbed the blood on his cheek with the handkerchief. "It would be better if there are no hysterics as you leave. I don't want her upset."

"And me?"

His tone brokered no reasoning, no pleading: "Better than you deserve."

"Come on, Mrs. Cranley," said Lyall, gripping her arm.

He dragged her into the hallway. At the bottom of the stairs, the front door was open to the fog outside. Waiting below, also in a black suit, was a pudgy man pacing back and forth. Over his arm was one of Madeleine's fur coats; in his fist, a revolver.

"Where are you taking me?" she asked.

A memory shrieked in her mind: the time the Nazis came for her father in Vienna. The pounding on the door, the house swarming with uniforms and weapons. Her mother had asked the same question. *Just some forms to fill out*, soothed one of the brownshirts. Papa returned two days later, his tie missing, shirt filthy, unable to stop shaking.

"It's all arranged," said Lyall. "Won't take long to get there."

Madeleine dug her feet into the carpet. Made her legs rigid.

Lyall forced her to the edge of the staircase. "My wife had a miscarriage once, silly old thing. Fell down some steps."

She struggled a moment longer, then went limp, hugging her stomach. As Madeleine was led away, she twisted round for a final look at her husband.

Cranley was framed in the doorway of her room. He glanced at her for a second, then went back to examining the blood on his handkerchief. At his feet were the names of the dead.

PART I

BRITAIN

All that he held dear—hearth
and family, belief and belonging—
had been taken from him.

—ELEANOR COLE
Letter to her sister, 1930

CHAPTER ONE

Schädelplatz, Deutsch Kongo
26 January 1953, 06:30

PANZER CREWS CALLED it *Nashornstahl:* rhino steel. It was supposed to be impregnable. A girder of it had been welded across the entrance.

There was a crackling boom, like thunder heard from within a storm cloud, and the door exploded. Shards of metal and flame flew down the corridor. Before the smoke cleared, Belgian guerrillas poured through the barricade, kicking aside the mangled girder. Among the Europeans were black faces.

Oberstgruppenführer Walter Hochburg felt a shudder of incredulity. Then the fury swelled in him, his black eyes glittering.

No nigger, no breathing nigger, had ever set foot in the Schädelplatz, his secret headquarters. He raised his rifle above the sandbags—it was a BK44, the one Himmler had awarded him—and lashed the trigger. Waffen-SS troops fired alongside him.

More guerrillas surged into the passageway.

"Stand your ground," roared Hochburg. His voice was a raw baritone.

To either side of him, men were retreating to the next redoubt. Hochburg followed with a slack stride, certain of his invincibility, his rifle searching out dark skin. He reached the second wall of sandbags and dipped behind them to reload.

"Oberstgruppenführer!"

Before him was his new deputy, Gruppenführer Zelman: flat-faced, blond, unblinking. The buttons on his uniform were as untarnished as virgin silver. He had emerged from a side passage.

"What news?" asked Hochburg.

Zelman huddled low. "A thousand guerrillas, maybe more, including artillery. The main entrance and southern walls have been breached. We can't hold out much longer."

"Where are my helicopters?"

"You must leave, Oberstgruppenführer. Immediately. Your bodyguards are waiting to escort you to Stanleystadt." Stanleystadt: Kongo's great northern city.

"And have the blacks in our sanctum? Never." There shouldn't be a single negroid within a thousand kilometers of the Schädelplatz. Hochburg slammed a fresh magazine into his BK44. "Get a rifle in your hand and fight. You, the auxiliary staff, kitchen porters, every last man."

"I didn't come to Africa to die, Oberstgruppenführer."

"Then you have no right to be here."

Not for the first time Hochburg regretted dismissing Kepplar, his former deputy. Whatever his failings, there was a man who would have relished defending the Schädelplatz. Zelman was a cousin of Reinhard Heydrich's wife and had been assigned to him after the invasion of Rhodesia faltered. *To keep an eye on me*, Hochburg told him the day he arrived.

A grenade landed between them.

Zelman grabbed Hochburg and yanked him into the side passage. The blast turned the entrance into a cascade of bricks.

"I would have thrown it back," said Hochburg as he got to his feet, swiping away the dust. When the attack woke him, he had put on his black dress uniform, the material straining against the brawn of his shoulders; now it was floured and torn.

Zelman led the way through the stone corridors of the Schädelplatz, till they turned into the main thoroughfare. Hochburg stopped abruptly.

He had been here fifteen minutes earlier, demanding the base at Kondolele get his gunships airborne. There should have been sentries by the door; instead, only the smell of the wind. He pushed his deputy to one side and stepped into the command center. The cloud-riddled dawn shone down on him, wands of orange and coral-pink light.

Hochburg felt a shifting inside himself. "It can't be . . ." he said. It sounded like his jackboots were treading on snails.

The command center had taken a direct hit. In the middle of the room, the table map of central Africa was broken in two; above it, jigsaw pieces of sky. The black triangles that represented units of the Waffen-SS lay scattered on the floor. Hochburg stooped to pick one up, rolled it in his fingers as if it were a divining stone. Bodies were strewn on the floor, cables sparked. Only the telex machines seemed unaffected: they continued the merry chatter of war. By now he should have been the master of Northern Rhodesia, its copper mines serving the Reich, its cities and dusty plateaus cleansed of the negroid threat. His panzers had invaded the previous year and found British forces waiting for them. The swift victory he'd promised became a protracted retreat, the British eventually crossing the border and encircling Elisabeth-stadt, Kongo's third city. A pendulum siege of attack and counterattack had lasted ever since. With Hochburg's army engaged in the south, the remnants of the Belgian Force Publique took advantage of the situation and launched a full-scale guerrilla war in the north. The Belgians, the previous rulers of Kongo, had been fighting an insurgency since the swastika was raised over the colony a decade earlier; now they were emboldened.

A female radio operator was beseeching her mouthpiece. Hochburg buried the black triangle in his pocket and placed his hand on her shoulder. Her hair was thick with dust, the right side of her face burned. "Any word on the helicopters, Fräulein?"

"We lost the line to Kondolele, Oberstgruppenführer."

"Reinforcements?"

"Stanleystadt reports that a new offensive started against the city an hour before dawn. They can't spare any manpower."

"You must leave," said Zelman.

Hochburg scraped his palm over his bald scalp. "No."

"With respect, Oberstgruppenführer, if you're captured, they'll parade you in the streets of Lusaka—"

"You think I care?"

"Germania* might, especially when you stand before a Negro court."

Hochburg sighed. "You would be more convincing, Zelman, if you weren't so desperate to save yourself."

"You can't command a counteroffensive from here. Stanleystadt is your better hope."

"This place is my home."

"There are no helicopters, not enough men. It's already lost."

The radio operator put up her hand to speak. "The Schädelplatz is more than the walls around us. It is an ideal. A beacon for our hearts." She was too shy to look at Hochburg. "As long as you survive, Oberstgruppen-führer, so will it."

"The girl's right," said Zelman. "We don't have to die."

Hochburg considered her words, unwilling to admit the truth. He

---

*Capital of the Reich, formerly Berlin.

patted her gently. "There's nothing more you can do. Come with us—you'll be safer."

"I shall stay, Herr Oberstgruppenführer. I'll keep trying to reach the helicopters."

"You see, Zelman. Give me a battalion of girls and this war would already be won."

He stormed from the room, his rifle held ready.

"Where are you going?" Zelman called after him.

Back in the passageways, the lights flickered above Hochburg. There were sporadic snorts of gunfire, and the shouts of Belgian guerrillas echoed along the walls. He was disappointed not to cross any as he made his way to his study.

The Leibwachen—his personal bodyguard—was waiting outside. He had dismissed them earlier as, goaded by Zelman, they fretted over his every move. All were dressed in dark combat fatigues with BK44 assault rifles. One held Fenris—his Rhodesian ridgeback—on a leash. Hochburg cupped the dog's face in his hands, inhaled his gamey breath.

The French windows of the study had been blown inward, showering the floor with glass. A spectral smoke clung to the air. "Bring me some gasoline," said Hochburg, casting his eyes over the walls of books. "Then get down into the square and secure the area. Somebody carry the dog."

He flopped down at his desk, unlocked a drawer, and took out a piece of tightly bound sacking. Inside was a knife. There was a blink of silver as he withdrew it. This was the blade Burton had wanted to drive into his heart.

Burton Cole.

He was to blame for the death of Hochburg's great love: Eleanor. Burton's mother. She had chosen her son over him and, in doing so, condemned herself to a savage death. Hochburg would never forgive Burton. All these years on, his grief for Eleanor remained as raw as his need for retribution. His desire to watch her son burn—literally burn; to luxuriate in each crackling scream—quickened his blood more than ever. It was the itch of a phantom limb, beyond relief. Burton was dead: torpedoed and drowned off the coast of West Africa. Hochburg had issued the order himself. It was a decision he had come to lament.

As the war in Rhodesia had spread back across the border to Kongo, he spent his nights imagining Burton's final seconds. The boy's panic as the ship began to list and fill with flames; the dilemma of surrendering himself to the fire or waves. A man would always throw himself overboard: the virulence of the human organism demanded that it preserve itself, if only for a few minutes longer. Inevitably, Burton would breathe salt water: that was the moment Hochburg regretted.

He had been cheated of his final look into the boy's eyes, its exchange of triumph and failure. Then Burton would descend into the darkness and oblivion, a release Hochburg had been denied. He knew who suffered the most: Hochburg lived with the pain of losing Eleanor every day.

A Leibwache entered carrying a canister that sloshed with fuel. Behind him, Zelman stumbled into the room. "They've reached the command center. We've only minutes to spare."

"What happened to the radio operator?" asked Hochburg.

His deputy went to the portrait of the Führer and flicked the switch hidden in the frame, doing so with a familiarity that made Hochburg bristle. The painting swung open to reveal a secret chamber. In the ground was a trapdoor that led to an underground passage out of the Schädelplatz.

"I'm not slinking out of here," said Hochburg, sheathing the knife.

"Oberstgruppenführer," implored Zelman. "We must go now." His voice was sucked into the passage.

Hochburg turned to the Leibwache with the petrol. "The books," he said. It may have been too late to save the Schädelplatz, but his enemies would not make spoils of his precious volumes. He supervised the dousing of his library, then ordered Zelman to burn them; striking the match himself would be too heartbreaking.

He stepped to the veranda. Below, the square was empty except for his men creating a perimeter. Streaks of light blazed on the hallowed ground as the bombardment continued overhead. There was one final object he had to save.

The most prized thing of all.

✦ ✦ ✦

Beneath his boots was an expanse of human crania. *Twenty thousand nigger skulls,* as Hochburg thrilled to tell visitors. This was the place that gave the Schädelplatz its name: the "square of skulls," the ground cobbled with bone.

In the rosy dawn mist, he allowed himself to savor the square one final time. It was the fortress of his heart: a vast quadrangle, the perimeter covered by cloisters, with guard towers on each of the corners, from which soldiers were firing into the jungle beyond. The northern wall was obscured in scaffolding where they were repairing the damage wrought by Burton and his team of assassins the year before. Burton had been hired by a cabal of Rhodesian industrialists and British intelligence; when Burton failed, Hochburg used this attempt on his life to justify his attack on Rhodesia. Flanked by the Leibwachen, Hochburg ransacked the workmen's equipment for a tool, then strode into the center of the square. Fenris bounded after him.

Hochburg raised the pickaxe above his head and brought it crashing down—once, twice—spitting mortar and chips of skull.

One of the guard towers vanished in a balloon of fire. There was a second blast and a section of the wall was punched wide open. A tank rumbled into the square; behind it came Belgian fighters, one of them carrying a banner of yellow stars against a peacock-blue background: the old flag of Belgian Congo and now a symbol of resistance. They wavered as they saw the ground.

"Where does a guerrilla army get a tank?" said Hochburg. It was an old British Crusader from the desert war against Rommel.

He redoubled his work, swinging the pickaxe with a fury, vigilant of the skull at the dead center of the square. The tank swiveled in his direction, fired, the shot reducing his study to a smoking wound. More SS troops emerged onto the square.

Zelman appeared at his side, clutching a Luger that reeked of packing grease. "Oberstgruppenführer, there's no time for this."

Hochburg shoved him away. The Leibwachen were a corona of gunfire around them. The pickaxe struck the ground again—and the skull at the center was free.

Fenris edged forward and sniffed as Hochburg carefully picked it up. He brushed flakes of cement from it, never believing that it had been disturbed, and stared into the hollows of its eyes. After Eleanor had chosen Burton over Hochburg, she'd fled into the jungle and been murdered by savages. Hochburg had hunted them down. The skull in his hand belonged to the first black he'd killed, a deed that saw the beginning of his mission to transform Africa. He had laid the square in Eleanor's memory.

His dreams, his ambitions for the continent weren't supposed to end like this.

Hochburg wrapped the skull in the sack he had taken from his study. He would defeat these insurgents: drive them into the jungle till the trees dripped scarlet. Then raise a new Schädelplatz, grander, more awe-inspiring than anything before.

The square was being overrun by Belgians.

"My garden," said Hochburg. "That can be our escape." He made a chivalrous gesture to his deputy. "Show us the way, Gruppenführer."

Zelman remained within the huddle of Leibwachen, unblinking.

Hochburg ran from the center of the square, Fenris at his heels, the Leibwachen struggling to keep pace. They reached the cloisters as another tank broke through the far wall. It trundled toward them, shielding more guerrillas, the Belgians concentrating their fire on the small band of Nazis beneath the colonnade. Hochburg's Leibwachen were falling around him. He fired his BK44.

"Save a bullet for yourself," said Zelman. "You mustn't be taken alive."

Hochburg ignored him: his final rounds would be for blacks. He grabbed Fenris by the leash and raced toward the garden gate. Close behind he heard the slap of Zelman's boots.

The second Crusader was armed with a flamethrower. A jet of orange and ebony roared through the quadrangle. Skulls that had been gathered from all six provinces of German Africa were reduced to cinder.

Shielded by the cloisters, his lungs charred, Hochburg reached the archway that led to the garden. It was his sanctuary. He tended it personally: dug the soil till his back ached, propagated every plant with his own fingers, the way Eleanor had taught him.

Now it writhed in flame.

He barely registered the intensity of the heat. Fenris broke free of the lead and galloped through the foliage to where cultivated land and jungle merged. For a long moment Hochburg stood motionless, his jaw listing and feeble; then he chased after the dog, into the inferno.

CHAPTER TWO

Suffolk, England
28 January, 15:30

"STOP THE CAR."

"We're not there yet."

"Just stop!"

The taxi driver braked sharply.

"Now back up. I saw something."

The driver went to reply, then thought better of it. He put the car in gear and reversed down the empty lane. On either side was a wall of dank woodland: oak, ash, elm. Fading sunlight cut through the bare canopy.

"Here."

The car came to a halt again.

Burton Cole climbed out and stared at the gap in the trees. He felt a tightening in his throat. Above him, branches creaked in the wind. He never should have sent the telegrams.

"It's well hidden," said the driver, following his gaze. "Yours?"

Burton shook his head. He had wheat-blond hair and eyes the color of an autumn afternoon, calm but alert, hard as a rifle butt. Concealed among the trunks was a black Riley RME. He put his hand—his right hand, his only hand—into his pocket and pulled out a banknote. "You can drop me here," he said, offering it through the window.

"No way I got change for five bob."

"Take the rest of the day off, buy yourself a drink. And if anyone asks, you never came out here. Or saw me."

"Is it the law?" The driver looked uncertainly at the money.

"Jealous husband," answered Burton with a forced wryness.

The driver gave an understanding nod and crumpled the note in his hand. "Couple of pints and I can't remember a thing."

Burton lifted out his haversack and shut the door. He was unshaven, wearing a sheepskin jerkin under a secondhand suit. The trousers and jacket were cut from scratchy brown rayon; sweat from a stranger's body lingered in the cloth. When Hitler had returned the Dunkirk POWs to Britain, rather than sending them in uniform, he'd ordered a quarter of a million of these "dove suits" hastily made. Few of the homecoming prisoners wanted their new clothes. They were to be found heaped up in rag-and-bone stalls, promised to clothe generations of vagrants.

The taxi made a three-point turn and accelerated away in the direction of the railway station where Burton had arrived earlier that afternoon.

Moments later—silence.

As soon as he was alone, Burton reached into his haversack. He took out his Browning HP pistol, inserted a clip, then secured it in his waistband. He was less than a mile from home, and knew this spot well. Before he bought the farm he'd parked here with Madeleine on several occasions. It was a discreet place to leave the car while they vanished into the trees to feel a bed of leaves beneath them. Perhaps the Riley belonged to a couple looking for some privacy.

He crossed over to it and touched the bonnet: the metal was cold. Peering through the window, he found nothing except an ashtray overflowing with cigarette butts. All the doors were locked.

Burton tugged the collar of his jacket around his neck; his breath smoked the air. This was no weather for lovers.

The mud revealed footprints—two pairs, men's—that had left the car and joined the road heading toward the farmhouse. Burton followed them, his pace soon quickening, boots drumming a lonely sound. They were the ones he'd acquired in Angola, taken from the feet of a dead man, the laces badly tied. He'd never imagined how difficult it would be to do one-handed.

He had been a fool to send the telegrams.

The first was from Cape Town, before he was admitted to the hospital, when he was delirious with exhaustion and self-recrimination. The message had been dispatched to Madeleine's house in London, all caution abandoned. Her husband had sent Burton to his death in Kongo—what might he have reaped back in England? YOU ARE IN DANGER, it read. LEAVE IMMEDIATELY! ON MY WAY BACK TO YOU. Even in his fevered state he changed the last words before they were tapped in: ON MY WAY HOME. He sent another from Mombasa and then one more from Alexandria, on Christmas Eve, the words identical, each message increasingly desperate. It was probably too late, but he couldn't bear any more days of unresting seas creeping by while he was impotent to help; he didn't dare to think what might have happened. There were no replies.

Woodland gave way to open fields. Ten minutes later, Burton was staring at a weather-beaten sign: Saltmeade Farm. This moment had sustained him on his long journey. He'd clung to the image of the windows burning bright, the smell of applewood curling from the chimney, Maddie opening the door in her cornflower-blue dress, her belly swollen with the baby she would soon have. Their first child. He would clasp her and sink to his knees, beg forgiveness for leaving her to kill Hochburg in order that he could forgive himself.

The sign brought neither relief nor welcome, only anxiety and the anger that had throbbed inside him since he'd left Africa.

Five hundred yards of potholed driveway led to the farm; from here the house wasn't visible. He hurried on, assuming it must be a trap, but the murmurings of hope were too strong. That's why he'd come to the farm first.

"Please, God," whispered Burton to the empty heavens. "Please."

He hadn't prayed since he was a child. Not after Hochburg took his parents, not at Dunkirk when German artillery turned the coast to offal. Not even when he lay trapped in the consulate in Angola with no hope of escape. Now the words tumbled from his lips, pleading for this one moment of grace. If only he had enough faith, Madeleine would be waiting.

A gust of air shrieked down the driveway. Nearby Burton heard the shimmer of a wind chime, its sound thin and mournful.

Suddenly he felt exposed: a man walking into the sniper's sights. He stepped away from the drive. He would reach the house from behind, screened by rows of apple and quince trees. It took him several minutes to make his way there. Once he slipped on the grass, almost fell; close to the ground, he smelled the night's frost gathering in the soil.

Rows of hawthorns created a natural barrier around the orchard to protect the fruit from the wind. As Burton approached, he sensed something different, something unnatural. It was as if the lay of the land had been distorted. He squeezed through a gap in the hedge and caught sight of the house: the windows were full of shadows, the chimney lifeless. But it wasn't the farmhouse that absorbed him; instead, his eyes took in the scene around him.

The breath died in Burton's throat.

He swayed, the haversack toppling from his shoulder. Then his legs sagged and he dropped to his knees.

+ + +

Cranley.

Only Cranley could have done this.

Burton had to look away. It was as if he'd taken a blow to his chest, its ferocity deadening his whole body. Two ravens watched him, like sentries in sleek black uniforms.

He had discovered the farm two years earlier. It had been April; he remembered that because of the morning's news: the Duke and Duchess of Windsor had accepted an invitation to the Führer's birthday festivities in Germania. People didn't know whether to be outraged or keep their heads down. Madeleine was at the family's second home, on the Suffolk coast, for a few days while her husband and Alice remained in London. Burton picked her up, and they drove inland, where there was no chance of meeting someone she knew. They went walking, exploring woods and meadows, stopping for lunch by a tumbledown wall that overlooked the farm. As they ate cheese-and-chutney sandwiches, they daydreamed about living in a place like this. It became one of their regular spots. They were both drawn to the farm's isolation and weary, dilapidated state. It was a place that yearned for renewal.

Then, the same week they had agreed to make a life together, a FOR SALE sign appeared.

"I don't believe in coincidence," said Madeleine, struggling to contain a smile as they drove past.

"Good," replied Burton. "Neither do I."

The owner's son had shown them around, apologizing for how ramshackle everything was. He explained that his father had recently died, that he himself had no urge to stay on: the work was too hard, the profits meager, all the more so given Germany's agricultural policies. With the vast fertile plains of Russia and endless bounty of Africa, Hitler had achieved his goal of autarky. Thereafter Germany began exporting food, undercutting British farmers.

"Of course there are the orchards," said the son. "That's a good business. People will always want English apples." He led them to the fruit trees, the branches ablaze with blossoms.

"These are quinces," said Madeleine, gulping down the scent.

"We have apples and quinces," said the son. "Pears, plums, damsons, cherries."

"Quinces are my favorite." She slipped her arm through Burton's. "Do you know what they represent?"

"Eve took one," he replied, thinking back to his childhood; his parents had been missionaries. "In the Garden of Eden."

"I don't mean fairy tales. In ancient Greece they were eaten by the bride and groom on their wedding night."

"Really?" He loved the way her mind was a trove of knowledge from a childhood spent in books. "But we don't believe in coincidences."

Three months later, after Burton had borrowed a fortune from his aunt, the farm and orchards were theirs. Sometimes Burton wondered if he'd done the right thing: the call to adventure was impossible to silence completely, no matter what he said to reassure Madeleine. There was more work to be done than he'd realized; he discovered he was less good with tools than weapons. But it was the first home he'd had since childhood, and there were moments—repairing a patch of roof, the aroma of burnt toast in the kitchen, Maddie's slippers nestled by their bed—when he felt a satisfaction he'd never known. A belonging life had denied him.

The grass was soaking into his trousers. Burton stood, his face hot, and startled the ravens. They took to the air, croaking with laughter, and soared into the low, red sun. Burton headed in the opposite direction, walking through the orchard.

Cranley had taken an axe to the trees, hacking them down. Trees that cropped showers of golden fruit, that had built their rings over decades, were reduced to stumps. It had been done some time ago, guessed Burton, before the winter: the exposed wood was blackened with frost. Split bowers lay strewn across the ground like bodies gunned down on a battlefield.

The act itself looked frenzied, as if Cranley had been unable to control himself. Burton heard him in his head: the terrible chopping sound, trunks cracking as they tumbled. Cranley howling. Not all the trees had been felled. Some showed gaping wounds but were still standing; others remained untouched altogether. Burton reached out for an intact one. Needed the reassurance of the bark against his palm.

Acid was swilling in his gullet; he wanted to vomit. And with it came a fury to surpass Cranley's, a fury that had been growing inside him for months.

He climbed over a trunk and continued to the house—

Stopped immediately.

He'd seen someone in an upstairs window. A face in the gloom, the outline of a white shirt and tie. Then the figure was gone, only the sway of the
curtain suggesting a stranger in his home.

Burton surveyed the destruction in the orchard. They were waiting for
him. Maybe Cranley himself.

Good, he thought, the rage leavening in him. *Good.*

He reached for his Browning, tugging it from his belt, and headed
toward the farmhouse.

CHAPTER THREE

FROM INSIDE HE heard a voice. A familiar, impossible voice: *"Africa has the shape of a pistol,"* it intoned, *"and Kongo is the trigger . . ."*

Someone had forced the back door open, the old frame standing no chance against a crowbar.

Burton pushed it inward with the stump of his arm. His left hand had been severed during his escape from Angola. In the months since, he'd learned to quell the anguish when he glanced at his empty sleeve, but the lack of weight beyond his wrist continued to feel unnatural. Keeping his gun in front of himself, he stepped into the kitchen.

He was expecting that homey smell of must and apples; instead, the stench of tobacco hit him. Fading daylight washed the walls and cabinets in a crimson gloom. Burton tried the light switch. Nothing. On the table was a heavy-duty rubber flashlight. Next to it a half-cut loaf of bread and a mess of crumbs; a jar stood open beside a spoon leaking jam. Cigarette ends had been stubbed out on the wood, leaving a score of burn marks.

The fury fluxed in Burton again. It wasn't the intrusion; it was the slovenly indifference of it, the act of someone who didn't care if they were discovered. He thought of the regimented order Cranley insisted upon in his house. Madeleine found it stifling.

The voice was coming from the hallway, and it had been intentionally amplified. He crept toward it, straining to hear, over the jowly intonation, anything that might indicate where someone was hiding: the creak of a floorboard, a suppressed cough.

". . . We must not allow the continent to become a German dominion," declared Churchill. In the background, a crowd was split between applause and jeers. *"I therefore urge the prime minister to reconsider the clever, shameful compromise of his foreign secretary . . ."*

The hallway was empty, doors opening off it onto sunless rooms. Burton glanced up the staircase: there was no face peering through the banister. On the side table was a Grundig transistor radio, one of those new portable devices from Germany that everyone seemed desperate to own and that neither Burton nor Madeleine was interested in.

"... to appeal instead across the Atlantic to the new president. The Nazis will only be contained with the assistance of the United States—"

He flicked the off switch with the muzzle of his Browning. Africa was the land of his birth, where he'd spent most of his life: first in Togo, then, after his parents' deaths, in the Sahara as a soldier of the French Foreign Legion. During the Nazi conquest, he'd fought across the continent as a mercenary. He hoped never to hear the name of the place again.

Burton sensed a rush of air. He lurched backward as a crowbar smashed into the wall. It swung a second time, wielded by a man in a suit who glided silently across the floor. Iron thumped Burton's shoulder. He dropped his Browning, watched it clatter past his assailant's socked feet: he wasn't wearing shoes.

Burton stamped on his foot.

The man tumbled forward, grabbing him. They both crashed into the table, then the floor, knocking over the radio. Churchill's voice boomed out again—"Britain is weaker than we admit; we need American might"—followed by a rainstorm of static.

Burton was on his back, a chubby weight on top of him, fists blurring his vision. He scooped up the radio and smashed it into the other man's head. His hand came away full of bloody transistor parts.

Upstairs, a door opened. Floorboards groaned.

In the hallway, the suit was already on his feet. He kicked Burton and sent him sprawling. Burton landed hard, something digging into his back. Through his jacket he could make out a metal L-shape; he reached for it.

The man in the suit towered over him, wagging the crowbar. "Lyall," he shouted up the stairs. "I got the bastard." He turned to Burton. "You broke my fucking radio. You know how much it cost me?"

Burton shot him in the kneecap.

The man dropped, clutched his spewing leg.

"Where's Madeleine?"

"Lyall!"

"What did you do to her?"

A hiss and nick of plaster as the wall behind him exploded. Lyall was at the top of the stairs, a revolver in his hand. He wore an identical black suit and dainty, slip-on shoes, his lips and chin masked behind a thick beard. Burton aimed the Browning and let off two blasts before charging after him.

By the time he reached the landing, Lyall had vanished; all the bedrooms were shut. It was like a game he'd played with Hochburg as a child: the three doors of the washhouse, Onkle Walter reducing him and his mother to terror and giggles as he burst from one with his lion roars. Burton's father had been a trusting doter to let Hochburg into their lives. He checked Alice's room first, pistol raised in front of him. It was dank, stripped bare except for a sleeping bag that didn't belong here; through the window the fields were growing dark gray. He wondered what lies Cranley had told Alice about her mother.

Burton moved to the next room—also empty—then the master bedroom. The axe that savaged the orchard had been at work here.

There were gashes in the walls and the wardrobe, one of its doors hanging from the hinges like a broken jaw. The bedsheets had been ripped off and the mattress slashed open. Burton's clothes were strewn across the floor; they stank of urine. The Browning faltered in his grip.

In that moment a revolver was pressed into his cheek, squeezing the flesh against his teeth. "Drop the gun," said Lyall. His voice was gravelly like an old woman's.

Burton let the Browning slip from his hand. *Clunk.*

"Hands on your head. Turn round."

He was marched out of the room, the revolver against the back of his skull, and guessed at once where he was being taken.

If Madeleine cared for one luxury, it was bathing. After fleeing Vienna, she told him, she'd gone years without a proper bath, instead scrubbing herself clean with a washcloth from a bowl or sharing the facilities, and sometimes gray water, at the public bathhouse on Merlin Street; for hygiene reasons, Jews were allowed only on Thursday evenings. After marrying Cranley, she could spend hours up to her chin in hot, scented bubbles. The one time Burton had seen her bathroom in Hampstead—the swirls of Italian marble, taps that glittered—his mood slumped; he wanted to give her the same. No, better. When he learned that the farm had indoor plumbing it was another reason to buy the place.

"Open the door," said Lyall.

They went through to a white enamel tub, toilet, and washbasin, below a mirror. The walls and floor were tiled, but crookedly. Lyall had prepared heaps of towels to make it easier to mop up after they'd finished with him.

"On your knees."

Burton hesitated until the revolver was prodded more forcefully against his head.

"You're Burton Cole," said Lyall. It was a statement rather than a question.

"No."

Lyall reached into his jacket to retrieve something; the whole time the revolver stayed against Burton's skull. "Who are you then?"

"I heard the place was empty; I thought I'd break in, see what I could find."

"Most burglars don't carry Browning HPs."

"It's from when I was in the army. I haven't taken anything. You can let me go."

Lyall found what he was looking for and tutted. He thrust a card in front of Burton.

It was Burton's military record; Cranley must have retrieved it from the War Office. On the inside was a photo taken against a white backdrop. It had been snapped a decade earlier, when he had signed up and immediately been demoted: his Legion service counted for little with the British Army. He hadn't cared; he wanted to fight the Germans. Burton looked at his younger self. *My God*, he thought, *what happened to that boy?*

"You were captured at Dunkirk," said Lyall, pinching the shoulder of Burton's dove suit.

"No. I got out."

"Lucky bastard." Thirteen years later, his voice bridled. "I spent six months in a POW camp, and Halifax* called it a victory." He cocked the Webley.

"Wait," said Burton. "There was a woman. Madeleine."

"You mean the Jew?"

"I came back for her. What happened?"

"Russell dealt with it. He was very keen. You know how it is with those kids who missed the war."

"Russell?"

"Mr. Russell. The little terrier downstairs. The one who's going to walk funny from now on."

"What did he do to her?"

No reply.

Burton twisted round. There was an unpitying expression in Lyall's eyes. "What did he do?"

Another prod of the revolver. "Keep forward."

_____

*Lord Halifax, prime minister after Churchill resigned; he had negotiated peace with Hitler.

Burton's gaze came to rest on the tiles in front of him. He'd been laying them the afternoon before he left for Africa, accompanied by the sound of Alice playing outside. He couldn't get the lines straight, no matter how hard he concentrated: as the tiles went beneath the bathtub, they grew more and more skewed. In the end, Maddie said she would redo it.

"You married?" asked Burton.

"I was."

"What if it was your wife? You've got to tell me. You owe me that at least."

"Four weeks we've been waiting for you. Four weeks in this shithole, Christmas cut short. No heating, no decent food. There's not even a pub nearby." A blast of stale tobacco breath. "I don't owe you anything."

Burton was still looking at the tiles. There was a stack of them under the bath where they had been lifted. Madeleine must have started it while he was in Kongo, using a chisel to pry them up, ready to be laid again, straight as a German road this time.

He could see the handle of the chisel, almost hidden from view beneath the belly of the tub.

"You've never killed before," said Burton.

"Don't be stupid."

"Then why aren't I over the plughole?"

"What?"

"There'll be less mess. You can wash it straight down."

There was a long pause. Downstairs, Russell was still bawling. Finally, Lyall grunted. "Go on then."

Burton shuffled forward on his knees, feeling the pressure of the revolver ease against his head. In the orchard, acid had swilled in his throat; now he let it overflow. He snatched Lyall's ankle, yanked it upward, sent him tumbling. There was an ear-bursting blast from his revolver. Burton reached under the bath, grabbed the chisel. Buried it in Lyall's groin.

Lyall shrieked, swinging his revolver. Another bullet sparked against enamel.

Burton spun round, found a fistful of Lyall's hair, and smashed his face into the washbasin. He yanked his head back up and this time drove it into the mirror. Once, twice—then in a frenzy. Glass cascaded everywhere. The fury that had burrowed inward since Africa was free; it came out howling. He thought of his failure to avenge his parents and slay Hochburg. He thought of all the men under his command in Africa who died; Patrick, his oldest friend, had been killed in Angola. He thought of Madeleine, and

Russell manhandling her. Had she cried out for Burton? The tendons in his neck were rigid. He smashed Lyall's limp body harder, a piston against the wall.

Then he stopped, chest heaving.

He let Lyall slither to the floor and put his stump out to steady himself, nausea rising. Around his boots was an archipelago of silver fragments. Burton caught crazy, distorted images of himself: his blood-flecked face; sleepless eyes that were darker than he ever remembered. A laugh escaped him. He imagined what Patrick would say, shaking his head at the pieces of broken mirror. *That's a barrel of bad luck, boy.* He chased away the voice: the guilt was too intense.

Downstairs, Russell had left a trail as he dragged himself toward the front door. It was almost nightfall. Burton stood over him and demanded to know what he had done to Madeleine.

When there was no reply, he pressed his boot against Russell's leg and relished the scream. He asked again before squatting by him, placing his Browning inside the hollow of Russell's good knee.

The man in the suit struggled briefly, then sagged, nodding his fleshy head. "We took her," he said. "From the house."

"You mean in Hampstead?"

He nodded once more, forehead studded with sweat.

"Where did you go?"

"It was the governor's orders. I was just doing my job."

Burton screwed the muzzle of the Browning into Russell's knee. "Where?"

Russell seemed in a daze, whispering something over and over. Burton couldn't make it out; he leaned closer to hear. The face below him turned to a snarl.

There was the flick of a switchblade.

Scalding filaments flared along Burton's shoulder. Russell withdrew the knife and went to thrust again. Burton fired. At such close range, the bullet whipped the fat man's body over. Burton rolled him back—his chest was a quagmire—and clamped his hand on the wound to stem the flow. Russell was convulsing, disbelief in his eyes. He sucked in sodden gulps of air.

"Where did you take her?" begged Burton. He applied more pressure to the wound and put his mouth against Russell's, desperately trying to breathe the life back into him. *"Where?"*

The blood between his fingers slackened and stilled. Russell stared through him, his lips locked in a cruel, self-satisfied rictus.

Burton sat up, wiping the dead man from his mouth, then reached around to check the wound in his shoulder. His shirt was sopping; pins and needles teemed the length of his arm to his stump.

"If it still hurts," said Burton, flexing the elbow, "it's not that bad." One of Patrick's sayings: the wisdom of the Legion. Patrick had been his commanding officer.

He returned his attention to Russell, checking his pockets for any indication of Madeleine's fate. Inside his jacket he found a money clip (four crimson-moist notes) and what felt like a wallet. He flicked it open and found himself staring at a photo of Russell. Opposite was a badge: Metropolitan Police, Special Branch.

+ + +

Burton dragged the two bodies out to the septic tank, lifted the cover, and dumped them, watching their faces as they were sucked into the shit. The violence had purged him: he felt calm, focused, the howling anxiety held at bay. He returned to the house and searched it by flashlight. Every room was the same.

It was as if Madeleine had never been here.

Her clothes were gone. Clothes, coats, shoes and stockings, woolen scarves, her toiletries, the bottles of nail polish, toothbrush, the hot-water bottle she kept in the airing cupboard and had nicknamed Clarissa. All the things she was gradually moving in, ready for the day she left her husband. Her books were no longer on the shelves, each volume removed individually, leaving only Burton's; the bookcase looked like a smile smashed by a knucklebuster. In the sitting room there should have been a painting of the synagogue where her parents had married, one of the few possessions Maddie managed to bring from Vienna. A lack of relics from the past was something she shared with Burton. Cranley disapproved of the picture, so Maddie had brought it to the farm. Burton skimmed his hand over the wall: whoever had taken the painting had also removed the nail that held it up.

He grew more frantic, needing to find some proof that they had shared this house. Even the Weetabix she ate in the morning with spoonfuls of white sugar was missing. Burton tried the cloakroom under the stairs. There was a long oval mirror on the wall where Madeleine combed her hair, the area beneath it always patterned with dark strands. Burton got to his knees and shone the flashlight the length of the skirting board. Someone had swept the floorboards dustless.

He traced the smooth grain of the wood, hoping to discover a stray hair, then rushed back upstairs to the main bedroom, lifted the bedstead, and heaved it over. The sound reverberated through the silent house. The effort made him wince: the pain in his shoulder was spreading. In the gloom, his fingers followed the grooves between the floorboards until he found the loose one, pried it up, and reached into the cavity below. Cobwebs brushed his hand. Out came the jewelry box; this was where he hid his gun when Alice stayed. He opened the box.

Inside was a pouch of diamonds: the initial down payment to assassinate Hochburg. When he'd accepted the mission, he had no idea that Cranley was behind everything or that it would provoke a war. He shook the pouch and heard the stones rattle against one another before shoving them into his pocket. He dipped into the box again and pulled out something much more precious.

In the flashlight's beam, the yellow looked jaundiced. It was Madeleine's Star of David armband, the one she'd been forced to wear in Vienna. He lifted it to his nose, hoping to inhale her scent. Nothing but an ancient mustiness.

"Oh, Maddie," Burton whispered. "What happened?" He slipped the band into his jerkin, wanting it close to his skin. "Where are you?"

But he was kidding himself. The final look on Russell's face had told him everything.

CHAPTER FOUR

Stanleystadt, Kongo
28 January, 12:30

EVERYWHERE HOCHBURG WENT, a single, detested word was only a breath away.

It was on the lips of the citizens, half-spoken by soldiers as they hunkered down in preparation for the Belgians' next attack. Worst of all, his generals were beginning to murmur it, the same generals who four months earlier had been poised to conquer Rhodesia and then all of southern Africa.

Surrender.

"Oberstgruppenführer, they're coming!"

Hochburg raised his binoculars and scanned the far shore: it was the Otraco district, with its rotting cathedral—the undeveloped part of Stanleystadt. He was on the opposite embankment of the River Kongo, in one of the gun emplacements hidden among the palm trees. Around him the city boomed and shook. The thunderclap of artillery hadn't left his head since he'd escaped the inferno of his garden. Combat fatigues were his uniform now, the material streaked like green tiger fur. Through the smoke he glimpsed a dozen inflatables laden with men, the same mélange of Belgian and negroid faces he'd seen in the Schädelplatz. The boats were marked with SS runes.

"The order was for everything—*everything*—to be destroyed on the far side."

"They took us by surprise," said the Hauptsturmführer next to him. "There wasn't time."

"These guerrillas have nothing. If they defeat us, it'll be because we gave them the means."

The air stank of tar and petrol. Hochburg wondered if the men in the boats could smell it. They were almost across the river, the sluggish current drawing them toward the wreckage of the Giesler bridge, the city's main crossing. Hochburg had ordered it dynamited the previous night; only stumps of concrete were left above the waterline. He'd always thought it too small; they'd rebuild with six lanes instead of four.

"Now?" said the Hauptsturmführer. He held an MG48 machine gun in a tight embrace.

"You see that?" said Hochburg, pointing to a wrecked kiosk. Only weeks before, it had served pretzels and *Lebkuchen* to Stanleystadters strolling along the embankment. "Inside are engineers. They await my signal." He revealed a flare gun. "Not a single shot is to be fired until then."

"But if they land—"

"You're eager to kill, Hauptsturmführer. That's a welcome change. But wait for my command."

A shell burst farther along the embankment. Palm fronds quivered above them.

Hochburg didn't need his binoculars now. He could make out the faces on the boat: the wild-men eyes and ruffian brows. Those Belgians with any wealth had fled abroad before the German invasion of 1944; the guerrillas mostly consisted of miners and stevedores, men with little option other than to stay and resist the Nazis. They had endured years of hardship in the jungle, fighting an insurgency. But then it was those with the least who made the most tenacious warriors. That was the lesson Hochburg was learning. It had made the Belgian guerrillas strong while the new German population—with their air-conditioned apartments, refrigerators, and shiny Volkswagens—had become complacent.

The first of the inflatables ran ashore. Boots hit mud, then slipped on a slope of oil.

Hochburg reached for the flare gun. The Belgians' expressions were a jumble of relief and suspicion that they were landing unopposed. He let the insurgents struggle halfway up the bank, their trousers weighed down with sludge, before he fired the flare. At his sign, the entire shore exploded in flames. The shore, the steps leading to the embankment, even the river itself, with its film of gasoline.

Hochburg stood mesmerized, the skin on his bald scalp wrinkling with the heat. The fire towered over Stanleystadt; it had a holy, shimmering quality. And as he watched it burn, a notion seized hold of Hochburg's mind.

If only he had the means to engulf the whole city. The whole of Kongo.

+ + +

Hochburg's jeep weaved through the streets, the driver spinning the wheel to avoid piles of rubble. Hardly a window had survived anywhere in the city. Chains of tattered lanterns festooned the buildings; serpents of tinsel, now clogged with brick dust, were coiled around lampposts. The battle of Stanleystadt had begun with a surprise bombardment the night before Christmas, or Julfest, as Nazi Party ideologues insisted it be called.

He returned to SS headquarters on Eiskeller Strasse and was met by Zelman. Even in the gritty smoke, his deputy's eyes remained unblinking. Sometimes Hochburg wanted to snap his fingers in front of them or find Zelman's wife and have her shot while he was forced to watch—anything to elicit a bat of the eyelid.

"Are my generals still here?" demanded Hochburg as they strode into the vestibule.

The space was dominated by von Kursell's portrait of Himmler: twenty-eight square meters of oil on canvas. The Reichsführer's face was askew and peppered with shrapnel, as if he were suffering from shingles. Despite the Reichsführer's eyes being in every public building, Hochburg ran Kongo with limited interference from Germania. So long as boats brimming with minerals, timber, cotton, and green bananas continued to flow to the Reich, Hochburg administered the colony as he saw fit, even if that meant war. To extend the borders of Kongo farther into southern Africa was Germany's right, he told Himmler. Its destiny.

Zelman handed Hochburg a damp towel. "The generals are waiting in the conference room."

"No tactical withdrawal to the bunker then?" he replied, mopping his neck.

A weak smile. "If you recall, Oberstgruppenführer, you locked them in."

The lift wasn't working. Hochburg bounded up the staircase, past bandaged soldiers slumped on the steps.

Zelman continued his update: "Insurgent units have surrounded the entire city. Every district reports heavy shelling. All roads out are blocked."

"And elsewhere?"

"Elisabethstadt says the siege is worsening. By the hour. They can't hold on much longer."

"What about the Reichsführer? Have you made contact yet?"

"We've opened a line to Wewelsburg, but communications are proving problematic." Wewelsburg: Himmler's castle in Westphalia, the spiritual headquarters of the SS. "We're still trying to connect."

"I want to know as soon as you have his office on the phone," said Hochburg.

He continued his rapid ascent, with Zelman struggling to keep up. Occasionally the building shuddered. On the seventh floor he stormed into the conference room. The blast curtains were drawn, leaving the room in a murky light. Most of the generals were huddled together over a map. Shaking heads, murmuring. They straightened their backs as he entered. In the corner was a decorated fir tree that no one had bothered to remove; beneath it lay Fenris, dozing with one eye half open.

"I hope you put my absence to good use," said Hochburg, taking his place at the head of the table. He gestured for everyone to sit. "What plans for the counterattack?"

Nobody replied.

Hochburg scanned the faces in front of him. The air-conditioning had stopped working. They all glistened, the collars of their uniforms wet. Outside: the relentless beat of artillery.

It was General Ockener who finally spoke for the group. He had a hewn face and thinning white hair atop a beach-resort tan. "Hochburg, we feel this is unacceptable." He spoke with the measured tone of a man who wanted to scream. "To leave us in here with no refreshment, nowhere to relieve ourselves—"

Hochburg smelled urine. "It would appear that one of you can't control his functions."

"You locked the door," shrieked a voice from the other end of the table. "This is the biggest target in the city. We could have been killed."

"If I hadn't, you would have fled. What example is that?"

"I will be reporting this matter to the Führer."

Hochburg was on his feet. "Then you can also tell him this."

He wrenched open the blast curtains, flooding the room with furious light. The city was pockmarked with columns of smoke. Otraco was obscured behind a convulsing orange barrier that followed the bend in the river.

Hochburg gave an exultant sweep of his arms. "Guard!" A sentry appeared. "The Brigadeführer here"—he pointed to the end of the table—"wishes to leave. Escort him outside. To the street."

"I am a general in the Waffen-SS. I will not be treated like—"

"You can leave through the door—or the window. I don't care which."

When he was gone, Hochburg flopped into his chair and rotated it toward Ockener. "You were saying, Herr General."

Ockener had been decorated at the Battle of Smolensk before chasing mass graves and medals across the Russian steppe; later he transferred to Africa and earned the nickname "Der Schnitter." The reaper.

"Your fire won't burn forever, Oberstgruppenführer. Meantime, the enemy's guns can strike anywhere."

"How did the dregs of Belgium's army come to surround an entire city?"

"Their ranks have been swollen by the Free French* and blacks who escaped deportation." Ockener was playing with a bauble taken from the tree. "We don't have enough soldiers to contain them. Too many were sent to Elisabethstadt. On your orders."

To relieve the siege of Elisabethstadt, Hochburg had sent contingents from the north of Kongo to the south. When they proved insufficient, he commandeered troops from Kamerun, Aquatoriana, and Madagaskar until the governors of these colonies complained that their own security situations were threatened. The Afrika Korps in Angola, whose commanding officer was mysteriously lost and whose soldiers were caught up in their own siege, was unable to offer support.

Ockener put down the bauble and glanced at the other generals. Hochburg noted their tacit nods.

"The position is clear, Herr Oberstgruppenführer." A pause. "We cannot continue to fight."

From the streets below came shell bursts of German artillery. To Hochburg they sounded like the heartbeat of a dying lion: inconceivable, dwindling, full of fury.

He leaned back in his chair till the leather cracked. "There was a time, not long ago, when the Waffen-SS was feared," he said. "Now I have generals like you."

"Give me a BK44 and a sack of grenades, and I'll gladly fill the drains of this city. The problem is the ranks."

"How dare you say that while you sit here. They are true white men."

"Half our numbers are ethnics. The rest, the pure Germans, too many of them don't want to fight."

"Nonsense."

"You promised them a swift victory."

---

*The remnants of France's army in Africa.

"It's been four months. You're telling me that's all it's taken to blunt their spirits?"

"They are a generation of conquerors. They have never known attrition, or the possibility of losing."

"We fought for a year to take central Africa," retorted Hochburg.

"A mopping-up operation," said Ockener, "of colonies whose European masters had been defeated. It was also a decade ago. All the fighting was a decade ago."

"Meaning?"

"The ethnics are here because the alternative is herding goats in Ostland. The Germans just want a plantation, an obedient wife, and enough workers so they don't have to get off their arses."

"It's the same in the East," muttered someone.

The Soviet Union had been defeated in 1943, with Moscow razed to the ground and scattered with meadow seed. Despite that, a guerrilla war churned like a meat grinder on the shifting eastern fringe of the Reich. An intractable conflict stretching from the Ural Mountains deep into Siberia that the Russians couldn't win and the Germans were weary of. But Africa, Hochburg believed, Africa was different. It wasn't a battle of political ideology; the clash of races was as stark as the midday sun and the dead of night.

"Perhaps one day," continued Ockener, "we will have the means to wage war without men. Such an army will always be victorious. Until then, we've grown soft on peace."

"The British, yes," said Hochburg. "Mired in imperial weakness. But not us."

"The same British whose grip around Elisabethstadt we've been unable to loosen? Who are supplying the Belgians with tanks and artillery? Their blood is up. You have underestimated them."

"You sound almost admiring, General."

"Then there's the matter of civilians. While you were away on your riverbank 'adventure,' the Belgians took the water treatment plant."

"And while they took it, you were in here. Or did a simple door lock flummox the cream of the Waffen command?"

"The sewage system is also damaged. In a few days, dysentery will be rife. Cholera will follow, typhoid."

"What would you suggest then, Herr General?"

Ockener lowered his voice: "Surrender."

"Those who do not want to fight in this world of eternal struggle do not deserve

to live," replied Hochburg, citing the Führer's book. He judged that the quote would be well known around the table.

"A cease-fire then. A truce."

"No."

"At least some form of negotiation."

"No."

An exasperated *Ach.* "Then a squadron of Heinkel bombers to flatten the city."

Hochburg roared with laughter. "There's hope yet." He swiveled his chair to gaze out across the city. The wall of fire was beginning to ebb. "Every soldier is to fight," he said. "Street to street. If they lack the guts for it, we shoot them where they stand." He spun back. "It's a matter of reasserting discipline. Punish the worst cowards and the rest will fall into place. If need be, we can start in this room."

Hushed words flitted round the table.

"It is not my wish that the civilian population suffer," continued Hochburg, "but it must also be mobilized. Give a rifle to every last man and woman. Remind the fair maidens of this city that these guerrillas, and the blacks among them, have the most base of needs, needs that will have been unmet in the jungle."

"And the children?" said Ockener. He was toying with the bauble again.

"Teach them what milk bottles and petrol can do."

"The civilians should be allowed to leave. They are German citizens."

"Who have been indulged enough. Most have lives better than anything in Europe. In Germania all they'd get is forty-four square meters of living space. Here they have sixty. They enjoyed the abundance of conquest; now it's time to endure for it."

"They may not wish to die for sixteen meters—"

The door opened. Zelman slid in, unblinking as ever.

"I have the Reichsführer's private office on the line."

"This city will rise!" said Hochburg, reaching for the phone on the table. "That will be all, gentlemen." Nobody moved. "Five minutes ago you were complaining about locks; now you won't leave? Zelman, get them food and drink. They have long days ahead."

As soon as Hochburg was alone he lifted the receiver and found some blossom in his throat. "Heinrich, it's Walter. How are you?"

The connection crackled and fizzed. "This is Fegelein." Hermann Fegelein: Himmler's chief of staff.

"I want to speak to the Reichsführer."

"He's at lunch."

"At lunch . . . Is he aware that the Schädelplatz was attacked?"

"Yes."

"That it has been lost."

"This he also knows," said Fegelein.

"And he has no response?"

The line squeaked: sixty-five hundred kilometers of static.

"The Reichsführer has always approved of your methods, Hochburg. Your thoroughness, your grasp of the 'biological' issues. But your pagan square is far from his only concern. He's preoccupied with the Jews again. In Madagaskar. Surely you know about this?"

"I've been preoccupied myself."

"We may have another full-scale rebellion on the island. Poor Globus is struggling to maintain control. He blames you for everything."

Globus: Odilo Globocnik, the SS governor of Madagaskar.

"That drunken satrap," said Hochburg. "Is he still whining about the men I commandeered?"

"It was an entire brigade," replied Fegelein. "He claims if they hadn't been sent to Kongo—to 'shore you up,' as he tells the Reichsführer—the Jews would be in their place."

"And as I like to tell Heinrich, half a million tons of copper was shipped from Kongo last year. What does Globus give the Reich? Fucking canned meat."

"You miss the subtlety of the situation, Oberstgruppenführer. Globus keeps us Jew-free. That is worth a thousand years of minerals."

"I wonder whether Germania will feel the same if Kongo is overrun by niggers." His tone became emphatic: "I need more men. If not from Africa, then spare me a division from the East."

"I doubt they'd make a difference now."

Hochburg's fingers tightened around the receiver. "What do you mean?"

"You've not heard?"

"No."

"Unreliable things, telex machines," said the chief of staff, and he went on to detail events. Even across thousands of kilometers of wire, the gloating was apparent in Fegelein's voice. The SS was riven with jealousy and petty rivalries: between Europe and Africa, between one governor and his neighbor, all kept simmering by Himmler to make sure no one challenged his position.

Hochburg listened in silence, his throat thickening.

"I hope the Reichsführer enjoys his lunch," he said when the conversation was at an end. He couldn't bear the gilded dining room at Wewelsburg, nor the fleshy droop of Himmler's lip as he chewed. He set down the receiver and listened to the funnel of his breath. A shell landed near the base of the building. The decorations on the Christmas tree tinkled, waking Fenris.

Hochburg leapt up and grabbed the telephone.

Hurled it at the window.

It bounced off, the wire yo-yoing it back into the room. He threw it again, this time with such ferocity that the glass cracked. Outside, the burning river was reduced to billows of smoke.

"Come, dog," he said and strode from the conference room.

The corridor was empty except for Zelman.

"I need a plane," said Hochburg, heading to the stairs.

"Technically," replied Zelman, "Stanleystadt is part of the no-fly zone."

Hochburg stopped at the edge of the steps. He fixed his deputy with his black eyes till Zelman averted his gaze. "I expect it fueled and ready to leave in fifteen minutes."

"At once, Oberstgruppenführer. What is your destination?"

"Elisabethstadt." Hochburg began to descend. "I have a firing squad to arrange."

CHAPTER FIVE

FROM STANLEYSTADT TO Elisabethstadt: fourteen hundred kilometers. Hochburg decided to pilot the plane himself, flicking away the concerns of Zelman and the ground crew: "How can a man rule the earth if he can't command the heavens?" He had learned to fly when he was the governor of Muspel,* soaring alone over the dune seas.

The plane was a Focke-Wulf Fw-189, a twin-engine propeller aircraft, nicknamed "Le Chambranle" (the window frame) by the Belgians because of its fishbowl cockpit enclosed in bands of metal; its primary function was reconnaissance. Hochburg dismissed the captain, kept the copilot and dorsal gunner. Fenris squeezed behind his seat and bedded down. The Focke-Wulf lifted off into a mesh of ack-ack fire, broke through, then turned south into empty skies. Hochburg fixed his eyes on the sun; it was too distressing to look back.

Following the outbreak of war in central Africa, Prime Minister Halifax had requested an audience with Hitler. To his surprise, the Führer issued a statement detailing how there was no need to intensify hostilities after so many years of peace: "If we say we are fighting the British empire to the death, then obviously we shall drive even the last of them to arms against us." He did not, however, leave his palace in Germania. Rumors bubbled: the Führer was ailing, had been incapacitated by a mystery illness; he refused to sign any document because he planned to pulverize Rhodesia from the sky. Some said that at sixty-three, now master of the world, he was simply bored with the diplomatic chase. Instead he sent Himmler's deputy, Reinhard Heydrich, chief of Reich security and, it appeared, also its highest negotiator.

---

*The common name for Deutsch Westafrika. Hochburg had administered the colony before taking up the governorship of Kongo. It was to the Sahara region of Muspel that the black population had been deported.

Heydrich met Halifax's foreign secretary, Anthony Eden, and a number of points were swiftly announced.

The conflict was deemed "local": a colonial border dispute confined to Kongo and Northern Rhodesia. Renegade British elements had provoked it; they did not represent official government policy. There would be no escalation. No reinforcements were to be sent from Europe or any other African colonies with the exception of support personnel; Churchill quipped that the Waffen-SS had more cooks in it than any army in history. To protect economic infrastructure and, as a secondary concern, civilians, a no-fly zone was to be established between the first parallel north and the sixteenth south. In the meantime, Germania and London would work to a negotiated settlement. Both sides agreed that the war in Angola was a separate matter and that Portugal (a small European country with disproportionately large African colonies) should come to terms with the Reich immediately. Word of the Führer's approval was passed on from his palace: for now, the Heydrich-Eden Pact was a mutually beneficial stalemate.

The Focke-Wulf stopped to refuel at Tarufa.

Hochburg left the aircraft and paced the landing strip to waken his legs and allow Fenris to drain his bladder. Dust rose from his boots. Deep in the cotton-growing region of Kongo, Tarufa was untouched by the war. A gaggle of boys had hurried to the perimeter fence when the plane touched down, hoping for some action. They quickly became bored and were now playing baseball, a craze that had spread through the colony from American prospectors working with the SS Oil Company; some fretted it would prove a greater threat than British tanks. One boy sat away from the others, his back to the fence. He appeared to be sawing something in his lap.

"You're not joining your friends," said Hochburg.

The boy made a show of being startled. He had the same unkempt black hair Hochburg had as a child. There was a familiar ravenous look in his eye, as if he wanted to consume the world.

"They hate me," he replied, then added, "but I hate them more."

"You're in the JVA?" Jungvolk Afrika: the continent's youth movement for boys between ten and fourteen.

"Everyone is; you have to be. I prefer being alone."

"But you enjoy it?"

"It would be better if they allowed girls."

A smile tightened Hochburg's face. "And what is in your lap?"

"I killed it myself." The boy lifted up a headless snake with yellow scales, the tail still twitching. Hochburg recognized it as a puff adder; its venom could kill a man in minutes.

"Does your mother know you hunt snakes?"

"She's dead. So is Papa. Malaria."

Hochburg wanted to comfort the child. "I lost my own parents when I was younger. My brothers, too."

"Who looked after you?"

"Someone special. I was older than you, already in my twenties, and lucky to find her."

"I live with my aunt now. She worries a lot." The boy snorted as if blowing a fly from his nostril. "Did your parents get malaria, too?"

"No. They were killed."

"How?"

"Butchered, by tribesmen."

Hochburg had been the sole survivor of his family. Afterward, sick with grief and nightmares, he was taken in by Eleanor and her husband. They were missionaries who ran an orphanage in Togoland; Burton was eleven when he first arrived. Hochburg had sobbed in Eleanor's arms and shared the horrors he'd witnessed; piece by piece, she made him whole again. Later they became lovers and eloped (Eleanor reveled in the romance of the word, perhaps because it obscured the reality of abandoning her husband and son). The two years they spent together were the happiest Hochburg ever knew. They lived simply, glutting in each other's love, until the regret began to trickle into Eleanor and she looked back guiltily to the life she had discarded. This time it was Hochburg she abandoned, fleeing into the jungle to Burton and her death. That Eleanor met the same fate as his parents could only be a calling. A portent.

"You must be very old," said the boy. "The niggers are gone."

"Alas, not all." Hochburg thought of the faces in the Schädelplatz. "What would you do if you saw one?"

The boy pondered the question, then held up the two bloody pieces of snake.

"Oberstgruppenführer!" The copilot beckoned to him. "We're ready."

Hochburg drew his pistol and unlocked the clip. He freed a bullet and passed it through the chain-link fence. The boy dropped his snake and took it with red fingers.

"Use it wisely, my child."

The Fw-189 lifted into the sky again. Two and a half thousand meters below, savannah drifted past: blots of jade and khaki like the camouflage pattern on an SS combat jacket. The sun beat through the glass cockpit. Sleep had been a snatched indulgence for Hochburg these past nights; drowsiness crept over him.

"How long till we land?" he asked the copilot.

"Another hour. Assuming we get through the British air defenses."

"Take control," said Hochburg, relaxing his grip on the lever. "Wake me in twenty minutes." He yawned, studding his eyes with tears, and let his head recline. Elisabethstadt filled his half-dreaming thoughts.

Before the siege it had been the mining capital of Kongo, with its rows of prim bungalows, world-famous botanical garden, ice factories, and a railway hub that whisked Germans as far south as Cape Town or to the pleasures of Roscherhafen. As with other conquered cities, Hochburg had planned to rename it; to do so was part of the psychology of victory. It affirmed the Reich's dominance as trenchantly as jackboots stamping the boulevards or the flutter of red, white, and black. For years he knew what to call it; he even had the approval of the Führer, who foolishly claimed to understand the Homeric allusion.

Then Hochburg's pen hesitated over the document that would have made it law. He looked at the city's new name stamped on the thick, lion-colored paper of official documents. Above it was the eagle-and-swastika seal. He meant it as her memorial:

Eleanorstadt

Minutes passed. A drop of ink ran down the nib and splashed onto the paper. Hochburg laid down his fountain pen, folded the sheet in half, quarters, eighths; later he burned it. When the bureaucrats puzzled over the change, Hochburg fended them off: *George VI won't always be on the throne. In the years ahead, the British will be reassured to hear their monarch's name so close to the border.*

He would offer Eleanor more than Elisabethstadt.

The whole of his Afrika Reich would be her immortalization: every stone that was laid, every garrison, town, city; the ports, the white roads cutting through the jungle, the babel of a million copper threads connecting the continent. A mausoleum of such glory that her name need never be written on it. That's why he'd been so impatient to invade Rhodesia: to consecrate more lands for her. Of course, they understood none of this in Germania. To the ministries on Wilhelmstrasse, Africa was a trove of mines and timber forests, its plantations existing solely to fill the bellies of the

German hordes. But to Hochburg, Africa was a kingdom of temples. The only way of keeping Eleanor present. So long as his heart drummed, the British and their ragtag allies would never prosper.

He would find a way to crush them yet.

His dreams were marauding. From Elisabethstadt . . . to his lack of troop numbers . . . to General Ockener's war without the weak souls of men, *such an army will always be victorious* . . . to a vision of the entire continent ablaze . . . Then the soothing lap of waves and the river by which he and Eleanor had lived together.

He was gliding with her in water as warm as amniotic fluid, below them a fathomless indigo black. A splash, a laugh . . . and they were lying naked next to each other in the mud, the sun filling their skin with light. He counted the freckles around her nose, which were as tiny as banana seeds. This was all he craved: this peace. If she hadn't chosen Burton, if she hadn't left Hochburg and been murdered, he would have watched the Nazis raise their edifice in Africa with indifference.

He took her hand, felt it so vividly: each silky finger, the creases of the palm. He traced his thumb along the life line till it came to an abrupt halt—

"Oberstgruppenführer!"

A roaring sound.

Hochburg dragged himself from the banks of the river. He rarely dreamed of her anymore and wished he could sink into the moment. His heart wrenched to let go of her hand . . .

"Oberstgruppenführer!" It was the gunner at the rear of the aircraft.

There was a flash of aluminum and olive-green paint.

"It's a Meteor," said the copilot. He strained in his harness to identify the plane in front. The cockpit bucked in the wake of its jet engines. "British markings. RAF."

Fenris was yelping.

Hochburg reached behind to soothe the dog. "Are there any others?" he asked the gunner.

"Sky's clear."

The Meteor was banking, ready to circle round.

"We can't outrun it," said the copilot.

"It's coming back!" shouted the gunner. "What should we do?"

The Meteor slowed till it was tailing them from above. A hundred meters of sky separated the two aircraft.

Hochburg shook off the last of his dream. "Is it armed?"

"Four guns."

"No British planes should be up here." Hochburg took hold of the controls and eased back on the speed. "We give it the air ahead," he said to the gunner. "If it returns for another pass, blow it from the sky."

"But, Oberstgruppenführer—"

"Or would you rather it be us?"

The Meteor overtook them. Banked sharply again.

"He's coming around. Five hundred meters. No sign of engaging."

"You have your orders."

"Five hundred," counted the gunner. "Four. Three . . ." He fired, blasting the British jet.

Hochburg's seat rocked. The Meteor streaked over, blinding them with smoke. As it cleared, he watched the plane plummet toward the grasslands below. The cockpit vanished; seconds later, the white poppy of a parachute appeared.

Suddenly the air around them was electrified with bullets.

The copilot slammed the stick forward, sending them into a dive. The propellers screamed.

The gunner was yelling into his mouthpiece: "There's another plane!"

A second Meteor whooshed overhead.

Hochburg caught a band of red and green on its fuselage: the Mozambique Air Force. Numbering twenty aircraft, it was considered more a vanity project than a threat, though recently Hochburg had seen intelligence reports that the British were training its pilots. So far Mozambique, Portugal's other African colony, had stayed out of the war and not supported Angola.

The gunner pursued the Mozambican jet. Clipped its tail wing. Then it vanished from view as it arced back through the clouds for a second run at them.

The Focke-Wulf was level again, the movement so abrupt that Hochburg's head bounced off the cockpit glass.

"Give me the controls," he said to the copilot and forced them into a steep climb.

More tracer fire flickered past.

"We'll stall," said the copilot.

They were rising almost vertically now, the whole structure of the plane shuddering. The sky above was bleached of color.

"Is it in range?" Hochburg asked the gunner.

"He's following. Four, five seconds to contact."

"Get ready," said Hochburg, straightening them out.

He drove the lever forward.

They dived—a lurching, bowel-flattening sensation—and in an instant were level with the belly of the Meteor. The *rat-tat-tat* of their cannon was louder than the rushing air.

The gunner whooped. A fireball shot past them.

Hochburg watched the Mozambican jet plummet from the sky. A shard of metal detached from its tail fin and spun toward them. It punctured the Focke-Wulf's port wing and fuel tank. The plane juddered violently, Fenris howling.

Gasoline streamed from the aircraft. It caught the sunlight, stretching and separating into globules as it was whisked away, sparkling like a trail of diamonds.

Hochburg battled with the controls. "Where's the nearest airstrip? We can glide down."

"There's nothing in this sector," replied the copilot.

Empty savannah filled the bubble of the cockpit. Slowly the fuel gauge dipped toward zero.

CHAPTER SIX

Suffolk coast, England
29 January, 03:15

THE SEA AND sky were the deepest black. He couldn't wait for sunrise.

Reluctantly, Burton pressed the bell. The second time, he let his finger stay till a procession of lights came on: the attic, the stairs, finally the lamps by the front door. Shivering, he squinted in the glare. His shoulder had grown stiff, the shirt plastered around it with blood.

There was a purposeful snap of locks, and the door opened. Burton found himself staring at the twin bores of a sawed-off shotgun.

"What do you want?"

It was Pebble, his aunt's maid, wearing a greatcoat over her nightdress, scowling with sleep; she looked ready to pull the trigger. Her husband had been a gamekeeper before being killed at Dunkirk. Burton noted that the safety catch was off.

"Sorry it's so late—"

"Who are you?"

"I've come to see my aunt."

The barrels lowered. "Master Cole?" The maid checked herself: "Burton?" He couldn't bear the servants calling him anything other than his first name.

Pebble, like her mistress, was a woman given to pragmatism. That her employer's nephew had arrived on the doorstep at three in the morning with a split face left her unfazed. Her only task was to find solutions.

She stepped aside to let him in.

Burton half-jokingly called this place "the sanatorium." This was where he came between bouts of carnage in Africa: a haven where he could let his wounds heal or lie in bed as tropical germs sweated out of him. Before he bought the farm, this was his imitation of home. With its white, colonnaded frontage, the house possessed a conspicuous grandeur; at the rear, the garden ran down to the North Sea. It had been built by his grandfather in the previous century and lost through brandy and bad adventures. His aunt had made it her duty to regain ownership of the house. Burton suspected that she'd endured years of sordid marriage, before being widowed, to inherit enough wealth to buy back the family property.

Pebble showed him into the drawing room. It was still warm, even though the hearth was dead. "I'll wake her," she said and slipped away.

All Burton wanted to do was sink into one of the chesterfields, but he ignored them. If he sat, the embers of his strength would desert him. Instead he patrolled the room, absorbing its familiarity: the deep carpet that smelled of ash and sea salt, the decanter half full of Madeira, the photograph on the mantelpiece that showed his mother and aunt before they were estranged—all legs, laughter, and Edwardian bathing suits, taken a hundred feet from this spot. In the corner a piano gleamed like a somber, polished sarcophagus.

Burton rested his hand on it. He became aware of how silent the house was. The first time he met Madeleine, she'd been playing this piano. That had been—what?—four or five years ago. He could never remember exactly: it was a chance meeting that foretold nothing.

It had been a blustery summer evening; plenty of cocktails and merriment on the lawn. Burton was at the sanatorium to shake off the last dregs of a bout of dengue fever. His aunt insisted that he show his face, so he came downstairs, planning to drift through the partygoers before returning to bed. In the drawing room there were calls for music. A slender, dark-haired woman volunteered to play. " 'Knees Up Mother Brown,' " called someone. " 'What's the Use of Getting Sober,' " shouted another. Ginned-up laughter.

The woman ignored them and began to pick out a classical piece. Burton recognized it at once, even if he couldn't name it. The music was mischievous, melancholic. He moved toward the piano and watched her. She was trying to play casually, a virtuoso tinkering at the keyboard, but he could see her knitted concentration. Her fingers were long and delicate. Every now and then a lock of hair would bounce into her face; he liked the way she flicked it behind her ear when the music allowed. Halfway through the piece, she gave up.

"Why did you stop?" asked Burton.

"Nobody's listening."

"I am." He moved closer and smelled her perfume; it was a musky barrier around her. "It's familiar—what is it?"

"Schubert," she replied. "The Hungarian Melody."

He nodded to himself. "My mother used to play it."

"She was a pianist?"

"On the gramophone," he said absentmindedly. "It makes me think of kerosene lamps and crickets."

The woman raised her eyebrows; they were finely plucked.

"I grew up in Africa. She liked to play her records in the evening . . ." Burton fought away the memory and studied the woman.

She was younger than he'd first thought, about the same age as him. Her eyes were blue with a tinge of pewter; he noticed that instantly, as he did the wedding ring. Her expression was bright, but beneath it he sensed something else, something forlorn, unconsoled; or maybe he was seeing himself. The mercenary in him noted the pearl earrings and expensive dress. Burton didn't know what else to say. They appraised each other for a moment that lasted too long.

She held out her hand: "Mrs. Cranley."

He took it. Her grip was assured, the skin soft, and yet in the palm he felt calluses that no amount of cream could smooth away.

"Burton," he replied.

"Ah . . . the famous nephew, back from Africa."

He let go, unsure whether she was mocking him. Her eyes gave away nothing. He searched for something to say and saw that her glass was empty.

"Another?"

"No. I don't much like parties. I only came because of your aunt."

"How do you know her?"

"We're neighbors. I have a house along the coast."

"But you're not from here."

"It's a country home. The rest of the time I live in London."

"I meant the accent. You're German?"

Her expression darkened. "Viennese." She replaced the lid of the keyboard and stood. "I left before the war."

"Es waren die guten Leute die gegangen sind."

She looked alarmed and, glancing around, replied in English: "My husband says it's best not to speak German. Or to men I don't know."

Sometimes Burton took pleasure in provoking his aunt's friends, with their settled, swanky lives, but watching Madeleine walk away, he was irritated with himself. "I enjoyed your playing," he called after her—in English this time. His father had been German and he grew up speaking both languages. If she heard him, she didn't turn round.

Twenty minutes later, exhausted by small talk, Burton retreated to his room. He stood by the window, ignoring the shouts of laughter from the garden, letting the sea breeze cool him. Then he closed the shutters and pulled the curtains tight. At once the air took on a hot, oppressive quality—he drew comfort from that. As for Madeleine Cranley, he didn't give her another thought. It was more than a year till they met again.

The piano was cold and lifeless beneath Burton's palm. His aunt couldn't play, and he wondered if anyone had sat at it since Madeleine. A deep quivering sob rose in him; he stifled it and blanked his mind. The minutes passed. Burton was beginning to wonder if Pebble had failed to rouse his aunt when she glided into the room. She was wearing an emerald dress, her face fresh with foundation, the white-and-blond curls of her hair tied tight.

"Poor Pebble is getting too old to be woken in the middle of the night. So am I."

Somehow she was never as stately or attractive as the image Burton kept in his mind. "I need your help," he said.

"Couldn't it have waited till morning?"

Burton parted his jacket, showing her the blood-soaked material beneath.

Without another word his aunt escorted him to the kitchen, where Pebble had put a kettle on to boil.

"I was going to make tea."

"That won't be necessary, dear. Check that Burton's room is made up, then get back to bed."

Burton was told to sit at the table. He peeled off his jacket and shirt, revealing the stump of his wrist. Above it, the forearm was burnt and disfigured where he had been branded in Kongo. Another scar from his failed mission.

"Good God, Burton!" His aunt tapped her breastbone. "What happened?"

"I need you to look at my shoulder first."

She reached for a tea cloth and dabbed the wound. "You'll live," she said. "But it's deep. You should see a doctor."

"No doctors."

"It needs stitching."

"Can you do it?"

Whereas Burton's mother had gone to Africa to save souls, her sister, always the more practical, wanted to save bodies. During the Great War she had volunteered as a nurse.

"Watch the kettle," she replied, heading for the door. "And find more tea towels."

She returned with iodine, liniments, a needle and thread, a spare shirt; she wore an apron over her dress. After cleaning the gash, his aunt took the needle and bent low. Burton felt her breath warm his neck. He shifted forward.

"It's been a long time since I had to do this," she said. "It won't be the prettiest of things."

Burton glanced at his stump and wondered what Maddie would have made of it. They'd once seen a legless beggar on the street, a veteran of Dunkirk, and she'd been horrified. "Doesn't matter."

The needle pierced his skin.

"So are you going to tell me?"

"There's nothing to say."

"I haven't heard from you since the summer. Then you turn up in the middle of the night like this." She tugged the thread. "I think you owe me an explanation."

Burton jigged his foot: blood was trickling down his back. "When did you last see Madeleine?"

"You mean Madeleine Cranley? Not in months, the poor dear. I didn't think you knew each other."

"What happened to her?"

"There have been all sorts of rumors, silly talk mostly. But what's it got to do with you?"

"Tell me."

She was taken aback by his intensity. "Madeleine is very ill. Had some kind of breakdown. I heard she'd been sent to an institution—though it's been hushed up because of her husband."

"What about him?"

His aunt paused to dab the wound. "He came to their house for Christmas with his little girl—"

"Alice."

"They hardly stirred. After the New Year they returned to London and haven't been back."

"Did you see him?"

"Only once, at the Vieux-Moines' and their Boxing Day drinks."

"How was he?"

"He'd had a glass too many but seemed in good spirits. I'm sure it was for show. Do you know him, too? Charming man; he'll do his best for Madeleine."

"She's dead." Traveling from the farm, he had warded off the thought; now he was sickened by how easily he spoke it. "Cranley had her killed."

The needle stuck.

"Burton! How can you say such a wicked thing?"

"It's true." He hesitated before continuing, glad that his head was dipped toward the table. "Madeleine and I were having an affair. She was going to leave him—that's why I borrowed the money to buy the farm. He found out about us: sent me to Africa, I don't know what he did with Maddie . . . except she's dead."

"I don't believe it," his aunt spluttered. "He works for the government, is highly respected. When I saw him at Christmas, I told him how sorry I was. He brushed away a tear."

"He took this." Burton raised his handless arm. "And the lives of the men I led."

"But killing his own wife, the mother of his daughter! He even has a CBE, the king pinned it on him."

"If a lord of the realm can call Hitler our friend, you can have a CBE and blood on your hands."

Somewhere a clock chimed: one, two, three, four, the sound dissolving into the cold. His aunt folded a tea towel and pressed it against his shoulder to absorb more blood.

"You have to believe me," said Burton.

"If it's true what you say, why did you go to Africa? You told me you were giving up that life."

"Cranley tricked me. Tricked me with the one thing I couldn't refuse." Burton hesitated again. "The chance to kill a man."

"Who could have mattered so much?"

He had waited till after his twenty-first birthday before writing to his aunt; any sooner and he feared he might be shipped to England and her custody. By then Bel Abbès, the Legion fort that made him a soldier, had been home for five years. Patrick offered him his quarters for some privacy. Outside, the dunes hissed as the wind beat across them. The sky was a dirty pink; Burton remembered the blush of the sunset on the paper. He wrote a simple letter, omitting the terrible details, and informed his aunt that his parents had passed on.

"I never told you the truth," he said, fixing his eyes on his scarred, misshapen arm. "There was no consolation in it. Mother didn't die; she left—vanished—years before, with no explanation. The man I went to Africa for, the one I wanted to kill, knew why."

"Who was he?"

Burton hadn't spoken his name since Africa. Now he came vividly to mind: his ogre's frame and bald head, those eyes—black as the devil's hangman. "Walter Hochburg. He was a pastor when he came to us; I was just a boy. Now he's the governor of Kongo. He vanished the same day as Mother." He had imagined countless possibilities for her—all of them foul. "We offered Hochburg kindness and charity, and he repaid us with misery. I wanted revenge."

"Revenge is vanity. Did Madeleine know any of this?"

"Everything."

"And what did she say?"

"She told me I was chasing ghosts, pleaded with me not to go."

"But you did, Burton." His aunt tossed the tea towel onto the table; it was soaked the color of wine. "If it's true about Cranley, you left her when she most needed protecting."

He had no reply. The needle broke his skin again.

His aunt sewed in silence till she finished and knotted the thread. She put a pad doused with liniment over his shoulder, secured it with a bandage, and draped the spare shirt over him. Then she took the blood-soaked tea towels to the sink and rinsed them under the tap.

Burton watched his aunt and wished he had told her about his affair with Madeleine long before—but he'd heard too many tales of his errant grandfather to share that confidence. He guessed she was offended by the lack of trust. What bound them was as shallow as blood: she'd needed a nephew to spoil, and he'd wanted a place to seem like home. That, and a woman they rarely spoke about. Burton had a sudden sense of his aunt when he was away and there were no party guests, only Pebble and the remorseless thud of the sea. He understood that loneliness, and so had Madeleine—that's why the two women had befriended each other.

His aunt wrung out the tea towels and flicked her hands dry. "You're as selfish as your mother," she said, speaking with an ancient resentment he had never heard before. "She went to Africa without a thought of what she left behind."

"It wasn't like that with Maddie. I needed the truth."

"Did you find it?"

He shook his head. "But I had to try. I wanted to lock up the past for good, and Madeleine understood that."

"Eleanor had her justifications, too."

"You always said she was a good woman."

"She was everything an older sister should be. Clever, beautiful, brave as a lioness." His aunt took off her bloodstained apron. "She was also feckless. Impetuous. A stupid, romantic fool chasing her dreams and to hell with the hearts she broke."

Burton met his aunt's eyes and realized that he had been wrong. It wasn't resentment; it was exhaustion, a lifetime's worth flowing from her as hot as it was futile.

"Your mother butterflied from one fancy to another," she continued. "When she found the church, that was the worst. I begged her to stay here and help me save this house. Later I begged her not to marry your father, because I knew that one day she'd wake up next to an old man while she was still young. There's no mystery, Burton, she ran off with this Hochburg. Nothing bad happened. And when her next whim came along, I'm sure she flitted away again."

Burton answered in a hollowed-out voice. "Two years after they'd vanished, Hochburg returned. Alone. Who knows what wickedness he'd done to her. He set our home alight, torched the orphanage. Father was trapped inside. The children were in their beds."

His aunt fell silent.

"I'll never forget the screams or the sound of the timbers crashing. I'll never forget that smell. It's what I think of first when I think of my childhood."

There was an unbearably long pause.

At last his aunt spoke: "It's too late to talk like this." Her whole demeanor looked eroded. "I need to sleep. You should rest, too."

They said good night. Burton went upstairs to his usual room and slid beneath the sheets. They were icy and reeked of musty lavender. He was still staring at the ceiling as dawn cut through the curtains.

+ + +

"I just remembered this," said Pebble, bringing in a package along with a fresh pot of tea.

They were at the breakfast table, the air savory with kedgeree and buttered toast. Burton felt warm and full, his hair damp from a bath. He was skimming the front page of the *Telegraph:* President Robert A. Taft, inaugurated in Washington the previous week, had announced his first visit to the Reich to voice concerns about the Jews in Madagaskar and reaffirm his country's neutrality; he would pass through London on his return. Burton took the package and checked the postmark. Lusaka, Northern Rhodesia.

"It arrived last year," said his aunt. "I'm afraid I opened it." Her face was smooth, but the foundation failed to hide the charcoal smudges beneath her eyes.

Burton reached inside: two passports, his and Patrick's. Prior to the Kongo mission, the team had been asked for next-of-kin addresses to send personal effects should the worst happen. He hadn't wanted Madeleine to learn of his death that way, so he had given his aunt's details; Patrick was of the same mind. He opened his old friend's passport and saw a familiar face scowling at him. Patrick gone, Maddie gone: could it really be true? The world seemed lonelier than ever. Patrick was American with a teenage daughter in Baltimore. Burton decided that he would find her and explain everything that had happened to her father. Give her a share of the diamonds in his pocket. It was a small penance, but it was all he had.

"I hope you're going to keep us company for a while," said his aunt.

"I want to catch the one o'clock train."

"So soon? You should stay—it's been too long since you were a guest. Your shoulder will need a few days."

"It feels better." He rolled it stiffly to prove the point; there had been no blood on the bedclothes.

An hour later they were walking the length of the driveway, to where a taxi waited. A mist had crept off the sea, shrouding everything in a bright whiteness that burned his eyes. Pebble had found him one of her husband's tweed jackets to wear: more dead men's clothes.

"You always have a home here," said his aunt.

Burton thought of the septic tank on the farm. "I know."

"It's what your mother would have wanted. I shouldn't have spoken so freely last night. I'm sure she was happy with your father. He doted on her, wouldn't have left her—that's what she needed. I never knew about Hochburg."

"I should have kept him where he belonged, buried in the past, like Madeleine said."

There was nothing else to say; it was all too painful.

He leaned forward to give his aunt the customary parting peck on the cheek. She took hold of him, hugging him as though she knew they would never meet again. He caught a ghostly trace of his mother. What would she have been like if she'd lived? Apart from their golden-blond curls, there was little resemblance between the sisters. The taxi honked its horn. He let go of his aunt.

"Where are you going?" she asked.

Burton had returned to Africa for the truth; it had led him through a maze to where he started from. "I need to find out what happened to Maddie. I can't grieve for her till I do." He swung his haversack over his good shoulder. "Then America—I've a promise to keep there."

"And Cranley?" Her eyes bored into him. "You're going to kill him, aren't you?"

Burton shook his head, a reassuring smile on his lips. "I want to hurt him more than that."

CHAPTER SEVEN

Kongo
29 January, 10:00

WALTER HOCHBURG READ with a single eye. The sign was peeling, pitted with open sores of rust:

Union Minière du Haut-Katanga
SHINKOLOBWE MINE
Est. 1922
"Good health, good spirits—and high productivity."

A thick black cross was painted through the words. In the top left corner a skull stencil had been added, along with the letters DESTA, indicating the SS earthworks company. Beneath the sign were a roofless sentry hut and a wall of mangy barbed wire; no gate.

He spoke to the man slung over his shoulder. The Focke-Wulf, its fuel tanks empty, had landed hard despite Hochburg's wrestling with the controls. It bounced off the savannah . . . then furrowed into the earth. One of the wings broke away; the cockpit buckled and shattered. The copilot's neck had been broken, but the gunner survived. Ignoring his own injuries, Hochburg dragged him from the wreckage and carried him through the rain-soaked night, driven by his need to reach Elisabethstadt. At least the terrain was easy: this was cattle country: rolling hills, few trees. "I promised you deliverance," he said.

When there was no response, Hochburg lowered the gunner and pressed two fingers against his jugular. His pulse was silent.

A girl emerged from the hut. She was no more than thirteen, with blond plaits and the fierce little teeth of a civet. Around her waist was a grimacing skull belt, in her hand a rickety Karabiner rifle.

Hochburg heaved the gunner back onto his shoulder and headed toward her. Fenris limped at his side.

"Halt!"

When he ignored her, the girl fired a single shot. Mud exploded centimeters from his boot. She drew back the bolt to reload the weapon.

"Identify yourself."

Despite the burrowing pain in his eye and limbs steeped in exhaustion, the sight of her skull buckle was welcome. A weary indulgence took over him. In their first months together, he and Eleanor tried to conceive a child. *Let it be a daughter,* she used to say. Often when he came face-to-face with girls he would look upon them and ruminate. Would Eleanor still have left him for Burton if they'd had a baby?

"We are a dog, a dead man . . . and Oberstgruppenführer Hochburg, governor-general of Kongo." Fenris sniffed around her knees. "And you, my young Fräulein?"

The girl's eyes widened, but she did not avert them. "I am not yet worthy of a rank, Oberstgruppenführer."

"But you wear the skull."

Remembering herself, she cracked the rifle to her side with well-drilled precision and held out her arm. "Heil Hitler!"

Hochburg indulged her once more—"Heil"—and motioned for her to stand at ease. "You are lucky this morning. Normally Fenris eats little girls."

They walked through the gap in the fence to a dirt avenue bordered by decrepit barracks. The ground was encrusted with the tracks of huge vehicles—but the impressions were old, like the clawmarks of prehistoric beasts. Above, the sky threatened to open again.

"How long has the mine been closed?" asked Hochburg. He recognized the name Shinkolobwe from the endless flow of paperwork that crossed his desk; there had been some export kerfuffle over it a few years previously.

"Since before I was born," replied the girl.

"Then why are you here?"

"The DESTA guards were sent to the front line, so we were brought in."

"Has there been news from Elisabethstadt?"

She shook her head.

"I need to send a message there at once and arrange a helicopter. It's urgent. Where is your commander?"

A puddle blocked their path. It was too deep and wide to cross, so they went round it. Fenris paused to lap the water.

"Interrogating prisoners, Oberstgruppenführer."

A prickle of despair. He should have pushed himself harder through the night and left the dying gunner. "The British are this far north already?"

The girl didn't answer but led him to a wooden hut painted marmalade red. Before entering, he laid down the dead man. Inside was a young woman dressed in the tan uniform of an Oberhelfer. Although SS membership was closed to women, a special corps—the SS-Helferin—existed for auxiliary roles: administrative staff, radio operators, camp guards. It was a boon for proud parents who only had daughters. She was talking on the phone, her voice as clenched and damp as her face.

". . . there must be someone with the authority. Try Stanleystadt again. You have to find me someone. I can't take responsibility."

She looked up.

"Oberhelfer Lampedo," said the sentry girl, "this is Oberstgruppenführer Hochburg."

Without another word, Lampedo replaced the receiver. Hochburg recognized her type at once. The Party liked to cultivate them, women who were wholesome, beautiful, but considered themselves plain to the point of indifference: effortlessly exploitable. She stood to attention and dismissed his escort.

"I shall see you are given the *Silberspange*," Hochburg called after her. The Silberspange was a silver clasp awarded to women of distinction in the SS.

The girl left beaming.

He addressed the Oberhelfer: "My plane crashed."

"There's no doctor here," she apologized, "but we do have medical supplies."

When the Focke-Wulf's cockpit had shattered, a shard of glass lodged in his left eye; by nightfall it was swollen shut, the throbbing as deep as his gums. "It can wait."

"It looks bad, Oberstgruppenführer. You must be in pain."

"My priority is Elisabethstadt. I have to stop them from surrendering. Can you get me a line?"

Lampedo was already picking up the phone.

"I hear you have prisoners," said Hochburg as they waited for a connection.

"We captured them last night."

"On patrol?"

She curled the telephone wire around her fingers. "In the mine itself. They had cut through the perimeter fence. Were taking samples."

"How many of them?"

"A team of four. One was shot trying to escape. We're holding the others."

"What have they told you?"

"Not much. I did try, Oberstgruppenführer, but they refused to cooperate."

"The arrogance of the British will be their undoing." He dabbed a bloody tear from his eye. "Elisabethstadt is not yet theirs, and already they steal our treasures."

Lampedo creased her forehead in confusion. "The British?"

"Your prisoners. You said they were taking samples. But they'll have nothing more."

"There has been some misunderstanding, Oberstgruppenführer. The prisoners aren't British."

"Then who are they?"

She glanced down, as if it were her fault. "Americans."

+ + +

Before interrogation, always a good breakfast.

Hochburg sent orders to Elisabethstadt to keep fighting; a helicopter was requested. While he awaited its arrival, he would chat with their American guests. Although supplies at the mine were short, teenage girls flitted in with salami, some stale *Schwarzbrot*, and coffee, most blushing and tongue-tied. His favorite sentry returned with some painkillers for his eye and a mango. Hochburg thanked them all and breakfasted heartily. He speared a slice of meat onto his fork, waved it beneath Fenris's snout, but did not feed him. Saliva drooled from the dog's mouth.

"Where are the prisoners now?" asked Hochburg, draining his coffee. A decade before, the Führer had insisted that the growing of coffee be a priority in German Africa: it would end the humiliation of having to import it from the British.

"At the top of the mine," replied Lampedo. "I left them out overnight, hoping it would make them more . . ."

"I believe 'amenable' is the current textbook term."

She nodded.

"They must be soaked. Take me to them."

Hochburg followed her out of the hut, Fenris at his side. The morning sun was shrouded in clouds. As they walked, he reached inside his tunic for Burton's knife and began to peel the mango.

"How do you know they're Americans?" he asked.

"I spent three months in New Jersey," replied Lampedo. "A student exchange between Freiburg University and Princeton."

Shinkolobwe was opencast. The avenue of barracks rose to a ridge and a gash in the earth's crust hundreds of meters deep. Down the sides were terraces where minerals had once been mined. The rock was the color of butter toffee, with seams of something darker and occasional slivers of turquoise and gray.

Kneeling at the edge were three men stripped to the waist, arms bound behind them, their boots removed. Lampedo had chosen her spot well, noted Hochburg. Inside a hut the prisoners could have plotted an escape, but here they were entirely visible: a suicidal drop in front, rifles at their backs. To have trapped Burton in such a position! There would have been no brief agony for him—instead, an accretion of torment and hopelessness that Hochburg could have prolonged for any period he desired.

"You did this?" he asked. The men's faces were swollen and crusted with blood.

"I wanted them to talk."

"And your girls captured them?" Guarding the Americans were a pack of teenagers: grubby cheeks, wisps of blond hair. No BK44s, no grenades or flamethrowers, only the Karabiners their fathers had used a decade before.

Lampedo nodded.

Hochburg recalled his words to Zelman in the Schädelplatz: *Give me a battalion of girls and this war would already be won.*

He paced behind the prisoners. Two of them had brawny torsos blasted by the elements, and he sensed they wouldn't talk even if beaten with iron bars; endurance was a quality they wanted to parade. The third was much paler, with a band of sunburn around his neck and hair recently cropped at the back and sides. Hochburg peered over their shoulders: below, the bottom of the pit was flooded.

"Fee-fi-fo-fum," he said, "I smell the blood of an Ameri-can . . . I am the governor-general of Kongo. Given your attire"—they were wearing camouflage trousers; nearby, Fenris sniffed three pairs of combat boots—"I will assume you are soldiers."

They offered no reply.

"Unless I am mistaken, your 1940 Neutrality Act is still in force, which makes your presence here . . . unfortunate." He contemplated this a moment. "And intriguing."

He finished peeling the mango, cut a slice, and ate.

"Have they been given food, Oberhelfer? Water?"

"Nothing. I even taped their mouths so they couldn't drink the rain."

"You possess a cruelty, Fräulein, that should be exported."

He cut another slice and offered it in turn to the three men. "Not the ripest I've had but refreshing all the same." The first two stared ahead; only the pale one glanced at the fruit. His tongue darted over cracked lips.

Hochburg shrugged to himself, swallowed the slice, and finished the mango. He sucked on the stone and tossed it into the abyss. "I want your names, ranks, and why you are here in Kongo."

Again, no reply.

Hochburg greeted their silence with laughter. "Good. I hate long introductions."

"He's called Nultz," said Lampedo, pointing to the pale one. "He was the only one to talk last night. We also confiscated these from him." She held up a pair of wire-framed spectacles, the ends curled to fit tight round the ears.

Hochburg stood behind the prisoner, studied the hunch of his spine. "I'm guessing that your background is academic, Herr Nultz, not military." His tone was emollient, attentive. "Where do you teach?"

"Berkeley—"

"Shut up!" spat the soldier next in line.

"Ignore him," said Hochburg. "Consider your position; think for yourself."

Nultz curled his toes but said nothing more.

There was a rumble of thunder. The clouds were congealing. Fenris lifted his snout and inhaled the approaching rainfall.

Hochburg sighed deeply. An unexpected weariness took hold of him that had little to do with trekking all night or his gnawing eye. Its sluggish distemper settled in his stomach. Why wouldn't they tell him what he needed? Why this defiance in the face of the inevitable? As if men secretly relished being the objects of violence. It was the only commonality he knew of that bound the races.

"One hundred and twenty kilometers from here, Elisabethstadt is close to capitulation. I need to get there with all haste." He straightened his spine. "How long till the helicopter arrives, Fräulein Lampedo?"

"Thirty minutes, Oberstgruppenführer."

"You see, Americans, time is short. So tell me what I need." He prowled behind them, his boots squelching in the mud. "I implore you, for my sake as much as yours."

Silence.

He cocked his eye toward Fenris. The dog was tense, staring at him keenly.

Hochburg kicked the first American with all his force.

His boot landed square between the shoulder blades. The man tumbled over the edge. A scream filled the air for a second. A second and a half. Then a wet, ripping thump.

Hochburg skipped to the second soldier.

"No, wait! I—"

Another kick. Another plummeting scream.

He rounded on Nultz. In Germania there was a worming paranoia that one day the United States would declare war on the Reich—despite the reassurances of presidents from Roosevelt to Taft. Hochburg had never shared the concern. The American below him was hyperventilating, a wet patch spreading from his groin.

He clamped his fingers around the man's neck, held his head over the precipice.

"What are you doing here?"

On the terraces below, his two compatriots lay buckled and snapped, outlined by rock pools of blood.

Nultz's stomach heaved.

Hochburg levered him farther over the edge. "You're with the British?"

"No."

"Then why?"

"The mine."

"Tell me something I don't know."

"I'm just a geologist."

"Look." Hochburg forced the prisoner's head down. One of his comrades was still alive, his arm held toward the heavens. Twitching. "If you're lucky, you'll land headfirst."

"Uranium," bawled Nultz. His beaten face dripped tears and mucus.

"It means nothing to me."

"It's a heavy metal," said Lampedo. She was standing well back from the edge. "They use it in X-rays."

"You came ten thousand kilometers for hospital equipment?" Hochburg dragged him to the very rim of the pit, the mud crumbling beneath his boots.

"Another use," said Nultz.

"What?"

"Can't say . . . please . . ."

"Tell me!"

When all he got was sniveling, Hochburg whistled to Fenris. He gave the dog a flick of his head, and the animal bounded to the terraces. He began picking his way down, moving with the agility of a famished belly.

"There was only breakfast enough for me," said Hochburg. He grabbed Nultz by the ears, locked his head in position. "Watch."

Fenris reached the first American. Began to gorge.

"Stop! Please . . ." Nultz was sobbing.

"Why uranium?"

"A weapon . . . a bomb."

"Tell me more."

For several moments, Nultz did nothing but quail; then he sagged. "I'll talk."

Hochburg dragged him away and threw him at the feet of the guards. One had turned away, her shoulders shuddering. The rest of the girls stared at the American with contempt. A few were peering into the mine, their eyes chasing Fenris.

"Give him some water," said Hochburg.

A canteen was tossed at Nultz. Hochburg squatted by his side, unscrewed it, and helped him drink.

"I want to know about this bomb. Why your government sent you all this way."

Nultz spoke in a babble: "Because of the Jews . . . as insurance . . . against Madagaskar."

"Jews don't concern me. The bomb."

"It's fifteen kilotons."

Hochburg possessed only a rudimentary knowledge of these things. He did the calculation in his head. No: *impossible!* Did it again. "Kilotons. Are you sure? A single bomb could—"

"Destroy an entire city." Even drenched in his own piss, sullied with snot and mud, Nultz couldn't keep a tremor of a boast from his voice. "American big talk and orgies of numbers," Goebbels called it.

"You've developed this weapon?"

"It's only theoretical."

"Why the uranium?"

"It's needed as fission material. That's where it gets the power. We're looking for a source."

"Oberstgruppenführer, urgent news!" said Lampedo. Next to her, one of the radio-hut girls was panting, a scrap of paper in her hand.

"It can wait." Hochburg already knew what it said.

He snatched a handful of Nultz's hair and hauled him back to the edge of the pit. Fenris looked up, disturbed from his feasting.

"You're lying to me," he said.

"I promise, no. You were developing one, too."

"Then where is this miracle?"

"All research was stopped. Your Führer's orders."

"Why?"

"You can check." He gabbled a roll call of half-recognized names, some of Germany's most eminent scientists.

"These men were working on it?" said Hochburg.

"Find them—they'll tell you."

"Do the British know?"

"Not from us."

"And this wonder weapon. It is as powerful as you claim?"

"I swear!"

Could it be so? Could one device, free from the limitations of men, obliterate an entire city? He would need only a dozen to rule the whole of Africa.

His eye flared, radiating needles of pain across his skull. He cupped the wounded socket, then held out his hand to Lampedo. She passed him the message with an ashen expression. There were three words on it. Hochburg read them and crumpled the paper in his fist.

If what the American said was true, perhaps it no longer mattered.

CHAPTER EIGHT

Hampstead, London
31 January, 00:20

WHY DOTH THE *wicked prosper?*

It was his father's nightly howl after they had been abandoned. Burton had asked the same question in the Schädelplatz as he was escorted between the colossal gilded lions that guarded the entrance, on his way to assassinate Hochburg.

As he watched Cranley's house, Job 21:7 tormented him once more.

Burton was enveloped in a thick cobwebby fog, the streetlamps above him fuzzy orbs. Even though he'd fastened all the buttons of his sheepskin jerkin and turned up the collar of his jacket, the cold squeezed his chest. Hidden in his sleeve was the crowbar he'd taken from the farm; his Browning was in his haversack.

Cranley was hosting what Madeleine used to describe as "one of his soirees" (she always laughed at the phrase). The windows were oblongs of peach light, and through them Burton glimpsed guests swilling champagne, heard shrieks of hilarity and swing music, the noise deadened by the fog. He knew these types from his mercenary days: in Congo and the French colonies, they thought the garden parties and cocktails round the pool were going to last forever. Every shout of laughter tightened his gut.

It would have been too suspicious to linger outside, so he kept walking round the streets, passing the house every ten minutes, like he had done on Christmas Eve two years before. Madeleine had lit a pair of candles for him: two flames in the window that promised they wouldn't spend another Christmas apart. Burton's plan was to watch the place for several nights, establish the household's routine, and strike early one morning.

Then he saw Cranley, and his hatred overflowed.

It was past midnight when he appeared, his figure distorted in the fog.

The windows remained bright, though the house was silent now. Burton had stationed himself behind a tree on the opposite pavement. Once he sensed someone nearby, but when his eyes searched the gloom there was only empty, shifting vapor.

He watched Cranley guide a woman in a full-length fur coat to a waiting Rolls-Royce. There was a slight wobble to their steps. They exchanged a few words, and Cranley threw back his head, laughing. He kissed her good night, then signaled to the driver with a rap on the car's roof. That gesture—so genial, so carefree—caused Burton to clench the crowbar. Cranley would go to bed full of expensive bubbles and relaxed cheer; he'd fall asleep as soon as his head sank into the pillow.

Burton darted across the road as the Rolls drove away but not fast enough to catch Cranley. The front door was shut before he reached it and too solid to kick down. He prodded the doorbell with his stump; there was a musical clanging. Through the obscure glass, he saw Cranley return, heard the sound of locks.

Burton dropped.

A weal of pain expanded from the base of his neck, causing his limbs to sag and eyes blur; his teeth felt as if they were going to scatter. The crowbar vanished from his grip. Next moment, the air in his lungs was warm. He heard Cranley's voice—*close the door . . . the dining room*—and was dragged through the hallway, up a short flight of stairs to the mezzanine level. *Tie his hands.* Burton was dumped in a chair, his neck lolling. The chandelier streaked in the murk of his consciousness.

Frozen fingers snatched at his arms. "Sir," said a woman's voice close to his ear, "what should I do?" His stump was forced into the air.

"What was Rommel's valediction when he retired? *'Ein Teil von mir wird für immer in Afrika bleiben.'*" Cranley spoke with the precise accent of a diplomat: *I leave a piece of me forever in Africa.* "Bind him to the armrests," he said, loosening his tie. "Use this round his feet."

While he was being bound, Burton was aware of Cranley crossing the room to fetch a telephone. He brought it back and placed it on the dining table, the cable taut.

"That will be all, Mrs. Anderson," he said. "I'm expecting some callers shortly. When they arrive, show them in here, but keep it quiet. I don't want to disturb Alice. Meantime, warm yourself. You did well tonight."

Burton pulled at his arms, but the rope was too tight. His mind was scrambling, sluggish. He heard the door lock behind him; the housekeeper's footsteps faded. Nausea blurred his thoughts.

Cranley clicked his fingers close to Burton's eyes. "Are you with me?"

When he got no reply, he tossed a glass of champagne in Burton's face. The liquid made Burton focus; with it came a surge of alarm. He scanned the room for any means to free himself. A coal fire hummed in the hearth. There were empty bottles and clusters of glasses everywhere; the table was laden with the remnants of a buffet.

"I expect your full attention," said Cranley, "especially since I'm going to thank you for what you did in Kongo." There was a quality to his voice, something affable and golden, that Burton struggled not to like. "It played out exactly as I hoped. We baited Hochburg with Rhodesia, his hubris did the rest: he overstretched himself. Elisabethstadt surrendered yesterday." He rummaged through Burton's haversack till he found the Browning. "The only shame is that Madeleine wasn't here. She always enjoyed parties."

"She hated them."

"I think I know my wife better than that."

The circulation was dying in Burton's arms. He tugged at the ropes again; there was the tiniest give around his stump. "What did you do to her?"

"I used to carry an HP myself," said Cranley, aiming the pistol at Burton's chest. "During the Spanish Civil War. It's lighter than I recall"—he weighed it in his grip and depressed the safety catch—"but a fine weapon. Very accurate, never jams. You were going to shoot me in my sleep?"

Burton knew it would be better to say nothing but couldn't contain himself. "I'm only here for Alice." His plan had been to snatch the girl, flee to America, and vanish. Cranley, with his wealth and prestige, his strings of power, would be left impotent.

"Then you know nothing of me. Take my daughter and I'd hunt you for the rest of your days."

"It was the least I owed Madeleine."

Cranley scrutinized Burton, running his eyes from his boots to his beard. Burton stared back. Neither of them blinked. Previously, he had only seen photographs of Cranley. Up close, Burton was struck by the symmetry of his face, the unblemished skin, the beauty of his mouth; he could think of no other description. There was also an itchy, repressed quality to his features. He remembered something Madeleine once said: first class was never good enough for him. The whole time, Burton kept trying to worm his arm free.

"I can't imagine what she saw in you." Cranley's eyes remained fixed. "She was from good Viennese stock. Though I confess it is intriguing to meet you, Major Cole. Is one's rival the same as oneself, only in more . . . 'concentrated' form? Or the complete opposite."

Finally he glanced away, a smirk parting his lips as if he had intended to avert his gaze all along. Near the fireplace was a liquor cabinet in the shape of a globe. It was antique: Russia stretched from Europe to the Pacific. Cranley poured himself a brandy, never letting the gun waver.

"Shall I tell you what distressed me most?" he said, perching himself on the table. "It's those things the Nazis say about Jews. That they're rodents. Unclean, conniving." He inhaled the bouquet of the brandy. "Claptrap, of course. But when I discovered what she'd done to me . . . Propaganda is most hateful when it's true."

"You killed her."

"What would you have done if it was *your* wife?" His jawline erupted in scarlet pinpricks. "If you'd given her a life beyond her imagination, then found her fucking some menial." He was calm again. "I didn't kill her."

"Like you didn't kill Patrick or the rest of my men in Kongo. You gave the order; that's enough. Russell told me everything."

"I doubt it."

Cranley picked up the telephone from the table and dialed the operator. "Scotland Yard," he said, specifying the extension number. While he waited to be connected, he examined the point of his shoe as if it were the most fascinating object in the world. Burton gave his arm another tug; the skin was chafing, but the rope felt slacker.

"One thing I am curious about. How did you escape the *Ibis*? I received confirmation that you were on board when it left Angola."

"A day out to sea, we passed a freighter headed for Cape Town. Even half-dead on morphine, I reckoned someone would hit us. If not you, then Hochburg. I changed ships."

"You are a remarkable man, Major."

"Then up the east coast to Suez."

Cranley nodded but was no longer interested. With a sardonic detachment, he watched Burton fight the rope before his attention returned to the phone. He identified himself as though his name were expected.

"That Suffolk business, the two dead officers, I have the killer here . . . in my house . . . No, I'm perfectly safe, he's not going anywhere . . . Good, send them quickly but keep it discreet—I don't want to alarm the neighbors."

He replaced the receiver.

"We assumed you'd come here; they're only minutes away." He sipped his brandy. "There will be a guilty verdict, Major, and a noose. Personally, I'd rather you rot in prison for the rest of your days, but the law is the law. Whatever reputation you might have had will be ground into dirt. Worth nothing."

Burton listened to those final words, the unrestrained thrill of them. "And in the dock, I'll tell them what you did to Madeleine."

"Which was?"

"You had her murdered."

"No. She's alive."

He showed his wedding ring as if it were proof.

Burton felt a murmur of hope before dismissing it. Cranley was toying with him. "I don't believe you."

"Of course I thought about it. How it would feel—that final, pleading look in her eyes." Another sip of brandy. "But as I said, I don't believe in death penalties. They're too kind. A bullet, or a rope, and it's done. But a lifetime of torment: that is retribution."

"So you sent her to the madhouse?"

"Is that what they're saying?" Cranley clapped his leg, the sparkle in his eyes genuine. "One can always rely on the tittle-tattle of society women!"

"Then where is she?"

From outside came the sound of an engine.

Keeping the Browning pointed at Burton, Cranley stepped to the curtains. "The police, two cars."

Burton twisted his wrist: just a few more inches.

"There's one last thing I have to tell you," said Cranley, returning to his perch. "Something for you to dwell upon in the months before you choke. The real reason why I couldn't kill her." He leaned in close, whispered as he prodded the Browning into Burton's ribs. "It's my baby."

"You hadn't touched her in months."

"Only an idiot would believe a woman who lived a double life. Every time she returned from your trysts, I visited her room, smelled you on her."

"You're lying."

Cranley's next words emerged with complete assurance: "She never loved you, no matter what she professed. I hope you understand that."

Burton tore at the rope. When it didn't give, he hurled himself forward with such ferocity that the chair toppled over and they smashed into each other. The wood around his stump splintered, allowing him to free his arm. Burton grabbed the tie around his feet, forced it over his boots, and released his legs. Next he reached for the rope that bound his right wrist to the armrest. His stump was useless against the knot.

Cranley rose. He watched Burton struggle but made no attempt to stop him. "After your telegrams, I had the security improved. The house is locked like a fortress. Even if you could get past this"—he poked the air with the Browning—"you'd have no way out."

"It isn't loaded."

Cranley pointed the pistol at Burton and fired. An empty snap. "You're right: it's not." He placed the weapon on the table, his poise unaffected.

Burton would enjoy beating the confidence out of him. He gave up on the rope and got to his feet, the chair still secured to his arm; its seat caught the backs of his knees, making him stand like a hunchback. He stepped toward Cranley, who made no move to retreat.

Outside the engines stopped; doors opened and were carefully shut. The click of shoes as men hurried to the house.

Burton heaved the chair above his head and swung.

It came crashing down as Cranley slipped out of range. Burton lifted it again and smashed it against the table. On the third blow it broke into pieces, freeing him, though the armrest remained bound to him like a baton. He spun round as Cranley charged.

Burton toppled onto the table, dragging Cranley with him. They smashed into serving dishes and glasses. There was a burst of crockery; uneaten puddings splattered everywhere. Cranley grabbed a champagne bottle and slammed it down. The impact reverberated through the table, inches from Burton's skull. The bottle flashed again, now a jagged neck of glass. Burton raised his hand to shield himself, the armrest deflecting the blow. He staggered to stand.

A fist cracked him in the ribs; then a second, harder punch to the gut, all knuckles.

Cranley hadn't learned this at the Colonial Office, thought Burton as the blows continued. Somewhere in his past he'd been a brawler.

He was lifted up and punched across the table. Slid right over it, falling to the ground on the far side in a cascade of broken plates. His back arched as he dropped next to the fireplace.

Cranley walked round the table, snatched up the poker, and swiped it theatrically like a rapier. He grasped it in both hands and raised it above his head: no longer a sword but an axe. His mouth was stretched with fury.

Burton kicked the grate.

Coals tumbled everywhere, spewing fire across the carpet. The hems of Cranley's trousers ignited. He dropped the poker and slapped at them till his hands smoked. Burton sought a flameless spot in which to lever himself up. From the hallway came the musical clanging of the doorbell.

Cranley retreated from the fire to the liquor cabinet and toppled it onto Burton. Alcohol fattened the flames. Burton forced the cabinet off and rolled beneath the table. In front of him was his discarded Browning. He picked it up and searched for his haversack. Across the room, Cranley had reached the door. He produced a master key and grasped the handle.

Burton saw what was about to happen, screwed himself into a ball. Covered his head.

There was a throaty noise as if someone had gulped sharply in his ear. Fresh oxygen was sucked into the room, the air sweet and lethal. A wave of fire rolled across the ceiling. The walls and furniture erupted in flames.

Burton's face felt like it had been plunged into frying oil. He got to his feet and slammed a clip into the Browning. Cranley had been knocked to the ground by the blast. Burton stood over him and fired an inch from his head. Recocked the hammer.

"Where is she?"

"You'll never find her."

He dropped to his knees, pinning Cranley down, and whipped the Browning against his face.

"Where?" he roared.

When he received no reply, he struck a second time. A gash spread from Cranley's brow to his cheekbone, the metal of the pistol coming away sticky. Each new blow was more frenzied and frustrated.

A pinging. Pieces of the chandelier fired into the room; it jerked from its fitting.

Burton stuffed the pistol into his waistband, grabbed Cranley by the throat, and dragged him deeper into the room, cocooning them in flames. He twisted the other man's face into the blazing heat.

"Last chance," said Burton. Each word charred his throat.

"I'd rather burn than let you see her again."

"I'll track her down."

"All the records are gone. Immigration, marriage. She never existed—"

The chandelier plunged from the ceiling. Baubles of molten glass spat everywhere.

Cranley threw his arms around Burton, clutched him in a tight embrace, and rolled them both into the inferno. Burton's jacket smoldered around his body, the ferocity of the heat searing his skin. The stink of scorched hair.

He cracked his head into Cranley's face and freed himself. A blazing barrier separated them. Through the flames he glimpsed his Browning on the floor, out of reach. Cranley crawled to retrieve it.

Burton stumbled backward till he found the open door. He took the key from the lock, singeing his fingers, stepped into the hallway, and slammed the door shut. Seconds later Cranley's fists were pounding on the other side. Burton turned the key and hurled it into the smoke.

Flames were creeping through the entire house. Burton covered his mouth and groped his way down the stairs, toward the front door. Mrs. Anderson was opening it, yelling in his direction. Three men hurried through: two in police uniforms, the other wearing a trench coat and carrying a tommy gun. Bullets sprayed the walls around him.

Burton doubled back to the mezzanine level, past a grandfather clock; it clanged crazily as its innards distorted in the heat. There was a pair of windows overlooking the street. He tried the first, found it locked and bolted. Through the glass he saw impenetrable fog, tinged orange; it had shrunk from the house as if it feared being scorched. The other window was similarly barred. Over the crackle of the fire, he heard Mrs. Anderson baying for him; one of the policemen barked orders. And between their voices he caught another: a cry from upstairs.

For an instant his heart skipped: Cranley had lied, Madeleine was imprisoned somewhere inside the house. Then he realized who he had heard. He scrambled to the main staircase and peered into the gathering smoke.

Not Madeleine. Alice.

CHAPTER NINE

BURTON AND MADELEINE became lovers in a grubby, second-class train compartment. Earlier they had talked themselves empty and decided not to see each other again. Better to end it when the only intimacies were grim tales of their pasts that they had never shared with anyone else and cautious kisses. Madeleine had wept too much to mean it. Through his own tears, Burton agreed with her reasons for the split—and, driving to the station, countered every one. They sat in silence on the train. Burton felt heartsick, pitted. He was thinking about a ruby he'd been given to save a Belgian industrialist from the Afrika Korps' advance on Stanleyville. He would have traded the gem in an instant to read Madeleine's mind.

"Are you sure we're doing the right thing?" he asked.

"Yes."

She rested her hand on his thigh, the movement unconscious; from early on she'd had an easy manner about touching him. At first he relished it; then he grew jealous, until he saw her around other men and realized how proper she was. Her fingers were cold through his trousers. He took her hand to warm it—she resisted briefly—and, when he failed, put it to his mouth and offered his breath. This time she didn't struggle.

"I don't want the train to arrive," she said. They were due in London by nightfall. Outside, marshland trundled by, the smoky sunlight glittering on the water like tinsel.

Madeleine took her hand back, hesitated, then twisted to cup his face. Her dress crinkled loudly as she moved. She put her lips to his, tentative at first, before an angry passion took hold. Their tongues met but not like previous times; he understood the abandonment in her, reckless and resigned. When he ran out of breath, Burton stood and stepped to the door. The corridor was empty; some of the overhead lamps had failed. He drew down the blinds and forced Madeleine's umbrella beneath the handle.

She had shrugged off her coat, loosened the buttons around her throat; her skin was flushed from her cheeks to her scalp. Madeleine carefully took off her pearl earrings. They kissed again, slipping down on the seats, with their dusty reek and layer of grime. He pressed his body against hers, eased up her dress, his palm catching on the clasp of her stockings. Her thighs encircled him.

Suddenly, she pushed him away. "What about Alice?"

It was only in the months that followed that Burton realized the significance of that question; he'd never fallen in love before. But on the train, aware of the heat surging through him, he was unsure how to reply.

"I won't leave her," breathed Madeleine. "Whatever happens, never ask me that." She spoke those last words in German. He didn't meet Alice for a long time after.

In the spring of 1952, Burton followed Madeleine on a trip she took with her husband to Germania. At a café on the Kurfürstendamm, they had discussed everything: her leaving Cranley, the end of Burton's adventures abroad, finding a home, the life they wanted together, everything except her daughter, perhaps because both were afraid that their hopes might vanish before a five-year-old girl.

"It's time you met Alice," said Madeleine several months later, as they cleared out the attic in the farmhouse.

Burton had sensed something unspoken in her all day, a stiffness to her good humor. Marriage had taught her to be cautious of sharing thoughts too openly, a habit she wasn't free of yet.

"We could have a day out," he replied, picturing families on the beach, ice creams, normality—that bright overworld that was so foreign to him. "Go to the seaside."

"I want her to come here."

Burton set down the box he was moving. "That's not a good idea. Not yet."

"One day this will be her home."

"What if she says something?"

"She won't—she's too young to understand."

"But if she does?"

Madeleine considered his words. "What's the worst that could happen? There's a scandal, people gossip. The Jewish maid is used to that."

"It's not right that he finds out that way."

But Burton relented and on the morning of Alice's first visit had gone to the local village to buy sticky buns and the linzer tortes that were colonizing bakeries throughout the country. It seemed the duty of every Briton to carp about them even as they consumed the cakes in vast quantities. Later the three of them sat at the kitchen table, divided by teacups. Maybe it was because he sensed so much of Madeleine in her, but Burton was surprised to find a burl of affection for the girl; he wanted to befriend her. She sat tight to her mother, swinging her legs, in a velvet dress that looked more expensive than every stitch Burton owned. She kept her hands fastened together, her eyes darting at the peeling window frames and ramshackle furniture, nose twitching at the damp. With Madeleine's encouragement, he managed to coax a few words from her.

When Burton was alone again, he threw away the leftover tea things. Alice hadn't inherited her mother's sweet tooth and had ignored the cakes, apart from a squeak of horror when a bluebottle settled on the icing. How much simpler it would be, he thought, if Madeleine didn't have a child.

A coldness swilled in him. He wondered whether his mother had ever felt the same way.

+ + +

The policeman with the tommy gun emerged from the blaze in the hallway, Mrs. Anderson at his side.

She pointed at Burton. "That's him."

Burton toppled the grandfather clock across the stairs to bar the way—a din of crashing cogs and chimes—then raced up the main staircase, into the smoke. A breath later and the air was fiery, mountain-thin, like when Hochburg burned down Burton's childhood home; he remembered how rapidly the flames consumed the building. Alice's cries had stopped, but he recalled that her room was on the third floor. By the time he reached it, the door was warping in its frame. He forced it open and found an empty bed, neatly stacked toys.

"Alice?"

He checked under the bed, then behind the curtains; the window was bolted. Burton glanced through it at a thirty-foot drop onto a brick patio. Protruding from the floor below was a downpipe. He resumed his search and opened the wardrobe, finding a mound of coats and blankets at the bottom. He lifted the top one. Alice was in her nightdress, the same dark hair as her mother's straggling over her face, eyes gummy with tears and squeezed tight.

"Alice," he said softly.

Her eyes remained shut.

"Alice, it's Burton." He reached for her. "You have to come with me."

The air was thickening with smoke. She shrank deeper into the blankets, but Burton grabbed a skinny wrist and lifted her out.

Over the years, plenty of parents had weighted his palm to carry their children, but this was the first time he'd held Alice. She was a squirming bundle, heavier than he'd expected. He smelled sleep on her and smoky laundry and, hidden inside these scents, the faintest trace of Madeleine. He buried his nose in her hair, hugged her tight.

She fought him off. "You're a spook!"

"No, I'm real."

"Daddy said you were dead. But not in heaven. You'd gone to the place for bad people."

"What about Mummy? Did he tell you where she was?"

She started to cough.

Burton let go of her and dropped to his knees so they were at eye level. "Alice, it's very dangerous," he said. He had no natural manner with children, feared that his words sounded like orders. "You have to come with me, do as I tell you."

"I want Daddy."

He wrapped a coat round her, clumsily fastening the buttons with his stump. When she saw the end of his wrist, she backed away and finished them herself. The coat had a fur collar; he told her to cover her mouth and breathe through it. Then he grasped her hand and tugged her from the room, into clouds of swirling black tar. Burton used the banister to guide them to the floor below; beyond that, the stairs descended into flame.

"Where's the bathroom?" he asked.

Before he could stop her, Alice broke from his grip and darted to the end of the corridor; Burton followed. Once they were inside, he began running a bath. The air was less noxious. He threw some towels into the water, rolled them into sopping coils, and blocked the gaps round the door frame. Next he checked the window: like all the others in the house, it was bolted shut. Burton wrenched the towel rail from the wall and pounded it against the lock.

The metal rattled—but didn't give.

Below them there was an explosion, shaking the whole room. Tiles pinged off the walls. The floor buckled, dropping several inches. Alice screamed over the sound of crashing timbers. A gash opened beneath the door; within seconds the air was blackening.

Burton smashed the lock again, battering it ferociously, till the window

burst outward. He sucked in gulps of air. The garden flickered below: a shifting semicircle of lawn that vanished into the fog. The previous time he'd
visited the house, even though it had been empty, he hadn't relaxed until
he knew how to get out. *An escape route!* joked Madeleine as he checked a
path from the scullery to the rear of the property. It was bordered by a wall
with a door that led directly to the heath.

Burton leaned out the window and found that he was able to reach the
downpipe he'd seen from Alice's room, its iron damp and slippery. He turned
to take her hand.

She was sitting in the bath, knees drawn to her chest.

"What are you doing?"

"I saw it at the circus," she replied. "You can't catch fire if you're wet."

He scooped her out of the water and put her on his back. "Arms round
my neck and hold tight. Like that time on the farm when you got stuck in
the tree." He levered them both onto the windowsill.

Alice's arms tightened around him. "Burton, I'm scared." Her face burrowed into his neck.

"Me, too."

He lowered himself till his boots found the drainpipe, then carefully
transferred his weight to it.

In the Legion, when he'd done *la corde*—rope training—he had been
taught to climb and descend with one hand, rifle in the other. *Your legs and
feet do the work*, the *sous-officiers* would shout. *Your hand is only there to guide
you.* Burton spent most of the day sprawled in the dirt.

He shinned down the first few feet, aware of how hollow and flimsy the
iron felt in his grip. There was a *boom* from above, like a mortar round. A
roof tile rocketed into the air, then shattered as it hit the ground. Alice clung
tighter, squeezing his windpipe, shifting her weight, threatening to topple
them. Burton froze and pressed his face against the brickwork. He tried
soothing her, then hissed at her to keep still.

The iron juddered in his hand, the fixings beginning to strain.

Burton worked his feet faster, the ground almost within leaping distance as the pipe broke away from the wall.

He twisted as they fell to cushion Alice, missing the patio but landing
with a hard smack that emptied his lungs. For a beat he lay there, resting
his face in the grass to soothe his skin. In the distance a siren was approaching. Burton untangled himself from Alice and checked her over. Her face
was sooty and there was a cut on her forehead, but nothing was broken.

"Fun?" he asked. "Want to do it again?"

She shook her head emphatically.

Over the roar of the flames, he thought he heard men shouting. Burton picked the girl up and darted through the garden, pausing only to kick down the door in the wall. Then on to the heath. The fog was dense and black, muffling the noise of the fire, until soon they were moving in silence. Once Alice asked where they were going; he lifted her onto his shoulders and kept running.

CHAPTER TEN

A COPPICE EMERGED from the darkness. Burton slipped between the trees, found a sheltered spot, and lowered Alice to the ground. The place had an indoor quiet.

"Pull your collar up," he said, catching his breath. "Keep warm."

Despite the numbing fog, he was soaked with sweat. He needed water: to clean his face, soothe his blackened throat. Burton used his forearm to wipe his brow.

"Where's your hand?" asked Alice, staring at his stump.

"I lost it."

"Will it grow back?" He shook his head. "Mummy won't like it."

"Do you know where she is?"

"No."

"It's very important, Alice. Did your daddy"—he could barely form the word—"say anything?"

"No."

"Anything at all?"

She dipped her head, scratching the ground with her feet; then her face puckered. Tears began rolling down her cheeks. "He said she was finished being my mummy. That they were broken up and she's gone back to her other family."

"That's not possible."

"He said it was your fault."

Burton knelt, dried her face with the cuff of his sleeve. Her eyes had the same sapphire glow that Madeleine's did when she'd been crying. "I love your mummy, and she loves you. I want to bring her home. So she can look after you. But I can only do that if I know where she is. I need some clue."

Alice hesitated. "I heard Mrs. Anderson talking to the maids. She caught me. Said if I told, I'd be sent there."

"Where?" Burton felt the urge to shake her, anything to get the answer. Instead he spoke kindly: "Mummy told me all her secrets. So can you."

"I wanted to know why they were laughing. Mrs. Anderson was angry. She said Daddy would lock me in the coal cellar for 'eve-dropping.'"

"No one's angry with you, Elli." He'd never called her that before. "But you have to tell me what you heard."

For a moment he thought she wouldn't reply; then she blurted out: "Mummy was sent south." Her words were full of a shame she couldn't comprehend.

Sent south. One of the expressions of the age: spoken with a wink and a grin in factories and pubs throughout the country, used by parents after a clip round their kids' ears. *Behave! Or you'll be sent south.*

Sent south like the Jews. Five and a half million shipped from Europe to the island of Madagaskar.

Burton dabbed at Alice's tears again. Could it be true? He absorbed what she'd said, his mind full of boundless, confused thoughts, and experienced a shiver of hope. He had been to Madagaskar before, as a mercenary, rescuing wealthy French colonists during the Nazi takeover.

From Hitler's earliest days, his avowed intent had been to make Germany *Judenfrei*—Jew-free. With the introduction of the Nuremberg Laws in 1935, and their institutionalized anti-Semitism, life became progressively more insufferable for Jews, until the outburst of Kristallnacht. That night, thousands were imprisoned, attacked, and killed, businesses destroyed, synagogues burned. The Nazis hoped a voluntary migration would follow; when it didn't, and other countries refused to take Jewish refugees, compulsory deportations began en masse. But as war stretched the boundaries of the Reich, Germany found itself not only reabsorbing the Jews it had expelled but acquiring millions extra in the occupied territories. A more radical and permanent solution to the Jewish problem was needed.

After the defeat of France in the summer of 1940, an ambitious diplomat named Franz Rademacher proposed a plan to deport the Jews to Madagaskar, a former French colony off the coast of East Africa now at Germany's disposal. The idea was not original to him, having been conceived in the previous century by the scholar Paul de Lagarde and later appropriated by the French, Polish, and British governments. Before he became prime minister, Lord Halifax had been involved in discussions on the matter; President Roosevelt toyed with a similar proposal (though his preferred location was Ethiopia).

Initially dismissed as a fantasy, word of Rademacher's scheme soon reached the SS where it was assigned to Adolf Eichmann, head of the Jewish Evacuation Department, for further development. Eighteen months later it was on the agenda at the Wannsee Conference, a meeting of SS and government officials to resolve the Jewish question once and for all. Heydrich adopted the "Madagaskar Projekt" as his own. *It's either that,* he said, *or we send them up in smoke.* There was a ripple of knowing mirth around the table.

The logistics proved more challenging than Rademacher or Eichmann had foreseen. The sheer volume of people to be moved threatened to overwhelm Europe's transport networks. After months of interdepartmental squabbling, as millions languished in transit camps, it was Himmler who eased the problem with his "Barbarossa Line" solution: all Jews living to the east of Germany's border on 22 June 1941—five million of them—were to be marched to Siberia; only those in the west would be sent to Africa. A fee of 360 reichsmarks for women, 310 for men, and 200 for children would be levied against every Jew to pay for their shippage. All Jewish assets would be transferred to a special bank overseen by Göring to finance this exodus.

Hitler approved the plan, insisting that Madagaskar must never become a Jewish state but would remain a "grand reservation" overseen by the SS. He appointed an old stalwart, Philipp Bouhler, as the first governor. Hitler saw another advantage of the Jews remaining under German rule. It would guarantee "the future good behavior of the members of their race in America," thus eliminating the possibility of conflict with the United States.

Within a year of Wannsee, the project was a reality—though by now the ambitions of the Führer had expanded. He wanted all of European Jewry resettled.

While the Council of New Europe had established the external security of the continent, the new threat to its stability was from within. In an amendment to the founding principles, every member state was required to transfer its Jewish populations, since they did "not belong to the community of white peoples, but to the area of habitation of the coloreds."

Peace depended on it.

Many of the council's member states responded with an efficiency worthy of the SS. In London, Foreign Secretary Anthony Eden stood in Parliament to confirm that he would also be honoring the country's commitment to the council, after receiving reassurances from the Colonial Office about the habitability of the island. " 'Madagascar is large, healthy, undeveloped, and sparsely populated,' " he read from the report. "It seems a chance for these wretched people." There were caws of approval till Churchill got to his feet.

Was this not the nation of the Balfour Declaration? asked the former prime minister. *Of the Peel Commission?* While Palestine remained a British mandate, it was their duty to try to establish a Jewish homeland there rather than yielding to the fanatics in Germania.*

Someone shouted "Lehi," referring to a Zionist terror group killing British soldiers in the Near East. A throng of other voices joined in: more Jews in Palestine could only stoke Arab nationalism and demands for self-governance; with India's imminent independence, anything that threatened further imperial losses was treachery. The British Empire was weak enough.

And what of the Jews currently living in Palestine? continued Churchill. *The Germans already call them a threat; must they be deported, too? I foresee a day when the Reich will have a hand in our territories for the sake of peace.*

Eden replied that he would address the matter with Foreign Minister Ribbentrop in due course. Later he was heard saying, "We didn't turn our back on France to hand our empire over to the Jews." His 1943 Evacuation Bill was decisively passed.

Eichmann identified 330,000 British Jews. Those with sufficient means were permitted ninety days to leave of their own accord; the Americas were still a haven for the wealthy. The remainder were interned at designated ports around the country before embarking on the journey south, two thousand every week. "Few in Britain are truly anti-Semitic," observed George Orwell as the first ships departed. "The majority, however, are indifferent."

---

*The 1917 Balfour Declaration called for the establishment of a Jewish homeland in Palestine. Twenty years later, the Peel Commission suggested the partition of the territory between Arabs and Jews. Neither was implemented.

CHAPTER ELEVEN

Madagaskar
7 February, 21:00

"COME ON, JEW, push!"

The nurse was wearing a tan uniform and black rubber gauntlets that went past her elbows. Patrolling the ward behind her was an SS obstetrician: a parody of the nervous husband, checking his watch, his jackboots drumming the floor. He had thick blond eyebrows and a scorpion smile. The night sky groaned and gurgled with thunder.

Burton, why have you done this to me?

Madeleine kept repeating the question to herself, her lips moving but no sound emerging. The contractions were coming faster, every twenty-five seconds. She counted the intervals between them as she had been instructed to when giving birth to Alice. That had been in a clinic in Harley Street with an abundance of meperidine and gas, sunlight rippling through the windows, vases ready to be filled with bouquets. Jared sat calmly outside.

Now she was in a long hospital ward of empty bedsteads. Bare white walls, concrete floor. Above the entrance hung a skull-and-palm-tree insignia—symbol of the SS in Africa—carved from a single turtle shell. Madeleine was naked, lathered in sweat even though the air was icy from air-conditioning. The mattress was thin enough for her to feel springs skewering her back, the sheets made from plastic. Each breath flooded her nose with the sting of antiseptic.

"Push!" urged the nurse between her open legs. "Push and we can all go home."

Why hadn't Burton listened? Why hadn't he stayed instead of vanishing to Africa? Why had he chosen Hochburg over her? She was ashamed of her anger yet clung to its sustenance.

Madeleine had woken that morning in Antzu, her new home in Mada-gaskar, with a tingle of excitement and a numbing sense of dread. Her body felt distended and open; she knew the baby would be born that day. Her water broke at two in the afternoon, and she tramped through the rain and muddy lanes of Antzu to the hospital. It was in an old rice warehouse that was too small to have separate maternity facilities; Madeleine was given a bed in a packed ward that rumbled with tuberculosis. An ancient doctor and midwife examined her belly, then drew a threadbare curtain around her bed. She caught their whispers:

—*We have to tell the SS,* the doctor said. His voice was fleshless, fragile.

—*It's not ethical,* replied the midwife.

—*If we don't, they'll put us on a work gang. Or worse.*

—*How would they ever find out?*

The doctor gave a bitter laugh. *Look how busy the ward is. Who wouldn't snitch for a scrap of meat and extra bag of rice?*

—*Do you think she knows?*

—*No. And it's better she doesn't.*

Madeleine called out to them: "Is there a problem?"

Whatever life promised on Madagaskar, she needed the baby. In the months since arriving on the island, she had spoken endlessly with the unborn child as if it were Burton himself, unburdening herself about her privations, the shaking fear that wouldn't let her sleep, her despair. Even the stinking humidity was easier to endure if shared, or the heartache when she saw a couple trudging the streets, cowed and hungry but able to clasp each other. The tiny beating heart inside her was the only tangible bond that remained with Burton; she needed to touch it, smell it, embrace it.

The conversation resumed in more hushed voices.

—*You can't hand her over to those SS butchers,* said the midwife.

—*I've got my family to think about. My patients.*

There was a long pause before the midwife spoke again. Her voice was pained but pragmatic, that tone heard everywhere in Antzu. *Very well, but I want nothing to do with it.*

—*I will make the call. Your conscience can be clear.*

Madeleine was left alone. She wished she had Burton's fingers to fill the gaps between hers. Every time she thought of him, tears surged like a wave that wouldn't break. The island was four months into the rainy sea-son; the roof thrummed. It was made from corrugated tin; geckos flitted in and out of the spaces beneath the cladding. Madeleine had a horror of one dropping on her, its sticky feet skittering across her stomach. She could feel the contractions now, building in speed and intensity, the pain sharpening.

An hour passed before the rapid approach of boots. Silence descended on the ward, and the curtain was yanked aside.

An SS doctor stood there in his death's-head cap and a dripping white coat. He gave his scorpion smile and kneaded her abdomen. His fingertips were soft, warm, the nails manicured like Jared's; there was a steeliness to his touch, as if he were molding clay. He parted her legs, Madeleine trying to resist, but his grip was too strong. Those probing fingertips again. Behind him stood two Jewish orderlies with their heads bowed. He clicked his fingers at them and Madeleine was transferred to a stretcher, strapped down, and carried out of the ward.

"I'm sorry," said the midwife, reaching out for her.

The SS doctor swiped her hand aside. "She will get the best treatment."

In the square outside the hospital, where lines of patients formed at sunrise, hoping to see a doctor, a helicopter was waiting. Its rotors began to turn as they approached.

Panic filled Madeleine. "Take me back!" she yelled, fighting against the straps.

Curfew in Antzu was at 20:00. In the darkness that followed, people huddled round to share rumors, the grislier the better, especially of the Eastern Sector: men and women too old to work dashed on the stone spikes of ravines; Romanian Jews forced to drink seawater until their stomachs burst. They reminded Madeleine of those months after the Nazis seized power in Vienna and the stories Abner, her younger brother, used to tell. He claimed they were meant to reassure, that no matter how grim life had become, things were worse elsewhere, yet the only person they comforted was himself. Provoking fear made Abner feel more secure. She imagined her fate as a cautionary tale: a pregnant woman taken high above the mountains and hurled into the air as an experiment for the SS, or maybe their amusement.

As the helicopter lifted into the clouds, she started hyperventilating, her hands jerking as if she was having a fit. The doctor leaned over with a needle. Madeleine felt a sting in her shoulder. Immediately, the world dimmed. She hoped to sink into oblivion; instead she hovered above unconsciousness, watching forest and verdant hills roll past.

"Come on, Jew, *push!*" The SS nurse sounded increasingly irate. Bobbing by her side was a *Blutsschwester*.

Madeleine was panting. The pain intensified with each breath. She screwed her face up, did as she was told. Harsh fluorescent lights poured their glare over her.

"Push!"

The doctor probed between her thighs. "It could be some time yet. Inform me when the head appears," he said to the nurse and marched to the door.

The *Blutsschwester* called after him: "Please, Herr Doctor, you must give her something for the pain."

The doctor turned on her. She dipped her head, scrunched her grimy apron in her hands. *Blutsschwestern*—blood sisters—with their clogs and Star of David armbands, were hospital menials, their purpose to mop up the fluids that no German wanted to touch. He considered her words and ordered her to follow him. She returned ten minutes later carrying an enamel mug and a handful of pills, and helped Madeleine into a sitting position.

"Aspirin," the *Blutsschwester* whispered into her ear.

Madeleine washed down the tablets with warm water as the nurse watched, hands on hips. "I had my three boys as nature intended," she said scornfully. "Thundered them out. It's a mother's duty to endure childbirth, as men must endure the battlefield."

The contractions were unremitting now, too fast to distinguish between.

Outside it was pouring again. Madeleine concentrated on the farm, picturing herself nestled with Burton as rain lashed the windows. The dry, musty bedroom, the feeling of security that the closeness of his body brought. That's where sanctuary was to be found, she thought, not in the grand peace treaties of nations or the promise of communities; she had drifted through too many of those—Vienna, London, now Antzu—to believe in their illusion. All she had ever needed was a few bricks, a few roof tiles, and the warm skin of someone who loved life the same way she did. The two of them had planned so many things for the future. How could he have left her like this?

Madeleine arched her back, cried out. The baby was leaving her protection.

The nurse heaved her legs wide open, over her shoulder the anxious face of the *Blutsschwester*. "Push, Jew! *Push!*"

Madeleine squeezed outward. Roared. Squeezed again: an agony like she had never known.

The nurse jerked away. "It's coming," she said and curled her mouth;

the bottom lip was fat and shiny. She told the *Blutsschwester* to take over, then reached for a telephone on the wall and dialed an extension.

The *Blutsschwester* combed her fingers through Madeleine's hair. "You're doing well," she cooed. "Keep going." She had parched skin and graying hair and reminded Madeleine of a waitress at Café Herrenhof, where the family used to go for cake and coffee every Friday when she was a girl. Such normality was too distant to seem possible anymore.

Madeleine clamped her teeth together, every muscle in her face rigid, and pushed with an effort that left her raw.

The nurse hung up. "There's no answer," she said to the *Blutsschwester.* "I must fetch the doctor." She hurried from the ward.

"Fast as you can now," whispered the *Blutsschwester* when they were alone. "Before they come back."

Madeleine didn't hear her. All she was aware of was an intimate tearing. She swallowed thickly, summoned the breath in her lungs, and heaved till it felt her spine had been flattened. She screamed again, the way she had when Russell and Lyall were driving her through the fog-bound streets of London and the immensity of Burton's death struck her.

"The head's out," said the *Blutsschwester.*

A final juddering contraction. And the baby was free.

+ + +

The rain continued to beat against the window, the sound exaggerated and savage in the stillness.

The *Blutsschwester* glanced up, her eyes locked with indecision. Shudders of relief that the pain was over coursed through Madeleine and, with them, a rising panic at the silence. The *Blutsschwester* scooped up a sinewy mass from between her legs. There was a syrupy cough, and her baby began to cry.

A joyful, rattling sigh escaped Madeleine. Her muscles were spent, but she sat up and peered at the child. "Is it a boy or a girl?"

When the midwife had presented her with Alice, a pellet of failure possessed Madeleine: even though Jared never mentioned it, she wanted to give him a son. He parted the swaddling and something unfathomable slackened his brow. She spent a long time puzzling over that expression before realizing that it was relief. Relief that there would be no male to challenge him in the future.

"Boy or girl?" Madeleine asked.

The *Blutsschwester* tied the umbilical cord, cut it with a pair of scissors, and reached for a blanket. She wrapped the baby and lowered the bundle to Madeleine.

A perfect penny of a face, messy with blood but beautiful. Squirming, yelling, alive. Madeleine could see Burton in the wrinkled features before her, that look when he dozed in the orchard after a day's work, when the late sunshine soaked his skin and napping freed him of troubles. She raised a finger to trace the child's nose. Wanted to kiss it and breathe in the blessed scent of baby skin. She offered her arms to take the child.

A contraction tore through Madeleine, her limp body rigid again, as if a current had arced the length of her spine.

The *Blutsschwester* took the bundle away. The hollows of her eyes flowed with tears. "Forgive me," she said. "Forgive me."

Another contraction.

She took the baby, laid it at the foot of the bed, and smothered it. The child's cries were stifled in the folds of the blanket.

"What are you doing?" screamed Madeleine. She struggled to sit up as another wave of pain crashed through her abdomen.

"It's for the best," said the *Blutsschwester*. "Trust me."

Madeleine flayed around for something to fight with till her fingers found the enamel mug on the bedside cabinet. She struck out feebly. The *Blutsschwester* hesitated, then mumbled, *I'm sorry, I'm sorry*, and pressed harder, burying the baby into the mattress. A terrified, bewildered fury filled Madeleine. She raised the mug and brought it down on the *Blutsschwester*'s head with all her strength. The blow struck her brow, splitting the skin. She stumbled backward, and Madeleine snatched up her baby, bringing it to her breast.

She parted the blanket and found a squashed face, eyes pressed shut. Madeleine blew gently into its mouth. The baby whooped and started to cry again.

Another spasm.

After she'd given birth to Alice, the pain had stopped almost at once and an exhausted euphoria crept through her. She must have some internal injury. "I'm hurt," she said, hoping it might placate the woman on the floor.

The *Blutsschwester* got to her feet. Lurched over to the bed and snatched at the baby, attempting to wrestle it away. Madeleine clawed her face, refused to let go. She saw Burton walking through the farm door on their final morning: his shoulders dark against the coral sky. *Never shout "Help,"* he once told her, *people will ignore you. But if you shout "Fire"* . . .

"*Feuer!*" yelled Madeleine. "*Feuer!*"

"Sssh," hissed the *Blutsschwester*. "I'm trying to help." She put her face up close to Madeleine's. "Listen to me. You've got to spare them. This is the kindest way."

"Get off me!" Madeleine shoved her back while wrapping her other arm around the baby.

"You don't understand. They'll take them, like they took my babies." Blood trickled down her forehead, darkening her tears; her eyes were frenzied pinpricks. "They do things to them. Here, in this hospital. Terrible things. Experiments."

From the corridor came a corrugation of noises: shouts, swing doors being kicked open, boots.

"Don't let them suffer," said the *Blutsschwester*. She held out her arms to take the baby. "Give them a mother's death. Both of them."

"Both?"

"You're having twins. That's why the SS wants them—"

The obstetrician burst through the door, a crowd of nurses and guards with him. He strode toward the *Blutsschwester*, his white coat flapping, and tore her away from Madeleine. "Get her out of here."

A guard dragged the woman across the ward.

"A mother's death, not theirs. A mother's . . ."

She was hauled through the doorway, still wailing. Then a thud and her voice was silenced.

"She's deranged," said the doctor. "Ignore her." He examined Madeleine carefully. "Your other baby is coming. All feels well. Keep pushing, like you did before. Everything is going to be fine, Madeleine." His voice was velvet, sharp with the reek of coffee.

She couldn't remember the last time someone had spoken her name. Exhaustion was darkening her vision. Her body wanted to expel the other baby and flee consciousness. The SS nurse pried the bundle out of her arms. Madeleine had no strength to resist.

"We're putting the firstborn in a crib," said the doctor. "There's room for another." A smile darted across his face. "Keep pushing."

There were nurses all around, hands swabbing and dabbing her like tentacles.

She heaved again, feeling her neck become a trunk of tendons.

And again.

Madeleine sensed her body splitting open, then a sickening hollow sensation. The cries of the second baby pierced the ward as the doctor sliced the cord between mother and child and offered the baby for Madeleine to see. Another perfect penny face, the ghost of Burton blinking at her once more.

"They look strong," said the obstetrician. "Healthy." His words had a mechanical ring now. "Too often conditions here stunt the fetus. This is a rare opportunity."

The second baby vanished from her sight. She heard the wails of both children, the creak of spokes. A nurse wheeled the crib away.

"Where are you taking them?" asked Madeleine. Her head was effervescent, spinning.

"We have special facilities here," replied the doctor. "They are the best specimens I've had for a long while. You will be sent back to Antzu."

He escorted the crib from the ward. There was a gust of wind as the door opened; it rocked the lights overhead, snatched the babies' cries. When the sound of them returned, it was already fading down the corridor.

Madeleine swung her feet off the bed, determined to follow. There was blood on the floor with a bootprint in it. A hand forced her against the mattress; straps pinched at her arms and ankles.

The sound of wailing continued to echo around the ward but was growing ever more distant. A door opened and slammed, muffling her children further. The moment when they would be replaced with silence was too much to bear.

She fought to sit up, her limbs thrashing against the restraints with such ferocity that the nurses flinched. Her stomach muscles buckled with the effort; she barely noticed. Something sharp pricked her shoulder. A cold sponge scoured between her legs. The stench of antiseptic.

Madeleine collapsed onto the plastic sheet and for a heartbeat was mute. The lights above burned her eyes. Then she opened her mouth and screamed. Screamed till her throat was empty.

PART II

ROSCHERHAFEN AND THE OAO

The Jews must pack up, disappear
from Europe . . . It's clearly not
enough to expel them from
Germany. We cannot allow them to
retain bases of withdrawal at our
doors. We want to be out of danger
of all kinds of infiltration.

—ADOLF HITLER
27 January 1942

REUBEN SALOIS WAS executed during the Mered Ha-vanil—the Vanilla Rebellion. His final resting place was to be an isolated beach at the southern end of Madagaskar. As dawn broke, they had been forced to dig a ditch: hundreds of emaciated Jews scooping out stony sand, not a spade among them. When it reached two meters deep, the Nazis ordered them to climb out, stand along the edge, and turn toward the waves. "See how fine the view is!" shouted the Hauptsturmführer. The sky was hot, cobalt blue.

"We must face them," said Salois, his voice serene, loose with hatred. He swiveled on his bare feet, urging the rest of the line to do the same. A few followed; most kept their eyes fixed on the ocean. The Jew at his side mumbled prayers. Salois pitied him: the heavens were empty—there had never been anyone above to hear the anguish of their tribe.

"Turn back around!" screamed the Hauptsturmführer. "Turn back around!"

Salois spread his withered arms and stared at the soldiers opposite. His pulse was hammering in his throat, but a stillness settled upon him. He had yearned for this moment many times; it was a relief finally to meet it. There were worse things than death.

"Turn back around!"

His last memory was of being blasted into the trench; the *thud-thud* of bullets raking the bodies on top of him; the distant noise of someone spitting. Then the crash and boom of the ocean fading to silence.

The Mered Ha-vanil began in March 1947 in the vanilla-growing regions of the northeast. Vanilla was Madagaskar's main cash crop and a profitable business for the SS; it controlled 90 percent of the world market. There had been resistance groups since the first Jews arrived on the island, but few dared to challenge the Nazis or had popular support. Dissent was met with a noose for the ringleaders, a further reduction in food for any community that supported them. Two months earlier, Cyclone Eva had battered the island, submerging swaths of agricultural land, drowning thousands. Half a million were left homeless as the rainy season continued. A typhoid epidemic followed. Heydrich's official report to the Council of New Europe estimated that 5 percent of the population had perished because of their lack of preparation; in private, and to the delight of the Reich Chancellery, the true figure was given at 15 percent.

With the vanilla crop mostly destroyed, an overseer named Sakle defended his profits by cutting his workforce's rations to an ounce an a half of rice per day. Shortly afterward, he was stabbed in the neck. When guards were sent to round up the perpetrators, they were beaten back with dinner bowls and rocks. The Jews torched their barracks, the farm, and the processing plant. Troops arrived from the garrison at Sambava to be slaughtered by the bare hands and starving fury of men who had nothing to lose. For the first time, the Jews realized that it was possible to do something against the Germans' will and power.

More vanilla plantations were burned, a sickly-sweet pall of smoke spreading rebellion from the north toward the heart of the island. When the eastern port of Salzig was captured by Vanilla Jews, Governor Bouhler was recalled to Germania. (He was later found in his Schwanenwerder mansion next to a suicide note.) Salzig was the disembarkation point for Polish Jews, the most numerous and despised of the Reich. More than 320,000 remained to be shipped, an operation now in jeopardy. In Britain, Lord Halifax said that support for sending away the Jews relied on a degree of security for them; deportations were temporarily halted.

Hitler raged. His vision of a Jew-free Europe had been stalled by Zionist plotting and the incompetence of the men entrusted with his dream. He censured Heydrich, who remained chief of the project; threatened to carpet-bomb the island. Finally, Himmler interceded, suggesting that the answer might be Odilo Globocnik, his disgraced protégé. He had done great things in the East and was ready for rehabilitation. "Despite all his mistakes," said Himmler, coaxing the Führer, "I think you need to recognize the intense fervor and dynamism of this man. He is qualified like no one else."

The new governor arrived with extended powers, three new brigades, and a fleet of Walküre helicopter gunships, the so-called Madagaskar Defense Force. His zeal was criticized by the Red Cross and American Jewish Committee, which lobbied Congress to intervene. Washington invoked the country's neutrality while dispatching a battleship to Africa and an undersecretary of state to Germania. "Keep him talking," Globocnik told Heydrich. "I need another six weeks."

Every pod of resistance was crushed. If five Jews defended a hut by hurling stones, twenty SS troops were sent in with machine guns, grenades, and flamethrowers. The settlements of Kandreo, in the Western Sector, and Brickaville, in the Eastern, as yet untouched by the rebellion, were razed to the ground as a warning to the civilian population. Salzig was retaken street by street, any Jew captured alive strung up from the palm trees that lined the seafront; clouds of gulls massed above the port. Within three months of his arrival, Governor Globocnik had regained control of the island, and ships laden with their human cargo were docking again. The following year, on 14 May 1948, Hitler gave an ecstatic speech to the Council of New Europe, declaring that his life's mission was complete. After two millennia, Europe was *Judenfrei*. In Germania, Globocnik was admitted into the pantheon of heroes; however, he was not yet finished with Madagaskar.

"The Jews blame everyone and everything for the uprising," he said in a speech to SS business leaders visiting Tana, the capital, that autumn. "Us for giving them a homeland, our European neighbors for letting them leave, America for abandoning them. Other times it's a lack of food, or housing, the climate, disease. Even the ring-tailed lemur is vilified!" Thunderous laughter from the audience. He became stern: "The true cause was idle hands. With nothing to fill his days, the Jew's mind will always turn to mischief."

With Heydrich's approval, Globocnik set the population to work, building new roads, dams, and a railway that ran the length of the island. Industries were established by the WVHA, the SS economic department, from bootlace manufacture to meat processing. Jews were permitted to own small businesses and pocket farms as long as they employed no more than five workers. To avoid spreading their "mercantile contagion" to the rest of the world, goods could be sold on the island, not traded internationally. There was only one buyer for their wares: the SS.

Under the original plan, Madagaskar was divided into four districts that equated to regions of Europe. The common languages of each district had allowed the Jews to conspire, declared Globocnik; along with Idle Hands, he set Operation Babel in motion, "to stir up the ethnic soup." The population was split between three sectors, with families randomly moved from one location to another.

The southern part of the island, with its spiny deserts, was partitioned along the Tropic of Capricorn and became Steinbock, the penal sector. Jews who had settled there were ordered north to join other communities or sent to work on the Betroka Dam, thirty kilometers beyond the new boundary. Meanwhile, another column was marched in the opposite direction, tramping barefoot into the arid hills with little water. These were the prisoners of the rebellion to be exiled in the south, far from the eyes of those they might inspire. For some this meant slave labor in mica and sapphire mines; for the majority: death. When the American Jewish Committee tried to intervene, Germania was unequivocal: these were criminals and terrorists. On clear days, workers at the Betroka site saw towers of smoke stretching toward the heavens.

Salois was roused by the ghostly caterwaul of a harmonica.

A guard patrolled the edge of the ditch, playing to ward off the quiet. Salois tracked his pacing till the sky darkened and the Nazi abandoned his post. Once he was alone, Salois checked his chest where the bullets from the firing squad had hit him—there was not a trace of a wound.

Corpses pressed around him, legs and lacerated feet at bizarre angles, arms locked rigid as if reaching for something. A butcher's harvest. He crawled through them to the air and listened for the Germans: silence except for the wind and ocean. The stench of petrol stung his nostrils, but no match had been struck. Near his face were the closed eyes of a dead man. They opened, the soul ready to flee, and for an instant Salois thought he was staring at his wife; she had been dead for so long he barely remembered what she looked like. With a trembling hand, the corpse reached inside the rags of his shirt and produced a tin of sardines in oil.

"Feast," he breathed, and died.

Salois pried the tin from his fingers. In the days and delirium that followed, he bound some planks together, dragged them into the surf. Sea mines the size of tanks bobbed past; he drifted beneath patrols that ignored the skeleton on the raft. Tiny nibbles of sardine sustained him, the oil thickening his tongue. The whole time, he recited numbers to himself, like funeral rites. To the west, the coast of Africa beckoned.

It was only later that Reuben Salois regretted his escape.

CHAPTER THIRTEEN

Kongo
1 April, 12:00

THE JUNGLE STREAKED past, dense with shadows and fever trees. Whether this was German territory or under the insurgents' banner, Salois no longer knew. For three years he had been fighting as a guerrilla, first as part of the insurgency against Nazi rule in Kongo, lately in the war that had spread across the north of the colony. A life of scavenging in the jungle, ambushes, and killing the enemy wherever he could. Now he sat in the rear of the jeep, shirt clinging to the seat, hands cuffed in his lap. On either side of him were military policemen in the uniforms of the Force Publique. His legs were unbound. If the guards had been German, he would have kicked the driver in the back of the head, thrown himself out of the vehicle, and run till they shot him. Instead, he sat resignedly.

"Where are you from?" he asked the boy on his left.

"Stanleyville."

"I mean the old country."

"Antwerp."

"My hometown," said Salois, and laughed. For seven centuries, it had been the center of Jewish life in Belgium. All he had left of the place was a smudged impression.

"What's so funny?" asked the policeman.

"That you found me. Arrested me."

The Nazis had retaken Stanleystadt in a ferocious counterattack, then driven deep into the surrounding jungle, routing out the insurgents; mustard gas had been used against the guerrilla stronghold of Bambili. Salois heard rumors of a second rebellion in Madagaskar and bloody reprisals. Yet in the midst of this carnage, someone had ordered these boys to track him down for a crime committed a lifetime ago.

"You're not being arrested."

Salois rattled his cuffs. "Then why these?"

"Orders."

The jeep turned off the level tarmac of the German highway and joined the old Belgian road, navigating its way through a tunnel of trees. Through chinks in the canopy, Salois saw the sun reach its peak and begin to descend. Later the forest gave way to baked grasslands.

"Are we in Sudan?" he asked. There had been no demarcation line, but they had driven relentlessly north.

"Almost there," said the driver.

The sky was ocher when they reached a dusty track that ended in brick pillars and a gate. A sentry waved them through to a convent with an imposing bell tower. Parked outside were tanks and military lorries.

Salois was escorted inside, toward the rear of the building. The air smelled chalky, and beyond he detected meat and gravy, not individual platters but the bawdy aroma of a mess kitchen. They reached a door set in a stone wall. The policeman from Antwerp knocked while the other undid Salois's cuffs and gestured for him to enter. He was in a large, bare room bathed in a tricolor of light: gold, red, and blue. The only furniture was a conference table, at its head an officer in navy whites. He stood and spoke in stiff French with a British accent.

"Ah, Major Salois, we've been expecting you."

"Sal-*loire*," he replied, correcting the officer's pronunciation.

"I'm sorry if our Belgian colleagues alarmed you, but we couldn't send British soldiers and feared you might scarper if you weren't cuffed." He had a face like the sides of a candle left to burn through the night, bags of flesh tugging at his eyes. "My name is Rolland. Vice Admiral Rolland, Royal Navy. Will you sit?"

Salois didn't move. "We're a long way from the sea."

A curt, bronchial laugh. "It was an invitation, not an order."

There were two other men at the table: one swarthy as an Arab, dressed in a blue-gray uniform Salois didn't recognize, the other in a suit, younger and well fed, with silver hair. He stifled a yawn behind his hand. Both reeked of suds and soft sheets, a life Salois hadn't known for a long time. He took a chair opposite them.

"First, a delicate matter," said Rolland, also sitting. "Not everyone speaks French, nor English, for that matter. In fact, our only common language is, well, German."

"*Deutsch ist gut,*" replied Salois.

"Excellent." Rolland gave the table a congratulatory tap. "Would you like some refreshment before we begin? Tea? A drop of the stronger stuff? I find a little Scotch cools the blood at this time of the afternoon." He spoke German more fluently than French.

"What about food?"

The admiral picked up a phone on the table. "We can find something."

Salois's eyes roved around the room. There were three ceiling fans above him, only one turning. Behind the table was a stained-glass window that depicted Abraham binding Isaac; it had no openings. Salois felt the heat soak through him, though he didn't loosen his collar or roll up his sleeves. It was not for these men to see the story his skin told.

For the first time, he became aware of a fourth person in the room, perched by the window, a half silhouette against the dipping sun and harlequin squares of color. He was wearing a linen suit that looked as if it had never known a patch of sweat, a silk shirt, no tie. His face was shaded by the brim of a Panama. Their eyes locked, the man scrutinizing him.

"It took an age to track you down, Major," said Rolland.

"Why were you looking?"

"You're a legend among the guerrillas of Kongo. The invincible Jew! The only man to have escaped Madagaskar."

"Am I really the only one?" The thought depressed Salois.

"No," said the man at the window. "But the only one foolish enough to stay in Africa." His German was impeccable, arrogant, and accusatory.

"I had no choice."

"Personally, I would have gone to America."

"If you'd seen what I have," retorted Salois, "you'd know that was impossible."

"You want redemption?"

"Madagaskar won't be free till Africa is. Hate kept me here."

"A misunderstood virtue," said Rolland. "You'll forgive my colleague. He thinks your involvement will only complicate matters. I, on the other hand . . . Your military record is remarkable, Major. We need your expertise."

"This is a debriefing?"

The admiral steepled his fingers. "Not exactly."

There was a knock on the door, and a staff sergeant entered carrying a tray laden with tea things. A plate of corned beef sandwiches was placed in front of Salois. He picked one up, a tongue of mustard easing from the bread, and chewed hungrily. In the jungle, he subsisted on a diet of wild yams, caterpillars, and monkey flesh.

"Sorry about the china, Admiral," said the sergeant as he poured the tea. "We're still waiting for the proper stuff from Khartoum. One of the Belgians nabbed this as they retreated from Stanleystadt."

The cups were as thin as petals, rimmed with a frieze of swastikas, gold on red.

"Good enough for a simple sailor." Rolland took a sip and let out a rumble of satisfaction. "You were telling us about the war, Major."

"The Germans can't win it."

"They've taken back Stanleystadt."

"For now. And it cost them dearly. Meanwhile, Elisabethstadt is under British control. The Nazis don't have the manpower, not while they're also fighting in Angola. Not unless they want to bleed their other colonies dry."

"So you guerrillas are in the ascendancy?"

Salois tugged at his collar; the heat was insufferable. "We don't have enough heavy weaponry. Or tanks. We can wound the beast but not slay it."

"What if the British joined the war?" asked Rolland. "Not just in Elisabethstadt or the south; I mean the whole of Kongo. A spearhead from Sudan."

"The Heydrich-Eden Pact killed that possibility. It's a border dispute, remember? No escalation."

"Major Salois," said the admiral, "we're planning an operation. Top secret. Something that could change everything in Africa—"

Salois put up a hand to silence him. "Last year, a commander of the Force Publique summoned me like this. He had something top secret. Promised it would change things. Do you know what?"

"To kill Americans," said the man by the window. "A team of oil workers to be exact, prospecting in the Kosterman district."

Salois had slit their throats as they slept, spared one man, and paraded around him in a black uniform, flashing his swastika armband.

"I assume the plan was to provoke the United States," continued the man at the window, "drag it into Africa. Very clever. Unfortunately, your witness made it back to Stanleystadt and was handed over to Governor Hochburg. He understood the delicacy of the situation and had him shot. The Americans were none the wiser."

"How do you know this?"

"I've been secretly arming the Force Publique for years." In the haze of the sunset, he may have been smiling. "When I told them we were looking for you, they furnished me with plenty of details."

"I don't like it."

"You should be gratified that we've taken such an interest in you."

Rolland intervened again: "Hear us out, Major. Official policy is to endorse the Heydrich-Eden Pact. We don't want the war to escalate or, heaven forbid, spread to Europe. However, there are those of us who think that's an inevitability. Unless we shift the balance of power."

"You mean fight a bigger war?"

"For the greater peace, yes." He drained his cup. "Bringing men from Europe isn't feasible. Not only would it leave us exposed at home, we couldn't move a force of any size through Suez without Germania knowing. Nor can we round the Cape—not unless we want to sail past every Nazi base on the west coast of Africa. Which leaves one alternative."

Salois understood immediately; he showed no expression. "Diego?"

The admiral glanced at the other men around the table and nodded.

Diego Suarez: on the northern tip of Madagaskar, one of the largest natural harbors in the world. The Nazis had militarized it as soon as they took control of the island, transforming the decrepit French port into a state-of-the-art naval fortress. Salois had worked in the gangs that built it, a minuscule dot of flesh among the stone and steel, like one of the slaves who toiled on the treasure cities of the pharaoh, aware that every brick laid, every girder hauled on blistered backs was reinforcing the Nazis' grip. He had sabotaged a batch of cement; when it didn't set, the guards had selected a work detail at random—twenty-five men—and shot every one. It was from Diego that the Reich's East Africa Fleet dominated the shipping lanes of the Indian Ocean.

"We have thousands of soldiers stationed in the Far East," said Rolland. "It would take a fraction of this force to make the difference. We're already preparing supply lines through Kenya and Sudan to this forward station. Once we land, we can have our troops on the border with Kongo inside a week, faster than the Germans can mobilize. If we join with the Force Publique, we could take back Stanleystadt."

"Then what?" said Salois.

"We drive toward Elisabethstadt, squeezing the enemy from the north as well as the south."

"But you can't get your men to Africa."

"Precisely. For two centuries, the Royal Navy has commanded the Indian Ocean." Rolland's mouth sagged with distaste. "Now we have to share it." He poured himself another cup of tea before leveling his eyes on Salois. "We want you to destroy the base at Diego Suarez."

Salois said nothing. He took another sandwich; the mustard burned the roof of his mouth.

"A large-scale operation is out of the question," continued Rolland. "Stealth and secrecy are our only hope. You will lead a team of four."

Salois shook his head. "Diego's huge, bigger than a city."

"We're aware that you know the terrain, Major. This is your chance to free Madagaskar."

"There would be reprisals. Worse than anything Globocnik did before."

"Think of it like gangrene," said the man at the window. "Sometimes one has to lose a limb to save the body."

Salois shifted his look toward the light. "Easy to say when it's not you on the butcher's block."

"After you torched a few vanilla farms, thousands joined the struggle. Strike at Diego and the whole island will rise."

There was truth in what he said. Salois also heard the impatience in his voice, the cynicism of his appeal. He turned back to Rolland. "Five men are not enough."

"Now is the time," replied the admiral. "A whole brigade was transferred from the island to fight in Kongo. Security will never be so thin."

"But five men."

"Your task would simply be to incapacitate the air defenses. We'll do the rest, from above."

"A bombing raid?"

The admiral indicated the dark-skinned man opposite Salois. "Colonel Turneiro, of the Mozambique Air Force."

"I didn't know they had one."

The airman puffed himself up. "A squadron of Lancasters, sold to us by the British."

"It will bring you into the war."

"Lisboa has decided. It's time we joined our Angolan brothers—what better way than with a famous victory."

Salois was thinking about the flat, scrubby hills above Diego: there was a runway that could land the latest jet fighters. "If I take out the guns, there must be a hundred Messerschmitts at Diego. The bombers will never get through."

"Which is why I'm leading a second team," said the man by the window. "To destroy the radar station at Mazunka. Once it's done, the whole west coast will be blind. By the time our planes are over Diego it'll be too late."

Salois glanced at the finish of his jacket. "You might get your suit dirty."

He let out an empty laugh. "Don't let this fool you," he replied. "I'm as happy in uniform. Happier, wouldn't you say, Admiral?"

Salois leaned back in his chair, feeling the upholstery shift around him, and tried to remember the last time he'd sat on anything so comfortable. He wanted to believe these men. Outside, the sun continued to sink, spraying the floor with color through the stained-glass window. He shook his head again.

"None of it makes any difference. Even if you can destroy Diego, even if you can land thousands of new troops, you and the Germans will slaughter yourselves to a stalemate."

"What would you suggest then?" asked Rolland.

"The one thing every Jew knows: America."

"You're ahead of us, Major. Something you proved when you killed those oil workers. Kongo is huge. If we fight in the north and south, that still leaves the west. Which is why once we open up this new front, the United States plans to attack from the Atlantic. It has been agreed at the highest levels."

Salois's eyes narrowed in disbelief. "Just because I've been in the jungle doesn't mean I don't hear the news. I know how Taft won the election; Americans don't want adventures abroad."

"Winning and governing are not the same. Fifteen years ago, their economy was in ruins. They rebuilt; now it's waning again. They need fresh resources, and Africa has them in abundance."

"Neutrality bought them a share."

"Which the Germans control," said the man at the window. "They could be choked off on Der Führer's whim."

"I still don't buy it," said Salois.

"What did Churchill say? 'America will always do the right thing, after exhausting all the alternatives.'"

"You see," said Rolland, "our paths may be different, but they wind to the same point." He offered a rheumy smile. "You're the best man to lead the operation, Major. The only man."

"And if I refuse?"

"This isn't the SS—we can't force you . . . However, there is one, well, awkward matter."

While the admiral took a sudden interest in his empty teacup, the man by the window stepped forward and removed a sheet of paper from his jacket. He slid it across the table. Salois saw him clearly for the first time and felt a twist of sympathy. Half his face was scar tissue, the color of plum flesh. Salois glanced at the photostat he'd been offered.

The ancient remorse filled him. No matter how deep he buried it, it was only a scratch away.

"Where did you get this?" he asked, hiding his nausea.

"Like I said: the Force Publique furnished me with everything I needed."

Salois studied the document. It was dated Antwerp, 1928, when he'd been at university studying veterinary medicine. His name was emblazoned on it—not Reuben Salois but his real name, the one he'd abandoned when he fled the country to join the Foreign Legion and a decade of brutality in the desert.

"It's meaningless," said Salois, pushing away the warrant for his arrest. "That Belgium doesn't exist anymore."

"True. In your case, however, I'm sure they'd honor it. The new Europe is prosperous, clean, law-abiding. It has no time for criminals."

"Except in Germania."

The warrant lingered in the open for a few moments more before it was stowed in the man's pocket; he returned to his perch. The movement reminded Salois of the furtive bartering in Madagaskar: a handful of salt, some bread, or a scrawny rooster briefly displayed, then hidden from sight until a price was settled upon. With so much hunger, the buyer was always the loser.

Salois took his final sandwich and chewed in silent deliberation. Outside, the sunlight weakened, the glow of the stained-glass window fading to gray. The four men watched him.

"I won't be threatened," he said once he'd swallowed the last mouthful, "but I will do it. Not for you, for me." He was completely still. "For what comes after. For hope."

Rolland seemed relieved. "I'm glad you look at these things so realistically," he replied. "You'll leave for Mombasa tomorrow, to join the others. Then to Madagaskar before Führertag."

Führertag: Hitler's birthday, 20 April. Across the Reich, from the festooned avenues of Germania to the ice floes of the north and the deserts of Südwest Afrika, Germans everywhere celebrated. Simultaneously, as far as the state apparatus was concerned, its enemies plotted. Security was ratcheted up in the days before; military bases were put on high alert.

"Everything starts returning to normal on the twenty-first," said Rolland, "which also happens to be Governor Globocnik's birthday. His own festivities begin on the stroke of midnight: a lavish party to which regional bosses are invited, including the commander of Diego; intoxication compulsory. We strike an hour before dawn the same morning."

"And after?"

"Considerable thought has gone into your escape, but we can discuss that later. First, time to introduce everyone properly. Colonel Turneiro you already know. And next to him—"

Salois was more interested in the man by the window. "What about you?"

"Ah, here we have the ringmaster," said Rolland. "He's coordinated between London and Lisbon—Washington, too."

He left the window again, striding into the gloom, and offered a burned hand: "Jared Cranley, British intelligence."

CHAPTER FOURTEEN

Roscherhafen, DOA
17 April, 10:30

TÜNSCHER WAS LATE. Tünscher was always late.

They had agreed to meet at ten that morning, during the rainy hours when there were fewer people around. Burton didn't bother arriving till half past and found himself at an empty table. Their meeting place was the Polar Café, festooned with sodden flags for Führertag; Hitler's birthday celebrations would reach their climax in three days. Burton sat opposite an enclosure of concrete icebergs where penguins huddled together in the steaming rain. A banana-leaf roof thrummed above him. This was Roscherhafen's Tiergarten, its zoo, designed by the Hagenbeck family and the largest in the world, as billboards proclaimed along every path: ninety hectares, a twelve-million-liter aquarium, more than ten thousand animals and seven hundred different species from across the globe.

Despite his torturous journey to Deutsch Ostafrika (DOA), Burton was calm and invigorated. It was as if Maddie had returned from the dead. The thought beat constantly in his mind, stoking him with hope, unveiling paths of light. He was closer to her than he had been in months and felt she must sense it, too. Burton imagined her cradling their child, the baby's tiny, translucent fingers clutching at hers as she whispered that the three of them would be together shortly. He had dismissed Cranley's claim to be the father. For all his posturing, it revealed his true nature: malicious, vindictive. For the moment, Burton didn't want to consider what lay ahead. He had escaped Britain, chanced his way back into Nazi Africa; somehow he would get them out safely. The hated air of the tropics, muggy and dense in his lungs, teemed with possibilities. Everything he and Madeleine wished for could come true, even if they'd never see the farm again. During their trip to Germania, when they had decided to make a life together, they had discussed moving abroad. Quinces didn't grow only in Suffolk.

Burton stilled his jigging leg and ordered a drink from a waitress wearing traditional Bavarian costume. There was no mango juice, so he chose a Reich Kola. Patrick had once told a tale about the Spanish Civil War and having to wait more than two days for Tünscher. When he finally showed, it was with a runaway whore and a bundle of stolen Miró canvases.

A family passed wearing lilac-and-blue KdF macs: father, mother, four blond kids, full of determined smiles despite their drenched socks and sandals. The youngest girl must have been the same age as Alice. She hung over the enclosure wall, gabbling something in a yokel accent. As if on cue, the penguins slid sullenly into the water; the girl clapped her hands in delight. Burton felt an unexpected reproach.

Alice couldn't come with him to Africa, and he had no desire to involve his aunt further, so he had walked the girl through the fog of Hampstead Heath to the glowing shadow of her house. He left her by the back wall, her coat lopsided where he had fastened the buttons with his stump. Through the mist came the roar of fire hoses, a woman's voice calling, *Alice! Alice!*

"I'll bring Mummy home," he promised.

"Not to the farm. I don't like the farm."

"Is that why you told your father?"

Alice was vehement: "Mummy said I should never tell anyone. Cross my heart and hope to die."

Three days later, he was booked on a Comet flight to Johannesburg. There were plainclothes policemen waiting at Heathrow, the same at Northolt airport and the Southampton docks. Each time he slipped away unnoticed. Finally, in desperation he strode up the first unwatched gangplank he found: a cargo ship for New Zealand. He hoped to pass another vessel en route and transfer to it. When there were none, he disembarked at Panama and caught a tramper back across the Atlantic to Cape Town, then another bound for Durban, and continued on overland through Mozambique.

Burton finished his Kola, ordered another. It was darker than the American equivalent, had a more syrupy, vanilla flavor. In the distance, distorted by the rain, he heard an oompah band. Screams from the roller coaster.

And then he saw him: strolling through the downpour, his straw-colored suit perfectly dry beneath a huge black umbrella. It seemed the years hadn't touched Tünscher. He was leaner, his shoulders still too broad for the rest of him, golden hair cropped tight against his tan. The same grizzled, sardonic features. How was it Patrick used to describe them? That was it: "a frontier face." By his side was a boy in Jungvolk uniform: black shorts and khaki shirt, his sleeve dark where the umbrella didn't cover him. It had never occurred to Burton that Tünscher might have a family.

They made their way into the café. Tünscher shook out his umbrella, then thrust his hand forward. Burton seized it, both men trying to crush the other's knuckles, and felt a wave of bravado at seeing his old comrade, as if Madagaskar would be no tougher than a raid on a Tuareg camp. Up close, one of Tünscher's eyes was puffy and bruised; his pupils had an empty look.

"What happened?" asked Burton.

"I was bored. Got into a fistfight."

"And is this your son?"

"Fuck, no! My sister's boy. I borrow him for business meetings—adds an air of . . . innocence, in case someone's watching. And I assume this is business." He spoke with an impudent drawl that had earned him nightly beatings from the *sous-officiers* in those first days of the Legion. "Your telegram was intriguing."

Tünscher beckoned the waitress over, glanced at her cleavage, and ordered cherry schnapps for himself, a Reich Kola for the youth.

"How did you know I was here?" he asked after the drinks arrived.

"Patrick."

"I've not seen him in years."

The two of them had fallen out in Spain and never spoken again; Burton had no idea why. "He kept tabs on you. Said you were back."

"And how is the old Yankee bastard?"

"Didn't you hear? It was broadcast across Africa."

"I don't listen to the radio. All that good news, the victories and everything, it depresses me."

"Patrick's dead."

A pause. "When?"

"Last year, in Angola. We were on a job together."

Tünscher fished in his pocket—underneath his jacket, he was wearing a woolen cardigan—and removed a cigarette packet. "I always hoped we'd square things one day," he said, lighting up. His expression remained inscrutable. "The dead are happier dead."

"He had a daughter, in America."

"I didn't know that." For the first time, Tünscher caught sight of Burton's empty sleeve. "Your contribution to the Angolan front?"

"Fishing accident," replied Burton. He hurried on: "What about you, Tünsch?"

"The body's still in one piece, but the heart and head have suffered. I joined the SS." He smiled—a line of crooked yellowing teeth—and watched Burton's reaction before his smirk broadened to a laugh. "Relax, Major, I'm no blackshirt. I joined up for the fight. A Waffen brigade."

"You were at Dunkirk?"

"The East; stayed after Barbarossa. I spent the last three years in the Urals and Siberia."

"What's it like out there?" asked Burton.

"Vast. Too vast ever to control. Cold. Desolate."

"I meant the war."

Tünscher sunk into his cardigan and considered his reply. "Like a good-time girl when the navy's in port," he said at last.

"What?"

"Fucked in every way. The Soviets are beat but don't know it; then there are the Eastern Jews . . ." He blew smoke. "I had to get out of there. Somewhere warm, civilized. So I thought I'd come home." Like Burton, Tünscher had grown up in Africa.

"And now?"

"What is this, an interrogation?"

"Just catching up with an old friend."

"I work for Section IX-c, the tourist department. The SS swallowed it up several years back. I take party chiefs to the Serengeti. Big-game hunting. They love going with old soldiers—gives them a heroic stirring."

"And the rest of the time?"

"I guess that's why you're here," said Tünscher. The boy next to him finished his Kola, sucking noisily through the straw. "The Section pays a pittance, but DOA is a good place to get rich."

"Smuggling."

"Booze, cigarettes mostly. Never girls, that's not my racket."

"You go to Madagaskar?"

"From time to time. Nosy Be is a good run." Nosy Be: an islet off the northwest coast of Madagaskar that the SS used for leave when not returning to Europe. It was notorious for its bars and brothels. "They turn a blind eye to keep the garrison happy."

Burton glanced around and produced a small box from his jacket. He slid it across the table. Tünscher removed it immediately, opening it in his lap: a tiny searchlight winked in his eyes.

"Five carats," said Burton. Inside the box was a single diamond from the pouch he'd hidden on the farm. "I need your help, Tünsch."

"That depends. Five carats doesn't get you far in this part of the world."

"I have more."

It had stopped raining; the café was getting busier. Tünscher drained the last of his schnapps, made a "stand up" gesture to his nephew, then turned to Burton. "I know a better place to powwow."

+ + +

They walked at a brisk pace through the Tiergarten, passing the elephant house and the pink ranks of the flamingo lagoon. The last time Burton had been to a zoo was with Madeleine in Germania, when the ground was scattered with daffodils. By the big cat enclosure was a billboard that showed one of Lazinger's fantasy portraits: Hitler in safari garb towering over a slain lion with Semitic features.

Whereas Kongo was a trove of mineral wealth, Deutsch Südwest Afrika functioned as the administrative center of the continent, and Muspel hid sand-lashed camps and military bases, DOA initially struggled to find a role beyond sisal production and fisheries. That it had once been a German colony, surrendered to the British after Versailles and not returned to the Reich until the Casablanca Conference, meant that Germania was keen to make it a glittering example of what National Socialism could achieve. It was the KdF that transformed it.

Kraft durch Freude (KdF: Strength Through Joy) was the Nazis' leisure organization, one of its goals to make travel available to even the lowliest factory worker—as long as he joined the party. It offered subsidized package holidays and by 1937 had become the biggest tour operator in the world. There were hiking trips to the Alps, a huge beach resort on the Baltic, and, most popular of all, a fleet of twelve cruise liners that conveyed passengers in spartan luxury to the fjords of Norway, the Mediterranean, and North Africa. As the Reich expanded below the equator, ever more exotic possibilities were offered; it was one of the inalienable rights of conquest. Hitler approved: "Every worker will have his holiday . . . and everybody will be able to go on a sea cruise once or twice in his life."

Robert Ley, founder of the KdF and later governor of DOA, first proposed developing the colony as a tourist destination. Its endless white beaches and German heritage made it an obvious choice. In five years from 1945, the capital, Roscherhafen (formerly Dar es Salaam), was transformed into a gleaming resort that accommodated half a million visitors a year from the cities and garrisons of German Africa. A new generation of cruise ships, big as aircraft carriers, brought a further three hundred thousand guests from the Fatherland itself.

As the number of vacationgoers increased, so did the need to occupy them. While safaris were the preserve of high-ranking officials, more immediate diversions had to be created for the masses. To the south of the city, KdF built its first "education and entertainment park"—a colossal site consisting of the zoo, the botanical garden, a military museum to commemorate Germany's East African campaign during the Great War, and a sprawling amusement park that offered the thrills of Oktoberfest all year long beneath broiling African skies. The British, with their decaying seaside towns and holiday camps, could only look on in envy.

Tünscher guided them to the fairground. The air smelled of wet cobbles and engine grease. There were shrieks from the log flume and the ghost train, the tinkling grind of merry-go-round music. If the crowds were aware of the war raging in Kongo, it didn't show in their smiles. Rising from the center of the park was the Roscherhafen Riesenrad, a monumental Ferris wheel; as with everything, it was the largest in the world, at over a hundred meters tall. Tünscher bought a string of tickets so they would have a cabin to themselves.

"I never feel comfortable in these things," he said, stuffing a handkerchief into the light fitting as they began to move. "Microphone," he explained. "Now we can talk."

"What about the boy?" replied Burton.

Tünscher leaned toward his nephew and sang to the tune of the "Horst Wessel Lied," the Nazi anthem:

When Der Führer says we is the master race
We quack quack quack in Der Führer's face
When Goebbels says we own world and space
We quack quack quack in the doctor's face

It was from a Donald Duck cartoon, a song that was banned everywhere in the German-speaking world. You could get five years in a concentration camp for letting it cross your lips. The boy offered a blank grin.

Tünscher gave his hair a playful tousle. "Stone deaf."

"What about the Jungvolk uniform? I thought you had to pass a medical."

"He failed. Bastards. I bought the clothes; he wears them when we go out together. You never saw a kid so happy."

The car was rising. With all the Führertag bunting, the park below appeared like a scarlet crater. To the east it gave way to a strip of beach and drab blue waves: what Burton still thought of as the Indian Ocean. He was keen to start negotiating but felt cautious, remembering how loose his old friend's tongue could be; his war record didn't help.

"It takes four minutes and forty-one seconds to go round," said Tünscher, unstrapping his watch. "You'd better be quick."

"I need to get to Madagaskar. To find someone."

"A Jew, I presume."

"Who else?"

"There are several SS brigades on the island. Perhaps you want to save one of the Schutzstaffel from himself."

"A Jew."

"They pay well?"

"Nothing."

"You sure? There are stories of treasure troves on the island. Hoards of gold smuggled from Europe."

"This is coming from my pocket."

A humph. "What town?"

"I don't know."

"Sector?"

Burton shook his head.

"Getting you on the island should be simple enough—for the right price. But without a location, forget it."

"There must be some way."

"It might help if I knew who this person was."

Burton would have preferred not to say, but the truths he'd withheld from Patrick remained livid inside him. He explained about Madeleine as quickly and with as little emotion as he could, then waited for Tünscher's contempt. In Bel Abbès, if a fellow legionnaire received a perfumed letter or admitted to falling for one of the prostitutes at Madame Maxine's, Tünscher was always the first to scorn.

Instead he stared out of the window and nodded gravely. The wind whistled and clanged around the wheel as they reached the highest point. "There may be a way to find out where she is, but I've never tried it. I'll have to ask around."

"I need to go tonight."

Tünscher let out a blast of laughter; next to him, his nephew gave a silent, gormless grin.

"The baby was due in February," said Burton. "I wasted weeks getting here. Anything could have happened—they could be sick, starving. Every single day matters." The thought had punished him since he'd left Britain.

"At least wait till after Führertag."

"And if she dies the night before? If I could have got there?"

Tünscher banged his sternum. "I should never drink schnapps, gives me indigestion. How many of those diamonds you got?"

"Keep the one I gave you," replied Burton. "That's your down payment. Help me find Maddie and the baby, get us all off the island, and there are four more."

"How do I know they're not fakes?"

"You don't."

"I'll do it for ten."

"Five. That's my only offer. Unless you want to spin for it."

Tünscher's expression darkened, as if he might lash out. "I gave up the gambling," he said. "It cost me too much." He wrapped his jacket round himself, fighting off an imaginary cold, then chased the anguish from his face and lit a cigarette. "No one cares if you're smuggling in brandy, Major. Jews are a different matter. Ten diamonds: I've got some serious debts to pay off in the East."

"Does brandy pay better?"

"No." He glanced at Burton's wrist, his eyes glassy. "But there are fewer fishing accidents."

"I can push to six."

"Nine."

"Seven. We have to live afterward, and the stones are all I got."

"They're worth nothing if you don't get off the island. Eight."

Burton tugged at his upper lip, feigned indecision as though weighing up who held the stronger position. It was a con—there were no more diamonds; he'd spent the last of them getting to DOA. *"Seven,"* he said. "That really is it."

The wheel was completing its revolution. Burton smelled pretzels and sausages wafting through the window. "You're lucky I'm so bored," said Tünscher, putting his watch back on. "Bored and broke. You just bought yourself Section IX's finest."

"I also need a gun," said Burton. "A pistol."

"What happened to that Browning of yours?"

"Gone."

"That'll be straightforward."

Tünscher retrieved his handkerchief. They got out of the cabin and meandered into the crowds.

"Give me twenty-four hours and I'll see what's possible. No promises, and"—he slapped his pocket—"I keep the diamond either way. Where can I find you?"

"Msasani Beach," replied Burton, giving the name of his hotel.

"You and ten thousand other people."

Tünscher nudged his nephew, pointed to his mouth, and mimed, *Wurst?* An excited nod. Then another gesture, indicating that they were going their separate ways. The boy turned solemnly to Burton and gave him a Nazi salute.

It was like the whole fairground was watching. Burton replied in kind, a fleeting raise of his good arm.

"I'll be in touch," said Tünscher, disappearing into the throng. There was a finality to his words, as if the meeting was a one-off.

"Wait!" Burton called after him. For the first time, he noticed Tünscher's feet: the hems of his trousers were frayed and ended in paratrooper boots. "Can I trust you?"

His old comrade flashed his yellow teeth. "No. But you can trust those diamonds."

CHAPTER FIFTEEN

Roscherhafen, DOA
17 April, 11:00

"IT COULD HAVE been worse," his wife had told him.

Brigadeführer Derbus Kepplar sat with his jackboots on the desk, staring at the wall, and became aware that the rain had stopped. He was an exemplary Aryan specimen: cropped blond hair, blue eyes, leanly muscular. To either side of him were towers of paperwork that he couldn't face: the minutiae of border patrol, customs, and immigration in Deutsch Ostafrika. The blinds were down, casting the room in a frowsty shade. Although his shirt clung to his back, he couldn't be bothered to switch on the overhead fan. He felt his victimhood strongly.

It could have been worse. They were the first words his wife said when he returned to Germania. She had perfect cheekbones, was a devoted and wholesome woman, but if the children hadn't been lined up behind her, if his heart wasn't so burnt, he would have removed his belt and thrashed her. She took to repeating her balm at every opportunity, till he snapped.

"How?" he demanded. "How could it have been worse?" The previous year, when he was still Hochburg's deputy, he had been tasked with apprehending Burton Cole and his team of assassins. When he failed, Hochburg insisted he take six weeks compulsory leave; after that he was dispatched to DOA. The black uniform of Kongo ceased to be his right; a silver diamond was docked from his shoulder lapel, reducing him from the rank of Gruppenführer to Brigadeführer.

His wife shrank from his outburst. "They could have sent you to the East. Or one of those punishment battalions you told me about in Kongo."

"Have you ever been to Kongo?"

"You know I haven't, my darling."

"Then don't presume to tell me about it. You understand nothing of

Africa." His palm found his chest. "To serve anywhere in Kongo, even with mongrel ethnics, would be an honor."

He stormed from the room, ordered her to sleep on the sofa after that, irate because she was right. His punishment could have been worse.

The security is atrocious in DOA, Hochburg had said. *You'll fit in well, Derbus.* It had been within the Oberstgruppenführer's power to retire him to Germania for good.

Kepplar pushed himself away from the desk. The walls of his office were blank, except for two framed photographs. He took the first down while keeping the other in the periphery of his vision.

It had been taken eighteen months before, snapped by an official SS photographer while they were on a routine inspection: Kepplar behind the wheel of a stationary Mercedes; Hochburg leaning against the bonnet, sleeves rolled up, laughing.

Kepplar traced his thumb over the Oberstgruppenführer's image; he wanted his laughter again. "Oh, Walter," he whispered; he was talking to the picture more and more, reminiscing about all they had achieved together. "This is agony."

Hochburg must have known it. An indefinite deployment to a corner office in the Zollgrenzschutz building was a sadistic punishment indeed.

Kepplar had devoutly followed the progress of the Kongo-Rhodesia war: wept when Elisabethstadt fell, bought champagne for his typing pool when the battle of Stanleystadt ended in victory. Several weeks earlier, he'd signed a dispensation for a flight stopping to refuel on its way to Germania that wanted to avoid immigration. The itinerary listed one passenger: Hochburg. Why his former master was bound for the world capital, Kepplar could only speculate; Walter hated the place as much as he did. He'd been tempted to visit the airport and plead with Hochburg for another chance. They hadn't spoken a word since that final day in the Schädelplatz, 19 September.

All because of Cole.

He replaced the picture of Hochburg and stood before the second. It was a secret Gestapo photo that showed Cole and Patrick Whaler, the American. He studied Cole's face as he had done innumerable times; his features were more familiar than Kepplar's family's.

His pursuit of Burton Cole was like a recurring nightmare. In the months since his failure to capture him he had reflected endlessly on his own shortcomings. What if he'd forced Cole's comrades to talk sooner? Or driven himself harder during the hunt, sacrificing the physical needs of his body. He shouldn't have involved the lower ranks, with their juvenile brutality; then again, perhaps a lack of brutality was Kepplar's mistake. If he had employed harsher methods, been careless and copious with death, not only in his orders but personally, maybe the outcome would have been different. That thought troubled him the most—success might have lain in his hands the whole time, if only he'd been prepared to bloody them. He had exposed his limitations.

He turned his back on Cole and peeked through the window blinds into an overcast brightness. The city was an amalgam of ornate, vaguely Oriental buildings from the previous century and severe white structures erected over the past decade. In the distance, Roscherhafen's most famous landmark, the giant wheel, rose from the KdF park like a shark fin. His eldest son begged to visit so he could ride on it. Beyond that were the dull waters of the OAO. He hated the ocean, perhaps because he was Austrian: there was something landlocked in his blood. Kepplar's eyes dropped to street level.

There was a rap on his door.

On the pavement, a cripple lurched past. He was dressed in black, with braces on his legs and crutches under his arms; Kepplar had the impression of an oversized tarantula. What must it be like to be so deformed, he thought, so pointlessly weak, and yet not have been spared by euthanasia? He felt an impulse to run down to the street and offer the cripple a handful of reichsmarks. Later Kepplar would remember that moment. The party was hostile toward religion and Hochburg scoffed at any mention of God, but for Kepplar it was as if someone had heard his prayers. The spider below was an omen.

Another rap, more urgent.

Kepplar returned to his desk, opened a report at random, and pretended to pore over it. "Come!"

An Untersturmführer entered, letting in the clack of typewriters. "Sorry to disturb you, Brigadeführer. Normally I would have dealt with this myself"—he offered a telex message—"but it expressly names you."

Kepplar took the sheet. According to the details at the top, the telex had been rerouted halfway across the continent: from Rovuma, in DOA, to Stanleystadt; to Windhuk; then back to DOA. A message in search of a recipient.

He read the first sentence and felt hot pins rise from his tailbone to the base of his skull. Kepplar reached for his right ear—the top half was missing, a subject never to be mentioned—and twisted the lobe. "Where did this come from?"

"Our border post with Mozambique—"

"Where in this building?"

"Third floor. Apparently it's been sitting there for a couple of days. You know how busy things get before Führertag."

Kepplar tore out of his office.

In the corridor, people froze to let him rush by. He didn't bother with the lift; instead he leapt down two flights of steps and through a set of frosted-glass doors. If his office was in shadow, then the third floor was like stepping into a sepia-toned photo: brown floors, brown furniture, countless bureaucrats in brown shirts with their muddy thinking. There was a hint of turpentine in the air. He strode through ranks of desks to Fregh's office.

The Standartenführer started as his door burst inward, spilling his midmorning coffee. On the desk was a plate of *Führerplätzchen*, a spiced biscuit popular at this time of year.

"Why wasn't I informed of this immediately?" demanded Kepplar, shaking the telex centimeters from Fregh's face.

"Herr Kepplar. What a surprise. Would you like some coffee? The biscuits are delicious."

"Why?"

Fregh put down his cup and read the message, tracing the text with his finger.

Kepplar had been at the top of his class in craniology; he believed you could judge everything about a man from his skull type. There were five strains: Categories 1 to 3 were Germanic; 4 and 5 were the *untermenschen*, the subhumans. The minimum requirement for anyone in public office was a Category 3. Because it was obscured by a layer of fat, Kepplar had never been able to discern the exact shape of Fregh's head. He suspected a trace of negroid in his hair, too. Fregh had married above himself, owed his position to his wife; it was well known that she had a taste for young eugenics students at Roscherhafen University.

Fregh nodded thoughtfully. "Ah, yes, very unusual. We received it on Wednesday."

"Then why wasn't I told?"

"Perhaps if you'd updated your orders, let them know you're with us now, you might have been easier to find."

During his pursuit of Cole and the American, Kepplar had issued a continent-wide alert to arrest them if they attempted to leave the borders of German Africa. It was unlikely that they would use a conventional crossing, but every possibility had to be covered. Now, seven months later, here was a telex saying that an American passport holder by the name of Patrick Whaler had been stopped trying to enter DOA from Mozambique at the border post of Rovuma Brücke.

"What can it mean?" asked Kepplar.

Fregh was staring wistfully at his biscuits. "Americans aren't uncommon here. They enjoy the big game."

"But this man, Whaler, was killed last year. Governor Hochburg saw the body."

"A mistake?"

The telex was back in Kepplar's hand. "It says 'stopped.' There's no indication whether he was taken into custody."

"It's best to leave these things. You're just making work for yourself."

"I need to get Rovuma on the phone."

Fregh opened his mouth to reply—a glimpse of coffee-black tongue—then thought better of it and dialed his secretary.

On the wall was a chart of Deutsch Ostafrika. Kepplar took down the map and spread it across Fregh's desk.

Rovuma Brücke: a byword for lax standards and one of the most sought-after postings on the continent—even a man of the lowliest rank could get rich there. After he took up his new role, Kepplar made an inspection and found things worse than he'd feared. A week later he was invited to the residence of Robert Ley, governor-general of DOA; it was as louche and luxuriant as Hochburg's study was austere. Over dinner they discussed the Führer's health and reports of a second rebellion in Madagaskar; then, unexpectedly, the governor said:

"I hear you are making changes at the Rovuma crossing."

"Security is a joke."

"We're known for our sense of humor in DOA."

Kepplar stopped chewing and put down his fork.

"Execute the occasional smuggler, by all means," continued Ley, "make an example of them, but remember, this isn't Germany or Kongo. We have a different approach here."

"You condone what happens?"

"Of course not. Sometimes, however, a more flexible approach to security has its benefits: to me, our most prominent citizens, the province as a whole." He sighed. "If ever you rise to a position like mine, Gruppenführer, you will understand."

Kepplar was obliged to explain his demotion.

He studied the map. From the crossing he could see only two obvious routes. One headed to the west and Songä; there was little there except tobacco plantations and archaeologists seeking dinosaur bones for the Linz Museum. The other road ran north, following the coast to Roscherhafen.

Kepplar pictured a team of armed troops swooping down on some innocent American who was in town to bag a lion's head and trawl the brothels. He'd start screaming about his fucking rights. The U.S. embassy on Kelele Platz would demand an explanation—and Germania was keener than ever on good relations since President Taft's visit to the Reich the previous month. They'd send Kepplar back to the Fatherland permanently this time, maybe give him a stint in a camp to calm his more erratic impulses.

But if he was right . . .

"We'll need to check every hotel room in the city," said Kepplar.

A belch of disbelief erupted from Fregh. "They say you never turn on your fan, Herr Kepplar, or open your windows. I think the climate's gone to your head."

"You will address me as Brigadeführer."

"But every room! We haven't the manpower."

"I see thirty of your men on their backsides for a start."

"They're not yours to commandeer," spluttered Fregh.

Six months earlier, no one would have dared speak to him like that. "I can get permission from the highest authority, but that will take time. Time you will be answerable for—"

The phone rang.

Fregh answered it, then proffered the receiver: "Chief of border control, Rovuma."

Kepplar pressed it to his good ear. An indolent, heat-soaked voice answered his questions: *Yes, Whaler . . . he'd stuck out; most Americans fly into Roscher, so it was unusual . . . He'd been stopped and questioned . . . No, not in his fifties, more like thirties . . . Blond, blue-eyed? Affirmative. No, he wasn't jumpy, his papers seemed in order . . . No, no other details—oh, except his hand. It was missing.*

That gave Kepplar pause.

"Do you still have him?"

"No."

"My orders were explicit."

"And seven months out of date, Brigadeführer. We tried contacting you. When we heard nothing back . . ."

"You should have arrested him."

The voice became more defensive. Kepplar wondered how many reichsmarks had exchanged hands. He was convinced it was Cole who had crossed from Mozambique. "On what basis? Keep the Yankees sweet, we're told. Your instructions say to detain suspects *leaving* our borders. Not entering."

"There must be a forwarding address."

The records were checked. "The Kaiserhof."

Kepplar knew it: a mock-Bavarian hotel close to the central train terminus. "You've been most helpful," he said into the receiver. "I will be including this conversation in my report."

He visited the Kaiserhof with two troopers carrying submachine guns. As he'd suspected, no one by Whaler's name or Cole's description had checked in. Afterward, he returned to the Zollgrenzschutz building and began organizing a city-wide search.

The breakthrough came ten minutes after four. Kepplar had spent the last hour in silence, his throat hoarse from bellowing orders. The staff on the third, fourth, and fifth floors were involved now, muttering to themselves when they thought he was out of earshot, glancing bleakly at their watches. The days before Führertag saw bands and pageants, balloons and scarlet cotton candy on the streets. That afternoon there was a parade along the waterfront; everyone wanted to be on the curbside with their families. The phone in Fregh's office—now Kepplar's temporary command center—rang. Fregh answered it with a blubbery sigh, wiped some crumbs off his shirtfront, then sat up.

"They've found him. At Msasani." Msasani Beach, the colossal KdF hotel development to the north of the city.

Kepplar snatched the phone and felt a tingle of self-satisfaction as the block warden described Burton Cole.

"Did you notice his hand?"

"Of course. We get lots of veterans here."

"Hold the line," said Kepplar.

He covered the mouthpiece and spoke to Fregh: "I'll need two cars: one for myself, you as backup. A truckload of your border guards. Armed. Plainclothesmen to watch the exits."

"Who is this man?"

"He mustn't be allowed to escape."

Fregh scowled at the clock and hurried out.

"I'm sure your wife will approve of you working so late," called Kepplar cheerfully before speaking into the phone again. "Where is 'Herr Whaler' now?"

"He went out this morning." There was a short pause at the other end; Kepplar heard the warden shuffling around. Then: "His key's not here; he must be back in his room. Shall I fetch him?"

"No," said Kepplar. Hochburg's eyes would glisten with gratitude when he delivered Cole. "Make sure he doesn't leave. I'll be there in fifteen minutes."

CHAPTER SIXTEEN

Tana, Madagaskar
17 April, 12:00

HOCHBURG STEPPED FROM the gloom of the palace and envied Globocnik. He crossed his arms and inhaled deeply, as if he could take the view into his lungs, breathing the clean air of the high plateau. In the distance were paddy fields worked by Jews and, beyond them, the smoky ring of the hills that surrounded Tana, the administrative center of Madagaskar. It seemed unlikely, but somewhere out there was the means to acquire his superweapon. A hot breeze licked his face.

"Magnificent," he said to the adjutant bobbing at his side.

"The stonework was imported from the governor's house in Europe." The adjutant had adopted the same jeering voice as his master; men stayed in Globocnik's service for decades.

Hochburg lowered his eyes. He was standing on gravestones etched with Hebrew. "I meant the garden." He strode down the steps through a lava flow of bright flowers, skimming his palms over the petals.

The adjutant followed. "Would you like some refreshment, Oberstgruppenführer? The governor keeps the best-stocked cellar in the Southern Hemisphere."

"Water will do."

"We have some particularly fine vintages—"

"Water."

"I'll have some brought out, and will tell the governor you are here."

Once he was alone, Hochburg filled his lungs again. After the cold rain of Europe, it was good to taste tropical air. He was in a jaunty mood.

At the bottom of the stairs was a terrace almost as expansive as the one at the Berghof. A wall separated it from a precipitous drop to the city below. Hochburg leaned against the bricks, feeling their warmth in his kidneys, and surveyed the palace with his good eye. The left one was still swathed in bandages; the surgeon had been unable to guarantee that his sight could be restored despite several weeks of treatment in Germania.

The governor's residence was an impregnable stone cube with turrets on each corner and a pyramid roof. It had been built in the 1830s by Ranavalona I, a bloodthirsty native queen who ruled the island with a grip not seen again till the SS. Bouhler, the first Nazi governor, gutted and modernized the building; since Globocnik's reign, a new frontage had been added in what he described as his neo-Mesopotamian style: stark, angular, dangerously modern. Descending from all four sides, recalling a ziggurat, were flights of steps surrounded by terraced gardens. The planting would have been too structured for Eleanor, but Hochburg spied many of her favorites: hibiscus, Rubiaceae, euphorbias. There were red and white roses, magenta cascades of the local bougainvillea. If only he'd had the time to create a paradise like this.

The adjutant returned with a Malagasy* carrying a bottle of Apollinaris water on a tray. Typical Globocnik! Only he would thrill to have an indigenous wait on him. That this maid had been sent when the palace must be teeming with blond servants was a deliberate provocation. Hochburg checked to make sure her negroid fingers hadn't touched the glass before pouring. Her face wore the signs of Globocnik's moods.

"I have informed the governor of your presence," said the adjutant. "He will be with you shortly."

"You mean he's still in bed. Or hungover."

"He has been touring the island for Führertag; didn't get back till early this morning."

Hochburg downed his water. "Tell him I haven't got all day."

The minutes passed; then five, ten, fifteen. Hochburg tracked a pair of Me-362 jet fighters as they howled across the horizon toward their base at Diego Suarez. Although the majority of the island was the responsibility of Heydrich's office and the SS, the northern sector came under the jurisdiction of the Kriegsmarine, the navy, an independence held as sacrosanct. Twice the adjutant appeared to reassure Hochburg that Globocnik was on his way. Finally, half an hour later, the man himself tottered down the stairs half-dressed.

Obergruppenführer Odilo Globocnik: the SS governor of Madagaskar, commonly known as Globus.

---

*One of the native inhabitants of Madagascar.

Born in Austria, a builder by trade, he joined the party in 1930 and rose to become the gauleiter of Vienna. After that his fortunes had swung like a weathercock, as Hochburg once heard them described. Within six months of taking the top job in Vienna, he was forced to resign because of an embezzlement scandal. He joined the Waffen-SS as an enlisted soldier, was decorated in the war against Russia, and subsequently made a police chief in the occupied territories by Himmler. After the Barbarossa Line division, Globus was tasked with resettling the Soviet Jews and spent several years evacuating them beyond the Ural Mountains to Siberia before once again a corruption charge brought him down. It looked as if he was finished for good until Madagaskar salvaged his reputation. His latest ambition was to leave the island and take up the governorship of Ostmark.*

"Governor Globocnik," said Hochburg when he made it to the bottom of the stairs, "I'm so happy you could join me."

They shook hands—their palms barely touching, a thick gold watch jangling around Globus's wrist—and appraised each other.

Hochburg hadn't seen him since the Windhuk Conference, the gathering of senior SS officials that decided the fate of the black population and their subsequent "resettlement." In the years since, Globocnik's mucky-blond hair had started to thin. His face was more bloated, the skin around his nose sunburned and riddled with a network of burst veins, eyelids drooping. He wore jackboots and tan trousers with the suspenders flapping at his side; his vest failed to contain his paunch. There was a yeasty smell about him.

"I never knew we shared a passion," said Hochburg, admiring the garden. "Or that you had such good taste."

Globus made no reply.

"Did you design it yourself?"

"No. Some Jew cunt."

A neat smile passed Hochburg's lips. "I'm glad to find Madagaskar hasn't tempered your charm."

"If I had my way, I'd concrete the lot," he replied in his lilting Carinthian accent. "But Mutti likes it."

"Your mother comes all this way to visit?"

"She lives in the palace with my sisters. They keep my wife company when I'm busy in the reservations; I'm overseeing their completion personally." He reached into his pocket for a bottle of pills. "Now, what do you want?"

---

*Formerly Austria.

At Windhuk, Hochburg had agreed to send Africa's Jewish population to Madagaskar; when Globus failed to reciprocate with the native Malagasy and instead established a zone for them in the northeast of the island, Hochburg had been furious. It was only later that he appreciated that the best way of dealing with Globus was crude fawning and implicit threat.

"My dear Globus," said Hochburg, using the Reichsführer's favorite moniker for the Austrian, though he allowed a hint of ridicule to speckle his words. "I come to ask a favor. From one governor-general to another."

In an instant, Globocnik's face was puce. "You've already had a brigade of my best men. I won't give you any more. I refuse—"

"That's not why I'm here."

"I've fought to control the island ever since. Keep taking my troops, and the Jews will run amok. If that happens, I'll personally tell the Führer it was your fault."

"Calm yourself, Obergruppenführer. We all know of your security problems, and who you blame."

"You should be in Kongo, winning back Elisabethstadt, not bleeding me dry."

"It's not your soldiers I want," said Hochburg. "I'm after a Jew."

"A Jew?"

Hochburg gestured toward the lowlands, with their shanty towns and work camps. "You have several million."

"What is it, mine clearance? Take as many as you want."

"A generous offer; however, I need only one."

Globus grew silent, as if suspecting a scam. He unscrewed his bottle of pills and tipped some down his throat. "They tell me you came direct from Germania. That's a long way for a Yid. He must be valuable."

"That's not your concern."

"My island, my Jew."

"It's a matter of the highest state security."

A derisive snort. "Heinrich will tell me."

"He doesn't know either."

His scorn vanished; this upturned the natural order Globus clung to.

"This Jew could be anywhere," continued Hochburg, "so I have a second favor to ask."

"Go on," said Globus, his curiosity aroused.

"With your permission, I wish to visit the Ark."

"Why don't you ask to fuck my sister?" The blood was throbbing in his cheeks again. "We're not allowed there, and you know it: all that shit Heydrich agreed with the Americans."

"I thought you said it was your island."

"Even I"—Globus thumped his chest to emphasize the point—"I haven't been there."

"A guided tour won't be necessary."

"The Ark's rotten, falling apart. You could break your neck. There are also the Jews who guard it—they might take you hostage. It's too much of a security risk."

"Then I will go without your permission."

Globocnik's neck bulged with fury. His temper was legendary: in the Urals he had turned mountainsides crimson simply because an order from Germania displeased him. He lumbered toward Hochburg, who moved away from him, taking a dainty sidestep as if they were dancing.

"The Jews want to destroy this island," said Globus, "destroy me." His voice was black with resentment. "For now they're divided. Squabbling. That's how I can maintain control despite you thieving my men. But give them a reason to unite—like stepping on the Ark—and everything I've built here will collapse. Do you know how that will make me look?"

"There are greater stakes than your career, Herr Governor. I need to find my Jew; I'm going to the Ark."

"I forbid it! You don't like that, take it up with Heydrich. Take it up with the Führer, for all I care."

He stormed up the steps, suspenders whipping his thighs.

A chill settled in Hochburg's chest; he gazed out across the city with his single eye. After the French had been defeated, its name was Germanized to Antananarivo; later, Globus officially shortened it to Tana. The rumor was that the original six syllables were too complex for his tongue. Hochburg returned his attention to Globocnik as he receded up the stairs, the back of his vest an oval of gray sweat. "How are your swine herds, Obergruppenführer?"

A falter in his step.

"What about your meatpacking plants? My troops fight best on a belly of Madagaskan pork."

This time Globus stopped. He swiveled around, his whole body tense. His neck still pulsed, but there was caution in his expression, a twitch of barely hidden panic in that bloated face. He descended, grinding his boots into the Hebrew etchings.

"Do you know what the Jews are calling this new uprising?" he said. "The Pig Rebellion. Just yesterday there was a revolt at one of the abattoirs. I had to shut it down, shoot the ringleaders, transport the rest to the Sofia Reservation. The Jews think that by attacking our industry they can beat us. But I won't tolerate their threats. Or yours."

"I have two armies fighting in Kongo. That's a lot of ration tins. A lot of profit for you."

"No one is cheaper," replied Globus, reaching the terrace.

"I agree. But Governor Backe, in Kamerun, is always telling me how nutritious his highland cattle are."

"Backe? That scrawny cocksucker. He'll charge double what I am."

"We have a long-standing interest in hunger and its uses. I'm sure we could reach an agreement on price. In turn, that would represent a substantial loss of revenue to this island." Hochburg shook his head in mock sadness. "And where there are losses, Germania sends its auditors. Of course, you're familiar with them: they follow you like flies chasing shit. Vienna, the Urals . . ." He flashed a smile. "Everyone knows your ambition to become governor of Ostmark—why ruin your chances over a single, meaningless Jew?"

Globus's jaw was quivering.

Hochburg watched him coil his fingers into a fist. The metal of his wedding rings glinted. He wore two: one from his own marriage, and the other from his mother's, a source of much gossip. He squeezed his fingers till the flesh swelled on either side of the bands, but he didn't dare swing a punch. The governors of Africa all held the title of Obergruppenführer, with the exception of Hochburg. As the architect of Nazi Africa, he had been elevated to the select position of Oberstgruppenführer. He outranked Globocnik.

"We have an archivist," said Globus in a more controlled voice. "He's Jew-friendly, allowed on the Ark. Give me your one's name and he'll find the details."

"I will do it myself. This afternoon."

A blast of consternation: "Who is this Jew?"

"As I've said, that does not concern you. I will also need a helicopter to take me there."

"You can't have a Walküre. I need them all to fight the uprising."

"I understand," replied Hochburg. "Gunships are essential against boys with stones." He offered a placating smile. "A Flettner will suffice."

Globus was twisting his two wedding rings round and round as if trying to unscrew his finger. He rolled his shoulders, sending a ripple of fat down his vest. When he spoke, his words crackled.

"My office will sort out some transport. After that, I don't expect to see you again." He strode up the steps. "Find your precious Jew, Hochburg. Then get off my fucking island."

CHAPTER SEVENTEEN

Roscherhafen, DOA
17 April, 16:30

EVERY ROOM WAS as cramped as it was identical: a basin, sofa, wardrobe, and two metal-framed single beds, the soft furnishings done in cream and brown. A holiday cell, thought Burton when he first walked in. He was on the fifth floor of KdF's gargantuan Msasani Beach hotel.

If Kraft durch Freude was to offer package holidays to all, it would need accommodations, and so a program of resort construction began. The first had been in 1936 at Prora, on Germany's Baltic coast, and it became the prototype for future developments. Designed by Clemens Klotz, a favorite of Speer's, the architecture was martial, uniform: continuous blocks of rooms on a megalithic scale. On the clearest of days, you could stand at one end of the building and not glimpse the other. At the center was a grand hall used for dancing and indoor sports and to celebrate the sacred days of the National Socialist calendar. There were bowling alleys, cinemas, heated swimming pools—one with a wave machine. Every guest was guaranteed a sea view.

After peace in Europe, an expansion of KdF building led to nine resorts around the globe, from Danzig (another Baltic favorite) to Gothenburg, on the Black Sea; the latest was in Argentina.

KdF Msasani, in DOA, was second only to Prora: a slab of white concrete six stories high that stretched unbroken for four kilometers and could house fifteen thousand guests. Originally it had been called KdF *zum Weissen Strand*—White Sands—but regardless of ideological concerns, Germans wanted something more African, something that conjured up exotic adventures when they returned to the factory. Eventually the beach's native name—Msasani—took over, despite *"zum Weissen Strand"* continuing to hang over the entrance in cankered Gothic lettering.

Burton sat on the bed. He had always found hotels depressing, even after he and Madeleine were lovers and they became secret places of promise and release.

I don't want to die in a hotel room, he'd told her that time in Germania; they were lying exhausted in bed. *Spare me that.* The walls smelled as impersonal as sand, the linen boiled.

She stroked his cheek. *With all my heart.*

There was a knock on the door. Burton got up and let in Tünscher. Under his arm was a box wrapped in shiny Führertag paper. He was glassy-eyed, in good spirits.

"I took your diamond to a jeweler," he said, chucking the present on the bed. "It's genuine, five and a bit carats, oval-cut, from the Kassai mines no less. With the other six it's a good deal, will pay off my debts."

Burton nodded. They had an expression in the Legion: "the corvus." Promising the world, delivering dust. Self-loathing squirmed in his gut. He made himself think of the time Tünscher conned him out of his water ration on a desert march. Or the fight he got into in Marseille when Tünsch waited till he was on all fours, drooling blood, before throwing his first punch. Or when he'd sworn Tünscher to secrecy about the black girl he'd lost his virginity to at the orphanage; by nightfall even the camels knew her name.

Most of all, he thought of Maddie and the baby.

Tünscher took out a chart of Madagaskar, opening it to the northwest quadrant of the island. "This is Nosy Be," he said, tapping the laminate. "You're in luck. My usual people are flying in tomorrow night, one last sortie before Führertag. You'll be bringing in two hundred cases of Krug for the celebrations." He traced his finger south. "And this, Major, is how we find your woman."

"Lava Bucht?"

"The Jews keep their records there on a junked KdF liner. They call it the Ark."

Burton had a faint memory of some deal struck between Heydrich and the Americans after the first rebellion to protect a registry of Jews. By then Madagaskar had been off the mercenary trail for years; he was yet to meet Madeleine. The island meant nothing to him; it was one more beacon of misery on the periphery of the new German empire.

"How do we get on board?" he asked.

"It's not well guarded," replied Tünscher. "We'll serve up some bullshit." He explained the rest of his idea, smoking a cigarette to the stub, vague but confident.

"What about after?" asked Burton when he was finished. "Once I've found Madeleine."

"We fly you to Somalia."

"South Africa* would be better."

"And too far."

Burton considered everything he'd heard. "It's a good plan," he said, handing back the map.

"Keep it," replied Tünscher. "One last thing." His tone became business-like. "None of this is coming cheap. Seven stones gets you there and out. It doesn't get me on the island proper. My skin's worth more than that. I'll help you find the records, but once you get them—you're on your own."

After Tünscher left, Burton took a cold shower in the communal baths, then returned to his stifling room. He unfastened the balcony doors to get a breeze and was hit by the commotion below. Five stories beneath him were landscaped gardens—palms, castor oil plants, violets imported from the colony's interior—and the foreigners' pool, radiating its tang of extra chlorine. A group of Spanish tourists played round it, laughing, yelling, the kids dive-bombing each other. The lifeguard's chair was empty; he stood away from the water, conferring with a man in a suit.

Msasani had been built with an eye toward the future and wouldn't reach capacity till the 1960s. Even when the massive KdF cruise ships were in port, occupancies were never more than three-quarters. To fill the empty rooms, *Ausländer* wings had been established—blocks where foreigners could stay at an all-inclusive rate of fifty reichsmarks per week, twenty more than Germans paid. These guests came mostly from Spain and Italy and were encouraged to marvel at the Reich's experiment in vacationing—as bold as any of its military or engineering triumphs.

From the gardens, a path led to the ocean. The sky was turning from tangerine to gray, clouds darkening the horizon; Burton smelled thunder brewing. Some 450 miles to the southeast were the Komoros Islands, where the Nazis had a submarine base. Another 250 miles marked the first ring of mines that surrounded Madagaskar like a lethal coral reef. And some-where beyond that, he prayed, Madeleine was safe and waiting for him. He was impatient to get there. Throughout his voyage to Africa, he'd pictured the moment when they met again. It stuttered in his mind, impossible to capture. Would she be shocked? Relieved? Furious at him?

---

*After the Casablanca Conference, and the redrawing of the continent, South Africa remained an independent, neutral state.

He yearned to slip his fingers between hers, to cup her face and kiss her. Every time he comforted himself with their reunion, she was as plump and happy as she had been the previous summer. He knew that couldn't be true.

Burton retreated inside and opened the bedside cabinet where he had stowed Tünscher's present. Next to it was a copy of *Mein Kampf*; every KdF room in the world held a cheap edition of the book. Hitler took no salary as Führer of the Greater Germanic Reich—but he was a multimillionaire author. *What does that tell you about publishing?* was one of Maddie's favorite gibes. He picked up the present and ripped off the paper to reveal a box stamped BERETTA, MOGADISHU. Inside was a pistol, an M1951, Beretta's latest model, the type used by the Italian African Police and recognized for its accuracy and reliability. Burton raised it to his nose: virgin gun oil. He missed his Browning.

He dismantled the weapon, holding it against the bedside cabinet with his stump as his other hand did the work. Once it was in pieces, he wiped off the packing grease, carefully reassembled it, then reached back into the box. Tünscher had included a spare clip and a case of ammunition. Burton felt another spasm of guilt.

The racket below was irritating him; he kicked the balcony door shut. As the din subsided, he thought he heard something from the corridor. The echo of boots stamping upstairs.

He stood and closed the balcony door completely to blot out the noise from the pool. The man in the suit was scanning his floor. It sounded as if someone was walking down the corridor toward him. Not a guest returning to his room, sandals flapping carelessly, but cautious, controlled steps. Hard soles against the tiled floor.

He crossed the room and put his ear to the door.

No one knew he was in Roscherhafen. It was probably some Jugenvolk playing a game . . . unless Tünscher had decided there was more profit in turning him over than in the Madagaskar job. Or he hadn't paid enough for his entry visa.

There had been no opportunity to acquire a fake passport, so he used Patrick's. It was less risky than his own, and he'd hoped that America's neutrality would ease his passage through German customs. He had removed the dead man's photo and replaced it with his own; scratched and inked the digits on the year of birth so that "1896" read "1916." Presented it with a bland smile. When they detained him at the border with Mozambique, it cost thirty reichsmarks for each of the issuing officers, another fifty for their supervisor, and a thick donation to Rovuma's Führertag kitty. Perhaps he hadn't been generous enough.

Burton reached inside the bedside cabinet and took out the copy of *Mein Kampf.* Dropped it with a thud.

The footsteps stopped at once.

He stilled his breath. Four, five, six seconds passed.

Then the steps again, consciously keeping quiet this time. Burton grabbed the Beretta's magazine, wedged it into his armpit, and began pressing in bullets.

+ + +

A thud.

Kepplar raised his hand at the two men behind him; both were carrying BK44s with the safety catches off. They were halfway along the corridor, approaching Cole's room at the end. The fire escape was covered by armed troops, as were the main stairs, lobby, and gardens.

When Kepplar arrived at *zum Weissen Strand*, a moment of boyish excitement took hold of him. Every time he stood beneath its walls, the immensity of the place made him feel like a child transported to a world of giants. It was claimed that when Peenemünde put the first National Socialist into orbit—*soon,* promised Goebbels, *soon*—the building would be visible from space. Then he went to work: organizing the men he had so there was no chance of Cole escaping. If only he still commanded the resources that were his in Kongo.

Kepplar lowered his hand and continued along the corridor, treading lightly so his boots wouldn't squeak on the floor and its diagonal lines of yellow tiles. From outside came the screams of children. His own offspring would never dare make such noise, but then scientists had proved it was the Mediterranean blood that made its people constitutionally rowdy.

They reached the door. In a whisper he repeated the instruction he'd given the men outside: "He must be taken alive."

Kepplar watched the troops level their rifles. Before he'd left the Zollgrenzschutz building he had unlocked his safe and retrieved his pistol, a Walther P38; its holster was heavy and ungiving against his hip. He felt no need to unbuckle it. His heartbeat was in his ear, his stomach spongy with exhilaration. All that separated him from Cole and deliverance were a few centimeters of plywood. He would hand him over to Hochburg, then bask in his former master's contrition.

Kepplar raised his jackboot.

Seven months earlier, on the morning he'd returned empty-handed to the Schädelplatz, Hochburg had raged at his failure, ordered him bound to a stake, threatened to burn him alive. It was the stake originally meant for Cole's execution. Kepplar recalled the smoke clogging his nostrils and the sparks that danced around him; his legs were buried in tinder.

"Herr Oberst, please," he yelled as Hochburg strode away. "Herr Oberst!"

Hochburg crossed half the square before he stopped and sauntered back. At his command, Kepplar was cut free, his uniform already singed. He crawled over to Hochburg and clutched his master's boots, splattering them in tears.

"Give me one final chance," he pleaded. He was on his hands and knees, arse in the air. "I won't fail you again, I will find Cole. I promise."

"You didn't really think I'd burn you?" asked Hochburg, his voice mellow and contemptuous.

"No, Walter, no."

"Of course not. Can you imagine the fucking paperwork!" He roared with laughter. "It's time to send you home, Derbus."

Now Kepplar kicked the door with all his ferocity. It buckled in the frame but didn't give. He smashed his jackboot into it again.

There was a crash from the other side.

"He's barricading it," said Kepplar.

One of the soldiers opened fire. Kepplar swiped the muzzle to one side: "No shooting!" Outside, the kids round the pool had fallen silent. He grabbed the rifle and used it to batter down the door. It gave way, shunting open enough for him to see that a wardrobe had been toppled across the entrance.

Kepplar squeezed his face into the gap and saw a figure retreating through the room to the window, upturning the bed and sofa as he went, to block his path.

"Burton Cole!" he shouted.

His quarry spun round—for the first time they were face-to-face.

It was impossible to know why Cole obsessed the Oberstgruppenführer so much. He seemed a man—just a man—a feeble threat to the world Hochburg ruled over. He was more haggard than his photograph, with longer hair, the skin around his eyes ringed and drab, the left side of his face mottled with scars. Kepplar knew those features so well it was like seeing an old comrade; part of him wanted to raise his hand in greeting. Later he realized that he had paid no attention to the shape of his skull.

Cole aimed his pistol, fired once, and threw himself off the balcony.

CHAPTER EIGHTEEN

BURTON HIT THE water hard, the impact concertinaing his body. Bubbles roared in his ears. He bumped the bottom, kicked to the surface.

Spanish tourists were gathered around the pool. They helped him out, babbling excitedly. Pushing through them were the lifeguard and the man in the suit.

There was an explosion of water behind Burton.

The Nazi he'd seen at the door had followed him over the balcony. In the second their eyes had locked in the room, Burton had noticed that he only had one full ear, that his face was etched with wrath and accusation.

Burton seized the lifeguard by the wrist, twisting the other man's arm, and brought his stump down on the elbow. He hurled him into the pool, then the man in the suit, then everyone he could grab. The one-eared Nazi fought through a logjam of thrashing limbs.

Burton ran, heading toward the ocean, through the leaves of castor oil plants.

Another suit stepped in front of him.

Burton rammed him off the path and into the bushes, kept running. From the direction of the pool came shouts, someone blowing a whistle.

The beach was busy, despite the lowering sun: swarms of kids, men with burnt bellies wearing shorts and sandals, women in black one-pieces; bikinis were considered subversive by the regime. Burton headed right, his soaked clothes weighing down every stride till he was panting. His long journey to DOA had left him more unfit than he'd realized. He steadied his breathing, drawing air deep into his lungs. At least the years in the Legion meant he was nimble over sand. He glanced over his shoulder: nothing but vacationers.

The foreigners' block was at the southern end of the development, near the city itself, with its traffic fumes and sewers that needed refurbishing. Burton raced along the beach watching Block 2, then Block 1 pass: an unremitting wall of white stone and square windows. Finally, the buildings came to an end and he could see the row of palms that separated the hotel from the road.

Clutching his side, he hurried toward the trees. Cars were visible between the trunks.

"Stop!"

Several troops appeared from the gardens on Block 1. A warning shot zinged overhead.

Burton reached the road and chanced another look back. The front of Msasani glowed amber in the sunset. By the entrance was a police lorry and two BMWs; a figure in a soaked uniform was shouting instructions. Burton ran into the road, dodging cars, which swerved around him. It was a dual motorway, the traffic on his side heading out of the city. He crossed the central median—another palisade of trees—and stepped out in front of a taxi.

A squall of smoke and rubber.

The car slewed to a halt, behind it a cacophony of horns. It was a cream-colored Volkswagen, as were all taxis in Roscherhafen. On the door was a shield bearing a lion's head and an eagle, DOA's coat of arms. Burton yanked the door open and climbed in.

"Drive."

The man at the wheel, in a turban, gesticulated angrily.

Across the road, the two BMWs were gliding out of Msasani. One joined the traffic and accelerated away, followed by the lorry: a hundred meters up the road was a turning point. The other drove straight across the motorway, navigating through the trees and onto the city-bound lane.

Burton stuck the Beretta between the driver's eyes.

"Now!"

The taxi surged forward.

"What's your name?" he asked the driver.

No reply, only a wail of prayers—then wretched fatalism. Like many of Roscherhafen's cabdrivers, he was an Arab, his race tolerated by the authorities because they were prepared to work long hours for a pittance and gave the city that alien quality so many tourists wanted.

The first BMW was closing. "Faster!"

The taxi swerved around other cars. The interior was decked with golden trinkets and beads, which jingled violently.

"Where you go?" asked the driver.

Burton's mind was racing. "The old town." He cleared his eyes of sweat.

"The Bazaar." Its maze of streets would be the ideal place to lose his pursuers: he'd tell the driver to keep going, vanish on foot into the Indiamarkt.

They were approaching a yellow light. The driver reached for the gear stick. Burton slapped his hand away. "Straight through."

The taxi flew across the junction, and the next, then slowed. There was a barricade across the road. A detour sign.

"Why is it blocked?" asked Burton.

"They close for harbor parade," replied the driver. "It's now. For Führer." He risked a sidelong glance at Burton, nervously adding, "Blessed be his name."

"Go right."

The taxi veered off down a side street, the two BMWs pursuing. Burton leaned out the window to take a shot but was bucking too much in his seat.

Apart from a few students, the streets were mostly empty. They sped past the old Anglican church, now boarded up. Approached the Deutsch Afrika Expo, on Ringstrasse. Outside the hall were six flagpoles, each bearing the outline of its respective province in Nazi Africa.

Burton grabbed the wheel, shoved it to the left, causing them to mount the pavement; pedestrians scattered. The BMWs followed, horns blaring. The taxi plowed through the poles, hitting them one after another:

Th-boom. Th-boom. Th-boom.

With each impact, the Arab invoked the name of God. The poles tumbled onto the lead BMW, wrapping its windscreen in banners. It skidded and crashed into the steps that led to the exhibition. The second car smashed into its rear.

The cab braked to a standstill.

Burton was thrown forward, cracking the dashboard. The driver opened the door and fled.

"For fuck's sake," snarled Burton.

He watched the one-eared Nazi emerge from the flags flapping round the wreckage, his legs caught in Kongo's ensign. He freed himself, took a step toward Burton's vehicle, staggered, then righted himself and stumbled toward the curb. He held out his arm, as though giving the traffic a Führer salute. He must be concussed, thought Burton, before he realized that the Nazi was flagging down the lorry.

Guards emerged from the expo building, rifles at the ready. From across the city came the cry of a siren.

Burton clambered into the driver's seat, fought to put the taxi in gear, and pulled away in third. The engine strained . . . and stalled. Beads shimmered around him. He tried to restart it. Nothing but the lifeless chug of valves.

In the rearview mirror, the lorry had stopped. The Nazi ordered the driver out of the cab and hiked himself behind the wheel.

Burton twisted the key as if he would snap it. The expo was reached by a plaza; the Ringstrasse was an open boulevard. If he got out and ran, he would make an easy target.

There was a snarl of exhaust fumes, and the lorry started toward him.

Burton screamed at the car, spittle flicking the windscreen. Engines had always hated him. One afternoon when he'd needed to get Madeleine home before Cranley, he had spent several minutes battling with his clapped-out Austin. They were running late, the windows misty with condensation. The frustration of being bullied by the clock, and of knowing he would shortly have to watch the door of Madeleine's house close behind her, welled inside him. He beat the steering wheel, cursed useless British engines. Maddie took his hand and nestled it beneath her thighs. She waited, then calmly gave the key a single turn; he had dropped her off by nightfall.

Burton tugged the key loose, imagined Maddie pressing it to her lips, then slid it back in.

The ignition caught on the first try.

He stamped on the accelerator as the lorry bashed into his rear bumper. Burton was thrown forward but kept his foot down. The taxi lurched away. He left his stump on the wheel, let go with the other hand to change into second gear, then third.

On either side, open shopfronts flashed by: white tiles hanging with sausages, coconuts, sacks of coffee beans. Pharmacies, a taxidermist. There was a sign for the harbor.

At the next junction, the light was red. He squeezed harder on the gas, hurling the taxi through the intersection as if faith and willpower alone would protect him from collision. The lorry followed, pirouetting aside a mechanized rickshaw.

Burton's foot remained on the floor: forty kilometers per hour, forty-five, fifty.

He darted through holes in the traffic, struggling to work out where he was in the city. There were so many shops, it had to be the Bazaar. He needed to cross what had once been India Street, then left at—

A group of students marched into the road. They were part of the recently formed 3K movement, carrying banners and placards. TAKE THE WAR TO THE BRITISH! KENYA—KHARTOUM—KAIRO: VICTORY IN '53!

Instinct forced him to swerve. As the VW hit the curb, Burton thought he should have plowed through them. He felt a tire blow, the chassis bouncing back onto the road. The lorry was inches from slamming into him.

Ahead was an alleyway. At the last moment he worked the clutch and yanked the wheel sharply toward it. The front of the taxi hit the entrance, rebounded, then careered down the passage.

The lorry shot past.

Burton kept both his hand and his stump on the wheel now. The alley was gloomy, barely wide enough for the car, and seemed to be narrowing. Halfway down was an intersection, then another stretch of alley, ending in a window of sky that shimmered red at the base.

Still the walls closed in. Burton eased off the gas as the wing mirrors pinged and vanished. He was sure he could just make it.

The taxi gouged itself into the walls. Ground to a halt. The engine died.

Burton glanced through the rear window: no sign of the lorry. He went to open the door and found it wedged tight against the brickwork of the alley. This time the car started the first time. He put it in reverse and, twisting to see over his shoulder, pressed the accelerator. The taxi didn't budge.

The light from the street dimmed as the troop lorry trundled back.

Burton pressed harder on the accelerator, the wheels howling as they spun—but the car was stuck solid.

The lorry rolled into the alleyway. Sparks flared from its side as it grazed the walls. It stopped, blocking any possible escape. The one-eared Nazi climbed out. At the tail of the vehicle, Burton glimpsed boots landing on cobbles.

He scrabbled at the door, trying to force it open.

A voice called out, the sound funneled and amplified between the canyon of the walls: "You cannot escape, Major Cole. Turn off the engine, put your hands on your head." Soldiers with BK44s were squeezing past the lorry. "You will not be harmed."

Burton reached for his Beretta, its weight and balance unfamiliar in his hand. He fired a random shot at the Nazi, then emptied the clip into the windscreen. He kicked through the remnants of the glass. Dragged himself through the hole, slid off the bonnet, and ran.

Bullets ricocheted along the walls, spitting clumps of brick.

"Keep your aim low!" shouted the Nazi.

Zigzagging, Burton sprinted across the intersection and into the next alley, toward the flowing red street. Ahead he heard the beat of drums, mechanical cheers; behind him, boots closing in, the one-eared Nazi demanding that he halt, his voice frantic.

Burton burst onto the Von Lettow Esplanade. In front was the harbor where Albrecht Roscher had landed in 1859, claiming the territory for Germany. Farther along the road was the memorial to the soldiers who died in the 1914–18 East African Campaign. During British rule it had been the statue of an *askari,* a native black warrior. After the colony was returned to the Reich, the bronze was melted down and a more domineering figure fashioned, complete with pith helmet and whiskers.

Rolling past the memorial, filling the entire length and breadth of the road, was a procession for Führertag. Troops in the bleached khaki of the Afrika Korps and ranks of SS in ceremonial uniforms. Horses drawing artillery, panzers and Pfadfinders, a band keeping a martial beat. And everywhere banners of red, white, and black. The pavement thronged with families enjoying the spectacle; kids waved flags.

Halt!

Burton pushed through the crowds, slipping into the procession. Moments later, he had vanished into a forest of swastikas.

+ + +

Kepplar returned to Cole's room at *zum Weissen Strand.*

The corridor was crisscrossed with tape; at the door was a guard. Kepplar dismissed him and stepped inside, trousers chafing around his groin; it was too muggy for his uniform to dry. There was a cut on his temple from when Fregh crashed into his BMW. The furniture had been righted, but everything else appeared untouched. His inspection revealed a doctored American passport and an empty haversack. In the wardrobe: shirts, spare socks, underwear. Impulsively, he lifted the garments to his nose; they gave away nothing. On the bed were a discarded Beretta box and some kind of chart.

Why was Hochburg so determined to catch Cole? He had plenty of enemies, from every Negro on the continent to the highest ranks of the SS, with their shifting, petty jealousies, so why was this one man paramount? Kepplar realized that his master's obsession had become his own.

A furious, frustrated sob threatened to overwhelm him. He had been so close, could smell Cole in the room despite the open balcony doors, his personal miasma of breath and sweat. The faintest hint of cigarettes. That surprised him; he hadn't thought of Cole as a smoker. Perhaps Hochburg was right: Kepplar wasn't worthy of the task. At no point in the pursuit had he unbuckled his holster.

He picked up the chart. It was from the SS cartography department, a map of Madagaskar folded in four. Facing upward was the northwest quadrant of the island. A ruse? No, he had taken Cole by surprise: the map wasn't meant for his eyes. Kepplar angled it toward the light.

The laminate revealed a cluster of fingerprints running from Nosy Be to Lava Bucht.

CHAPTER NINETEEN

Western Sector (South), Madagaskar
18 April, 10:30

AS HE'D STRIDDEN from the helicopter, Hochburg had demanded two things of the Untersturmführer: some hot food and all his men's shaving mirrors.

Now he stood in the rain while the work gang was assembled. He had followed a trail from the Ark to this punishment detail, though there was no guarantee the Jew he sought was here or even alive. Hochburg wore a black leather mac, the collar wrapped around his ears. The bandage covering his wounded eye was sodden. When a guard came forward with an open umbrella, he waved him away.

Behind the workers, the road ended abruptly: a tarmac precipice, then fifty kilometers of dirt to the Betroka Reservation. This was part of Globus's Idle Hands project: to build a highway linking Tana with the southern port of Daufin. During the dry season, the unbroken ground was like flint; this morning, a man might drown in the mud. On the verge were tents for the guards and a bamboo structure with a frond roof to shelter the Jews. Cauldrons of boiling asphalt sweetened the air.

"I'm looking for number 1215132," boomed Hochburg as the Jews fell into ranks.

When no one stepped forward, the Untersturmführer ordered them to raise their arms. Hochburg checked the first few tattooed wrists before realizing it was pointless: their skin was too filthy to read.

Water trickled down his skull. The Ark might have given him 1215132's location, but his investigations in Germany had furnished him with the details. The Gestapo had a file on the man, including a photograph taken in 1931. It showed a full, smooth-chinned face, brittle white collar, belly pressing against the buttons of a double-breasted suit. Feuerstein addressed the camera with the arrogance of a man who thought his world would last forever. *That mien belongs to us now,* thought Hochburg. *We pose in our uniforms as if we rule the very light that immortalizes us.*

He lowered the picture and studied the gaunt, scabby Jews in front of him. There must have been a hundred men, their bodies hidden beneath striped uniforms. The photograph would be useless.

"Which one of you is Julius Feuerstein?" asked Hochburg.

He tucked the file behind his back and walked down the ranks, his jackboots squelching. The Untersturmführer followed, along with a guard carrying a BK44.

"Dr. Julius R. Feuerstein. Born Vienna 1900, Marc Aurel Strasse. Attended the Akademisches Gymnasium and then Franz Josef school; top of your class in mathematics. Left 1915 to enlist but turned down because of your age. Traveled to Munich a month later and this time lied. Served three years with the Bavarian Army, Tenth Infantry Division. Wounded at the Battle of the Marne, awarded the Iron Cross, second class."

Hochburg scrutinized the faces. None stirred; they were all bowed toward the mud, their shoulders slumped beneath sopping uniforms.

"Scholarship student at Munich University 1919, studied under Professor Somerfeld. Doctorate from Heidelberg 1927. Two years later, a professorship—till the Nuremberg Laws were introduced. Granted an exit visa to the United States 1938." Hochburg glanced at the guards, took in their barbed-wire expressions and dripping rifles. "A wiser man would have used it. Interned Mauthausen 1941, then Trieste transit camp. Arrived Madagaskar July 1945." Hochburg slipped the file inside his mac. "Married to Evelyn, and father of five."

A decrepit Jew stepped out of rank as Hochburg passed. *"Apfelsaft,"* he said.

"What?"

"Apfelsaft." Apple juice.

Hochburg shoved him back in line. "I don't have time to waste."

The Jew stumbled, his hands vanishing to the wrist as he landed in the mud. "Give us our apple juice and I'll tell you where the doctor is."

Mumbles of dissent from the other Jews.

"What's he talking about?" Hochburg asked the Untersturmführer.

"This one's a troublemaker."

The old Jew pushed himself up and stood half-hunched. "The JDC send us juice from America, but the guards steal it." JDC: the Joint Distribution

Committee, a Jewish organization that dispatched food and medicine to the island.

"Is that true, Untersturmführer?"

"We keep it as a reward. An incentive to make the prisoners work harder."

Hochburg turned to the Jew. "Tell me who Feuerstein is and the apple juice will be yours."

"Juice first."

The Untersturmführer slapped the old Jew, knocking him back to the ground. "How dare you! Shall I have him whipped, Oberstgruppenführer?"

"Not today. Bring them their apple juice."

When the Untersturmführer was gone, Hochburg lifted the Jew out of the mud; he was as flimsy as a girl. "Where is Feuerstein?"

"Don't tell him, Papa."

A boy stepped in front of the old man. Hochburg swiped his pistol from its holster and prodded it against the youth's forehead. "A live Jew or a dead Jew, it makes no difference to me." He swiveled his good eye back to the old man. "Where?"

A familiar pride flitted across his features. He whispered something to his son, then said, "I am Feuerstein."

"You're lying."

"Look at your dossier. I refused my visa to America because it didn't include my family. How could I know that?"

"An educated guess."

"Why make it up?"

"Perhaps you think I'm here to save you."

"Or murder me, like so many others."

Hochburg looked at him more closely. "You're too old to be Feuerstein."

"This island would wither any man. I was born on the twenty-first of April, 1900."

Hochburg checked the date. "The very same day as Governor Globocnik. He's holding a party—perhaps you'll be invited: the Jew of honor." He motioned to the guard, and Feuerstein was led away.

So this striped sack of bones and sores was the man to change his fortunes. The man to help him win back Africa. Hochburg followed, watching the Jew move: his hunched gait, the way his arms swung loose like an ape's. On his feet was a pair of brogues obese with mud, the soles flapping.

They headed toward the guards' tents; the largest belonged to the Untersturmführer. Hochburg had ordered it cleared of everything except a table and two chairs. They entered through a flap. The interior was lit with lamps, the air dry and heady with kerosene. From the roof hung two dozen shaving mirrors, dangling on cords at face height. The scientist was unlikely to be biddable, so Hochburg wanted him to see the depths to which he had descended. It would foster compliance. A draft rolled through the open flap, rocking the mirrors. They clinked off each other, the sound reminding Hochburg of Eleanor and her wind chimes. Pendulums of half-reflected light skipped along the canvas.

Feuerstein gazed at the mirrors, reached out for one. Stilled it. He glanced at his image, angled his neck to examine his profile, but offered no reaction other than a passing grimace.

Hochburg commanded him to sit, then took the chair opposite. In the enclosed space the Jew stank, his soggy uniform radiating all the odors a body could produce. Hochburg thought back to the man's photo: the spotless starch of his collar, hair slick and scented. How long had it been until the shame was nothing, till he no longer noticed smelling worse than a navvy's pig? How long would any man take?

"*I have borne it with a patient shrug,*" he said, "*for sufferance is the badge of all our tribe.*"

"An educated Nazi," replied the doctor. "Whatever next?"

Hochburg leaned forward, the leather of his raincoat creaking. "You speak bravely for a Jew." His voice was low, intense. "I could have you shot for less—"

"At least you didn't ask if I had hands, dimensions, passions."

"You and every man out there."

"But you won't, Oberstgruppenführer."

"Such confidence."

"I know why you're here. I knew that if I survived, eventually one of you would seek me out, no matter what your Führer says."

"Go on."

"There's nothing for the guards to do here but beat us and gossip. We know about the war in Kongo, the victory of the British at Elisabethstadt."

"We're turning the tide," said Hochburg defensively. "Stanleystadt is ours again; the rest of Africa will follow."

"But you're not convinced. The Reich has reached the edge of its power. Now you need more—why else would you be sitting opposite me?" There was a faint smirk on Feuerstein's lips. "I refuse to help you."

"Then you should help yourself."

Hochburg whispered an instruction to the guard, who brought in a trolley laden with flasks and serving dishes, crockery, cutlery, and wads of napkins. "Leave us," said Hochburg and lifted off the nearest lid. The aroma of roast chicken and ginger swirled around the tent.

Feuerstein made no effort to hide his contempt, or his hunger. "You think you can buy me with a plate of dinner?"

"Nothing so crude, Herr Doctor."

"Unlike your mirrors. This is no revelation." He tugged on a bristly jowl. "I've seen what I've become. Seen the reflection of a beast in puddles." He folded his arms. "You'll have to do better than that."

Hochburg was silent for a long moment, the wet gauze of his bandage pressing against his eyelid. Above them, the rain beat on the canvas. "I've insulted your intelligence," he said at last. "For that I apologize. But it's no reason not to dine with me."

Feuerstein's eyes flicked over the dishes; the corners of his mouth oozed saliva.

Hochburg reached for the flask and filled a bowl with steaming water. He placed it before the scientist. "You will want to wash."

The Jew slipped his fingers below the surface, closing his eyes in instinctive pleasure as they were enveloped in hot water. Then he remembered where he was and opened them with a jolt. The water had turned black. When he was finished, he withdrew his hands, chewed on a nail like a cat pulling a claw. Hochburg tossed him a napkin and served them on two plates: grilled rooster (its neck had been wrung upon Hochburg's arrival), steamed rice, a salad of beetroot and tomatoes.

Feuerstein didn't bother with the cutlery. He shoveled the food in with his hands, each mouthful a mess of sucking meat and clacking.

"Do Jews disgust you, Oberstgruppenführer? Do I disgust you?"

Hochburg took his fork, buried it in the other man's rice, and ate.

Feuerstein laughed, splattering the table. "I've lived like this for ten years now, the last two on the roads. I've seen men much stronger than me fade in weeks. You know how I survived?"

Hochburg shook his head. "Intellect?"

"It's worthless here. No, savagery. I realized I'm no longer a man: I'm an animal." He took a drumstick and ripped the meat from it. "With all the primitive instincts animals have to survive."

"Men can be as base."

"Not like a beast."

"And what is it you wish to survive for, Dr. Feuerstein?"

"My boy out there. To see my other children. Hold my wife."

Hochburg chewed on his chicken—the meat was all leathery sinew—and decided to be frank. "When I was in Germany I spoke to a colleague of yours, Professor Mannkopff. I wanted information, something to coax you with. He said there would be no leverage with your family."

"Once he was right," replied the scientist. "They were the accessories of my position. But Madagaskar taught me more than university ever did."

After that, Hochburg let him feast in silence. When Feuerstein finished, he began to lick his plate. Hochburg stopped him, piled on more food. He continued to eat ravenously till his hands dripped sauce and his beard was studded with rice.

"I want to save some for my son."

Hochburg filled a napkin with the remaining chicken, cleared away the dinner things, and slid a box onto the table.

"They may be a little stale," he said, opening the lid, "but I doubt you care."

Feuerstein peered inside, putting his fingers to his lips. "Mannkopff talked a lot."

"He sends his regards. He's sorry for what happened to you."

Feuerstein snorted and reached inside the box.

After Europe had been declared *Judenfrei*, there remained a taste for Jewish cuisine in Germania. Delicatessens served salt herring and hamantaschen with furtive glances; cholent was available from illicit nosheries. Hochburg had gone to a baker on a side street off the Ku'damm where it was rumored Göring sent his chauffeur to buy "Jew treats." Dressed in black, he strode to the curtain at the rear of the shop, swished it aside, and descended to the basement. The girl at the counter had been shaking as she placed the *Mandelbrot*, almond biscuits, in the box. Hochburg was so amused he gave her a fifty-mark note and told her to keep the change.

The scientist chewed slowly, savored. "You're wise enough to realize that biscuits are more persuasive than a fist, Oberstgruppenführer. But it won't make any difference. I will not do it for you."

"Surely you know you are going to die here. Not just you or your kith—every last Jew on this island. Humanity has abandoned you."

"That may be so, but I don't want the responsibility of destroying it."

Hochburg thought he heard some of the man's former arrogance. "Is it truly that powerful?"

Feuerstein fished out another biscuit. "Do you know why I started work on it? It was after Versailles. I remember our utter humiliation, the years that followed. I wanted us to be great again."

Hochburg had never felt such bitterness toward the peace treaty; it had transferred Germany's African colonies to Britain, which brought him to Eleanor. The carnage of the trenches was a fair price to pay for that.

"When I began my postgraduate research," continued Feuerstein, "I soon understood the implication of what my generation was working on . . . It's more powerful than you can possibly imagine."

Hidden at the back of the tent was an attaché case. Hochburg retrieved it, aware that he had little to threaten the Jew with. A human body—especially one as abused as Feuerstein's—could endure only so much before it expired. Then he would be denied the one mind capable of developing this new weapon. Hitler had forbidden the pursuit of "Jewish physics"; most of the scientists Hochburg quizzed were ideologically bound to say it was impossible. Professor Mannkopff was a voice of dissent. He spoke of a secret program from the 1930s that was later canceled by Himmler; he believed that the Americans might be working on something similar. Although Mannkopff's position excluded him from any further research, he had suggested Feuerstein as one of the few physicists gifted enough to deliver.

Hochburg removed a notebook from the case and placed it on the table. "Touch it," he encouraged Feuerstein. "Feel it."

The Jew's fingers hovered over the leather, his face a bewilderment of emotions. "I . . . I want to clean them." Hochburg poured him another basin of hot water; this time, Feuerstein methodically washed each digit.

The notebook was foolscap, bound in buckskin. It had taken Hochburg considerable effort, in the stationers of Germania, to find one that didn't bear the swastika. Feuerstein opened the cover, his eyes blurring, and caressed the paper. It was thick and luxurious, the color of fresh cream.

"Are you still an animal?" asked Hochburg, reaching inside his tunic for his fountain pen. With its black ink he had signed the documents that created Muspel and Kongo. He'd put his signature to the Windhuk Decree when everyone else at the table—Himmler and Globus included—had refused. "Write me the details of your wife and children, and you will all be free by nightfall."

"I can't give the Reich this weapon."

"You're not. You're giving it to me, the regime will be unaware."

"I can't!"

"Then you condemn your family."

"You don't know what you're asking. Millions will die."

"If you don't, you will die. Your wife will die; your sons and daughters.

Which means more?" Hochburg slipped the pen between the Jew's gnarled fingers. "Write."

Feuerstein hesitated, then put the nib on the paper, as gently as a father kissing his newborn son. Hochburg watched him scrawl the name Evelyn— hesitantly, the muscles only half-remembering how—and weep.

"I haven't written in years . . . Not a single word."

"You take my life," said Hochburg, *"when you take the means whereby I live."*

This time there was no retort from the scientist. He completed the names of his children, finishing with a full stop but not lifting the pen. A blot spread out from the nib.

He whipped the page over.

Began scribbling words, numbers, equations. They might have been coherent, they might have been nonsense; Hochburg couldn't tell. He filled a page, then another, then—

"Enough!" Hochburg slammed his hand on the book with such violence that the mirrors rattled. Shivers of light darted around the tent. "How quickly could you build this weapon?"

"It depends what type of resources you'll give me."

"Everything Africa has to offer."

He wiped the tears from his face. "Three, maybe four years."

"You're unwise to mock me. I give you six months."

"Impossible. Every aspect of the technology has to be developed from nothing."

"Eighteen," said Hochburg, masking his disappointment.

"Two years. And there can be no interference. Mistakes are inevitable. Punishments won't help; they'll only set the project back."

"You have my word."

"And I can't do it alone," said Feuerstein breathlessly. "I will need other men. Colleagues, Jews. If they're alive, there are some brilliant minds on this island."

"You have your book: write the names. I will find them."

"Their families, too."

"Don't push your luck, Herr Doctor."

"A man works best if he knows his family is safe."

Suddenly, Hochburg understood.

What had Feuerstein said? *I knew one of you would seek me out.* He must have played this scenario in his head a thousand times. Rationalized the ethics till he knew he would agree: anything to avoid a pickaxe in his blistered hands again; to be free of a life measured only in gnawing hunger, exhaustion, and, for the lucky, death. His refusal had been to win as many concessions as possible. Hochburg had misjudged the Jew.

"The cargo hold of my plane will take fifty people," he said. "Choose your names wisely."

Hochburg left the table and stood apart, catching a dozen reflected images of Feuerstein hunched over the notebook. If he was returning to the Ark, he would need to conceal his tracks from Globus. He took out Burton's knife and began cutting the cords from the mirrors. Behind him came the scratch of pen on paper.

CHAPTER TWENTY

OAO
18 April, 14:30

IT HAD BEEN renamed by the Germans in 1943: no longer the Indian Ocean but the Ostafrikanischer Ozean, or OAO, as Nazi maps showed it. Salois had traveled its fickle, azure waters before. The first time was during his deportation. It was like crossing the Styx.

The Wannsee Conference designated the ports of Trieste, in Italy, and Gotenhafen, on the Baltic, as the "primary expulsion conduits" for the Jews. When they failed to cope with the numbers, Marseille, in France, and Salonika, in Greece, were added, and later Constanta, to remove Romanian and Bulgarian Jews. A special fleet was created from the North German Lloyd and Hamburg-American lines, supplemented by the KdF's older cruise ships: 120 vessels in total. The initial route to Madagaskar was via the Cape of Good Hope; after the Casablanca Conference, Britain opened up the Suez Canal, reducing the journey to thirty days. Relays of ships chugged through the Red Sea and down the eastern coast of Africa to the processing stations of Diego Suarez, Mazunka, and Salzig, a journey of at least six thousand miles. They headed to the equator tottering on the waterline; returned empty.

After Salois's capture at Dunkirk, he spent the summer as a POW before being identified as a Jew (a fellow Belgian gave him up for a handful of cigarettes) and taken to the Breendonk labor camp. He was finally shipped to Madagaskar in December 1942, in the first weeks of the monsoon season, on seas so violent his blood ran yellow. He was a lucky one, assigned a cabin at the top of the ship, sharing sixteen square meters with as many strangers. Thousands were crammed below, where the floor sloshed with vomit. Talk of mutiny was silenced as soon as they were herded on board, the captain informing them that the hull was mined: any trouble and he would scuttle the ship. The decks were patrolled by kapos, Jewish criminals used by the SS to keep order. They were armed with whips and notorious for their brutality.

To reach the targets set by Wannsee, 83,500 Jews had to be shipped from Europe each month, initially men of working age—known as pioneers—to build the new towns and military bases of Madagaskar; later women, children, and the old followed. Thousands never arrived, dying of suffocation or dysentery from the bubbling toilets or simply because their spirits could no longer endure the endless plunge and roll of the voyage. Eighty kilometers from arrival, the liners stopped to disgorge their dead. A rabbi was permitted to say a few words; then the *splosh—splosh—splosh* of weighted bodies hitting the waves. In these stretches of water, it was rumored, the sharks were too fat to swim.

The dhow carrying Salois, Cranley, and the marines had left Mombasa three days before. It was a rickety spicer, honeycombed with smuggling compartments, its sails alternately billowing with downpours and hot wind. At present the sun was beating between the clouds. Salois sat at the stern of the vessel, by the kitchen, cross-legged in the shade. They had eaten at noon, but his belly was soon aching for more. He'd filled a bowl with left-over rice, okra, and scraps of fish in an oily red sauce and was loading his mouth. Cranley and the marines were at the prow, sharing round a pair of binoculars; they seemed expectant, jittery. Cranley detached himself from the others and headed toward Salois. Even though the swell was gentle, he swayed with each step.

"We're approaching the first of the Rings," he said. His burnt face was peaky.

The Rings of Madagaskar, "a marvel of our nautical engineering," as Governor Bouhler once described them, were a triple chain of sea mines, five kilometers from the shore, that encircled the island to prevent ships from approaching. Each mine was set twenty meters apart; as long as the waves remained calm, the dhow was small enough to slip between them.

"Can you see land?" asked Salois.

"On the horizon. Take a look yourself."

Salois returned to his food. "We'll be there soon enough."

Cranley joined him in the shade, mirroring his position. He was already in camouflage fatigues and had insisted that everyone else dress the same, despite Salois's advising against it. The plan was to pass through the Rings and reach the first landing point on the northwest coast by sundown; there, Salois and his men would disembark. Next, the dhow would turn south and drop Cranley's team in the mangroves around Mazunka. Although it would have been less conspicuous to wait till after dusk to change, Cranley had been eager to get into his combats. It proved something.

Cranley watched him gorge. "I don't know how you can stomach it," he said.

"You've never been hungry," replied Salois, not raising his eyes.

"I've had lean times. When I was in Spain, fighting with the Nationalists, we had days when there was nothing except potatoes." He considered this. "You're right, I don't know hunger."

"I've beaten men for a piece of orange peel," said Salois, "gnawed bones after dogs have finished with them." He chased the last grains of rice round the bowl. "That kind of hungry never leaves you."

After he was finished, he dabbed his lips with his sleeve and studied Cranley. In their time together, the Englishman had offered no explanation for his burn marks. The fire had spared most of his hair except for his eyebrows, which were bald. The left side of his face was charred, the skin taut, poreless, and matte; when the sun became too fierce, he smeared himself in cold cream. Despite his disfigurement, he remained handsome. He had a strong jaw, with an unblemished lath of flesh under the bone. When he addressed the men there was an affable superiority to him. Yet he unsettled Salois.

"I still can't see why you're with us," he said.

Cranley smoothed his camouflage. "This doesn't persuade?"

"Rolland's a uniform man, Turneiro with his airplanes. But you . . ."

There was a belch of noxious smoke, and the engine started. The dhow's crew of Indians and Arabs began furling the sails.

"Last year," said Cranley, "I planned an operation to curtail the Nazis—"

"Like this one?"

"We wanted to save Africa from itself. If you don't bridle faraway lands, one day faraway lands will bridle you." Something furious darkened his gaze. "It was almost a disaster. I can't let the same happen in Madagaskar."

"But you don't care about Jews."

"My department has been supplying the Vanilla Jews for years. Weapons, medical supplies. I don't condone what happened to your kind, or you being shipped to the tropics."

"Britain could have stopped it."

"Or the CONE*," Cranley replied impatiently, "or America. In which

_____
*Council of New Europe.

case every last one of you would have been transported to Siberia. Perhaps you'd rather freeze."

"Madagaskar's no better."

"The past can't be undone." His voice was level again. "Diego is the key to Africa now. That was our mistake during the Casablanca Conference: not involving the United States. It pains me to admit it, but we need their intervention to redraft the world; Britain is no longer the power she was."

"During the Ha-Mered, we prayed for America to join the struggle. Or rein in Globus. Each new atrocity convinced us they would. There was only silence."

"Then you misunderstand their politics. Americans only back winners. That's why we have to squeeze Kongo: so they'll land in the west."

"You and Rolland are no different. You're not fighting for Africa, whatever you say. You just want to keep Britain at the trough. That's the real reason you're here."

"Think what you will. I'm on this boat because I fear for the future. What parent doesn't?"

Salois was surprised; it seemed an unlikely justification. "You have children?"

"A daughter."

"How old?"

"She'll be seven this year. Such an intelligent child. I'll have to watch her when she gets older." His voice was tender, boastful. "She already speaks French and German. Plays Schubert on the piano. A few months ago, I thought she'd been taken from me. It was the most wretched thing I could imagine."

"What happened?"

"For the first time, I understood what it was to hate. To want to punish. I thought I knew before, but those few moments alone were an education. After I'm gone she'll be wealthy, cosseted. But I want to leave her more: a nation, a homeland, she can be proud of, Reuben, not a relic of a once great empire." He had never used Salois's first name before; there was a hint of irony in it.

Salois snorted. "You're an idealist."

"Nothing of the sort. I'm selfish. The seed of all idealism."

"And your wife?"

"Dead."

He said it abruptly, as if the word, with its finality, its hinterland of grief, anger, and yearning, had no significance.

"I was married once," said Salois. "Or going to be."

"In Madagaskar?"

"When I was at university. Her name was Frieda. She was pregnant—the child would be an adult now." He had nothing to prove that his former life had existed; even the memories no longer convinced him.

"So why leave and join the Foreign Legion?"

"You saw my arrest warrant." Salois held up his hands as though they were still bloodied. "I had no choice: it was North Africa or the hangman."

"You were only young," replied Cranley. "As a student, you must have been from a respectable enough family."

"A Jewish family."

"Which means money. You could have bought your way out."

"I had a hateful temper. Was arrogant, vicious." The desert had cured him of all three. "I didn't deserve leniency."

"Then you should have surrendered yourself."

Salois thought of the document Cranley had placed in front of him in Sudan. "If I'd said no, would you have used the warrant against me? Sent me back to Belgium?"

One of those barren smiles. "Of course—"

"Colonel Cranley! Major!"

It was Sergeant Denny, at the front of the boat, clutching a pair of binoculars. He had dark hair, a matinee idol's jawline, cauliflower ears; he'd boxed at the 1946 Olympics in Nuremberg. He beckoned them urgently.

Salois and Cranley hurried to the prow, the huge knobbly orb of a sea mine drifting past on the starboard side. Ahead, set five hundred meters apart, were the next two rings and, several kilometers beyond them, a dark wall of jungled shore. The clouds were knitting together. Salois had expected a well of emotion on seeing the island once more—terror, defiance, shame, possibly the cold thrill of hope. There was a hardening in his chest, nothing more. It was just rock, the same rock his people might have seen a millennium before. When the bureaucrats had presented Hitler's plan for Madagaskar to the Council of New Europe, they had summoned a wealth of anthropological evidence proving that the first inhabitants of the island were Jewish.

"You'd better look," said Denny, passing him the binoculars.

Salois put them to his eyes: a blur of blue-and-white wool. He lowered the lenses to scan the sea, adjusting them till the horizon was a sharp line. Abruptly, the eyepieces were full of gray tiger stripes, guns, a fluttering red, white, and black ensign. These were the craft that patrolled Madagaskar's coastline, ensuring that no Jew escaped. Salois offered the binoculars to Cranley.

"It's an S-boat," he said. At its prow was a battering ram that would turn the dhow to splinters.

From behind them came the clap of bare feet and a waft of piquant sweat: Xegoe, the dhow's captain. He was dressed in a sarong and a black beret. "They signal us to stop."

"Can we outrun it?" asked Salois.

Xegoe had treated Salois with superstition from the moment he stepped on board, refusing to meet his eyes, whispering that he stank of death. The captain addressed his answer to Cranley: "Not possible. But we meeting plenty German boums-boums before." He flashed his teeth. "They be liking your gold."

Denny clutched his rifle. "We can handle this."

"It's a routine patrol," replied Cranley. "We let them on board, buy them off, and they'll be on their way." He looked seasick again. "We don't jeopardize the mission."

"Sergeant," said Salois, "take the men to the hold. Hide all the equipment, then yourselves."

"And if they search the ship?"

"No one does anything unless I or the colonel says so."

"I show you smuggler safes," said Xegoe. He appeared excited rather than concerned. "They not find you there."

"We need the parrot," said Cranley, tugging off his camouflage jacket. "And we'd better get out of these."

"I told you," said Salois.

Their sailor garb was stowed in the cabin they shared. They stripped in the cramped, dingy space, Cranley revealing a patchwork of burns on his body. Previously Salois had undressed in private. He hesitated before removing his shirt and trousers; he wished it were darker. For the first time Cranley saw his companion's bare torso, his arms and legs. He went still; there was a click as he swallowed.

"Dear God . . ."

Salois ignored him and reached for the burgundy caftan he'd been wearing since they left Mombasa; it had an authentic pirate stink. He rolled down the sleeves and buttoned it to the throat, concealing his body again.

CHAPTER TWENTY-ONE

FROM ACROSS THE water came a metallic voice: *"Stop your engines! Prepare to be boarded!"*

Salois watched the patrol boat close the gap. Two of its three cannons were pointed at the dhow. There were a dozen soldiers on deck, all with BK44s, waiting to board.

Cranley pulled out a pistol with an ivory handle. Salois recognized it as a Browning HP. "You told Denny no fighting."

"A precaution," said Cranley, concealing the weapon beneath the flaps of his shirt. In his other hand he was cradling the stuffed parrot he'd retrieved from the cabin. "My German's better; I'll deal with this."

"You've never had to talk for your life," replied Salois. He tasted the fish and rice repeating on him. "Let me do it."

Cranley handed over the bird. "Make sure they take this." The parrot had blue-black feathers and a breast of intense green. The head screwed off to reveal a stash of gold reichsmarks. "And let's pray they don't strip-search you. You should have warned us in Sudan."

"Rolland said I was the only man for the job."

"One glimpse of your skin, and we're finished."

The S-boat drew abreast, hulking over the dhow. A gangplank was lowered; then came the tramp of boots as soldiers marched on board. They were followed by an officer. Salois watched him stride across, tiny bubbles of hatred rising from his gut and popping in his throat at the sight of his black uniform. He had blond hair shaven close to the scalp, and half his right ear was missing.

+ + +

Hatches opened and slammed; Kepplar heard the sound of material ripping, axes splintering wood.

He stood with one jackboot resting on a crate, his holster a goading weight against his thigh. He had been wrong-footed by the parrot, till he removed its head and saw the innards glint. He thanked the smugglers graciously—then ordered his men to search the entire ship, *a gold coin to each of you for your efforts.* The Hindoos had been forced to their knees at gunpoint; the two white men were allowed to remain standing, hands on their heads. The blond—with his Category 1 skull and burnt, well-upholstered cheeks—looked an unlikely smuggler.

"Where are you from?" Kepplar asked.

The thinner man replied; another potential recruit to the SS, a Category 1 or 2, wrapped up to the chin despite the temperature. "Antwerp," he said in rough German.

"A Wallonian." Wallonia: Hitler's name for Belgium; he had considered making it Germany's northwest province. "What is your course and cargo?"

"Nosy Be. 'Gifts' for the Führer's birthday."

"Nosy Be? You're seventy kilometers due south."

The blond shot a glare at the kneeling crew. "Useless niggers."

Kepplar permitted himself a wry smile that hid his frustration before calling to his men. "Anything yet, Oberbootsmann?"

"Lots of liquor. No stowaways."

"Keep looking," he replied, deciding this was to be the last board-and-search of the day. Although relieved to be free of his desk, he had exchanged one desperation for another.

The waters around Madagaskar teemed with contraband-laden dhows. As long as the boats brought their cheap wares—and no Jews were smuggled out—the trade was overlooked. Governor Globus encouraged it, to keep the booze flowing for his troops while siphoning off the expensive stuff for himself. Kepplar couldn't continue patrolling these waters and stopping every vessel that appeared on the horizon. The map he'd found in Cole's hotel room might be his best lead—but it was maddeningly vague. The area it covered was too vast, larger than the swath of Kongo that had been his hunting ground for Cole last time. What was it the Führer once said? "On land I am a hero, at sea a coward." Somehow he needed to systemize his approach and utilize his meager resources to narrow the search. Yet faced with the futility of his task, a question had crept up on him.

Why Madagaskar?

Cole had nearly been killed escaping Africa, the rest of his team annihilated; only a madman would risk returning—and to the island of Jews, of all places. So why?

Kepplar pictured Fregh, with his cake-flaked mouth and splays of paper-work. If he were tasked with tracking down Cole, he wouldn't leave his chair, he'd simply shuffle documents till he found a solution, then go home to his cuckold nest. Kepplar always hoped his own wife would take a lover. During his long tour of Kongo, he sent emissaries to Germania with mes-sages for her, implying how lonely his wife was, how they might seduce her. Her persistent loyalty disappointed him.

Kepplar dismissed the thought of her, Fregh too, and brought Hochburg to mind. The reward of serving as his deputy again had sustained him across the kilometers of empty ocean. As this was technically Kongo business, he had put on his black uniform, not least to impress the sailors. Throughout German Africa, the SS wore tropical uniforms, except where Hochburg was governor. He insisted that his subordinates dress in black, despite the pun-ishing heat. To do otherwise was tacit acknowledgment that the negroid races owned the color, and they deserved nothing: not light, not shadow, not air. Hochburg hadn't finished with the blacks yet—undoubtedly his most important work—so why his fixation with Cole? It seemed an unnec-essary distraction. If Kepplar understood the root of the animosity, he might be a more efficient hunter.

There was a kerfuffle at the far end of the boat, a shout of surprise. The two prisoners showed no response.

"What is it?" demanded Kepplar.

One of the sailors held up a Labrador puppy.

"Take it," said the blond. "A present for your children."

There was a presumptive quality to his tone that Kepplar disliked. "What if they hate dogs?"

He resumed his speculation. Kepplar knew nothing of his master's life before the SS. Perhaps Cole was in possession of some secret that Hochburg wanted permanently silenced. This wasn't uncommon among the highest echelons of the leadership. It was said that Heydrich had removed the names on his parents' gravestones to obscure any hint of Jewish ancestry. Might Hochburg be the same? No, thought Kepplar. His racial purity was beyond doubt: he had a perfect Category 1 skull; Kepplar had always admired it. Perhaps Hochburg came from a background of pacifists and Negro lovers. Yet a man was not his family. Kepplar's father died of septicemia during the Great War; he barely remembered him. His mother had called him, her only child, a traitor to everything decent when he joined the party.

Kepplar twisted the lobe of his half ear, envious that Cole might know more about Hochburg than he did. The stuffed parrot the Wallonian had given him was still in the crook of his arm. He stared into its blank eyes. Whatever secret bound Hochburg and Cole, it was beyond his comprehension. One day, when it was all over and they were sitting in the intimacy of his Schädelplatz garden, he'd ask Walter directly. For the moment, he would finish on the dhow and return to the base at Lava Bucht; there had to be a better method to apprehend Cole.

The Oberbootsmann approached, carrying a long metal container. "Everything is in order, Brigadeführer, apart from this."

Kepplar opened the box. Inside was a Panzerfaust 350: a handheld rocket launcher, the warhead primed. He removed it from the casing—it was the first time he'd held such a weapon since his training at the Vienna Colonial Academy—and showed it to the Wallonian. "Explain."

"Protection, from other pirates."

"A reasonable excuse," conceded Kepplar. "Anything else, Oberbootsmann? Any hidden compartments?" In one of the vessels they had stopped, a hollow wall revealed three Polish whores.

"Nothing, Brigadeführer."

"It seems everything is in order then," said Kepplar, preparing to leave. There was a final question he wanted to ask, one he'd posed on every vessel boarded that day. "Where is Burton Cole?"

The Wallonian remained blank. "Who?"

Kepplar fixed his eyes on his companion. The sunlight caught his flaxen hair as he shook his head.

It was infinitesimal. Only someone who had spent months obsessing about such a juncture could have noticed it: the tiniest tightening of the blond's mouth; a shadowy wisp of rage, incredulity, and something Kepplar was unable to decipher. For some reason, he thought of Fregh. A thrill traveled up his spine.

"Oberbootsmann, search the ship again. Tear it apart if you have to. No, wait—"

Kepplar had a better idea.

CHAPTER TWENTY-TWO

"WHAT ARE YOU doing?" There was panic in the Oberbootsmann's voice. The other soldiers scattered.

In Roscherhafen, as Kepplar had watched Cole disappear into the scarlet procession, he had been unable to free his Walther P38. Violence was merely a technical matter—one he found unbecoming, a task to be assigned, not achieved with his own hands. Hochburg's expectations, with their messy immediacy, made him feel awkward. Yet if he had learned to master his squeamishness, he wouldn't be on this boat. He wouldn't have wasted seven months in Deutsch Ostafrika.

Kepplar put the Panzerfaust on his shoulder, aimed at the deck, and fired; his whole body recoiled from the blow. The rocket flashed through the ancient timbers—a bolt of fire and sawdust—shaking the entire vessel. Shards of wood flayed the air. Kepplar blundered backward, smoke excavating his lungs. He was proud of himself: Hochburg would have done the same; simultaneously he felt a nugget of distaste at living out someone else's mania.

"Burton Cole!" he yelled when he'd regained his footing. His words were flattened, heard through a tumble of bells. "Surrender, and I'll spare the crew."

A snapping noise ran the length of the vessel. The dhow jerked and dropped in the water.

"Brigadeführer, we must get to our ship!"

"Not till Cole shows himself."

The blond was back on his feet; there were splinters in his hair. "He's not on board."

"Where is he?"

"I have no idea what you're talking about," he replied angrily. "None of us do."

Kepplar stared at him, unsure all of a sudden. But it was his denial that gave him away: it was too controlled. "Cole!" he yelled again. "Show yourself and save your companions." He looked to the hold entrance, expecting to see him emerge.

Another snap. Then a succession of them, like a back being broken vertebra by vertebra. A wave of oil-patterned foam spread across the deck.

"We take him," said Kepplar. He tossed the spent Panzerfaust away and retrieved the black-and-green parrot, with its belly of coins. The blond was dragged with them at gunpoint, hands on head. Next moment the gangplank was kicked away.

Kepplar called up to the bridge: "Put thirty meters of sea between us." He watched the ocean open up; the dhow was listing, chasing its own stern, smoke billowing from it. The Wallonian raced to the hold while the native crew skittered around—yelling, wailing—before abandoning ship.

A man materialized on the sloping deck, vanished back into the hold, then reappeared with several others. They were in battle dress, grasping carbines. Kepplar leaned over the railing to see if any were Cole. He thought he heard the ghost of a voice, coming from inside the stricken hull . . . *You're going to die.* The Wallonian joined the others, arguing with one of the Hindoos, who hurled a sack at him.

Ahead, the second ring of sea mines was approaching.

The S-boat's main gun rotated toward the dhow. There was the booming clatter of shells spewing on the deck. Small-arms fire flashed between the two vessels.

"Hold your fire!" shouted Kepplar at his soldiers. He planned to pluck Hochburg's prize from the waves. "I want Cole alive."

"You idiot," said the blond. "He's not on board."

"You're lying. You sacrificed the ship to save him."

"Watch. It will sink for nothing." Despite having his hands on his head and a rifle against his ribs, he made no effort to conceal his disdain.

Kepplar was irritated by how impregnably sure the man was. He decided to take him to Lava Bucht: they had interrogation specialists there who had honed their skills during the rebellion. It would be interesting to test the limit of the man's arrogance.

He stepped closer to the prisoner till their bodies were almost touching, making the leather of his boots and belt creak the way Hochburg used to. "You know Cole," he said. "You think you can hide it, but it's seeping from every pore. Where is he?"

"The last I heard, on a boat to Panama. You've got the wrong ocean."

"Yesterday he was in Roscherhafen."

Their roles were reversed. The blond searched his features to see if he was telling the truth. None of his poise left him.

Kepplar prodded further. "I am certain he's headed for the island. On your boat or the next. Tell me where and I'll save the others—"

There was a shout of alarm, then rapid bursts of BK44 fire. Along the deck, soldiers were targeting the dhow.

Kepplar craned his neck to see what was happening. "I said no shooting!"

The blond dropped his hands from his head. One swiped against Kepplar's neck, rigid as a spade, sending him to the floor; the other reached behind himself, drew a pistol, and leveled it between the guard's eyes. He fired without hesitation.

These were the swift, practiced movements of a man at ease with violence, thought Kepplar, not a smuggler. Slumped on his knees, he watched with envy.

+ + +

From beneath Salois's boots came distorted yells and the pounding of fists on wood. The hold smelled of tarred timbers and cloves; it was dingy, stacked with crates.

"How do we free them?" he asked Xegoe; he had dragged the captain with him.

Xegoe toppled the cases in front of him to reveal a hatch. He lifted up a floorboard next to it and reached inside for the lever. He pulled it twice.

"It kaput," he said. His eyes were jacked open with fright.

Salois took his place and tried the lever himself. It was as heavy and limp as a broken arm. In the coffee-ground light he searched for a tool with which to pry open the hatch, till he found a harpoon; the crew used it to spear mahimahi fish that got caught in their nets. He drove the point into the groove between hatch and the floorboard, forcing his weight on it; a gap opened. Instantly, fingers appeared.

"Xegoe!" he called. "I need your help."

The captain had already fled.

Salois heaved again, his elbows and thighs rigid with exertion. The hatch broke open. In the compartment below were Denny and Private Grace, chest-deep in bilge. Salois helped them out before moving the next tower of crates. Denny watched him work, then scrambled out of the hold.

"Denny!" shouted Salois after him. "You coward!"

Grace was fighting with the next lever, his golden hair dripping. He shook his head as Salois slipped the harpoon between the slats of wood. The hatch rose a few centimeters—the slosh of a drowning chamber, frantic yells—before banging shut. Another heave: the steel of the harpoon was bending.

"Out of the way!"

There was barely time to move before an axe buried itself in the floor. Denny pried it out and swung again, breaking a hole. Salois put his hand in and lifted the cover free. Below, the marines were up to their chins in bubbling water.

Salois took the axe from the sergeant. "Collect as much food and equipment as you can. Make sure you get the explosives for Diego. Then find us a way off this boat."

There were two compartments left. They freed the men from the first before Salois ordered everyone but Grace on deck to help Denny. The pounding beneath their feet became louder, more desperate and frenzied, reverberating through the floorboards and up the walls till Salois felt he was inside the ventricle of a huge wooden heart.

Seawater began to surge from the hatches they'd opened. The beating fists slowed.

"You're not going to die!" shouted Salois, struggling to position the harpoon.

The trapped marines were Perabo and McCullough: part of his Diego team. They had both been at Dunkirk, professional soldiers who had known the shame of digging potato fields prior to being returned home in their dove suits. The night before, McCullough had told him that after Diego, after they'd won in Africa, it would be better for all if the Jews stayed in Madagaskar. *Not under the Krauts,* he clarified, *but you can't come back now.*

The hold shook and cracked, the ocean churning around Salois's knees. He fought to lift the cover. When the harpoon buckled he squatted, water whipping his chest, and tried to wedge his fingers under the hatch. The thump of hands grew weaker, then silent. Private Grace stared at him with childish disbelief.

They staggered out of the hold, onto a deck flowing with dark red liquid; Salois thought someone's throat had been slit. The dhow was slumping into the waves, its main mast toppled, the sails unfurled and snapping. Aboard their vessel, the Germans lined the gunwale, watching indifferently. Salois made his way through the smoke to Denny.

"The life raft?" he asked. The air was fruity with alcohol fumes and brine.

"Those fucking wogs had it." Denny pointed out to sea. The dhow's crew was rowing away from the S-boat, toward the horizon, the raft half empty. "We're going to use barrels," continued Denny. "Swim to shore."

The other marines were emptying kegs; round their boots gushed Burgundy meant for the officers' mess on Nosy Be.

"It's too far."

"Then you surrender, Major. Or drown."

Salois looked toward the land. It was at least two kilometers, but the shore was distinct for the first time: a sliver of sand and the dark protective shawl of the forest. "Get everyone off the starboard side," he said. "It'll give us more protection."

A whistle.

Xegoe stood at the edge of his boat, a sow-skin purse swinging from his neck. It was the one Cranley had given him, full of gold reichsmarks for their passage to Madagaskar.

"You bringed this on us," he shouted at Salois. "You demon!" He tossed him a sack and leapt overboard, swimming toward the rest of his crew.

Salois retrieved the bag, which gave a wine-bottle jangle, and peered inside. The marines were rolling the empty barrels to the far side of the dhow. Salois stepped round them, scanning the swilling debris on the deck. The sack contained three rocket heads.

The dhow bobbed through the second ring of mines, so close it threatened to scrape against one.

The S-boat's main gun erupted. Salois flattened himself against the floor as shells poured overhead, dismembering the life raft. Xegoe was caught between it and the dhow, a bawling brown head in the ocean. Two of the marines took up covering positions and returned fire. There was an instant reply of BK44s, then: *"Hold your fire! I want Cole alive."*

Salois found the discarded Panzerfaust. He wiped it down, speared on a rocket head, and got to his knees, focusing on the S-boat through the sight. The Germans saw him; there was a cry of alarm, and bullets whistled through the air. A stillness took hold of Salois; all the noises in his ear—the crackle of rifles, Xegoe screaming—faded to whispers. He searched the Nazi vessel for Cranley, thinking of the daughter he'd described, a spoiled girl with no mother, as blessed as the orphans of Madagaskar were shunned. When he failed to locate the Englishman, he squeezed the trigger.

The command deck exploded.

Without pausing, Salois loaded another warhead and targeted the main gun. The rocket smacked into it—a burst of star clumps—hurling men and munitions into the sky. A lingering satisfaction filled Salois as he squinted through the scope for a third time.

A hush descended: the immense silence of the ocean disturbed only by the rumble of smoke and Germans shouting, their voices tiny as they battled the fire. Two inky columns spiraled from the S-boat. It remained seaworthy but was listing, the waves teasing it away from the dhow.

A head emerged from the burning sea between the two vessels, gasping for air. Salois lowered the rocket launcher. It was Cranley.

"Major!" On the other side of the deck, Denny had ushered the rest of the marines off the boat. He thumped an empty barrel. "See you on the shore."

"Watch for sharks," Salois replied, turning his attention back to Cranley. He swam away from the S-boat, using a graceful front crawl. The one-eared Brigadeführer grabbed a life jacket and dived in after him.

The final ring of sea mines was approaching. The dhow drifted toward them, close enough for Salois to distinguish the detonation nodes. Cranley motioned at him to leap.

Salois rolled the last barrel overboard. There was a saying in the Legion: Lose your weapon, lose your mind, but never lose your boots. A maxim for the desert, not for a soldier at sea. Salois yanked them off his feet, tied the laces together, and dangled them around his neck. Then he hugged the soles and stepped barefoot to the edge of the deck. He'd never been a good swimmer.

The nearest mine rose from the water like the hump of a black whale.

CHAPTER TWENTY-THREE

Tana–Diego Railway, Madagaskar
18 April, 14:30

IT WASN'T THE Nazis who put a stop to Madeleine's plan; it was the other Jews.

She was hunched over the floorboards, sawing as quietly as she could, her arm sore with the effort. A greasy tarpaulin screened off the toilet—a hole in the corner to squat over—from the rest of the passengers. The train rocked with a soothing rhythm. *Like a cradle,* thought Madeleine.

She banished the image and focused on cutting through the wood. Since she'd left the hospital, her mind had been absorbed by mundane activity, burrowing into itself to a place that was nebulous, numb. In the abattoir she'd been sent to, surrounded by Polish Jews with their ghetto stoops and incomprehensible talk, she'd worked for twelve hours a day in a trance, churning shovels of salt and cloves to make brine, scalding pig carcasses to remove the bristles. In that state, one urge dominated: to escape. It was a familiar thread in her life: escape from Vienna, escape from Cranley. Now this island.

After she had given birth to Alice, her body took months restoring itself, and she'd suffered a bout of depression, but in the meat plant Madeleine healed as rapidly as the lice that bred in her hair. It had been shaved to the scalp a month before and was growing back in spiky black tufts that itched. As her strength improved, she was moved from checking the labels on cans to more grueling duties, constantly shifted round the abattoir till she was familiar with its layout. Every place she went, she was occupied by the gates and fences, whether the windows were barred or not, when the guards took cigarette breaks, always alert for some chink that would allow her to break free. Several times she was convinced she had seen Burton—a pair of shoulders the same as his, a similar gait—and for an instant her haunted brain struggled to understand why he had joined the SS.

Finally she was assigned to the *Müllschlucker,* a series of chutes at the rear of the complex where the waste was flushed away into a slurry lake. The work gang had to keep the chutes clear, sweeping the detritus of industrial meat processing into the water. On the far shore was a mangy barbed-wire fence and an unmanned guard tower. The air broiled and stank.

"I've been watching you," said one of the women during the midday break (ten minutes of rest, a mug of water, squabbles over green bananas). "You're thinking you can swim to the far side and break out. It's only a couple of hundred meters." She spoke in German, her voice mocking and resentful.

Madeleine's mouth and nose were covered by a scarf; she tugged it down. "Has anyone ever tried?" The words emerged haltingly. It was the first time she had spoken in weeks; her throat felt narrow, cracked.

The woman was startled. "I'm sorry. You're German."

"Austrian."

"I thought you were just another peasant girl, a Pole. I can't bear them—they're so uncouth. Uneducated. And the Nazis say we're all the same." Her tone became more hospitable; like most people starved of conversation, she wanted to chat. "How come you're here?"

"It doesn't matter."

"I shouldn't be in the Eastern Sector, either. We're from Berlin, me and generations of my family. Where did you live in Austria? I love Vienna. Sitting in the Burggarten, drinking a cappuccino. I was a teacher once, linguistics and riding." The joke that followed was automatic: "I could have taught horses to speak! Now I'm in this pit. I swear, Jehovah above can smell it. I got mixed up in a work detail and lost my papers. That was a year ago. A year talking Yiddish. I'd forget my mother tongue if it wasn't for the guards; they're my only conversation. I keep telling them I'm a German Jew, shouldn't be with these animals . . ."

Madeleine wasn't listening. "Did anyone escape?"

"Several. I've thought about it myself, getting back to Antzu. My daughter's there."

"Why don't you?"

"Swim through that?" She looked at the crust of excrement and bobbing offal, and made a puking noise. "Breathing it is bad enough. And afterward, kilometers of barren plateau, no food, no shelter. The last time someone got away, they didn't bother with patrols—just picked up the bones. Hung them from a gibbet on the parade ground to let us know."

"You'd be free," said Madeleine.

"Free?" She cackled in response. "No, I'll follow the paper route. I put a request in to the Ark. When my documents come through, they'll send me home. I used to help the vet at Governor Quorp's stables . . ." She became silent, staring at Madeleine through the haze. Her lips narrowed; they were blistered from the sun. "But I can see that you, girl, you are looking to hang."

There was a whistle blast.

"What's your name?" asked Madeleine.

"Jacoba."

The women pulled their scarves over their mouths and went back to work, Madeleine's eyes fixed on the far shore; her senses were lighting up. In the days that followed, she studied the guards' routines more closely and stole food from the production line: pig ears meant for the guard dogs, trotters she could save for the journey and suck marrow from. Everything was ready. For the first time in months she woke with a fleck of hope. She would hide in the chute on Führertag and escape that evening when the Nazis were filling their veins with toasts to Hitler. Then the others ruined her plan.

In the dingy light of the train's toilet, Madeleine flowed with sweat. She was wearing the factory uniform of sallow-gray pajamas; on her feet were the hobnailed boots she'd stolen from one of the Polish workers. They were a size too big and she had no socks, but they were stout enough to take her miles. She was hacking into the urine-soaked planks around the hole. If she could cut through two of them, she'd be able to pry up the others and get under the railcar.

The first slat had almost given way when someone tried to open the curtain. Madeleine cursed Jacoba, who was supposed to be keeping watch, and grasped the screen.

"You going to be much longer?" asked a man's voice.

"I've got the shits," she replied, startled by her own ferocity.

"You're not the only one." Beneath the curtain she saw a pair of bopping feet with twisted black nails.

"Give me a couple minutes."

Her arm pumped more vigorously. She sucked in mouthfuls of stinking air and ignored the blots in her vision. The last thing to pass her lips had been a bowl of broth so meager she'd counted the rice in it, all twenty-three grains; that had been hours ago. The knife continued its creeping journey through the wood. Madeleine had lifted it from the factory; it had a serrated edge and was meant for pig flesh, not three-inch timber. Her palm was blistering. Beyond the curtain, she heard the desperate pad of feet.

When she judged that she'd cut enough of the second slat, she released the blade from the wood and yanked at the board. After the first tug it gave easily; another plank and she would be free. She removed it and eagerly stared down at the ground below: the rush of crossties, the smell of damp stones and steel.

The wood slipped through her fingers and bounced on the filthy floor. The bottom of the railcar was reinforced with a row of iron bars. Even a child wouldn't be able to squeeze between them. A deadening crept through her, a deep despondency like the one that had overcome her two nights earlier, in the abattoir.

Madeleine never knew if it was spontaneous or long planned. There had been no whisperings in the barracks after lights-out, despite rumors of revolt elsewhere on the island. Her first sense that her escape might be jeopardized was when the alarms started to shriek. From somewhere in the factory came the ring of single gunshots; later, shouting and automatic weapons. Soldiers arrived at the chutes—agitated, screaming—and ordered the workers to the parade square. Already Madeleine was cursing whoever was responsible for this nonsense; in the coming days the guards would be more vigilant.

They stayed in the square all night, beneath curtains of drenching rain. At dawn there were two volleys of gunfire in quick succession; a helicopter arrived. Madeleine and the hundreds of other workers continued to sit outside through a magic lantern of sunshine, downpours, and stars. Next morning, before the sun rose, they were herded through the factory to the transport pens where the pigs and cattle arrived. An empty livestock train waited for them.

Madeleine replaced the floorboards. She hoped the guards would think it too demeaning to check the shithole. If not, she would accuse one of the Poles. The ease with which she blamed others continued to shock her. Whenever she felt guilty, she heard Burton encouraging her: survival had its own rules.

"Hurry up!" pleaded the voice beyond the curtain.

Madeleine dropped her trousers and tied the knife to her inner thigh. Smuggling the weapon on board the train had been a risk. Some guards were repulsed by frisking Jews; others groped with a dedication the

Reichsführer would not have extolled. She pulled the waistband back up and sedately opened the curtain. Outside was an old man, clutching his belly. He resembled one of her father's colleagues from the clinic, except tatty and starved.

"Sorry," she said and let him pass before making her way to Jacoba.

The cattle car was misty with the coughing and sneezing of two nights in the rain. Jacoba lolled beneath one of the high grilled windows that let in ventilation and a wan light. She was fanning herself with a large reed hat and wore her usual look of repulsion; she hated being close to so many bodies. "You were gone a long time. Gripes again?"

"I wasn't using the toilet."

A sigh. "Do you remember bathrooms? I mean proper ones, a lavatory seat that was your own and a bath—wallowing up to your neck in water. Hot water!"

Jacoba shifted on the floor, making a space for Madeleine—but she didn't take it. She stood on tiptoe and stared out the window. Through the bars she saw a valley crowned with hills and knee-deep grass. Several hours earlier, they had passed Tana and she'd glimpsed the governor's palace, white as a sugar cube, atop the city's highest hill. After that she counted the miles till she figured they must be in the Mandritsara region. That's when she hurried to the toilet, the knife rubbing against her thighs.

Mandritsara: the constant, aching void in her. Mandritsara: the hospital where her babies had been stolen..

Madeleine grabbed the bars and rattled them, tears scalding her eyes. Then a voice from above:

"Was machst du da, Jüdin?"

A hatch in the ceiling opened, letting in drizzle. Blocking the sky was a guard in a khaki-spotted poncho, aiming his rifle at her. Each car had a soldier riding on the roof, in addition to the contingent of troops at the rear of the train. Madeleine had glimpsed their car as she shuffled on board: wide windows revealing padded seats, baskets of fruit, a steaming canteen. The scent of coffee and warm milk tortured her stomach.

The guard flicked the muzzle of his rifle. *"Abstand halten."*

Madeleine wanted him to pull the trigger, to be embraced by the same darkness that had swallowed Burton. Then she heard the wail of her babies fading down a hospital corridor and she uncurled her fingers from the bars. She stepped back, made a display of her open hands, and slumped to the floor.

"You look like you've got a fever," said Jacoba, flapping her hat in Madeleine's direction.

Fetid wafts of air cooled her face. She thought she had been so clever, waiting for Führertag to escape. "I should have gone as soon as I was ready," she said bitterly. "I'd be free now."

"I'm glad you didn't. Imagine being on this stinking train alone."

Madeleine glared at the woman opposite. She had no idea how old Jacoba was—too old to bear any more children. She had a witch's chin, made sharper by emaciation, and a tobacco-croaky voice, though she couldn't have smoked in years. Cigarettes were banned for Jews: the Nazis didn't want them to benefit from their soothing effects in the humid air.

"We're heading north," continued Jacoba, "which means the Sofia Reservation. I've heard it's easy enough if you keep your head down. We can live together, keep an eye out for each other." She glanced around the train car. "Because none of these Poles will."

"I'm going to escape."

"Not from the reservations. That's why they're sending us there."

"What about your daughter, getting back to Antzu?"

"They call this railway the 'Line of Fates.' It decides where you're taken, who lives or dies. What your future holds." Jacoba rubbed a filthy sleeve across her nose. "Perhaps I'm not meant to see my daughter again."

"The Nazis worship fate. I never have. I'm not giving up."

"You're kidding yourself," replied Jacoba softly. "Wherever you break out, you're still in Madagaskar. The sooner you accept it, Madeleine, the sooner every one of us accepts it, the simpler life will be. There's no way off this island."

Madeleine didn't want to speak after that. If Jacoba tried to reminisce—about Berlin or the apple macaroons she used to bake—she ignored her. Even when Jacoba mentioned her husband—he'd been a horse trainer, had died in 1932 and been spared the future—Madeleine met her with silence.

She gazed at the blank steel sky, her mind creeping toward her babies but not daring to imagine what might have happened to them. She thought of Alice and was ashamed of the crushing realization that the twins meant more: they were the reliquary of all she had treasured with Burton. *They. Them.* She hated thinking of her own children as nameless bundles of newborn flesh and screams. Never before had she appreciated how a few letters gave substance to the soul.

During their final morning together, before Burton left for Africa, they had discussed what to call the baby. To her surprise, Madeleine had slept deeply, waking only as Burton slipped out of bed. She sensed that he had watched the dawn break.

"Burton?" she called after him.

"You sleep."

She put on her nightgown and followed him downstairs, to the chilly kitchen. In Hampstead it was the domain of the servants, a room she rarely visited. Soon all her mornings would begin here. She found the thought humbling and wholesome. Burton made them breakfast: toast and butter, quince jam from the pantry, black coffee from Kamerun. Jared refused to have German groceries in the house; Madeleine approved except for coffee. The Germans were better at it, the Nazis' one contribution to the world. The only time she drank *Kaffee aus Deutsch-Afrika* was at the farm.

Burton was gazing at her.

"Are you sure you're happy about the baby?" she asked.

He nodded.

She saw gold in his eyes, hesitant but happy. When she'd been pregnant with Alice, her excitement had been cautious. Carrying Burton's child filled her with dance and birdsong. "What about names?"

"Depends if it's a girl or a boy."

"A girl," said Madeleine. "I want another girl."

Burton paused. Laughed apologetically. "I can't think. What about you?"

"I like Calliope. For the muse of poetry—it means beautiful face."

"What if she inherits my looks?"

"Or Josephine. Or maybe we could name her after your mother," she said. "Or your father if it's a boy."

Burton's voice was quiet: "No."

"How about Jane?" She knew how much he loved the Tarzan films. "Or . . . or . . ." She couldn't summon a single other name.

He offered his hand across the table and she took it, their fingers interlacing. The kitchen grew brighter, the August morning streaming through the windows. Eventually Burton stood and made his way upstairs. Madeleine heard floorboards creaking, the flush of the toilet, the clock in the hallway striking six. It was ten minutes fast; Burton could never get it to keep time. Such ordinary sounds, and yet that morning, each one made her heart shrink. Then another noise, something unfamiliar.

Whump.

Madeleine strode to the hallway. Through the window she could see a car approaching, black as a hearse.

"My ride," said Burton from behind her. "I'm going to get Patrick. He'll watch my back, make sure I get home."

She threw her arms around him, hugged him till she knew it was hurting. *Calliope,* he whispered, *it's beautiful.* Burton had brushed his teeth, and when she briefly tasted his mouth, the mint burned. All her reasoning against going to Kongo and killing Hochburg shrieked in her chest again. That neither the truth about his mother nor revenge mattered.

"Mummy!"

Alice was between their legs, tugging at her nightdress. Her daughter's face was blotted with sleep.

"Elli and Cally," said Burton, forcing the joke. "Heaven help us." He squeezed her hand, then moved to the door. "I'll be back on the eighteenth. I promise."

After that, Madeleine's memories grew indistinct. Their parting words were lost in a haze; she couldn't recall her final glimpse of him. All she remembered was watching the empty driveway for what seemed like hours, trying to convince herself that he would be safe but hoping he'd change his mind, that any moment the black car would trundle back into view. Sunlight pressed coldly against her; Alice told her not to cry. Standing there, she couldn't fathom his need to go to Africa and chase ghosts. Such inconsolable vengeance was a mystery to her.

Only now did she understand why he wanted to own Hochburg's last breath.

On the train, Madeleine squeezed her thighs together and felt the rough handle of the knife. Despite Jacoba's warning, she planned to find a way to Mandritsara and to escape this accursed island. Then one day she would stand before Jared Cranley again, knife in her hand. And bury the hilt between his ribs.

CHAPTER TWENTY-FOUR

16:00

MADELEINE WAS HURLED forward. Other bodies flailed around her in the gloom. Shouts of panic. There was a long, sparking screech of train wheels. For several seconds Madeleine was squashed into Jacoba's bony chest; then the forward momentum slackened and she tumbled backward.

The train shuddered and stopped. Silence except for the wheezing beat of the engine.

From the roof came the thud of boots, guards yelling. Madeleine struggled to stand and pressed her face against the window bars. They were in a valley: rugged hills with taller peaks in the distance, a scattering of mango trees. It was no longer raining, though the sky remained dark.

"What's going on?" asked Jacoba, picking herself up. She swatted the air around her with her hat. Others were crowding around the grille to look outside. A solid reek of sweat-stained uniforms.

Madeleine ducked as troops sprinted past on the ground below. "Something's blocked the track," she whispered. "I can't see what." She heard the splatter of more boots dashing to the front of the train. Then a voice, feeble and blood-spotted:

Don't stop! It's an ambush!

Madeleine's eyes darted round the cattle truck. "Danuta," she said. "Come here."

Danuta was one of the orphan girls who had shared the same barrack block with Madeleine in the abattoir. Five hundred women crammed into a space fifty meters by eight. The first night Madeleine lay there was the only time she wished she hadn't met Burton Cole; that when they had gone to Germania and discussed the future, she had jilted both their hopes. She yearned to be curled up in the snowy down of her sheets in Hampstead, grateful for everything Jared had given her. Mosquitoes drilled in her ears;

her back was hard against solid slats. And all around, the ceaseless coughing and snoring and corkscrewing of so many bodies that she thought she'd
never sleep again. (After a few weeks, she dropped easily into unconsciousness.) With so many women left childless, Danuta was a favorite, always
being given extra scraps of food; Jacoba was teaching her German. She was
a few years older than Alice, with a boy's crew cut and eyes as wide and
watchful as an owl's. Madeleine rarely spoke to the girl; she found it too
painful.

She knelt next to her so they were the same height. "I need your help,"
said Madeleine in clumsy Yiddish. "I'll lift you up, you look to see what's
happening."

Danuta nodded.

She was lighter than a sack of twigs; Madeleine felt a wrenching for
those afternoon teas with Alice where the scones and cupcakes were left
to go stale. "What can you see?" she asked when the girl was in position.
Danuta was able to squeeze her head through the bars.

"Lots of soldiers. They're so angry. Or scared."

"If they see you, jump down straightaway. What's at the front?"

Danuta peeked farther through the window. "There's a man on the
tracks. He's very fat, in guard clothes. A Sturm-shar-führer." The word
sounded ridiculous in the mouth of a child.

"What's he doing?"

She answered in Yiddish, Madeleine able to understand only a few
words. When she was growing up in Vienna, her father insisted that the
family speak German. Yiddish, with its ironic humor, suffering, and superstition, was the language of the street. She knew enough to speak to ven-
dors and beggars, no more.

"He's fastened to a cross," translated Jacoba. "Like a big X, in the middle
of the track—"

It's an ambush!

"—the soldiers are trying to untie him."

The crack of a bullet, the sound rolling from left to right.

There were startled cries from the guards. Another shot. Then gunfire
erupted on both sides of the train. Furious bursts from machine guns punc-
tuated by the steady, distant snap of rifles. The earthy boom of a mortar
roared over them; mud peppered the roof.

Madeleine dragged the girl away from the window. "He's shot," said
Danuta, wriggling in Madeleine's grip.

A bullet zinged through the carriage, leaving a spyhole in the wall inches from Madeleine's head. She threw herself on the floor, covering Danuta with her body and pulling Jacoba down. The carriage erupted in a fight for floor space. More bullets punctured the side of the train, letting in shafts of greenish light. Someone howled in agony.

The gun battle lasted several minutes before the shooting became sporadic, then stopped. Madeleine listened for any commands in German. Nothing but the chug of the stationary train and occasional sighs of steam.

"Are you hurt?" she asked Danuta. It was good to have a child in her arms.

"The fat man got shot," she laughed.

Madeleine stood beneath the roof hatch and heard no boots above. "Help me up," she said to Jacoba.

"You don't know what's out there. We should wait."

"This is our chance."

The older woman muttered something and knitted her hands together. Madeleine slipped her foot onto them, used them as a step to the ceiling. She lifted the hatch a sliver to check for guards, then flipped it open.

"At least let one of the Poles go first," said Jacoba, straining.

Madeleine clasped the sides of the opening and levered herself up the way she had done in gymnastics at school; it was one of her favorite classes. As a girl she dreamed of competing for Austria, till she realized she would never be good enough. Her innards threatened to buckle, but she managed to haul her body onto the roof. The air was mulled with cordite. She surveyed her surroundings—the world had never felt so broad or unbolted—then called below to Jacoba:

"Tell the others we're safe. I'm going to open the doors."

The train was littered with dead Nazis, most showing the single-shot wounds of snipers. Striding down the valley were parties of men, a few on horseback, rifles slung over their shoulders. Madeleine recognized them from their attire: stolen SS camouflage trousers tucked into socks, grimy white shirts, black waistcoats. Some wore trench coats that flapped around their heels. Every man had a flowing, wild mane. On an island where the length of your hair was dictated by bureaucrats, tresses were the first act of rebellion. In the markets of Antzu, Madeleine had seen wigs bartered for a month's worth of food.

The men were Vanilla Jews.

Despite the failure of the first rebellion, and the mass executions that followed, Globocnik was unable to eradicate the Vanilla Jews completely. The privations of the island meant their numbers soon began to swell again, and this time they were stoked by the Zionist imagination. Zionism—the movement to create a Jewish state in Palestine—had no place in the new world order, so an alternative, pragmatic version had evolved. If inhabiting the soil of Israel was a lost dream, the possibility of self-determination remained an ideal to fight for.

Madeleine clambered down the ladder on the side of the carriage. She wanted to deliver the other passengers into the light and air, not the men strutting toward her. Flecks of soot pattered her cheek. She landed by the track and stumbled down the embankment, sliding to a stop next to the body of a dead soldier. He was facedown in the mud, lying protectively over his assault rifle. Ignoring the hole in his head, Madeleine checked his pockets for food, found a tin of candies, and stuffed a handful into her mouth. They were half-melted, with a sickly strawberry-toffee taste. She took some more and was debating how many to save for the journey ahead or whether to share any with Jacoba and Danuta when she sensed someone watching her.

Crouching beneath the wheels of the train was a guard, his uniform patterned with mud. Blood was running from beneath his cap to his chin, tracing his jawline. Madeleine reached for the weapon at her feet, tugging it from under the dead soldier. She'd never held a gun before. Its long, curved magazine gave it unwieldy heft, but it was lighter than she'd imagined, an arrangement of metal and wood that made her feel more substantial.

The guard was holding a rifle similar to Madeleine's, the muzzle drifting toward her. She'd been to the pictures enough times with Burton to know that people died for want of releasing the safety catch; she risked a glance at it.

Her legs were weak and bandy, the weapon in her hands drawn to the ground as if the mud were magnetized. How often had she reveled in fantasies of justice and death? From watching Papa wipe away the spit from his face to lying hollowed out in the maternity ward. But the man in front of her wasn't responsible; he was Ulm, a drone. She'd seen him joking with workers at the abattoir, offering them the stubs of his cigarettes; she'd seen him swipe the butt of his rifle into a back for sport, laugh as Jews slipped in overflowing vats of blubber.

Madeleine eased her finger through the trigger guard.

Ulm glanced over her shoulder and crept out from beneath the train. "I want to surrender." His eyes were almost the same color as Burton's.

He raised his gun toward her.

Madeleine stumbled backward. The trigger seemed immovable against the tip of her finger. Her eardrums were thundering. She concentrated on the German's autumnal blue eyes.

There was a single shot, like the sound of a hunting rifle. It reminded Madeleine of the time Jared had taken her to the Highlands to hunt stags: the lone shots echoing across the fells while she stayed in the lodge. It was during that trip that Alice was conceived.

Ulm was blasted between the wheels. His body rolled over the tracks and vanished below the embankment. A spasm of breath caught in Madeleine's throat; she turned. Behind her was a crowd of waistcoats and dark, billowing hair. One of the Vanilla Jews lowered his rifle. His face was a toothless leer.

Madeleine let the machine gun fall from her grip, bridling with shame.

+ + +

The train was a relic from the French period, the engine powered by wood, not coal. With no one to stoke its firebox, the smokestack's output withered to nothing. The cattle cars were unlocked, and passengers helped one another onto the trackside. It was stewingly hot, the sky solid gray and ready to rain.

The Vanilla Jews corralled them round a single carriage, saying that Ben-Ze'ev, the commander of this band, had important news to share. Madeleine hoped they also had some food. The candy had left her ravenous, and she needed some sustenance before trekking to Mandritsara. Next to her, Jacoba was twitchy and bad tempered; Danuta had found a spent bullet casing and was blowing on the tip as if it were a recorder. Madeleine wanted to clasp the girl's bony body. No matter how betrayed by Alice she felt, she missed hugging her daughter, missed the glossy smell of her hair and her bumptious moods. It could only be Alice who'd told Jared about the farm, yet how could she blame a six-year-old? Madeleine understood that she was angry with herself for being so naïve, for not listening to Burton in the first place when he'd said not to bring her there. She stroked Danuta's head, then fixed her hands behind her back.

A group of men had positioned themselves on the roof of the train. They wore black waistcoats that fitted perfectly, no missing buttons, some embroidered. They parted for their leader. He limped to the front and waited for the crowd below to fall silent. His face was fierce and scarred, enclosed by hair as long as a Hasidic's and a wolf-colored beard that reached his belt. The brim of his hat kept his eyes in shadow.

Ben-Ze'ev summoned his breath. "My fellow Jews," he said in German, his lungs sounding charred, "you have been freed, but you are not safe." On the roof, two others began to speak, shadowing his words in Polish and Yiddish. "I wish to tell you of a place, the haven we all desire." Some of his words weren't loud enough to carry; the throng edged closer.

"It is a land where we govern ourselves," he continued. "There are no sectors, no work camps, no summary executions. Gunships do not rain fire on us." He peered out, seeking the eye of every man, woman, and child. *One of the demagogue's tricks*, thought Madeleine; she remembered watching Hitler's speeches before the *Anschluss*, captivated and not quite afraid enough to believe his words. Jacoba removed her hat and fanned herself as Ben-Ze'ev cast his gaze in their direction. His voice dropped: "Do you know where this place is?"

"Palestine!" shouted one of the Poles.

"Antzu!" called another. There was a ripple of laughter.

Antzu, where Madeleine had lived before she gave birth, was the capital of the Western Sector and seat of the Judenrat, the Jewish Council. It was also the island's only free city. The Red Cross and American officials were encouraged to make inspections; Goebbels had allowed the BBC to film there.

Ben-Ze'ev glared into the crowd. "Do not think of Antzu as some paradise! Even there we live in the shadow of the green house, ruled by the regional governor with his enormous wife and five greedy children." He spat the words out. "They have Jews for servants, Jews to tend their garden, Jews to muck out the stables—"

The mention of the stables roused Jacoba's attention. She was proud of having worked there. Ben-Ze'ev continued:

"—their horses are better fed than us. In the city itself: disease and curfew, sewers open to the air, thick clouds of mosquitoes, neighbor spying on neighbor. Is that what it is to live?" He was overtaken by a fit of coughing and hunched over, his beard trailing his boots. One of the translators stepped toward him; Ben-Ze'ev flicked him away.

He resumed through gasps of air: "I speak of a land where no Nazi dares tread. Where the Ark holds the names of free men, not captives. Shall I tell you where this place is?"

Silence.

"Madagaskar. Our new homeland. But we have to seize it, we have to drive the Nazis into the waves." He was panting. "Then the works we've undertaken, the road building, the factories and farms, the vanilla that has made men millionaires won't be for the Reich—but ourselves. Now is the time! Thousands of our enemy are away fighting in Africa. They don't have the numbers to control us."

Once again he erupted into coughing; this time he couldn't regain his breath. He stepped back, motioned for one of his subordinates to take over.

Jacoba shook her head. "Stupid, stupid," she whispered. "Look what happened with the last rebellion. This kind of talk will get us killed."

Another of the Vanilla Jews had taken the place of Ben-Ze'ev, looking awkward in front of so many people. He was a few years younger than Madeleine, scrawny and sunburned. Unlike many of the others, he wore his waistcoat half-buttoned. He massaged his jaw where the molars were, wincing occasionally. Speech welled in him, didn't come, then burst out.

Tears pricked Madeleine's eyes like when she'd imagined she had seen Burton in the abattoir. "Oh, my God . . ." she whispered, clutching Jacoba's hand.

"W-we don't ask the old to join us," he said, "nor ch-children or anyone whose nerves are ruined. We understand what you've suffered. You will be escorted to Zimety, the Malagasy reservation in the northeast. We have a camp there; the conditions aren't the best, but you'll be safe till the island is ours."

At first Madeleine couldn't believe it was him; as soon as she'd heard him speak she knew it must be. He had the same nurring voice and hint of a stutter, only deeper now, older. She wondered if he was still furious with her.

"Everyone else, man or woman, should take up the cause. A second rebellion—the Pig Rebellion—has started; this time we cannot fail. If we strike hard enough, the Americans will help our struggle."

"Like they did before?" cried a sarcastic voice from the crowd.

"They have a new president; he has already spoken out against this island. The American Jewish Committee is calling for intervention. We must fight heroically, endure loudly, so the world cannot ignore us. That's why we waited for this train. We heard what you did in the slaughterhouse. You may have been canning meat, but there's vanilla in your blood—"

"They shot the leaders," shouted someone. "We're just workers."

"Then go to Zimety—there's no shame in it. It's ten days on foot." He pointed behind himself; the clouds were at their bursting point. "Before you go, think on this: a generation from now, Tana will be our new Jerusalem. The Totenburgs won't be monuments to the German dead but engraved in Hebrew. This island will be a beacon to our people wherever they roam. You will live safe, comfortable lives, and your children's children will ask, What did you do?"

He finished on an expectant note, looking to the mob to be moved, for an ovation of mutiny and rage. Nothing except the echo of his words in Polish, then Yiddish, then the breeze.

Madeleine thought of Alice and the twins and hoped their children wouldn't be able to find Madagaskar on a map. She was unable to contain herself: she raised her hands and clapped. Another pair joined her, then another, missing the irony of her applause. Next moment it was taken up by everyone. There was an ebullient roar, whistles. The Jews on top of the train tossed handfuls of lychees into the throng. Jacoba crossed her arms.

"Don't tell me you're going to join them," she said as the cheering subsided.

"You should take Danuta and go to Zimety."

"Danuta has plenty of mothers, and I'm not going to live with a tribe of blackies. I want to go back to Antzu and my daughter." She put on her hat. "We could go together."

"I'm heading north. To Mandritsara."

"If they let you," replied Jacoba.

The Vanilla Jews were marshaling the others: to the rear of the train for Zimety; in front, where pineapples were being skinned and doled out, to join the fight. The valley echoed with barked orders. Jacoba shook her head. "They sound as bad as the Nazis."

"They won't stop me," said Madeleine. "I need water and supplies. Abner will help."

"Abner?"

She indicated the Jew who had taken over from Ben-Ze'ev. He remained astride the roof, wearing his familiar round spectacles now, and seemed to be scanning the crowds for someone.

"Why would he help?"

Madeleine was suddenly self-conscious. "He's my brother."

CHAPTER TWENTY-FIVE

Northwest Madagaskar
18 April, 16:50

ONLY FOUR OF them made it ashore.

Reuben Salois crawled through the surf and collapsed; his muscles didn't have a single stroke left in them. More than once his arms had failed and he had let himself sink, the urge to open his lungs to the sea irresistible. Cranley hauled him back onto the barrel, chided him to keep swimming: *Too many Yids have died already.* Now it seemed impossible that there was solid ground beneath him: thirty meters of salt-white sand leading to the jungle. Each breath was sweet and painful. For several minutes, no one moved.

The memory of arriving in Mozambique foamed in Salois's thoughts. By then he'd lost count of the days since he'd escaped Madagaskar, drifting across shimmering gray waters, time measured by the withering of skin around vanished muscle. Sharks circled and sang him songs: first in the voices of beautiful young women, later a raucous chantey of drunkards accompanied by a fiddle and timbrel. He woke to find the raft nudging the shore. Rolled himself off and almost drowned in a hand's depth of water. He dragged himself away from the ocean, pausing every meter to sink his face into the sand and summon the dregs of his spirit. Ahead, always out of reach, was a succulent strip of purple.

Salois shook off the memory and rose from the waves to check the others. His boots remained around his neck, salt burned his mouth; he imagined gorging on ripe papaya or crushing a lime onto his tongue. Of the marines, only Denny and Private Grace were with him. A dozen meters away lay Xegoe, clutching his purse to his chest, his beret lost.

"Where's Cranley?" asked Salois, his lungs jagged. The force of the currents had split the group apart as they approached the shallows. "The rest?"

No one replied.

Salois freed his boots as if unwinding a garland, then scanned the shore-line in both directions: there were no figures emerging from the waves. Out to sea, the Nazi patrol boat continued to drift and smoke. He ordered the marines to their feet, and they dragged their equipment out of the surf, to the remnants of a crater blasted in the beach. Its sides were smooth, the bottom scattered with pink shells. The men huddled together.

"What did we salvage?"

Denny rummaged through the bags. "Explosives . . . smoke flares . . . hand grenades. They seem dry enough. Detonators. No radio."

"Cranley had it."

"Medical kit . . . some ammunition. That's all."

"What about ration tins?"

"Nothing." Denny picked the sand out of his ears. "What do we do, Major?"

"Find the others. Then continue as planned."

"And if they didn't make it? Diego's pointless unless there's someone to take out the radar."

Private Grace spoke up: "The sergeant's right. It was over the moment the Nazis boarded the boat."

Grace—Gracovitz—was a fellow Jew who had escaped Madagaskar as a teenager; he'd considered himself uniquely experienced until Salois joined the mission. He was tough, angry, depressive. The other marines called him the "golden Jew" because of his hair. He sucked incessantly on aniseed candies. "The only thing to do now," said Grace, "is cross the island. Get to the extraction point."

"No, Cranley's alive," replied Salois. "If we can't find him, we find a way to call the radio."

"How?"

"First we get off this beach."

While Denny divided the equipment between the rucksacks, Salois pulled on his boots and walked over to Xegoe, who was lying in the surf. Salois offered his hand to help him up. The captain swiped him away and stood upright, stowing his purse.

"You are the cause that go kill my sailors," he roared in Salois's face, "sink my boat." He shoved Salois back, flashed a dagger with a curved point. "You and your devil skin!"

Before he could attack, Grace swept the captain off his feet. Xegoe stumbled, cursing in his native tongue, then scuttled up the sand.

"No, wait!" yelled Salois. "You can't survive on this island without us."

Grace aimed his pistol at the retreating captain. "If the Nazis capture him—"

There was a deep crump; the ground shook beneath Salois's boots.

Xegoe vanished. In his place, a stalk of writhing smoke.

An instant after the land mine detonated, offal and a sprinkling of gold reichsmarks rained down on them. The patter of gore ended as abruptly as it began. The only sound was the beat of the waves and *mesite* birds calling from the jungle.

Grace wiped the blood from his eyes. A spasm ran up his neck. "Why did I come back?"

"Same reason as me. Three nights from now, Diego Suarez will light the sky. The whole island will see. The Americans will come."

Xegoe's knife lay on the ground, his hand still attached to it. Salois pried the fingers loose and followed the captain's path, stepping only where Xegoe's footprints dented the sand.

"What about the kit?" asked Denny.

"Leave it. Once we've secured a path, we'll come back."

"I'll take the explosives," said Grace, wanting to make up for his misgivings. "In case we get stuck. We can't blow Diego without them."

When Salois reached the smoking crater, he lowered himself onto his belly and delicately slid the blade into the sand until it was buried to the hilt. He withdrew it, shuffled forward, and inserted the knife again, probing for mines.

Probe. Secure. Shuffle.

Probe. Secure. Shuffle. They edged forward in centimeters.

The land between Kongo and Rhodesia was said to be mined. Salois had heard stories that when the Waffen-SS invaded, Jews were in the vanguard: a shipment from one of the penal gangs of Steinbock, sent to central Africa and ordered to stamp their way across the border, five hundred men abreast. The advance was rapid, the Germans not losing a single vehicle.

Grace, then Denny, followed his path. The air was heavy and hot. They had covered ten meters before the tip of the knife contacted metal. As the breath solidified in Salois's lungs, he eased the dagger from the sand.

"Here," he said to the others, marking an X in the sand.

"Now what?" asked Grace, his voice barely a murmur.

"You don't have to whisper. They're not that sensitive."

"You're not wearing a backpack full of dynamite."

Salois prodded the ground to his left, tested the entire length of his body, and, when he was confident it was safe, slid over. He repeated the procedure three times before edging forward once more. They'd covered another five meters when Salois stopped again. The taste of salt was acrid on his tongue; he should have asked Grace for one of his aniseed candies. His fingers trembled.

"Another mine?" asked Denny.

Salois's face was feverish. "I just need a few minutes."

He pressed his cheek into the ground. The crust was warm, but below the sand was cool and moist, as it had been in Mozambique when he'd crawled up the beach. At the top he had found a carpet of purple and blue flowers and gorged on the petals till his saliva ran magenta and his stomach boiled. Then he slumped, gazing stolidly across the Mozambique Channel, ready to die. He counted numbers to himself. As the sun reached its zenith, a fisherman chanced by. He was wizened, wore his nets over his shoulders like a cloak. When he bent in close, Salois tasted his ethereal breath. *A morte não o quer mesmo levar,* he had said and laughed.

"Major!"

Salois brought himself back, mopped the gritty sweat from his face, and slipped the dagger into the sand. He heard a distant drone, like a hornet trapped in a can.

"Major! We have to move."

"This can't be rushed."

"We don't have a choice."

Across the ocean, the clouds were darkening to gray. Circling above the stricken S-boat was a Walküre helicopter. It dipped its nose and headed toward land.

Salois stabbed the knife into the ground, moving as swiftly as possible till the blade nicked something hard. "Another mine," he said, pricking the area to his left and changing course. It was fifteen meters to the trees.

The gunship reached the shore, screamed low overhead, its downdraft whipping grains into Salois's nose and mouth.

"It missed us?" said Grace.

"No," replied Denny. "It's coming round for a better shot."

Probe, shuffle, probe, shuffle.

The knife touched metal. The mines were becoming more concentrated, their purpose to kill men escaping the jungle rather than those emerging from the sea.

The Walküre completed its loop, came low over the breakers, its front minigun perfectly lined up with them.

Grace scrambled to his feet and sprinted. Salois reached out to stop him as he darted past, kicking up puffs of sand. *We're always running*, thought Salois, *running to the Germans' starting gun*. The protective shade of the jungle beckoned to Grace.

A crimson geyser. Then, a fraction of a second later, a blast wave as the explosives ignited.

Salois shielded his face from the debris, crying out when something bit into his forearm.

The Walküre opened fire, its cannon whipping the sea. Denny scrambled to his feet.

"Walk!" commanded Salois, taking the lead as he followed Grace's tracks. He made each stride as long and measured as possible, as if pacing out dimensions.

The ground reverberated as the helicopter's guns chewed into it. Salois kept focused on the gloom in front of him: he could already distinguish vines and patterns of bark. There was an explosion, another scream. Blood and sand lashed his neck.

One more stride—and he was beneath the boughs.

The Walküre slowed, hovering above the canopy. Its rotor blades battered the trees. Leaves and brightly colored birds whirled around Salois, streaks of white, emerald, indigo. He ran, following forest paths that split and crossed at random, stumbled on roots, felt branches bounce off his head. He kept running till the forest darkened around him and he could no longer hear the chop of the gunship. Only then did he stop.

Salois's caftan was sodden—though whether with sweat or blood, he couldn't tell. A throb trilled up his forearm to the elbow, and he lifted the sleeve to examine it. Buried in the skin was a molar, complete with its roots, a nugget of mercury in the center; Grace—Gracovitz—and his aniseed sweets. It made a popping noise as he extracted it. A familiar guilt washed through him, the chastisement for being alone, and he heard the laughter of the fisherman who found him in Mozambique. *A morte não o quer mesmo levar.*

The old man had saved his life, fed him peppery broth and sheltered him, before Salois was taken along the coast to the mission at Inhambane. There, one of the Jesuits spoke French, and he had asked what the words meant. The missionary offered him a scornful, earnest eye.

Death doesn't want you.

Salois rolled the tooth between his fingers, like a jeweler, then tossed it into the undergrowth.

CHAPTER TWENTY-SIX

Tana–Diego Railway
18 April, 17:00

"ABNER?"

He was standing over a pile of dead Germans as Madeleine approached, his back toward her. Other Vanilla Jews were stealing the trousers from the bodies. They had collected a stack of weapons.

Her brother twisted round. A searching look from behind his glasses, followed by a blossom of recognition; finally, blankness descended. Up close he was more ravaged, his skin walnut-red from sun and cyclone, the flesh below his cheeks sunken. The cake-plump boy she'd last seen fifteen years earlier was long gone. His lanks of hair were ridiculous; she always remembered him with cropped back and sides. *You look like one of those Nazis,* their mother used to scold.

"Do I know you?" he asked. The black of his waistcoat shimmered like a peacock's feathers.

"It's Madeleine."

His stare remained blank.

"Madeleine Weiss," she said, suppressing a pang of hurt that became embarrassment. "Your sister, for God's sake!"

"My sister's in England, married to some big man."

"You received my letters? But I never heard back from you."

"We used to write all the time before the rebellion . . ." He massaged his jaw and scrutinized her. "Leni?"

One day, when she was twelve or thirteen, Abner returned home from his wrestling class and started calling her Leni. Soon he had pestered the rest of the family to adopt the name, all except her father. She hated it. Nobody had used it since she fled Vienna. An unexpected sob rose in her; she covered her mouth to hide it.

"Leni? Madeleine?" He was incredulous, laughing, cross. "It can't be."

Her brother hugged her fiercely, his embrace so consuming that she couldn't free her arms to hold him. It was like being gripped by a skeleton. Madeleine sensed that he had recognized her from the start and was playing a game.

He released her, the laughter gone. "Why are you here?" he demanded. "You should be in Britain, safe as the king." He'd been angry that she fled abroad and he had not. He bombarded her with questions, his breath rank with tooth decay.

"The king died last year," she replied stupidly. "There's going to be a queen." Her brain felt cracked—how could she explain everything that had happened to her?

Buried in the detail of Eden's Evacuation Bill to remove the British Jews was a queasy subclause that covered mixed marriages. The simplest solution was a shotgun annulment that led to deportation. Those who chose to stay married had to obtain a licence for their spouses. Any offspring were subjected to strict conjugal guidelines: no child of a Jewish parent could marry another part-Jew; nor could their children or grandchildren. Thus, within three generations the problem would cease to exist (as defined by the Nuremberg Laws). The lawyers in Germania fumed until Hitler was reported to have said they should "turn a blind eye to certain little irregularities." He wouldn't fall into the trap of starting a world war over a handful of defilers. Before Madeleine was flown to Tana, Lyall and Russell made her sign the divorce papers Cranley had prepared. The ink removed her legal protection.

"I was deported," she said. It was all she could manage.

"What about your husband? Why didn't you move to America? You were rich."

She shook her head.

"You should at least have been sent to the Western Sector."

"I was. Antzu."

"Then what are you doing on the train?" Every question sounded like an accusation.

Jacoba appeared at her shoulder; she had been admiring the horses. "I told you, the Line of Fates! It brought you together."

"Who's she?"

"My friend."

"I'm going to Antzu," said Jacoba. "Back to civilization."

"Good. You can take Leni with you." Abner had always presumed to tell her what to do: the tyranny of the younger brother. "If you walk through the night you'll be there by tomorrow."

"No," said Madeleine.

Her brother made a scornful tutting noise. "Don't tell me you're joining the rebellion. Leni, you were never a fighter." During their clashes at home, no matter how viciously she struck him, Abner remained unscratched; the slightest thump in return and her skin was mauve. "Stay with your friend," he said.

"I'm not going to Antzu!"

"It's the safest place on this island—"

"Ben-Ze'ev doesn't think so."

"That's just propaganda, to make the Poles think we have it as bad as they do—to get them to fight. We need their numbers. But you've got a chance they never will." He unhooked his glasses and looked at her with naked eyes. "I still don't understand why you were on the train. If we hadn't ambushed it, you'd have ended up in the Sofia Reservation."

"I was in the hospital—"

"You're ill?"

"They took my clothes, my papers . . . everything. Afterward, I couldn't speak."

The shock of the birth had made her mute. When she was discharged, her voice was still dead. She stood in the office of a Hauptsturmführer who demanded to know what sector she was from, where her documents were. Her unblinking, rag-doll silence incensed him. He bent her over his desk, loosened the buckle of his belt; she didn't care what he did. She counted six lashes, none of them provoking a single murmur. All sensation had narrowed to the knife point of a single image: Cranley examining the blood on his handkerchief as she was led away. Before the seventh blow, the Hauptsturmführer was tear-stricken, babbling on about the pressure he was under, the things they made him do, how much he missed his wife and daughters. He scribbled a chit and thrust it at her. A lorry drive, then a train journey, and she was at the abattoir. Of the days before that—the tests and probing, her weeping, unsuckled breasts—she refused to think.

"I'm going back there," she said, unshakable. "To Mandritsara."

"It's in the Sofia Reservation," replied her brother. "What the Nazis call a 'special treatment facility.' " His tone became kinder. "I've just found you, Madeleine. I don't want to lose you again."

"I was pregnant. They stole my babies."

"Then they're already dead."

He was so matter-of-fact that she wanted to slap him. Madeleine searched his eyes, refusing to believe him, and for the first time she realized that her younger brother had known too much death for it to startle him.

"The doctor said they were good specimens. He wouldn't kill them."

Abner reached for her. "I'm sorry, Madeleine. Men with the fight of Samson are taken there and never return." His tone remained flat. "We hear stories of experiments, people injected with malaria, typhus. Drugs they use on us like we're lab rats—"

Madeleine covered her ears as though she were a child and howled. "How can you tell me this?"

"To stop you from going. To spare you." His voice swelled, then caught. "The b-best you can hope is they were too young to know w-what was happening."

There was a cry from the train: "Abner!" On the roof, one of the Vanilla Jews pointed toward the ridge of the valley. Silhouetted against the rain clouds was a line of men in pith helmets carrying rifles.

"The Jupo," said her brother, hooking his glasses on. "We need to move."

"What?"

"Police."

"But they're Jews."

"Yes."

"So why do we have to go?"

The Jüdische Polizei (Jupo) had been instituted by the SS, its role to maintain everyday public order and badger the resistance groups.

"Stay here," said Abner. "I'll be back as soon as I can." He grinned, revealing a glimpse of rotten teeth. "I'm so glad I found you, Leni."

Once he was gone, Madeleine strode toward the open grass and peaks in the distance. The sun was dipping in the sky.

Jacoba caught up with her, tugging her sleeve until she stopped. "Your brother's right. He's only trying to save you."

"My children are alive. I know it." She rubbed the nape of her neck, that spot Burton loved to nip. "Neither of you can stop me."

"At least say good-bye. I never had that chance with my daughter. What if you never see him again?"

The Vanilla Jews bustled around them, preparing to move out. Through the gaps between the cattle trucks, Madeleine saw a procession being led away toward Zimety by men on horseback; at the rear Danuta and the few other children were skipping along. Madeleine thought of the newsreels she'd seen of Soviet Jews being marched to Siberia: human lines five, ten miles long, trudging endlessly east. Halifax had said no British Jew need suffer that wretchedness.

"Ben-Ze'ev is sending me to Antzu," said Abner when he returned. He was carrying a rifle, a knapsack, and water bottles, his hair tied in a ponytail. "The Jewish Council needs to know that more of us are being sent to the reservations. They can't ignore it anymore."

"Jacoba can keep you company," replied Madeleine sourly. "She's keen to get back to her job at the stables."

"Leni, please, we don't have time to argue. The train's about to be blown. That will bring more police."

"But they're Jews—what does it matter?"

He started marching her away. "Last time we came across them, it ended in blood. The Jupo wants to confiscate our weapons, hand us over to the Nazis."

The locomotive exploded.

On the ridge, a cry went up from the Jewish Police. They streamed down the slope as if charging into battle, before being overtaken by mounted officers. The horses were wild and half-starved; the ground thundered with hooves. Madeleine and Abner fled in the opposite direction, wet grass whipping their knees. Jacoba couldn't match their speed; Madeleine had to keep slowing to encourage her.

Soon the three of them were alone in a dark emerald landscape beneath bulging clouds. The air was hot and asphyxiating. Apart from the chill of the hospital ward, Madeleine had no recollection of being cold since she'd arrived in Madagaskar. She yearned for cooler weather, like the long, freeing walks she and Burton used to take on the Suffolk coast when the sea vanished in hoary mists and the only sound was the crunch of their boots in the shingle. Or hiking in the Tyrol with her father when she was a girl; every year he took her on a trip alone. They drank in the mountain air, walked in silence for hours, Madeleine comforted by his solid pace and the tick-tock of his thoughts, even if he rarely voiced them. Abner fumed because he wasn't invited. When she returned home, she found buttons missing from her blouses, her secret tin of sweets depleted.

A question settled among her memories, one she should have asked earlier. "Abner," she said quietly, "what about our parents?"

His hand was clamped around his jaw. "Only now do you think of them." He shouldered his rifle and began to roll up a sleeve. "Papa's gone to America."

"And left the rest of you?"

A miserable snort. "One of our expressions. He died on the crossing. No illness, nothing from the guards. He woke one morning and had . . . given up. Just empty eyes and barely a whisper for us." His grief sounded fresh. "Three days later, they dropped him in the sea, somewhere off Südwest Afrika."

She felt Jacoba take her hand and was grateful for her sweaty palm. "Mutti?"

"She's still alive."

"Did she ever forgive me?"

"She talks about you all the time: *Madeleine was such a good daughter, so clever to leave for England—let's be thankful one of us is safe.*"

"When I arrived in Antzu, I spent weeks searching for her, for all of you. I knocked on every door in town."

"Even if you'd tried the Ark, you wouldn't have found us. After the first uprising, we left for Zimety; it was safer. She's there with Leah." Madeleine's elder sister.

"How are they?"

"Mutti's old, sick. She has malaria. Leah got married, here in Madagaskar. It was a happy day—for once you could forget the rain and mosquitoes and Nazis." He smiled at a memory.

Madeleine thought of her lonely wedding. To avoid being overwhelmed by guests on the groom's side, Jared had made it a small affair—though she suspected it was to save their embarrassment as much as hers.

"And baby Samuel?"

"He joined the Vanillas after me. Grew to be a fine man." Abner's voice wavered. "Also gone to America, a few months ago, on a raid. One of the first martyrs of the new rebellion. See for yourself."

He finished rolling up his sleeve and offered her his forearm. At the wrist was a tattooed number: 6112195. Above it were a series of other digits, eight in total, crudely inked on the skin. Abner pointed to the last one, which was laced with scabs. "That's Samuel."

"I don't understand."

"A tradition among the Vanillas. Each time a comrade falls, one of us adds his number to our own, so they're not forgotten. We're walking memorials. A day will come when we mark every number in stone."

"Who are the others?"

"Men who fought for a better future." He sounded so pious.

Madeleine stared at the list of numbers on his arm. During her first months in London, she wrote to her parents every week and received curt replies. Then the letters from Vienna stopped. For years afterward, she tried to find out what had happened. She didn't know where her family was on Himmler's Barbarossa date, whether they had been shipped to Madagaskar or Siberia. No one could help at the Red Cross; the Foreign Office rebutted her and the lines of other Jews with painstaking indifference, before the refugee department was transferred to the Colonial Office. She beseeched and complained her way through tiers of officials, till her tenacity brought her to the office of Jared Cranley. He was so considerate, insisted that she have a cup of tea and a biscuit while they chatted, paid no attention to her shabby dress. By then her search was habitual; it filled the few lonely hours when she wasn't working. She was resigned to the belief that her mother and father, brothers and sister were dead—or, if not burned or buried, as out of reach as her childhood. Madeleine had mourned them long ago, said Kaddish for eleven months—for herself, not God—then taken a pair of scissors to the ends of her hair.

Hearing their fates now, she experienced the shallow, passing sadness of someone else's tragedy, as if reading death notices in a newspaper. Her heart was too full of grief for Burton and the twins to accommodate any more.

She stopped walking and touched her brother's arm. "Which one's Papa?"

"He died before we were numbered. Globus brought that in. One of his 'innovations' to control the population. I keep Father here." Abner patted his chest. "You broke his heart when you left."

"You broke mine when you stayed. We could have gone to New York. All of us. As a family."

"The world closed its doors, remember?" His voice became mild, sly. "Mutti would never forgive me if I added your number. Don't go to Mandritsara, Leni."

She showed him her unmarked wrist. "I don't have one."

"How come?"

Madeleine shrugged, then said, "You can't stop me." She stepped away from him.

"And what are you going to do after?" He spoke in the same mocking, cross tone from their childhood, as though the privations of Madagaskar had changed nothing. "Swim to England?"

"Hush now," soothed Jacoba.

"You're going to swim with her?"

"No. But let the girl have some hope."

Suddenly Madeleine wanted to be alone. The oppressive script of family life, softened in her memory by separation, was in full voice again. When she'd first arrived in London, she'd sometimes thought it wasn't only Hitler she'd fled.

Abner lowered his gun, not aiming it at her but allowing the muzzle to float in her direction. She ignored him, took a bearing from the fading sun, and determinedly walked away. As if a switch had been flicked, it began to rain.

"Where are you going?" he called after her. When she didn't reply he shouted, "Silly girl! You're heading in the wrong direction."

"Mandritsara's north."

"Not from here. You passed it on the train twenty kilometers ago. You don't even know where you are, Leni."

Madeleine stopped, the chaff of her hair plastered to her scalp. She twirled round, trying to orient herself.

"Listen to him," said Jacoba. "Please."

Her brother trotted to her side. "Sorry, Madeleine. I'm playing the fool, I don't know why. But there's no point in going alone to Mandritsara—you might as well lie down here and breathe your last. If you want any chance of saving your children, come with me to Antzu." He was full of coaxing. "We'll talk to the council, see if we can raise some men and weapons."

"Since when has the council done anything but talk?"

"I know one of the elders; he'll help us."

She couldn't decide whether to trust him. "Only if I can go with you to Mandritsara. To the hospital itself. They're my babies."

"I told you, you're not a fighter."

"Lives change."

He shook his head. "Leni, I saw what happened under the train. With the soldier."

"What?"

"You couldn't pull the trigger. Whatever's happened to you, you don't have the heart." There was longing in his expression, gratitude. "Or the hate."

"I don't need a lecture about hate. I'll fight." She steeled her voice. "I'm not afraid."

Abner studied her eyes, then bent toward her, the rain trickling down his face. "You will be," he whispered. "You will be."

CHAPTER TWENTY-SEVEN

Lava Bucht, Madagaskar
20 April, 02:00

THE SMOLDERING DAMP of the forest came to an abrupt end, and he was at the water's edge. Burton looked up, arching his neck to read the name on the cruise liner. A cliff face of albino steel filled his vision.

The *Wilhelm Gustloff* rose out of the night, listing and cankered, scoured pale by salt winds. She was seven hundred feet long, the glass that remained in her portholes cracked, a scar of rivets running down her bow to the waterline. The communication masts had been cut down, every lifeboat removed. Only curls of smoke from the funnel suggested that there was life in her.

The *Gustloff* first set sail in 1937 as the KdF's flagship, a liner with berths for fifteen hundred passengers. After Dunkirk she had been readied as a troop carrier for Operation Sea Lion, the invasion of Britain, and when peace was declared, she'd been converted into a hospital ship to bring back the wounded of Operation Banana, Germany's conquest of West Africa. On the eve of her return to the KdF as a tourist boat, one of Eichmann's deputies at the Foreign Ministry calculated that the *Gustloff* could carry six thousand Jews per voyage to Madagaskar. When the KdF protested, Himmler intervened personally, declaring that a Europe free of Jews was more desired by the German people than the so-called glamour of tourism.

Tünscher emerged from the trees. Now that they were on the island he was tense, his swagger more guarded.

"I see you found it," he said, lighting a cigarette and gazing up at the ship. A Star of David had been painted on the smoke stack. "The Ark."

She was moored in the middle of the bay, her rear low in the water as if weighed down by an immense load. A series of bamboo jetties, lit with sporadic lanterns, connected the *Gustloff* to land.

Tünscher removed a small, collapsible telescope from his pocket and put it to his eye. "And that's Analava," he continued before handing the spyglass to Burton. "A Jew town." Farther up the shore, among the mangroves, was a ramshackle mass of huts raised on stilts; the stench of sewage simmered above it. "It's run by the Jupo, the local police. They guard the ship."

"Why?"

"The record of every last Jew is on the Ark. If that's all there was to prove I was alive, I'd keep a close eye on it." He took a drag on his cigarette, the tip flaring. "Beyond the town, out in the dark, are Vanilla Jews—who don't trust the police to do a good job."

"What about over there?" asked Burton, swinging the telescope to the far side of the bay.

Across the water, ringed by fences and lights, was a cluster of barracks. Burton glimpsed Walküre helicopters, hovercrafts.

"An SS base," explained Tünscher. "To watch the watchers, and tell the American Jewish Committee to go fuck itself. Don't worry, they're not supposed to come here. Part of the agreement."

"So why these?"

They were both dressed as Sturmbannführers, not in the black cloth Burton had worn to disguise himself in Kongo but in the tropical uniform of Madagaskar: jacket with shoulder yokes and *Tropenhosen* trousers (both made from tan cotton), straw-colored shirt, Sam Browne belt, and a soft cap adorned with silver skulls.

"All the Jews here are going to know each other," said Tünscher. "We can't pretend to be one of them. We're also too well fed." He finished his cigarette and flicked the butt away. "Besides, it's going to be a brave Jew who argues with an SS major. Trust me, this is the easiest ticket on board."

Tünscher guided them along the mud to the nearest jetty, Burton following closely. A seaplane, crewed by Italian smugglers, had brought them from DOA earlier that night, landing in a bay several miles south of the Ark. Burton and Tünscher had rowed ashore and picked their way through the tamarind trees; they traveled with no equipment except sidearms. As soon as Burton located Madeleine, he would pick up his kit from the plane and head into the interior alone. Tünscher would wait in Roscherhafen before flying back to collect them—or "cash in my diamonds," as he put it.

The jetty was guarded by Jewish policemen armed with sticks. Tünscher passed them with a stride that dared any objection, one hand resting on his pistol, then along the bobbing walkways to a tower that rose against the middle of the vessel; the stairs creaked as they mounted them. Up close, the *Gustloff* was leprous with rust and yellow streaking. Below, Burton saw sea mines encircling the ship like a string of black pearls.

"I'll do the talking," said Tünscher as they reached the top.

They stepped off the tower into a reception area. It was bare except for a mural showing three rabbits chasing each other's tails, and a table with two bespectacled Jews behind it. They were dressed in shabby uniforms.

Tünscher circumvented the table and yanked at the door to the ship. "Open it," he said when it didn't budge.

"Herr Sturmbannführer," said one of the Jews, rising from the table, "I must respectfully ask for identification and your letter of authorization." He indicated a leather-bound book on the table and steadied his voice. "You will also need to sign the ledger."

"What did you say, Solomon?"

Although Burton was useless at this type of thing, Tünscher relished it. Patrick had once said that he should have joined a theater troupe rather than the Legion.

The Jew spoke to Tünscher's feet. "It's protocol . . ."

"You hear this?" Tünscher said to Burton. "The fucking Yids are giving the orders now." He took off his cap and thrust it into the Jew's hands. "You see that?" Tünscher rapped the death's-head badge. "That's all the authorization you need. Now open the door!"

"Please, Sturmbannführer."

Tünscher took out his Luger, grabbed the Jew by the ear, and dragged him toward the exit. As he passed Burton, he winked.

"Are you with the Oberstgruppenführer?" The second Jew was on his feet.

Burton and Tünscher glanced at each other.

"He was here earlier." The Jew indicated the ledger. "If you're on the same business, I'm sure we can overlook the usual formalities."

"Of course we're with him," said Tünscher, shoving the other Jew away. "Why else would we be in this shit-sink?"

"Then, please . . ." Blinking behind his glasses, the Jew unlocked the door and dipped his head in welcome. Tünscher strode through it.

"We're looking for Section C," said Burton.

"The decks are arranged alphabetically, top to bottom. C is this level, toward the front of the ship."

"And W?"

"Bottom deck. The lights aren't so good down there. You'll find lamps in the stairwells."

Burton ducked into the ship.

For several years, the *Gustloff* ferried between Trieste and Diego Suarez, until 1947, when her hull was ripped open as she approached Madagaskar. It was during the first rebellion, when the United States sent a battleship to the region. The passengers, having seen the Stars and Stripes, believed they were going to be rescued; they mutinied. A court-martial agreed that the captain had no choice other than to scuttle the liner. Hundreds drowned in the aft compartments. The damage was patched up, but when engineers said it would be too costly to restore the ship, the *Gustloff* was towed to Lava Bucht—Lava Bay, an inlet on the northwest of the island—and left to rust, until Heydrich found a new use for her.

As the uprising and its brutal repression continued, America's Jewish population demanded that action be taken, regardless of the country's neutrality. Washington edged toward an ultimatum, insisting that the Jews of Madagaskar must be the guardians of their own records: while the SS controlled the files, Globus could act with impunity. This was to be the cost of nonintervention, and America's conscience. Heydrich convinced the Führer that it was a pittance to pay.

The door slammed with a clang that wanted to reverberate along the walls but was instantly strangled. The air was noxious: the stench of a mausoleum dense with rotting damp and fried meat. It pressed against Burton's throat.

He was in a dim corridor, buckled floorboards beneath his boots, dripping metal rafters above. This was the covered promenade deck where once Germans on vacation would have strolled to the strains of Mozart played over the public address system or dozed in deck chairs before the next round of compulsory activities. Now it was crammed with row upon row of filing cabinets. Hundreds of them, stretching in both directions, with only the narrowest channel between to squeeze through.

Burton flapped the air in front of his mouth. "You could have been easier on the Jews," he said.

"Got us in, didn't I?" Tünscher retorted.

The cabinets consisted of five drawers, the highest as tall as Burton. On each drawer, written in Gothic script (and, below it, in Hebrew) were three letters indicating the names of the files within. Burton read the nearest: CAL.

They headed toward the bow of the ship, past CAL . . . CAM . . . CAN, till the CAs gave way to CEs. Burton felt the pressure of the names around him, the silent cacophony of millions of files. In places the floorboards had caved in, and they had to navigate their way using the iron supporting beams beneath as stepping-stones. Their boots slipped on the girders as they continued past the CHs.

There was a sudden rap of metal.

Burton started; he'd been absorbed in watching the floor for weak timbers. One twisted ankle, and the terrain between the Ark and Madeleine would prove impossible. Tünscher had knocked on one of the cabinets.

"What is it?" asked Burton.

"COL," replied Tünscher, indicating the label. He wasn't good with confined spaces; the claustrophobic gloom had stunted his poise. He grinned, trying to regain some bravado. "Stick here long enough and that's where you'll end up."

Finally they reached CRA. Burton began opening drawers, searching for "Cranley," though he suspected he wouldn't find Madeleine here. Each one was solid with files; the smell of moldering paper burrowed into his nose.

Tünscher wedged himself between two cabinets and lit a cigarette.

"Do you think that's a good idea?" said Burton. "One stray spark . . . "

Tünscher shrugged, inhaled deeply. The glowing tip illuminated his pupils; they were tiny black holes.

Burton frowned. "You're smoking a Bayerweed?" He should have noticed in Roscherhafen.

Tünscher nodded and offered him a puff. When Burton shook his head, he sucked in another lungful.

Bayerweeds were cigarettes laced with heroin, initially prescribed for soldiers with respiratory injuries in the air of Siberia. A trade in them soon spread to every garrison east of the Urals, until Germania outlawed their production. In the months that followed, there was a rapid increase in the number of soldiers suffering nervous breakdowns. The ban was quietly forgotten.

"It's not a concern," said Tünscher, taking a final, deep drag and squashing the butt against a cabinet. "These things keep my head clear. And the stink at bay."

Burton went back to the files, working through them with tense determination. Sweat trickled down the sides of his ears. He took his cap off and screwed it up in his pocket. In the end he found thirty Cranleys, none of them Madeleine. He slammed the drawer shut, the sound echoing away to nothing.

"Now what?" asked Tünscher.

"We head below, look for Weiss."

"Weiss?"

"Madeleine's maiden name. Her Jewish name."

CHAPTER TWENTY-EIGHT

"LOUDER!" SHOUTED GLOBUS as he staggered to the cockpit. "Make us roar!" He was wearing his dress uniform, and in his fist was a bottle of cognac: VSOP, thirty years old, his second of the evening.

The pilot dipped the throttle, the hovercraft skimming across the bay. There were three ships: the troop carrier Globus and his guests were in and two smaller escort craft mounted with machine guns.

As the armies of the Reich had penetrated deeper into Russia, they overran research facilities before the Soviets had a chance to destroy their secrets. Once purged of Communist ideology, this work proved a trove of new weapons. The initial design for the BK44, the Nazis' ubiquitous assault rifle in Africa, had been stolen from an engineer called Kalashnikov. In Gorky, a prototype hovercraft was discovered, perfected, and put into service. Globocnik employed the craft during his time in the East and subsequently added them to his arsenal for Madagaskar: they were ideal for patrolling the mangroves of the west coast.

"Come on, man!" Globus thumped the pilot's shoulder. "Give it more! I want to wake the whole town, let those Yids know what we got."

The display wasn't only for the Jews. He returned to the cabin and slumped into his seat. On the bench opposite, ankles splayed but knees tucked together, were his sister-in-law, Gretta, and Romy, one of his secretaries, both in cherry-red dresses he'd chosen for them, sequins flashing; their eyes were hazy with booze.

Earlier, the three of them had visited the base at Lava Bucht: part of his Führertag tour of the island. He was visiting as many garrisons as possible, except in the Diego region, which was under the Kriegsmarine's authority. He was determined to prove that his control remained ironfisted. Globus always took girls with him on inspections; it was good for the men's morale to see a bit of skirt. They had eaten white sausages and pretzels with the base commander, drunk Riesling and brandy, and sung folk songs before Globus got to his real reason for being there—and suggested an excursion across the water. While Gretta and Romy thrilled at the idea of setting foot on the *Gustloff*, the commander blanched.

"Counting Herr Hochburg, your visit will be the third in the past forty-eight hours," he said. "The Jews will be watching by now; the forest is full of rebels. I can't guarantee your security."

An impatient wave of the hand. "Next you'll remind me that we're not allowed there."

"I wouldn't presume, Obergruppenführer. But no hostage could be more valuable than yourself." He chewed his lip. "You should take an escort—a radio and flare gun, too. Let me put the base on standby."

Globus grinned at the two girls. "You see how my commanders fret about me?"

The hovercraft glided from the water onto the mudflats at the base of the *Gustloff*, the jetty lamps swinging as it settled. Globus helped the girls out, took a swig of cognac, and passed the bottle to them. The air was brackish.

"Once I'm free of this armpit island," he trumpeted, "once I'm governor of Ostmark, the KdF is going to name a ship after me." A boyish delight spread across his face. "The cruise liner *Odilo Globocnik*, biggest in the world!"

He led the group up the tower to the entrance; along with Gretta and Romy, there were six soldiers with BK44s and Hauptsturmführer Pinzel, the liaison officer between Tana, Lava Bucht, and the Ark. He was a blond oak, with spectacles and the starchy manner of the graduates of the Colonial Academy in Vienna. There were increasingly more of his kind in the SS. Globus feared for the future: men whose piss had frozen in fifty degrees of frost had built the empire, but one day the schoolboys would take over. At least Pinzel seemed keen to prove that there was more than diploma in his trousers, even if Globus didn't like the way he kept glancing at Gretta. The Hauptsturmführer had informed him of Hochburg's second—unauthorized—visit to the ship, which was why Globus was here now.

"This is the governor-general," announced Pinzel as they reached the entrance to the ship. He had a glockenspiel voice. "Extend him every courtesy."

There were two filthy Jews at a desk; Globus saw them exchange terrified, conspiratorial glances. He planted the bottle of cognac on the table and flicked through the ledger to the final entry. The handwriting was as neat and small as typewriter print: Walter E. Hochburg.

"What did he want?" asked Globus.

The Jews were sticky-throated. "To . . . to see a file, Obergruppenführer," replied one when he found the courage to speak.

He belted the man who'd answered. "Do you think I'm stupid? Of course to see a file! Which one?"

"We're only night guards . . . you need Ratzyck. He's one of our archivists . . . showed the Oberstgruppenführer round the ship."

"Bring him to me."

"His daughter is expecting tonight . . . he's in Analava."

Pinzel yanked the Jew to his feet. "That is not the governor's concern. Fetch him."

As he scurried out, Globus kicked his arse. "Run, Jew!" he called after him. His voice rolled across the stinking town. "I want to be back in Tana by dawn." If she wasn't too weary, he planned to show Romy his trophy room. It was in the bowels of the palace; no one would hear them there.

He had a dozen secretaries to deal with the paltry amounts of paperwork his office generated. All were perfect blond specimens, employed on a six-month basis, none older than twenty-four. Being able to say that they had worked personally for Governor Globocnik promised them the pick of jobs when they returned to Europe, or so he assured them. Each girl was flattered, taken on tours round the island, her tears dabbed when she was homesick or complained about the others' bitching—but he never touched them until the end of their stint. He'd learned that from experience. Instead he waited till they had only two weeks left on the island; before he was bored of them or they could whinge about being used, the girls were already on a plane home. Romy's flight to Germania left on May Day.

They waited for Ratzyck, Globus pacing up and down, humming "Anything Goes" to himself. He poured more brandy down his throat, offered it to the girls, who dutifully swallowed. He could see they were growing bored.

"How much longer is your Rat going to be?" he demanded of the remaining Jew, pleased to hear the girls titter.

"He's an old man, Obergruppenführer. Can't move fast."

"Are you sure? Your friend, the one I kicked, wouldn't be spreading word I'm here?"

"No—"

"Because anything stupid and I'll burn your Yid town to the ground. Send you to the reservations. I don't give a shit." That wasn't entirely true, but the Jews didn't need to know.

Although Himmler was adamant that all disobedience be crushed, Heydrich—still overlord of their project in Madagaskar—advised restraint. He appreciated how testing the situation could be, but brute force only antagonized the Americans, and they should be wary of Taft, the new president; he was soft on Jewry. There were other methods, advised Heydrich, subtler methods, to deal with the island's inhabitants.

Globocnik stalked to the door and looked out across the jetties to Analava. The town was in darkness, a thin, mustardy veil hanging over the roofs. Dashing from the town were two figures: the Jew Pinzel had sent and an old man struggling to keep up. Globus twisted his two wedding rings and waited.

"Tell me what Hochburg was looking for," he said when Ratzyck finally reached him. The Jew was bent double, fighting for breath. He wore pajamas with a waistcoat thrown over the top; his feet were bare.

"I don't know . . . what you mean . . . Obergruppenführer," he panted.

Globus sighed: the patience he needed with these people. He picked up the ledger, opened it wide, and thrust it into Ratzyck's face.

"He's been here twice." He indicated Hochburg's prissy writing. "You helped him."

"You're mistaken."

Globus slammed the covers shut, trapping the Jew's head. "What did he want?"

There was a muffled squawk like a bird being crushed. Romy tittered again, her laughter nervous. Globus pressed harder.

"He told me not to say a word . . . My daughter had a child tonight, he promised to help us."

"Just as I promise to hang them if you don't tell me. We can start with a string for the newborn. Now, what did he want?"

"First time he was looking for a name."

"And the second?"

"He brought bars of soap and chocolate. We went all over the ship; he took at least twenty files."

Globus mulled this over before turning his attention to Gretta and Romy. "Want to poke around, girls?"

They nodded, a look of illicit adventure in their eyes; Globus was a connoisseur of that look. He released the Jew, positioned two sentries to watch Analava, then ordered the door unbolted. The hinges groaned. Once they were inside, Pinzel went to close the hatch.

"Keep it open," said Globus, irritated to find himself unsettled by the interior. It had to be the brandy, he thought; even the best stuff affected his mood.

"This way," said Ratzyck, leading them toward the rear of the ship. He was too shaken to walk alone, and his nose dribbled blood. The Jew who had fetched him stayed at his side.

The open door sucked gusts of wind through the holes in the deck. They shrieked and boomed, reminding Globus of raids in Siberia when they ran out of ammunition and buried villagers alive. Those ghoulish thumping sounds that rose from the ground. He still heard them in his nightmares. Luckily the girls hadn't noticed his mood. They huddled close to him; Romy covered her mouth and nose.

"Disgusting, isn't it?" boomed Globus. He needed the reassurance of his own voice. "What could Hochburg want in a shithole like this?" He spoke to Ratzyck: "I bet he got spooked, couldn't wait to leave."

"He showed a lot of interest in our work. Was very polite."

Globus shook his head in despair. To him, Hochburg was an *Ausländer:* a foreigner, born in Kamerun. A nigger in all but skin. In the 1930s, when Globus had been battling in the streets of Vienna, Hochburg lived the soft life, troubled by nothing more than insect bites and the sun. Hochburg had no right to be here, meddling with his island—Africa had always been separate from Madagaskar—but Globus was reluctant to protest about it back home, in case it made him look weak.

The group picked their way through the maze of cabinets to a set of double doors that led into a black space.

"This is where I took Herr Hochburg first," said Ratzyck.

From the echoes Globus guessed they were in a large, vaulted room, the air circulating more freely. The Jew supporting Ratzyck flicked a switch from a bank: a single, feeble lamp came to life. Walls covered in mosaics glimmered in the shadows.

"I can't see a fucking thing." Globus kept his voice boisterous. "Turn on the rest."

The Jew hesitated. "With respect, Obergruppenführer. The wiring can't cope. It might blow the fuses on the other decks."

"It's true," said Pinzel and offered his flashlight.

Globus swung it around the room, catching the faces of gods and nymphs before it came to rest on Romy's patent-leather heels. He had a vast collection of women's shoes in the basement of his palace—shoes, jewelry, dresses—doled out as gifts for his favorites.

He killed the beam. "If I want light, I get light."

"But the two Sturmbannführers," said the Jew. "They asked about W section; if they went below—"

Globus scowled. "What Sturmbannführers?"

"They arrived before you did. Said they were with Herr Hochburg."

He rounded on Pinzel. "You allowed this?"

"No."

"What is Hochburg's game? It's a conspiracy."

He pushed the Jew out of the way and flicked all the switches. Dirty light swamped the room. Globus handed Pinzel's flashlight to him. "Find these two Sturmbannführers," he said. "Bring them to me. If Hochburg won't talk, they will."

CHAPTER TWENTY-NINE

THE BLACKNESS WAS instant, subterranean.

"That'll help," said Tünscher.

Burton searched in his pocket for his lighter. There was the strike of a match, and Tünscher's face appeared; he lit another Bayer.

When they had first reached the bottom deck of the *Gustloff*, Burton thought there was a mistake: there were no filing cabinets, only an empty passageway lined with doors, and the feeble pulse of wall lamps. Every patch of shadow clicked and scratched with unseen creatures. The air was more fetid. He had eased the nearest door ajar. Inside, the cabin had been gutted: furniture looted, every fixture ripped out, a clump of wires dangling from the ceiling. Around the edge of the room were the filing cabinets, one shifted forward from the rest to allow a murky light through the porthole. They passed by several cabins, reaching one whose files began with WEB before the lights in the corridor flared and died.

"I saw some lamps in the stairwell," said Burton. "I'll get them. You keep checking the names."

He had just found the lanterns when he heard someone coming down the stairs. One of the Jews checking on them? No, those were boots ringing out on metal, descending rapidly, a cyan beam scything the darkness. Burton touched his lighter against the lantern, its meager reservoir of kerosene catching as the steps halted on the landing above him. He raised the lamp and in its glow saw a hulking figure in a uniform identical to his.

"Who are you?" he asked.

"Pinzel." In his grip he held a powerful flashlight; he pointed the beam at the four pips on Burton's collar. "And you, Sturmbannführer?" His voice was fluty, conceited.

"I'm checking some records."

"Whatever your rank, entry to this ship is strictly limited and only through the authorized channels. Namely, me."

"This is unofficial business."

"Meaning?" When Burton made no reply, Pinzel let out an irritated *pfft*. "I am here with Governor Globocnik. He wants to talk to you."

"Give me ten minutes."

"Now! Or I get my men, Sturmbannführer, and bring you to the governor at gunpoint. Except that won't look good in front of the Jews."

There was only one response.

Burton hurled the lamp at him and freed his Beretta. Before he could pull the trigger, Pinzel aimed the flashlight at his face. A dazzling corona burned the back of Burton's eyes. He fired blind.

There was a clanging as Pinzel fled up the stairs. Burton stumbled after him and fired again, the new weapon unwieldy in his hand. The bullet sparked off the handrail, but the Nazi was out of range. Burton didn't waste another shot. He grabbed two more lanterns, lit the first, and hurried to the corridor. Tünscher was running to meet him. "I heard gunfire," he said.

Burton handed him the unlit lamp. "We haven't much time."

"Jews?"

"Your fellow countrymen."

"How many?"

"I don't know. You carrying anything more than your Luger?"

Tünscher reached into his trouser pockets and fished a grenade from each. He moved them up and down as if he were about to juggle. "They sort of balance me up."

Burton marched away from the stairs. "We'll be quicker if we take different sides of the corridor."

"No need," replied Tünscher, putting a match to his lamp.

"You found her?"

"Best see for yourself."

They jogged into the darkness, Tünscher in the lead, the sway of his lamp stretching and shrinking the shadows with each footfall. An excited tension fizzed through Burton. After all the months and journeys across Africa and oceans, he sensed how close Maddie was, almost as if he were chasing the scent of her round the farmhouse. He must be passing cabinets that held her family's names. Had she sought them out? He hoped someone had protected her and the baby, but he feared the consequences; he had no means to get them all off the island. What if she refused to leave without them?

Tünscher stopped outside a cabin. "The records for Madeleine Weiss are here."

Burton reached for the handle—but Tünscher held out a restraining arm. He swung the lantern farther down the corridor.

"Also here . . . here . . . and here. I stopped checking after that."

Burton's voice flattened. "There must be thousands."

"Tens of thousands. You should've found a girlfriend with a less common name."

+ + +

Romy was gawping at the mosaics: fish, nymphs riding dolphins, a watery underworld. They were covered in cracks, many of the tiles loose. In the center of one was a bearded man with a stallion's physique, holding a trident. "Who is it?" she asked.

"Neptune," replied Gretta. "God of the sea."

Unlike her sister, Gretta had studied at university, something Globus disapproved of. He'd agonized over schemes to bed her but was aware that the Reichsführer frowned upon such couplings—"frankly incestuous" he declared them—and things were difficult enough with Germania as it was. Before Hochburg had stolen a brigade of his men and let loose the Jews, his governorship of Ostmark, land of his birth, had seemed assured; it would crown his career. Now his calls with Himmler were growing cooler by the week and ended with the same warning: *My dear Globus, I've dragged you from the mire twice before, but even I won't be able to resurrect you a third time, especially if you're bested by Jews.*

"Girls, away from the wall," he said irritably. "It might not be safe." He motioned at the soldiers to move them.

Below the Neptune mosaic was an empty swimming pool; ten by four meters, thought Globus, smaller than the one at his palace. On either side were fluted pillars, completing the Roman-bath look. Although he admired classical design for the great buildings of Germania, he found the obsession with it elsewhere vulgar. He preferred the harsh lines of modern architecture—a preference the Führer constantly rebuked him for. The pool had been drained and was chock-full of filing cabinets.

"Hochburg went down there?" he asked Ratzyck.

"Yes."

"You were with him?"

"I was sent outside."

"But you saw which cabinet?"

The Jew pointed to one in the far corner. Globus put his hand on the stepladder to climb down, then wavered: Himmler's voice was in his head again.

Be careful of Walter, he had once cautioned. *He's one of our best but cunning as a crocodile. And much more dangerous.*

Globus stepped away from the pool. "Get down there!" he bellowed at Ratzyck.

The Jew climbed down the steps and threaded his way through the cabinets.

"Odilo." Gretta was by one of the portholes. "Something's happening in the Jew town."

Too much to drink, thought Globus and ignored her. He watched Ratzyck's progress as he reached the cabinet in the corner. "This is the one Hochburg wanted? You're sure?"

"Yes, Obergruppenführer."

"What does it say?"

"FEU."

"Open the top drawer. I'm looking forward to this secret."

Ratzyck did as commanded and removed a sheaf of papers. He flicked through them. "They're all Feuersteins."

"Feuerstein?" Globus scratched his balls. "Who's he?"

"Odilo!" called Gretta again, her voice quavering. Romy had joined her; they were both staring out of the porthole.

"Not now. Try the next drawer," he ordered the Jew in the pool. "Hochburg must have left some clue."

Ratzyck returned the wad of files, closed the drawer, and reached for the one below. It didn't budge.

"Pull harder," said Globus. "Unless you want me to come down there."

The Jew tried again. The runners were stiff; he gave the drawer a hard yank—and it sprang open. Globus heard a metal click, like the fastener on his gold watch.

There was a blinding flash.

+ + +

Burton's jaw ached, his chin burned. The lantern hadn't cast enough light when placed on top of the cabinet; the only way for him to flick through the files one-handed and read was to grip the lamp's handle between his teeth.

A sense of impossibility, of finding one name among so many, was rising in him; the panic of being trapped in a well as it flooded.

With it came a tiny doubt: that he was risking all this when the baby might be Cranley's. He strangled the thought.

Each drawer was choked with filthy, mottled files, each sheet covered in grids of names, places, figures. The bureaucrat's vision of the world. *Country of origin, hometown, last tenancy address. Names & origins of grandparents, parents, date of birth, sex, occupation, congenital/communicable diseases. Internment camp (Europe), exit port & vessel, date of arrival in Madagaskar, registered assets in reichsmarks. Forwarding location: sector, town, street.* All stamped with a swastika and eagle. These were the records that traveled with Jews to their new life below the equator. Many had handwritten notes at the bottom with new addresses dated after the first rebellion.

Madeleine Weiss.

Madeleine Weiss.

Madeleine Weiss.

Over and over till the name held no meaning. None was Maddie.

Burton finished the top two drawers of the first cabinet, unable to contain the thought that many of these Madeleines must be dead. The whole time, he'd been listening for the stairwell door to open. He freed the lantern from his mouth, resting his jaw, and called to Tünscher in the next cabin. "Any luck?"

"This will take forever."

Burton opened the next drawer—and saw it at once. He snatched out the file: Madeleine Weiss, aged forty-six from Lyon, deported October 1951. This was how they'd find her! He hurried to the next cabin.

"Still nothing," said Tünscher petulantly.

Burton handed him the file. "Look."

"It's not her."

"I know that. The paper." It was crisp, the color of ivory.

"So?"

"Most of the files go back years, to the original deportation." He indicated the drawer Tünscher was propped against and its moldering records. "Maddie arrived six months ago, so her documentation has to be new. We only pull the clean ones."

+ + +

The swimming pool writhed with flames.

Gobbets of blazing debris had been blasted from the cabinet and were spreading. Files spiraled and danced in the smoke. There were fire buckets around the walls; the Jew who'd fetched Ratzyck grabbed them, pouring sand onto the inferno.

Globus stood unsteadily, his nostrils clogged with the stench of incinerated paper, and moved to the two girls. Romy was quaking, her face streaked black; the front of Gretta's dress had been shredded, revealing the lace of her brassiere. Globus slipped off his jacket and put it around her shoulders. Then he jostled them along the promenade deck, surrounded by soldiers, toward the exit. Yellowish-brown smoke floated above their heads.

"Twenty minutes from now," he boomed, "we'll be back in Lava Bucht. I'll get the commander to open a fresh bottle, and we can watch this ship burn. Fireworks for Führertag!"

The sentries were waiting for them by the door, alarm on their faces. "Obergruppenführer, you mustn't leave the ship—"

Globus pushed past them, reaching the stairs that led to the shore below, and froze. His bladder felt bloated. The momentary fright was chased away by a clot of rage that throbbed inside the muscle of his jaw. He twisted his two wedding rings, baffled as to why he'd ever listened to Heydrich and his talk of moderation. The man might be his boss but was eighty-five hundred kilometers away, far from the stench and threat of the Jew, immune to the realities of this island.

Where they had left the hovercraft, the mud was empty; the machines were now circling the bay. At the base of the *Gustloff,* filling the jetties, lining the shore, were hundreds of Jews, with more emerging from the mangroves. They bore clubs and sticks, and some unrolled hose pipes. These weren't Jupo; these were the gnashing teeth of the rebellion.

Romy began to cry. He wrapped his arms around her; she was chubbier than he'd imagined, her flesh springy. "No need for that—you're safe with me." He was aware of a prickling in his crotch and did nothing to disguise it. "These bandits wouldn't dare touch us."

The Jews had spied him. They began chanting, the first of them creeping up the stairs.

"Torch the tower," Globus ordered the sentries. He held out his hand. "Who has the radio?"

No one answered till Gretta piped up: "You said not to bother with it."

"I never."

"You should have taken the commander's advice. Not brought us here."

Only Romy's sobs stopped him from letting his sister-in-law feel the back of his hand.

The nearest lad proffered a flare gun and a pack of cartridges. Globus snatched them from him. "The bridge," he said, and they were moving again, wading between the filing cabinets. As they approached the aft staircase, Pinzel emerged through the smoke. Globus didn't slow.

"I found one of the Sturmbannführers," said Pinzel, keeping pace. "The bastard tried to shoot me."

"Take three men, go back down there, and fetch him by the balls. Don't take any shit this time. The Jews are running riot; I have to protect the girls."

"What about the Ark? If it goes up, there'll be hell with the Americans."

"Hochburg is to blame for this disaster. If he won't answer for it, his deputies below will."

Globus reached the bridge, harried Romy and Gretta inside. There was a spiral staircase that led to the viewing platform above, with banks of levers and dozing lights. By the wheel stood a lone, myopic Jew.

"Where are the others?" demanded Globus. It would take several of them to man the bridge.

The Jew peered at him, blinking, before his face melted in fear. He doffed his cap. "Gone to fight the fire, mein Herr. To save the records . . ."

Through the windows Globus saw a filthy mass swarming up the tower. Others were using grappling hooks to climb the side of the ship. "Power up the engines," he instructed the Jew.

When he got a blathering, incomprehensible reply, Globus slapped the man so hard his cap was thrown across the room. The Jew picked himself up and began working the levers.

+ + +

Each cabinet held only a few fresh records, some none at all; it took only minutes to collect them. Burton knelt and fanned the sheets across the floor. All of the files had mug shots in the top left-hand corner. In 1940, Heydrich had become the head of Interpol. After Europe was declared *Judenfrei*, the organization's primary function was the apprehension of Jews who had escaped the net. Viewed as a particularly pernicious threat, these illegals were indexed and photographed before being sent south. Many died during their arrest.

Burton checked the first few photos and gave up. They were identical: dark-haired, bluntly lit women hunched before the camera with the same cowed stare. He might look at Madeleine and not recognize her.

"I hear boots," said Tünscher. He was by the door, eyes blank, an unlit cigarette in his mouth.

Madeleine had been born ten months before Burton, in December 1915.

He sifted through the files, focusing on the year of birth. His fingers trembled.

1927
1895
1918
1920
1903
1922—

"Sturmbannführer!" Pinzel's voice rolled down the corridor. "I know you're here—I smell the Bayerweed. Enough games. The governor wants to talk to you, that's all."

Burton snuffed out the lamp and continued by the light coming through the porthole.

"Four of them," whispered Tünscher, peeking through the door. "All with BKs. You're paying me a smuggler's wage, not a soldier's."

Burton didn't look up. "Then hand yourself in. Tell them you're Section IX, or whatever you are."

"I'd rather take my chances with you than Globus."

Burton turned the last file: in his rush, he had missed her. He calmed himself, started again from the top, slowly, methodically, licking his finger to separate each sheet, calling the years out loud.

"Sturmbannführer! The Jews are taking control of the Ark—"

". . . 1922 . . . 1937 . . . 1910 . . ."

"—for your own sake, time to hand yourself in."

Burton reached the end again, his heart guttering. "She's not here," he said to Tünscher. He felt clouded, bewildered. "She's not here."

CHAPTER THIRTY

TÜNSCHER'S VOICE WAS terse. "We have to go," he said. "Now!"

"We must have missed the file. *You* must have missed it."

"I went through every cabinet."

"The Bayers have made your head fuzzy. We need to start again. Be more careful."

Burton opened the nearest drawer, rifled through the files, then lifted them out in great wads, throwing them into the air. Papers fluttered around him like the wings of bats.

From the far end of the corridor came the banging of doors as Pinzel and his men searched the cabins.

"Her record might not have been transferred here," hissed Tünscher. "Or maybe it was misfiled."

"Go if you want. I'm staying."

"Not without my diamonds."

Burton felt an angry urge to tell him the truth.

The cabin lurched. A grinding screech reverberated through the walls as if the hull were scraping rocks.

Burton fought to keep his balance. "The ship's moving."

"Impossible."

"Sturmbannführer! I told you the Jews were on the loose. Surrender yourself and we can all get out safely." Pinzel was no more than four or five cabins away.

"Thirty seconds from now you'll be chewing a BK," said Tünscher. "Then it really will be over for Madeleine."

"If I leave, I'll never know where she is."

"We'll find another way." Tünscher's face was lit from the porthole: a pale-blue oval, his eyes agitated, sincere.

Another cabin door banged.

Burton clutched the records to his chest. Could Alice have gotten it wrong? Could Cranley and his housekeeper have made sure she overheard a lie? Concocted a plan to send him to Madagaskar, as far as possible from wherever Madeleine really was? Burton let the files spill to the floor and reached for his Beretta. Tünscher was holding a grenade. He blew on it as if it were a lucky die, pulled the pin—and bowled it through the door.

+ + +

Ever since he was a boy Globocnik had wanted to do this; it was like whisking the cloth out from underneath a table set for dinner. That was one of the Führer's tricks at the Berghof—though only he was permitted to do it. Globus grabbed the *Gustloff*'s wheel and spun it round completely, spun it till it locked and the horizon began to shift. The tremor of the engines shook the floor.

He positioned a soldier by the door and guided Gretta and Romy up the spiral staircase; they needed no encouragement. He left another guard on the top step.

"You see," he told the girls when they were on the viewing platform, "big enough for a helicopter." Romy was shaking, her cheeks teary with mascara. Perhaps he didn't want to fuck her after all.

Smoke billowed from the rear of the ship. Across the water, the base was coming to full alert. Globus heard alarms ringing and saw crews sprinting toward their Walküres. The Jews continued to scale the sides of the ship, but they were irrelevant now. Let them and their records burn. The first helicopter lifted into the sky.

He inhaled deeply, the tang of the Ostafrikanischer Ozean blowing across the bay, and experienced a rare sense of satisfaction. All his life his father had been a source of humiliation to him. Even his name, Globocnik, had an embarrassing Slavic sound; Globus had considered changing his. But at that moment he wished they were standing side by side so he could show the old man the world he commanded. Globus reached to the heavens and fired three flares in rapid succession. The whole bay was bathed in a bloodred light.

The *Gustloff* strained at her anchor, drifting toward the chain of sea mines that surrounded the hull.

+ + +

A barrage of BK44 fire. Burton dived to the ground, Tünscher with him, and they crawled to the nearest cabin door, hunkering for cover as bullets flashed off the walls. There was a violent jolt, and the ship lurched beneath them again.

Tünscher counted down the rounds to silence. "Reloading," he said, getting to his feet.

They both sprinted through the swampy darkness, lit by gobs of fire from the grenade. At the far end of the corridor was the stairwell for the rear of the ship, if they could reach it—

The thunderclap was so loud Burton felt it as a physical pressure; his ears popped with a deafening whine.

The blast tore through the corridor, chased by a gust of invisible fire. Burton was whipped off his feet, his chin cracking the floorboards as he landed. He had the vertiginous sensation of the corridor shifting and rolling. Darkness pressed against his eyes, deeper than the gloom of the ship, a velvety warmth flooding through him . . .

Next moment: high-pitched squeaking, scurrying. Tiny claws pressed against his eyelids.

Burton sat up—a giddy rush—and tore the rat from his face. There were hundreds swarming around him and Tünscher, fleeing a tongue of water. He stood; within seconds his boots were submerged.

"We can't sink," coughed Tünscher. A layer of smoke rolled along the ceiling. "The bay's not deep enough."

"What did Patrick teach us? You can drown in an inch of water, even in the desert."

The corridor was at an angle, the sound of buckling steel echoed along its length. They splashed toward the stairwell, the water bubbling around their shins like a foul-smelling spring. Soon it was at their knees, then their thighs. Burton reached the door and tried to push it open—it didn't budge.

Tünscher shoved him out of the way. "You can't do it one-handed." He heaved against the metal, heaved again, his mouth contorting with the effort. When it refused to give he knelt, water up to his chest, and examined the lock.

"Forget it," said Burton. "The rats had the best idea." He waded away from the stairwell.

An electrical cable had been wrenched from the wall and was sparking violently. With each flash, Burton saw the silhouettes of three figures submerged to the waist.

"Governor Globus wants you alive," said Pinzel, waving his gun. "I could say you drowned."

Suddenly, Tünscher grabbed the scruff of Burton's neck and propelled him toward the Nazis. Burton twisted to fight him off and saw the stairwell door. It was bulging outward, jets of foam tracing its outline. A rivet fired from the bulkhead, lethal as a bullet. It struck one of Pinzel's men in the chest.

The door burst open.

Burton tumbled backward, wheeling in a surge of bubbles, his nose flooding. He felt weightless, as if he would fall forever—like he had in Germania.

Madeleine pushed him back onto the bed. The buttons of her dress were torn open, underwear discarded on the floor. She looked drunk. He remembered the colors of the hotel room vividly—the deep-burgundy furnishings—and, through the window, the virescent copper dome of the Great Hall looming above the city. He landed, bouncing on the mattress, the sensation protracted, as if it would never end. Madeleine mounted him, pinning his wrists down, her mouth so close he tasted the cherry, pistachio, and milk of ice cream on her breath.

"Make me one last promise," she said. Earlier that afternoon they had pledged their futures to each other.

"Anything."

"We'll live together, grow old together, but we won't marry."

Marriage: an undesired country. He'd never imagined exchanging vows with Madeleine, yet her words brought back some of the old vulnerabilities. She had consented to Cranley—why not him?

"But—"

She pressed a finger against his lips, showed him the indent where her wedding band went; she always took it off when they were together. The skin was hard and shrunken.

"I never want to wear another ring."

The current slackened. Burton staggered to his feet and fought his way through the foam. Tünscher was at the stairwell, his hand reaching for him. They ducked through the punctured door frame and Burton craned his neck: there was a square of fiery light at the top, water cascading on all sides.

Tünscher took the lead, mounting the stairs two at a time. "Right to the top," he yelled. "We can get out that way."

The ship continued to twist and strain around them—with the sound of metal being eviscerated—pitching the staircase to the left. Burton followed, using his one hand to steady himself. His boots slipped on the metal steps.

"Sturmbannführer!"

Pinzel was below, in the frothing water. He raised his BK44 as Burton pressed himself against the wall. Without slowing, Tünscher lobbed his final grenade over the side.

A spout of smoke and spray.

The stairwell continued to rotate. Burton felt like he was climbing through the inside of a tree trunk as it was felled. Soon they were half-clambering, half-crawling. A sign marked A–C told them they were on the deck where they had entered the ship.

"Two more," said Tünscher, wheezing.

Burton could already feel gusts of fresh air when he stopped. A thought had taken hold of him: illogical, unlikely—but a possibility. How could he have not considered it before?

"I'm going back," he shouted at Tünscher, sliding down the way they'd come.

"You got to be kidding me."

Burton ignored him, returned to the deck below, through double doors and onto the promenade deck. It was clogged with smoke and a burning-autumn-leaves stench. Most of the filing cabinets had toppled over, like dominoes. He scrambled across them, chased by Tünscher's calls. The door they had originally entered the ship from was bolted shut, fists pounding on it. Burton kept going till he reached the cabinets marked COL. He started righting them. "I need your help," he said when Tünscher arrived.

"Look outside!"

The liner had broken away from its mooring and shifted in the bay. Through the cracked portholes, the SS base on the opposite shore was visible; a Walküre gunship was taking to the sky, and the bay was dotted with hovercrafts.

"You want your diamonds, help me."

They righted the cabinet together. Burton yanked opened the drawers, scanned the wad of brown documents. Nothing. They lifted the next cabinet. Dead center in the second drawer was a line of clean paper. A nauseous energy surged in him; he plucked out the file.

Tünscher read over his shoulder: " 'Madeleine Rachel Cole.' "

"Born December 1915," breathed Burton. He glanced at her photo: her eyes were widow blank, like his father's after Mother vanished.

Tünscher pried the paper from his grip. "It says she's in the Western Sector, Antzu. That's fifty clicks from here. You could be there, back, and away in two days—*if* we get out now."

Burton took the sheet from him and hid it inside his tunic. They clambered over the remaining cabinets, headed toward the bow of the ship. The smoke was thinning. Burton's head was full of gold, full of everything that Madeleine was: her kindness and vitality and occasional seriousness; how when she wore blue it lit up her eyes; her minxy shyness when the bedroom door closed. The sense of belonging she gave him. He stifled the urge to laugh and charged through the exit that led to the main deck.

On the horizon, the first shreds of dawn peeked between bulwarks of rain clouds. A helicopter, lights blinking, swooped over the bay. As it neared the Ark, its rotors beat the wind in Burton's direction, choking him with the smell of bodies that hadn't known soap in years. Acrid sweat and oily hair, clothes washed in muddy streams. An inhuman scent, feral and furious.

It was seventy feet to the edge of the ship. The deck in between was crowded with Jews in black waistcoats.

Burton retreated a step and bumped into Tünscher.

"They're behind us, too," he whispered.

The Jews glared at their uniforms. They crept closer till the nearest man was an arm's length away. Burton kept his expression blank, made no eye contact.

A hand reached out for the collar of his jacket, tore off the skull-and-palm-tree lapel, and held it aloft for all to see before crumpling it. Then other hands were on him: grabbing, slapping, punching. Burton was dragged down into a scrum of fists and bare muddy feet.

CHAPTER THIRTY-ONE

THERE WERE EIGHTY different types of lemurs on Madagaskar. Globus's ambition was to make a trophy of every one.

Once he had been hunting the sifaka species through the desiccated forests of Steinbock. He'd glimpsed a flash of white fur, fired his rifle, heard the animal thud to the ground. His beaters—Malagasy who knew the terrain well—had searched for the body in vain. Then came cries of horror. Globus followed their voices and found his lemur. His shot had not killed it; the creature lay panting, mewling. And surrounding it was an army of ants, each the size of his thumb. They swarmed over the wounded animal till its fur teemed and vanished, then dragged it away to their nest.

Watching the two Sturmbannführers, Globus recalled that lemur. The soldier next to him aimed his BK44 below. Globus pushed the muzzle away. "Let's see what happens."

"Odilo!" shouted Gretta over the clatter of the approaching helicopter. "Do something!"

"Why? It serves them right." The *Gustloff* continued to burn. "The Americans are going to crucify me for tonight. Which means more grief back home."

"But you can't let Jews kill them."

She had a particular way of saying *Juden*—vicious and submissive—that excited him. He took his sister-in-law's hand, kissed it, his lips lingering on her knuckles. "Especially for you then, Gretta." Globus snatched the BK44 from the soldier and raked the deck below. The vermin scattered.

Gretta covered her ears. "Are they safe?"

Globus fired again till the magazine was empty.

The helicopter came in low to land. It was a troop carrier, the ferocity of its downdraft beating away the last of the Jews. Globus watched the Sturmbannführers struggle to their feet and make for the railings along the ship's bow. He put one arm around Gretta, while the other reached for Romy, and escorted them onto the waiting aircraft. The soldiers who had been guarding the bridge joined them.

"What about Hauptsturmführer Pinzel?"

"The Jews will have him by now." It was a pity, thought Globus, but for the Ark liaison officer to have gone missing might have its advantages; he'd also been the last one to see Hochburg.

Hochburg! What could this rotting hulk offer that he had visited twice? Who was Feuerstein? For someone of Hochburg's rank to show such interest in a Jew was indecent. An unexpected idea seized Globus. Hochburg had always been one of Himmler's favorites; perhaps he'd been sent by the Reichsführer to prod him into action and solve the current crisis. The calling card Hochburg had left in the cabinet was gutting the ship, something Globus had never dared risk. Perhaps Himmler was at last heeding what he'd protested ever since Heydrich signed the Ark away: whoever controls the records controls the population.

Perhaps, perhaps: he was too exhausted to think. All he knew was that the throne of Ostmark was less certain with each new Jewish outrage. He made sure the girls were fastened in—they were shaking with laughter and gratitude now—and took the copilot's seat. The helicopter lifted into the air.

Globocnik sagged, the adrenaline leaving him as fast as if he were pissing it out. Below he caught a glimpse of the two Sturmbannführers; they had leapt off the ship and were swimming toward a waiting hovercraft.

"Make sure those two clowns are picked up," he said into his headset. "They've got a lot of explaining. And send word to Tana: I want to know where Hochburg is."

+ + +

Burton's stump beat sluggishly against the waves, his boots tugging him down; Tünscher had reached the nearest hovercraft. It slowed, chasing its tail to keep afloat. Tünscher clambered on board and hurled the pilot out. The rear gunner stood to protest, but already Tünscher was aiming his Luger. For an instant the cockpit filled with light.

The *Gustloff* was listing as if it might topple over. Great orange whorls billowed from its portholes. On the shore, Jews watched and wept.

"You know how to pilot one of these things?" Burton asked as he heaved himself out of the water.

"I used to race them in the East, in the spring as the Tobol began to thaw. Fifty reichsmarks a go."

"You win much?"

"As much as I lost. Strap yourself in the back."

The gunner's seat was positioned behind the pilot's in a raised Perspex dome mounted with an MG48 machine gun, its lateral range limited to 135 degrees to avoid the rear fan. Burton slipped into the chair, ignoring the dead body at his feet.

Tünscher pressed the accelerator. The hovercraft surged toward the mouth of the bay and the indigo-black ocean beyond. Burton felt the thunder of the fan through his shoulders.

"Where are you going?" he shouted.

"To the plane, before those chickenshit Italians leave."

"What about Antzu?" He recalled the map Tünscher had given him: Lava Bucht lay at the inlet of the river that led to the town. "We could be there in an hour."

"That was never the plan."

"Things have changed."

"Not for me," replied Tünscher. "I got more than I bargained for on this trip already."

Two other hovercrafts were gliding in wide circles around the bay. A Walküre roared overhead. It rose over the *Gustloff*, heading toward the mangroves that bordered the shore. In this chaos, thought Burton, they could take the hovercraft down the river before anyone noticed. That had to be better than returning to the seaplane, then trudging alone through the forest; after tonight, it would be crawling with patrols.

"Turn us around," he said. "We're going to Antzu."

Tünscher pressed harder on the throttle, guiding them away from the Ark and the SS base. One of the other hovercrafts tailed them.

"Turn us around!" Burton pressed the Beretta against his friend's head.

Tünscher spat out a laugh. "You're going to shoot me?"

"All I want is Maddie."

"I said I wouldn't go inland—that was our deal. I got debts to pay; I can't do that if I'm dead."

"Your debts die with you."

"Not this one."

Burton cocked the pistol close to Tünscher's ear.

"Those lousy wops won't hang around for long," he said in response. "Not with this going off. If I don't get back to that plane, Burton, they'll fly. And if they go without me, they'll never come back. You and Madeleine will have no way to escape this island."

Tünscher steered them to the port side, out of the bay and into the open sea. At once the waves started bucking the hovercraft. Spray obscured the windows.

"I'm warning you, Tünsch."

Tünscher shrugged off the Beretta and searched for the wiper controls.

Even over the blare of the fan, the shot was deafening; it punched a hole in the windscreen. Burton returned the smoking muzzle to Tünscher's skull.

The wipers came to life. Tünscher eased off the throttle.

"You idiot," he said. "It's too late."

The seaplane that had brought them from DOA was skimming the waves, its four propellers a blur. It was flying dark, all lights extinguished. In the gunmetal of the dawn, Burton could make out the two pilots in the cockpit gabbling at each other. It took to the air, its undercarriage trailing water.

The plane vanished.

A balloon of fire whooshed into the sky, spitting debris.

The Beretta sagged in Burton's grip. He watched the Walküre fire another rocket at the plane, then leaned toward Tünscher, his voice dreary and caustic: "So much for your Madagaskar plan."

PART III

MADAGASKAR

All attempts to create a sovereign
Jewish nation must be eliminated.
At the same time it is necessary to
prevent any objections to this,
especially those coming
from the USA.

—"MADAGASKAR-PROJEKT,"
15 August 1940

CHAPTER THIRTY-TWO

Tana airport
20 April, 06:15

WALTER HOCHBURG WAS sketching a new Schädelplatz, hoping to ward off the despondency that had crept hold of him. It was the despondency that always accompanied success.

He sat in the cabin of his private jet, eager to leave before the explosive device he had planted aboard the Ark was discovered. The plane was a converted Junkers Ju-387 bomber: white leather seats, air as cool and dry as aerosol vapor. Through the window, the wings shimmered steel blue and gold as the sun sneaked over the hills of Tana; a ground crew busied themselves with fuel hoses. The Jewish scientists he'd spent the last forty hours scouring the island for were being loaded into the hold. All he needed now to possess his superweapon was patience, and yet with his hunt on Madagaskar at an end, the loss he'd spent a lifetime trying to dampen felt present again. Each triumph only made him yearn for the next distraction.

He drew in the notebook he'd given Feuerstein, using precise, confident pen strokes. His draftsmanship came from his days as a cartographer, dispatching secret maps of British Africa to Berlin. This new Schädelplatz would be a fortress built on a scale not yet envisioned on the continent: turrets thrusting into the sky like the towers of a fairy-tale castle, a deep catacomb of offices below, the walls so thick tank shells would barely dent them. At its heart, instead of a quadrangle, he planned a great circle of skulls. Not twenty thousand this time—a hundred thousand. Concentric rings of nigger bone, then British and Belgian skulls and all the breeds of men who defied his rule. The outer rim would be reserved for the disbelievers among his own ranks. Once Feuerstein delivered, Hochburg would oversee the construction himself.

A sudden idea possessed Hochburg. His dissatisfaction vanished, replaced by a cold rapture.

At the center of the circle he inked a black hole, out of scale with the rest of the drawing, like the vortex of a whirlpool. He had intended to fill it with the skull he'd salvaged from the original square in Kongo—but that could be put behind glass in his private collection. A more gratifying alternative had come to mind.

Feuerstein emerged from the steps that led to the hold and locked the door behind himself. Hochburg had given the scientist the key and ordered him to travel above: that would establish his authority over the others while creating a seedbed for potential resentments, something that might prove useful later. Feuerstein lingered by the chair opposite, his hands plucking at the pockets of his trousers. He wore a mouse-gray suit that once belonged to a teenager but was ample for his frame. A razor blade had exposed coarse jowls.

"You don't have to wait to be asked," said Hochburg, not looking up from his sketch. The smell of disinfectant emanated from the Jew. "Sit, and tell me how your fellows are."

"They wish me to express their thanks again. They are grateful to a man." The scientist slipped into the seat and chose his next words carefully. The bestiality that had sustained Feuerstein on the road gang had deserted him. He was contaminated with hope, fearful that the slightest impudence might return him to the life he had escaped. "However . . . some on my list are missing. Dr. Pavel, for instance."

"I found all the names I could," replied Hochburg. "Pavel was in Marana." Marana: Madagaskar's largest leper colony. "If he's essential to your effort, you're welcome to fetch him yourself." He put down his pen. "But that's not what you meant to say, Herr Doctor. So get to the point."

"My wife is not here."

"She was the first I sought," said Hochburg. His intention had been to conceal the truth and use it as leverage against Feuerstein to make him work harder. But the scientist's expression—so anguished and expectant—stirred Hochburg's sympathy. "She's dead."

Feuerstein's eyes darkened and blurred. "Do you know how?"

"I traced her to a cocoa plantation in Banja. They told me she died in an industrial accident last year. I'm sorry."

There was a long pause. "I was a poor husband," said Feuerstein at last. "She deserved more."

"Then be a good father," replied Hochburg. "You have five children below. Be thankful for that. Work hard for them and none of you need suffer again."

"My colleagues have their wives. It will be hard seeing them together."

"We can leave the women if you prefer."

A hint of his former defiance returned to his voice. "No." He paused once more, watching the ground crew as they reeled in the fuel hoses. "Do you ever think, Oberstgruppenführer, that we all lived our lives long ago? That this world is the punishment for our previous sins."

"I thought the scientific mind was more rational."

"When I worked on the roads, I reasoned it through endlessly. It seemed the only possible explanation for my fate." His voice was parched. "For this new torment, knowing I can never make amends, it's more plausible than ever."

Hochburg contemplated this and the decades of suffering that had been his own life. "If you're right," he replied, "then I must have been wicked indeed."

How much kinder it would have been to have died in Eleanor's arms, the two of them taking their last breaths together. In the days after her death, he'd contemplated suicide—it was his bridge to her—but he soon abandoned the idea: he wanted to honor her memory. Avenge her. The Jew's words had unsettled him. His wretchedness was because justice had not been served: Burton had not suffered commensurately. His pursuit of the boy in Kongo had been meant as a prologue to untold agonies. Hochburg cursed himself for sinking the HMS *Ibis*.

He returned to his sketch, pressing his pen into the central hole of the Schädelplatz until the ink soaked through to the pages beneath. Once he was the master of Africa again, he would raise the sunken *Ibis* from the Gulf of Kamerun, presenting it as an act of conciliation toward the British, though his true purpose would be to search the wreck for Burton Cole. Somehow he would recognize the corpse; perhaps Kepplar, with his obsessive knowledge of craniology, could help with the identification. *Then I will remove the boy's skull*, he thought, *take a trowel, and fill the hollow at the center of the circle*. As for Burton's bones, he would grind them to make his bread, tear the loaf in half and eat it warm as he surveyed his new home. The man who consumes his past will be free of it. It was the only gesture that could compensate for his mistake of killing Burton so swiftly. Perhaps then, at last, he would be at peace.

The cockpit door opened, and the copilot entered.

"Oberstgruppenführer, the plane is ready to depart."

"Good. I'm sick of this island."

"We've also received a message from Governor Globocnik. He wants to speak to you. Urgently."

Hochburg gave a dismissive bat of his hand. "Get us in the air." He hoped never to return.

"Where are we going?" asked Feuerstein as the jet engines fired up, one after the other; the cabin walls began to hum.

"To Muspel," replied Hochburg. "I have a secret facility where you will not be disturbed."

"And the uranium?"

"As I told you last night: that is not your concern." Hochburg had sent instructions to General Ockener to begin a drive south: not to counterattack the British at Elisabethstadt but to secure the Shinkolobwe mine. Hochburg was fearful that the Americans would send a second expedition. That pockmark in the earth's crust was more valuable than Kongo's great southern city now. He was still struggling to understand America's interest in the weapon. The United States clung to its isolationism as though it were a remote island state, a position that suited the Reich. Even Britain, the diminished leader of the Anglo-Saxon world, preferred it this way (despite Churchill's goading). America had no need for such destructive power.

The Junkers taxied to its takeoff point, the sound of its engines swelling.

"I've never flown before," said Feuerstein. "I understand the principles, of course, but . . ." He shifted on his meatless buttocks.

Hochburg pressed himself into his seat and closed his good eye. The other had stopped throbbing overnight and was lifeless behind the bandage: he sensed he would never see out of it again. There was a momentary lull in the turbines, then a full-throated roar. The aircraft sped along the runway. It was six hours to Aquatoriana, where they would refuel, another eight after that to their final destination. When they arrived, Hochburg would take an icy shower. His skin was layered with filth from the Ark.

Suddenly Hochburg was thrown forward, only his seat belt saving him from landing in the Jew's lap.

"Something passed us," said Feuerstein. His eyes were terrified and accusatory, as if Hochburg had been playing a trick on him all along. Through the window, the wing flaps stood erect to slow them down. The plane juddered, its frame creaking, and swerved to a halt.

Hochburg unbuckled himself and strode to the cockpit. The two pilots looked up from the controls.

"It's blocking our path," said the captain.

A hundred meters ahead was a black jeep.

"Globus!" snarled Hochburg.

The jeep rolled forward, ensuring that the Junkers could not take off. When it was below the nose, the vehicle stopped, the dawn light gilding the skull-and-palm-tree insignia on the bodywork. The passenger door opened.

"Keep the engines running," Hochburg told the pilots and moved back into the cabin. He opened the hatch, letting in a blast of aviation-fuel-soaked air, and kicked the emergency steps free.

"Whatever happens," he shouted at Feuerstein before leaving the aircraft, "say nothing, no matter what you're threatened with. Globocnik must not learn of our plan. Your life and that of every Jew on the plane depends on it."

+ + +

At the far end of the runway, in the window of the control tower, figures had gathered. The Junkers's engines continued to lacerate the cool morning air.

Before the hatch opened, Kepplar felt a flutter in his stomach at seeing Hochburg; now he was fighting to contain his laughter. He had never seen his former master look so startled. Kepplar's mirth turned to concern.

"What happened to your face?" he asked, reaching out for the bandage.

Hochburg flicked his head away; his single eye pulsed with fury. "There better be a very good explanation for this intrusion, Brigadeführer." His voice was low, dangerous.

I have loyally served the Oberstgruppenführer for years, thought Kepplar. *I come with good news; I have nothing to fear.* He held Hochburg's gaze for as long as he could—it was like staring into an abyss, black and bottomless—till he averted his eyes. Plumes of cloud were gathering in the far west; a swastika windsock snapped in the breeze. Kepplar smoothed his black tunic across his chest and spoke briskly: "Burton Cole is alive, here on Madagaskar."

"Don't make a fool of me!"

"I swear it, Herr Oberst. I've been pursuing Cole for the past three days. Dozens of others can verify it." He wanted a detail that substantiated his claim. "Cole has lost his hand—"

"You've seen him?" Hochburg stepped closer. "You're sure?"

"As sure as you stand before me."

"Then where is he?"

A familiar sense of deficiency sluiced through Kepplar. For the first time he understood that Cole was the sum of his failures, that he felt inferior to Cole despite his rank and the exemplary structure of his skull. "He was an arm's length from me."

"Alive."

"There have been casualties, here and in Roscherhafen."

The faintest look of elation played along Hochburg's mouth. "But why Madagaskar? It makes no sense . . ." He glanced behind him at the Junkers. Through one of the portholes a scraggy, scared face peered out. "He's looking for a Jew," said Hochburg.

"That was my conclusion, too—a recent arrival," Kepplar replied, impressed and irritated that Hochburg had understood so quickly. His own moment of realization had come as the patrol boat limped back to base. The helicopter sent to pursue the dhow's castaways reported seeing two separate parties make it ashore. He was set to follow the blond into the jungle when the purpose of Cole's trip unlocked itself.

"I spent the evening at Interpol's bureau in the city," said Kepplar. "They make carbon copies of all new deportees' papers before the records are sent to the Ark. I went through every man, woman, and child for the past six months." It had been a tedious, desperate night. He was assigned a small office (harsh electric lights, a jug of water that tasted of earth), where he scanned each document for some clue, slumping with hopelessness when he reached the bottom of the pile. "Then I went back twelve months."

He handed over a file.

Hochburg opened it and spoke deliberately: "Madeleine Rachel Cole. Deported London, October 1952."

"His wife, I assume. Reason to risk coming here."

Silence. Hochburg stared at the open document, unblinking, his mood strange. As the seconds dragged by, Kepplar wondered if he had made an error. He felt a twinge of envy again, sure that Cole knew some secret about his master that he didn't. "The file indicates that she was sent to Antzu," he said.

Still Hochburg said nothing. The wind from the jet engines tugged at the bandage covering his eye; he held the paper tight between his fingers. His expression was blank—but concealing something. A tiny tremor of rage? He dominated the space around himself less than Kepplar remembered, his frame somehow not as powerful. It was a disappointment Kepplar didn't want to admit. If his master seemed diminished, it was his fault for exaggerating him.

Finally, Hochburg closed the file. "Did they treat you well in DOA?"

"I hated every second of it."

"Governor Ley telephoned me after your transfer to complain. He suggested that you be sent to Siberia. I refused him."

"All I want is to serve you again, Oberstgruppenführer."

"Then board my plane and make sure its cargo is delivered safely to Muspel." He rolled up the file and tapped Kepplar's chest bone with it. "You have done well."

"If you please, Herr Oberst, I wish to be at your side. Complete what I began in Kongo."

Hochburg considered this, then snorted. "It seems you have the scent, Derbus. Very well, we shall find Burton and his bride together."

"And then?"

"Justice. It is overdue."

"I meant, what about me?"

Hochburg made no reply. Instead, he clambered inside the Junkers, leaving Kepplar on the apron. He stood there stupidly for several moments, absorbed by the Me-362s lined up opposite him and the runes on their tail fins. Despite Himmler's efforts, Tana had only a token squadron of jet fighters; the main air base was at Diego Suarez, under the command of the Kriegsmarine, not the SS. Then he strode to the jeep and ordered it to clear the runway.

After he had found the file, he'd leapt up with a yelp and paced his tiny cell; then his mood darkened. He had picked up Cole's trail without the need to bloody his hands, which should extol his methods; yet he felt a sense of shame, as if he hadn't given enough of himself—unlike the sailors who had been killed on the patrol boat (men who weren't even his to commandeer). He was in the basement of the Interpol building, where the archives were kept, the odor of paperwork pressing around him like a hand over his mouth. *Paperwork.* He saw himself in the Schädelplatz again: slumped on his knees, uniform singed, Hochburg laughing. More than anything else, he wanted to bring his master Cole, but if he pursued him and failed, if he squandered this second chance, there would be no path back. He wanted Cole to burn as he himself had been threatened with burning. Better to supply Hochburg with the intelligence, then let him take the risk of the pursuit. When he sought out the Oberstgruppenführer and discovered that he was already in Madagaskar, the decision was made.

Hochburg descended from the Junkers, the hatch closing behind him.

"What's on board?" shouted Kepplar as the jet rolled past them, returning to its takeoff position.

"The fate of everything we have built in Africa. Send her your blessings."

The plane roared into the sky, the two men watching in silence. Kepplar glanced at Hochburg: his profile was masked by bandages, but there was a triumphant thrust to his jaw. Kepplar returned his gaze to the aircraft. It soared toward the west, dwindling to a point, and then, at some indefinite moment, was swallowed by the clouds.

CHAPTER THIRTY-THREE

Lava Bucht
20 April, 06:20

IT WAS LIKE watching an entire civilization disappear.

The Ark continued to blaze, lighting the dawn sky more intensely than the sun. Although the hovercraft's hatch was shut tight, the smell of charred paper stung Burton's nose. He had a sense of dismay—and indifference. These weren't his people; he had no people. He remembered enough of his Old Testament to know that this had happened to the Jews before, and not just God's chosen people. Countries and cultures had repeatedly been wiped away. In the Legion his commanders spoke of the Sahara as if it were impossible to conceive of a time when it wouldn't be French; a decade later, the sand was German. It would happen again, in perpetuity, till one day Britain, America, even the Thousand-Year Reich were gone.

Or so Burton told himself. All that mattered was that he had saved Madeleine's record: that one sliver of paper meant more than all the others.

Tünscher swung the controls round, taking the hovercraft in a loop away from the flaming wreckage of the seaplane, back into the bay; the Walküre did not follow. They flashed past the other hovercrafts, then the Ark, and continued on to the Analava River in a direction that would eventually take them to the address inside Burton's pocket. Once they rounded a bend, the scene of the night before was hidden. Mangroves gave way to forest and hillocks of mud rising from the water.

Burton was squashed in the rear with the dead gunner at his feet. He rebuked himself for firing his Beretta; threats seldom worked against Tünscher. He leaned down to speak to him. "We going to Antzu?"

No reply.

Burton caught his friend's reflection in the cockpit. He was staring ahead, his eyes empty and furious. A tiny shard of disquiet. "Tünsch?"

"Shut up, I'm thinking." The hovercraft bounced on the river. Then: "You're fucked, Burton. I can get myself to Nosy Be or some other base. You're trapped."

"Hand yourself in and they'll lock you up after this."

At Bel Abbès, Tünscher was forever being thrown in the brig, its baking, claustrophobic walls the only punishment to curb his insubordinate streak. He feared being caged.

"I supply enough of the top brass—I can bribe my way off this island."

"Bribe them with what?"

"There's always you."

Burton's grip tightened around his pistol. "The only thing that matters is finding Madeleine."

"Then what? You going to live here like a Jew?" He eased off the speed. "You'll die like a Jew."

Tünscher steered them inland, searching for somewhere to land. Behind, the river was empty and emerging from the night. The hovercraft's wake caught the sun as it rose over the trees: a trail of oxblood foam.

A *crack*.

The stuffing in Tünscher's seat erupted. Burton reached forward to touch it. A small round hole had appeared in the cockpit glass.

The left bank exploded into light and noise. Bullets, slashes of pink tracer fire, arrows. In the tangled gloom of the trees Burton glimpsed men in waistcoats, their faces fierce. Tünscher rammed the throttle, and the hovercraft surged forward. The metalwork sparked around Burton. There was a hollow bang—and black smoke began pouring from the rotor fan.

They sped on until they passed the barrage, a prolonged wail of fear and despair following them. Tünscher fought the controls, the hovercraft slewing from side to side.

"There," said Burton.

Ahead were some mudflats, a spot where crocodiles might once have basked before SS game hunters and Jews desperate for meat had driven their numbers to extinction.

Behind them, the forest burst into fire again as new targets entered the ambush. Burton spun round as far as the gunner's chair permitted: two hovercrafts had appeared. One slowed, pirouetting till it faced the Jews; its gun spewed metal into the trees. The other raced forward in pursuit.

Burton watched it close in, then roar past in a whirl of leaves, blocking the waterway, forcing them toward the shore. He worked the breech of the MG48 mounted in front of him, loading it with ammunition.

"No!" shouted Tünscher. "We can still talk our way out of this."

"You can. What about me?"

Burton squeezed the trigger: a stream of bullets sliced through the other hovercraft's fan, cockpit, fuel tank. The river vanished in a pall of orange flame and smoke. Debris clattered down on them, smashing the glass, the wind tearing through the interior. Tünscher cried out as if he had been struck. They lurched to the starboard; a warning light began to flash on the console.

Burton was aware of the floor sinking. The constant din of the fan had been replaced by an intermittent chugging, as though the blade couldn't draw in enough air. Behind, the second hovercraft's gun was scything the forest; bodies toppled from the branches.

"Pad's losing pressure," Tünscher shouted. "We'll never outrun them."

"Then let's turn round. Hit them first."

Tünscher's response was biting: "I'm not dying today, Major."

He steered between the pillars of a washed-away bridge, then round a bend to a meandering stretch of river. From his elevated position in the gunner's seat, Burton saw that the trees were thinning, giving way to a scorched, desolate tract of agricultural land. There was a cluster of buildings set back from the water and a warehouse with a gaping, burnt-out roof.

Burton tapped Tünscher's shoulder with his stump and directed him to the shore. "There's a place to hide out."

They hit the bank with a jolt that bucked Burton in his seat. Tünscher forced the control stick forward with his entire body weight, driving the craft up and over the mud, across the fields, the engine stuttering. As they approached the warehouse, a flock of birds burst through the exposed rafters, into the air. On one side was a large sliding door left open just enough for a man to squeeze through. Burton clambered out of the cockpit and tugged on it till it could accommodate the hovercraft. Tünscher steered inside and killed the engine; the pad deflated, reminding Burton of that slumping roll when a camel knelt for its rider to dismount.

He returned the door to its original position and peered through the gap toward the river. The banks were screened by banyan trees. For several moments the second hovercraft continued its assault; then its engine powered up. It streaked by, heading inland.

Burton watched the foam from its trail settle till the river lay lapping and luminous, bathed in a yellow-and-pink light, like the sunrises he used to watch on the farm with Madeleine. Battenberg skies, she called them after the similarly colored cakes she enjoyed so much. They had both been wounded, wandering people for so long that neither quite believed that the farm, with its sturdy quince trees, was their new home. Sometimes they talked all night, not realizing the hour till the sky had lost its darkness; they'd knot their fingers together to greet the new day.

The unexpected beauty of the scene stilled Burton's breath. Despite everything they had lost, he sensed the durability of what he had made with Madeleine. He vowed not to start another day without her.

"I'm going to Antzu," he said, turning to the hovercraft inside the ware-house. The pilot's seat was empty.

Rapid footsteps approached him through the gloom. Next moment Burton was swept off his feet, fists clobbered his face. He took the blows, remembering this ritual from the Legion. "Pricking," Patrick used to call it: a drop of blood to draw Tünscher's mood. His knuckles were barely warm before he stopped. He stood panting for several moments, then offered his hand and yanked Burton up.

They stared at each other, Burton wondering how his old friend would react when he discovered the truth about the diamonds. It would take more than a pricking then, for sure. Burton broke from his gaze. The interior of the warehouse was bare, its walls blackened; the only source of light was the hole in the roof, which cast a ragged oval of dawn on the ground.

"What is this place?" he asked. There was a faint stench of rotten fruit.

"How am I supposed to know." Tünscher reached into his pocket for his cigarettes, sighed. "I guess it was part of the rebellion. They must have shipped the workers to the reservations." He lit up.

"You should have told me about the Bayerweeds," said Burton.

"These are the least of your worries."

"So what next?"

Above them the birds had returned to the rafters; they were cooing and shitting.

"You haven't left me with much choice." Tünscher took a cheek-hollowing drag. "We get to Antzu, find your woman."

"I thought you were going to bribe your way home."

His friend shrugged. "The only thing that matters are those diamonds. Remember the stakes in the Legion? *À quitte ou double.*" Everything—or nothing. Gambling for cash met with severe punishment, so vast quantities of dates exchanged hands. "Unless you want to pay me now."

Tünscher had the same woebegone look Patrick had worn in Kongo when he realized the extent of what he'd been sucked into. Burton felt a wash of guilt, then anger at himself for depending on a lie. "What about getting Maddie and me off the island?"

Tünscher stubbed out his butt and walked to the hovercraft. "You'd better hope I can think of something. Maybe the fishing fleet at Varavanga." For the first time, Burton noticed that he was clutching his right flank.

"You okay, Tünsch?"

"Ecstatic," he replied and hauled himself inside, rooting around for equipment that might be useful, checking the dead gunner's pockets. He handed Burton a compass, canteen, packet of jerky, medical kit.

From outside came gunfire. The sound rolled over the rafters, scooping up the birds and scattering them noisily. It was impossible to tell how close it was.

"We'd better go," said Burton.

"The river's too dangerous," Tünscher replied. "We should head inland. It's a five- or six-hour march."

Five or six hours: it sounded like nothing to reach Madeleine. "You know the way?" When Burton had been here before, as a mercenary, it was in Tana; he wasn't familiar with this part of the island.

"We keep due southeast through the jungle." Tünscher donned his cap, placing it at a rakish angle. "After that we should be able to see the governor's house. That will guide us in."

They were already outside, darting between the buildings, when Tünscher stopped.

"Wait," he said. "I got an idea."

He hurried back to the warehouse and dragged the body of the gunner from the cockpit, then the spent MG48 casings on the floor and any other junk he could find. Burton looked on in bemusement as Tünscher collected a helmet and a postcard of Hitler in Tyrolean costume that had been tacked to the control panel.

"The partisans used to do this in Siberia, after they'd ambushed our patrols."

"What does it mean?" asked Burton.

"Fuck knows." Brass shells glinted in his fingers. "We'd waste hours trying to make sense of it. If they find the hovercraft, it might buy us more time."

They left as soon as he was finished, following a muddy track into the forest; tendrils of mist were gathering around the tree trunks. Burton was aware of a bounce to his boots.

Behind them the gunner sat propped up against the hover pad: helmet back to front, one hand cupping his groin, left leg jackknifed, boot and sock removed. Dotted around him were geometric shapes made from the empty casings and the word KÜRBIS. Pumpkin. The postcard of Hitler had been ripped in two: one half rolled up between the gunner's toes, the other poking out of his mouth.

CHAPTER THIRTY-FOUR

Sofia Dam, Western Sector (North)
20 April, 10:45

HOCHBURG STARED AT the file on his lap, oblivious to the din and the cramped cockpit of the helicopter. He was trying to imagine the color of Madeleine's eyes. She would be his by the end of Führertag: the bait with which to capture Burton. He looked forward to talking to the boy again, maybe reminiscing, before his punishment began. If Burton's body could endure it, the years ahead would be long. The gifted practitioner of pain understood both cruelty and palliation.

"Can you imagine the blacks doing anything so bold?" Kepplar was squeezed in the rear of the Flettner, his voice heard through his headphones.

Hochburg glanced up. They had flown from Tana, their final approach taking them through the Mandritsara Valley, over a dense grid of barracks and the trickle of the Sofia River, to the dam that blocked it. Overnight, Jews had defaced the wall of the dam with streaks of paint fifty meters long. As Hochburg deciphered the shape of the graffiti, his mouth curled in amusement. This was the island's northern reservation: the Sofia Reservation.

"Jews are more technically minded," he replied, thinking of Feuerstein; the scientist would be flying over DOA by now. "That's what makes them dangerous."

Hochburg ordered the pilot to circle the dam and its orange-red reservoir, and caught sight of Globus. He was dressed in riding jodhpurs and a short-sleeved shirt, cowing men with orders as he strutted along the top of the dam. Spurs winked on his boots.

On the highest ridge overlooking the valley was the control center for the hydroelectric plant. There was a cluster of pylons and a landing pad; extra flags had been raised for Führertag. The Flettner touched down next to a trio of other helicopters, one an American Bell 47 with diplomatic markings.

"Why do we need Globus's permission?" asked Kepplar as they disembarked.

"He's bound to be testy about Antzu," said Hochburg, stretching. "And we are going to commandeer his men. Better to stick to the formalities; it keeps the Reichsführer happy." The valley below swayed with mist. "Wait here."

Inadvertently, it was Hochburg who was responsible for Madagaskar's dams. Although Tana and Diego were illuminated after dusk, most of the island remained black, and in the darkness, Globus feared, the population could plot against him. Coal was too expensive to import, and the SS forestry department wanted the native trees for lumber and profit, not lighting up Jews. Then, on his return from the Windhuk Conference, Globus had taken a night flight and seen the cities of central Africa twinkling beneath him: Hochburg had harnessed the continent's rivers. The Inga Dam, powered by the cataracts of the Kongo River, was the largest in the world. Globus commissioned a team of engineers to survey Madagaskar for its hydroelectric potential. Several rivers were identified as possibilities, though their tendency to silt raised doubts about their viability. Globus ignored the naysayers and, as part of his Idle Hands project, set the population to work building the Sofia Dam in the north, Betroka in the south.

Along the top of the dam was a two-lane road that linked the sides of the ravine. Crews of workers were preparing cradles to be lowered over the edge. Behind them, the reservoir was at maximum level because of the rainy season. Up close its surface was the color of rust, the air pungent with brine. Globus stood apart from the workers, conferring with a man in a suit. He looked as irate and defensive as he had a few days ago, on the steps of his palace.

"Here he is," said Globus. The reek of stale alcohol billowed from him. "While Oberstgruppenführer Hochburg is visiting, he's the most senior official on the island. Perhaps he can explain things." Globus introduced the man in the suit with a barely disguised resentment: "This is Herr Nightingale, the American envoy to Madagaskar."

When Washington had intervened to safeguard the records on the Ark, it had also established a small diplomatic mission, partly to reassure American Jews with familial connections to the island. It joined the Council of New Europe's and the Red Cross's representation in Tana, all three housed in the old colonial quarter of the city.

"He's new," continued Globus. "Wants to make a name for himself."

Nightingale stepped forward, his palm hovering, unsure whether it should be offered to shake or raised in a Führer salute. Hochburg spared him his predicament and grasped it. There was something effeminate, almost pretty about the American. His skin was so smooth it looked as if he shaved before every meal. He had feathery silver hair falling halfway down his forehead, tinged with sweat.

Globus fixed Hochburg with hungover, bloodshot eyes. "Have you heard the terrible news? The Ark burned down last night. How could such a disaster have happened?"

"The ship was gutted," said Nightingale in a soft, sticky German. "Hundreds of thousands of records destroyed, maybe millions. It contravenes every agreement we signed."

"Hochburg visited the Ark yesterday," said Globocnik. "And the day before. Perhaps he knows what happened."

"I left it perfectly intact."

Globus turned on the American. "You see. The Oberstgruppenführer had special permission to visit. Other than that, it's out of bounds. Be careful what you imply, Herr Envoy. You're new to the island and don't understand how things work yet."

"Unlike my predecessor?"

"At least he enjoyed our hospitality."

"The situation is unacceptable," replied Nightingale. "I've had firsthand accounts of SS officers boarding the ship. Reports of sabotage."

"And how did you come by this? The Jew lies as he breathes. I swear it's a conspiracy to stir the muck between us."

"I have informed Washington and regret to say that a military response has not been ruled out. We might have to send a warship to the region, like we did in forty-seven."

The American's tone remained measured, but Hochburg heard the conviction; he waited for Globus to explode. Instead the governor of Madagaskar offered a careless snort. He hooked his thumbs into his jodhpurs, pressed his belly out.

"And I've told Germania that the Jews were to blame for the Ark. They're using it as an excuse to spread their rebellion. Look what they did here last night. But they will fail. Now, if there's nothing else, I have work to do." He stalked off to supervise his men, the spurs on his boots jangling with each step.

Hochburg went to follow, but Nightingale stopped him. "Can I speak privately with you? It's important."

"I don't have the time."

"Your troops in Kongo will not thank you if you walk away."

Hochburg frowned, curious, and let himself be guided toward the far end of the dam. Nightingale lowered his voice and spoke in English.

"I know who you are, Herr Oberstgruppenführer, I know you have Himmler's ear. I need you to pass on a word of caution."

"I'm not an errand boy."

"This is unofficial."

The mist below had become patchy, offering glimpses of the valley. Near the base of the dam were the barracks Hochburg had flown over: thousands of huts nestled among the rocks, built from new logs, the thatched roofs still green in places. Globus's dam scheme had been an epic waste of toil: as the experts warned him, the Sofia River carried too much silt to drive turbines. After an initial burst of power, the dam's reservoir turned from blue to yellow-brown and then orange as the sediment built up and the electricity stopped. The same happened in the south. Then the second uprising began, and Globus found a better use for his follies. Any community that offered resistance was transported wholesale to the dam valleys, where, confined by the geography, they were easy to control. In the distance the river curved out of sight to Mandritsara and its hospital, a place Hochburg knew only by reputation. The doctors there occasionally shared their research with their colleagues in Muspel, some of it reaching Hochburg's desk; it made for grisly reading.

"I don't think Governor Globocnik appreciates the severity of the situation," said Nightingale. "Or the potential consequences. Every day I receive news of summary executions, food being restricted, whole towns and factories transported around the island as if they were toys. The reservations were meant as a short-term measure." He indicated the city of huts below; the sound of hammers drifted up through the mist. "They look permanent to me."

"He has a rebellion on his hands," replied Hochburg. "What do you expect?"

"The reservations have to stop. At this rate every man, woman, and child will be cooped up in them."

"Tell Globus, not me."

"I tried. His answer is to send me girls and hard liquor." In the rising humidity, Nightingale loosened his collar. "Now the Ark. We both understand the significance of the names."

"Then let me reassure you: he had no hand in it."

The American's tone was quietly imploring: "For all our sakes, Germania needs to recall him."

"I am here on a private matter, Herr Nightingale. I have no sway over events."

"President Taft was elected on a declaration to keep America safe behind our oceans."

"A neutrality the Reich respects."

"It took a lot of money to secure the White House." His tone became confidential. "Jews are wealthy in my country."

"He's in their pocket?"

"That would be to oversimplify matters. But they're not without influence. My predecessor was considered too accommodating to Globus and was recalled—"

"—as soon as Taft came to power," said Hochburg. Nightingale nodded. "So you're sympathetic to their cause?"

The American responded sharply. "I'm saying that the Jews could trap the president into acting against the best interests of the United States. Into a confrontation we don't want."

Hitler had long warned that the Jews of America wished to provoke conflict. Hochburg was skeptical. He thought of Nultz sniveling at the uranium mine and his admission that they wanted the weapon for insurance, not attack. Only America could conceive of such a device without wanting to wield it; that spoke of their national character. "That will never happen," he said.

"I wish I shared your confidence."

"You believe America will go to war?"

"Madagaskar is a German mandate, your security arrangements your own. But if there were a major atrocity, something on a scale that couldn't be ignored . . . Two weeks ago, at one of his 'folk nights,' Globocnik threatened to gas the whole Betroka Reservation."

"That was the wine talking."

"A drunk shouldn't be in charge of a powder keg. He's losing control."

"Globus is a brute, I agree, his methods crude—but he wouldn't dare. He wants the governorship of Ostmark too much."

"With the Ark gone, he could do anything."

Hochburg shook his head. "Such an order could only come from the Führer, and the Führer has no desire for war between our two countries."

"I pray you're right." Nightingale radiated sincerity. "Think it over, Oberstgruppenführer, for your sake, if not mine. One of our warships off the coast will not help you in Kongo."

The envoy excused himself and walked away, his footfalls making no sound. At the orphanage, Eleanor had devised a taxonomy for the children under her care. Her husband thought it fatuous, so she shared it only with Hochburg, the two of them adding terms over the years. There were the "hooligans," "heathens," and "please ma'ams," the "honey badgers" and "boys who need sun in their hearts" (*Like you,* she used to tease him). On occasion she called one of her wards a "spike beneath the snow": soft and cold on the surface, but you stepped down hard at your peril.

Hochburg hadn't thought of the phrase since his life in Togo; watching Nightingale leave, it came back to him. Whoever had dispatched him from Washington had miscalculated. The envoy's manner was too subtle for Globus's thuggish mind to take seriously. That was a danger.

"Will your country really send a warship?" he called after the American. He was weighing the implications.

Nightingale made a noncommittal gesture. "Rein in the governor, halt the reservations."

Although Hochburg had never feared a direct American attack, a U.S. presence in the region might bolster British aggression. Churchill was forever talking about Anglo-Saxon unity. If the British in Kongo couldn't be defeated, they had to be contained long enough for Feuerstein to work his sorcery. He considered the weapon the Jew would create for him and its sublime, decisive power. Then the Americans' interest in it. What had Nultz meant by "insurance"? *An insurance against Madagaskar* had been his exact words.

Hochburg strode to Globus and the men lowering the cradles over the dam. For now he wanted to get to Antzu and find Madeleine Cole.

"I thought you were leaving," said Globocnik.

"A change of plan. I have another favor to ask."

"Not now. I need to get below and survey the damage."

"It's important. I'm sure the Reichsführer would approve."

Globus rubbed his temples. "You told me Heinrich didn't know what you were up to . . ." He took out a vial of pills and knocked back a handful. Then: "Do you ride?"

Hochburg was wary of horses—their placid, knowing faces, all that untamable muscle between himself and the ground. "No."

An unpleasant grin spread across Globus's face. "If you want a favor, you'd better learn."

CHAPTER THIRTY-FIVE

GLOBUS HAD ALLOWED his sister-in-law to name the stallion. He kept stables all over the island, with horses imported from Arabia and what had once been the Russian steppe. For weeks his new mount had been nameless, till one morning he was riding with Gretta and she christened him "Kansas." It was stupid, but it made her girlishly happy, and he had to admit it was growing on him.

Kansas was seventeen hands, a pale dappled gray with a charcoal mane. He was not fully broken, tugging at the bit and bucking, always threatening to bolt. *He's a Jew horse,* Globus joked. *He needs to be taught who's in charge.* Globus had ridden since childhood and was an expert horseman. On the rare occasions when Himmler visited Madagaskar and they took to the saddle, the Reichsführer enviously praised his skills.

The sun was chasing away the mist. Globus shortened the reins and glanced over his shoulder; he was still too close to see the extent of the Jews' vandalism. Word of it had come in while he was resting with the girls at Lava Bucht, the three of them sipping coffee with cognac and whipped cream as the Ark toppled into the water. Immediately Globus had taken one of his injections—a concoction of amphetamine and vitamins—and flown to the dam. Since then there'd been a constant peck-peck-peck in his ears of other outrages as news of the Ark spread. Across the island his commanders were clamoring for orders on how to respond, though he was unsure himself. His first reaction to the dam was to scramble a squadron of Walküres, but he had to play it carefully . . .

The other governors of Africa had it easy, thought Globus. They were autonomous; so long as they paid tribute to Himmler, kept the ore and the bananas flowing back home, they were left alone, something Globocnik resented. He was accountable to Germania. To Himmler *and* Heydrich. To the RSHA, the security department; the race and resettlement department; the economic department. He even had to contend with the Kriegsmarine, whose naval base he guarded but whose officers always reminded him that they were independent of the SS (they, too, had been fussing about the Ark). Yet Globus had the toughest job of all: dealing with the great stinking salad of Jewry.

What a way to spend Führertag! Normally it was with the family, preparing for his birthday party the next evening. His only consolation was that the situation couldn't get much worse. He had one of his katzenjammer hangovers, the blood thumping through his eyes, his throat parched. Fifty meters behind him, Hochburg was following like a peasant on a plow horse. At the stables Globus had insisted that he take a black colt—"to match your uniform," he said sarcastically—but Hochburg refused, choosing a nag instead.

"I need your help," said Hochburg as he approached, "not a riding lesson."

Globus was enjoying the other man's discomfort too much to end it so soon; it might be his only fun of the day.

He squeezed his spurs into Kansas's flanks and cantered through the valley, through veils of warm mist and sunlight, climbing up to a ridge that looked down on the Sofia Reservation. This was one of his favorite spots; he slowed Kansas to a walk and admired his creation. It was on a scale Speer would appreciate: countless rows of huts constructed in a grid pattern, much more ordered than the ghettos he'd policed in Europe or the shantytowns elsewhere on the island. Above the barracks, the hillsides glinted with rows of barbed wire, vineyards of steel, ensuring that the Jews were trapped below.

"We'll make a Cossack of you yet," he laughed when Hochburg caught up with him.

Hochburg looked flushed. His riding hat was squashed down over his bandaged eye, the strap pinching his chin. "I thought you liquidated the Cossacks."

The track was wide enough for the two of them to ride abreast. From this elevation it was possible to see the railway siding where new arrivals disembarked daily. In the distance, a herd of bulldozers was leveling a hill.

"What are they doing?" asked Hochburg.

"Nothing for you to see." Globus directed his attention back to the valley. "There's room for three hundred thousand already," he said, using his crop to point below. "Add the Betroka Reservation, in the south, and that's almost twenty percent of the population, and we're still building. Long term, the plan is to do away with the sectors and herd every last Jew in here. Heydrich's idea."

"A containment policy?"

"This island is rife with tropical diseases. We hole the Yids up for a couple of generations and let nature take its course. 'Natural diminution,' Heydrich calls it. There's no blood, so it keeps the Americans off our backs."

"It's a risk," replied Hochburg. "I experimented with something similar in Muspel. In such confined spaces, disobedience can spread faster than you can control it."

"Not with my dams. The first sniff of trouble and the water supply gets shut off, like today. I'll teach those vandals a lesson. If there's open revolt, I raise the sluice gates."

"Your vandals scaled the dam in darkness, under the eyes of your men; they might be able to disable the gates."

Globocnik gave an irritated flick of his whip and trotted ahead. Himmler had given him a similar warning.

My dear Globus, he had said more than once, *you should mine the dams with dynamite.* Yet every time Globus asked for the order in writing, nothing came; often, with the Jews, it was a murk. Globus thought back to the Cossacks. How simple that had been: a communiqué from Germania, printed instructions, a signature. Since this new Pig Rebellion, Globus had been expected to find a permanent solution to the island's problems, always torn between Himmler and Heydrich—the servant of two masters. Both claimed to speak for the Führer.

The sides of the valley were once thickly wooded with cassias and traveler's palms. These had been chopped down to supply timber for the barracks below and to ensure that the hills were bare and easy to watch over. Globus picked his way through the stumps, Hochburg close behind, before climbing to the summit of the ridge. Stretching in both directions, at intervals of fifty meters, were guard towers. Patches of sickly sunlight were breaking through the mist to reveal the dam clearly for the first time. Globus yanked on the reins and brought Kansas to a standstill; his hands shook.

Overnight the Jews had climbed the dam and painted a colossal Star of David, only dawn interrupting their work. Every brushstroke took Globocnik farther from Ostmark.

"You have to admit it's impressive," said Hochburg.

"At the control center," replied Globus, aiming his whip in its direction, "there's enough TNT to demolish the dam. That's what Heinrich says I should do: wash the scum away."

"Don't be a fool. Blow the dam and you'll provoke the Americans. Taft may have no choice."

"Is that what you and Nightingale were whispering about?"

"You heard what he said. They want to send a warship."

"That's just big talk."

"You underestimate him."

Globus gave a contemptuous blow of his lips. "I'm not being bossed around by some Yankee Jew lover."

"Heydrich will want your head if the U.S. Navy sets sail. Himmler too."

"So Heinrich didn't send you?"

Hochburg climbed off his ride and unbuckled his hat, relieved to be back on the ground. "I don't know what you're talking about."

"I thought maybe he'd sent you to the Ark to give me a nudge. Show me the way."

Hochburg stared at him blankly. "I came here for a Jew. Now I'm looking for another."

"Are you collecting them?"

"I also need a team of your men."

"Why?"

"I'm going to Antzu."

The pulse fattened in Globus's neck. "Antzu is our show city," he spluttered. "You take a raiding party there, on Führertag, of all days . . ." His voice echoed along the valley. "The whole fucking island will erupt!"

"I will be less than an hour."

"You've caused me enough grief. I know about your bomb on the Ark—I could have been killed."

"A tragic loss."

"I let you in there, Hochburg, but this I refuse. Step one foot in Antzu and I'll call it treason, I'll have you . . ."

He was too choked to find a threat.

"Have me what, *Ober*gruppenführer?" said Hochburg calmly. "This may not be mainland Africa, but you'd be wise to remember your rank."

Globocnik felt his face burn. "You should remember whose island this is!"

He dug his spurs into Kansas so hard he must have broken the animal's skin; the horse reared up, threatening to trample Hochburg. Then Globus was galloping along the ridge. He bent low into the wind. Startled guards watched his charge from their towers. He followed the curve of the valley till he saw the hospital at Mandritsara and its complex of carmine buildings. Beyond it was a Totenburg: one of the memorials to the Germans who had died during the first rebellion.

He rode till Kansas was exhausted, his pale flanks foamed with sweat. Then he slowed and dismounted, working the tender spots behind the animal's ear to calm him.

Behind there was no sign of Hochburg, but he had a clear view of the dam, its monumental graffiti continuing to mock him. He watched his men in cradles scrubbing the paint off. If a photo ever reached home, he would be so humiliated that a Luger in the mouth would be his only option. He rubbed his throbbing temples and heard Himmler's voice coaxing him. As he rode back, it kept creeping into his head: what men would take hours to clean away, dynamite could do in an instant.

CHAPTER THIRTY-SIX

Antzu
20 April, 14:20

MADELEINE KNEW THEY were approaching Antzu when her ears began to hum and whirr with mosquitoes; soon the air was thick with them. She was too weary to bat them away. Her clothes were drenched, the bones of her feet sore. Jacoba looked even more exhausted.

"If only we had horses," she'd said a few hours earlier as the rain lashed them.

"If only you'd quit carping," said Abner in reply.

For a long time, zeal had driven Madeleine on—right foot forward for the twins, left to stab Cranley in the heart—but by dawn she was flagging. Only Abner seemed indifferent to the miles. As they trekked through the night, ranging over hills, he grumbled at them for being so slow, sighed every time they stopped to rest. Madeleine admired his fortitude without once telling him. For the past few minutes he had been searching the roadside. The temperature had risen, warming the saturated ground; mist snaked around them.

Finally he found it: a tangle of bushes like any other, except this one meant something to him. He removed his waistcoat, screwed it into a bundle, and hid it along with his rifle. Next he tied back the lengths of his hair, hesitated—then lifted the wig free of his head.

Madeleine stared at her brother, caught between mirth and pity. He was mostly bald, what little fuzz that remained on his scalp dotted with sores. "Why?"

"My hair stopped growing," he replied. His voice was defensive, embarrassed. "It's common here: lack of vitamins . . . the strain of it all." He stowed the wig in his backpack, exchanging it for a leather cap.

"I meant, why have you taken it off?"

He rolled down his sleeves to conceal the tattoos on his forearm. "Vanilla Jews aren't welcome in Antzu."

"Then how will you convince the council to help me?"

Instead of an answer, he put his fingers to his lips and touched Samuel's number before covering it. Madeleine's youngest brother had been ten the last time she saw him. At home she always regarded him as a chore: a timid, messy kid she was made to look after when their mother was busy. Perhaps if she'd known what lay ahead, it might have been different.

"I should add Samuel," said Madeleine, baring her wrist. "In case something happens to you."

"And spoil those pretty white arms?" Abner softened his tone. "Nothing's going to happen. We'll be safe once we're there." The prospect buoyed his mood. "It's not much farther."

They reached Antzu at midday, arriving at the southern gate.

In the 1930s, Poland considered deporting its Jews to Madagascar and sent a delegation to scout for settlements. Antsohihy, as it was then known, was a small village accessible to the coast by the Analava River. Because it was bounded by swamps and its people suffered from endemic malaria, it was deemed uninhabitable for large numbers—a point noted by SS officials when they chose it as the administrative center of the Western Sector. Within a few years it had become a sprawling city of shacks. Here the Judenrat, the Jewish Council, liaised with Tana, issuing papers, carrying out its orders. Antzu's citizens, with their relatively easy lives, had shunned the first rebellion; the council went further and demanded that the Vanilla Jews cease their self-defeating struggle.

By way of reward, and with an eye to Washington, Heydrich allowed Antzu to remain the island's only free city. Globus's protests were overridden; after so much bloodshed, it played well with the Americans. There was an SS garrison just beyond the walls, and the regional governor maintained a house that overlooked the city, but Antzu was policed by the Jupo and during daylight hours Jews could live as they pleased. "It is a model," Heydrich told a journalist from the *New York Times*, "a model of obedience and the freedoms therein for the rest of Madagaskar to aspire to."

A palisade had been erected around the city, not by the Nazis but by locals. *Jews have existed for so long behind walls,* Madeleine had heard it said, *that we can't live without them.* Several Jupo, dressed in their uniform of beige rain capes and pith helmets, manned the gate. They were gossipy, agitated. Coconut shells burned around them to keep off the clouds of mosquitoes.

A warden (as they liked to call themselves) came forward to see their papers while the others continued to whisper and shake their heads. He had the eyes of a man who was owed something. Abner handed over his documentation; Madeleine noticed that it was in someone else's name.

The warden gave the papers a cursory glance, keen to share bad news. "Have you heard? The Ark's been burned down."

Abner was appalled. "When?"

"Earlier this morning." He gestured at the other police wardens. "We reckon it was those bastard Vanillas, trying to force our hand. Make us join their revolution. But the council is too wise for that." He dropped his voice, wanting to show off a secret: "They're in session as we speak. An emergency meeting to denounce the Vanillas before we all go up in smoke."

"They wouldn't attack the Ark."

The warden eyed him mistrustfully. "How can you be sure?"

"We know the rebellion is bound to fail," replied Abner with bland conviction. "In the days after, the Ark will be our only safeguard."

The warden grunted and held his hand out to Madeleine. "Your papers." He had long, filthy nails.

"Silly girl," Abner replied for her, "she left them at home. Her and her friend both. We can fetch them if you want." He slipped some coins into the warden's hand. "Or you can accompany us back to check."

The warden glanced at his palm, then at his colleagues to see if they had noticed. "Where do you live?"

"Boriziny Strasse," replied Madeleine.

His attitude changed. "Next time, don't forget," he said and waved them through the gate.

Abner waited till they were out of earshot, walking past drab buildings and walls patterned with algae. "Boriziny?" He sounded impressed. "Mutti wanted to live there—she applied for years. How did you do it?"

"That's where I was sent when I first arrived."

"No one lives in Boriziny without something exchanging hands. Maybe your husband paid for it."

"I doubt it." The mention of him sent bleak emotions swilling through her. "Did you mean what you said," she asked her brother, "about the rebellion failing?"

"I said that to get us through the gate." He sighed and for the first time appeared weary. He became reflective. "Maybe it's true. I don't know, Madeleine; I'm exhausted by it all. We need America to have any chance."

"How?"

"It was my great dream. We spent months, thinking up a plan to draw in the U.S."

"Maybe it'll be different with Taft."

"The best we managed was to fight hard, fight everywhere. If the Nazis slaughter enough of us, the Americans will have no choice."

"That'll be a comfort," said Jacoba, "when we're dead."

They trudged into the city, the streets more deserted than Madeleine remembered. Abner stayed in front, encouraging the two women to go faster. Her brother's constant chiding and the arduousness of the journey had brought Madeleine closer to Jacoba. She reached out for her hand; the older woman had shown an unexpected stoicism. Now that Jacoba was inside the walls of Antzu, amid "civilized people," she seemed more secure.

The mist became heady with sewage and paint fumes and, wafting through it, another scent, warm and comforting. Fresh bread, thought Madeleine, her belly clenching. She couldn't remember the last time she'd eaten any; in the abattoir, the diet consisted solely of rice. Images filled her mind: crusty white loaves dusted with flour, rye bread, croissants, the challah her mother used to make, with its elaborate braids of dough. Soon they reached streets she recognized; ahead was a general store where she had bought bread before.

"Have you got any more yellow?" she asked Abner. The official currency for Jews was the gelbmark, commonly called "gelb": yellow.

"I spent the last of it to get you through the gates."

"You must have something." As a boy, he'd hoarded his pocket money. "I'm starving."

"Me, too," said Jacoba, sniffing the air.

"We have to hurry. With the Ark burned down, it's even more important I get to the council." He rubbed his molars through his cheek. "I thought that's what you wanted."

"It is, but . . ." Madeleine halted outside the shop. "My blood's like water. I can't take another pace."

Abner irritably searched his pockets and tossed her some change. There were no gelbmark notes, only coins made from zinc in denominations of ten, five, two, and one (known as a "rupee"), plus halves and quarters. The entire currency had been minted in the 1940s, with no additions since, the money supply maintained by restrictions on how much individuals could own and the shrinking population.

As Madeleine and Jacoba entered the shop, the smell of the place—grimy spices, last season's rice—almost made Madeleine faint with hunger. It was dingy, the meager stock of food stored in jars and containers behind the counter to stop thieves.

"Have you got any bread?" asked Madeleine.

"Not today," replied the woman at the till, pointing to an empty rack. The bottom shelf was covered by a thick rectangle of uncut honey cake.

"What about that?"

"Y'don't want any. They're *Bienenstiche*. Bee stings."

"How much?"

"Delivered this morning and not a single one sold. Quite right, too." The woman was from London, with a guttural East End accent.

"Why?"

"Came from the Nazis. A gift to every shop in town, so we can celebrate their Führer Day."

"If there's no bread, I'll have three pieces."

"You mustn't! They set fire to the Ark this morning. It's y'duty not to eat it."

"Three *big* pieces."

"Y'sick, girl. And now those Vanillas will use it as an excuse to spread their trouble. I tell ya, we'll end up in the reservations."

Jacoba tugged at her arm to leave. "I'm not hungry anymore."

Madeleine was undecided, then slid her coins across the counter. "I'll have as many as I can buy."

+ + +

Back on the street, Abner was cleaning his glasses. He looked out of place. Elderly couples passed him, infants and young mothers, but no men of fighting age. To subdue any chance of rebellion, the Jewish Council had decreed that males between the ages of fifteen and sixty were not allowed to reside within the city unless they were married with children or devoutly religious. Abner harried Jacoba and Madeleine through the mist, all three cramming their faces with cake. Madeleine swallowed in half-chewed gulps, the honey burning her throat.

They reached the Spanish quarter: a warren of sun-starved lanes that led to the docks and river. Untouched by Globus's Operation Babel, Antzu remained divided by national identity. Every building was hidden behind bamboo scaffolding. On the highest levels, old men with tins and brushes watched them pass.

"What is this?" asked Madeleine.

"You'd know if you lived here from the start," replied Abner with a hint of accusation. "It's an annual ritual: painting week."

"I don't understand."

"Wood weathers badly here. It needs preserving, but the Nazis control the paint. They say the chemicals in it can be used to make explosives, so they only give it the week of Führertag. To keep us out of mischief."

From the Spanish quarter, past a single block that accommodated Liechtenstein's Jews, and finally to the Altreich district, the oldest part of the city, where Germans and Austrians had made their homes.

Boriziny Strasse had been the main thoroughfare before the Jews arrived, a long snaking road, wide enough for a motorcar, that stretched from one end of town to the other. The pioneers had developed it, building better houses than anything that followed: they were raised on stilts against the rain, had roofs of corrugated tin and small gardens. There was even a rudimentary sewage system. At the northern end, under the shade of papaya trees, was a cluster of chalets from the French colonial period. This was where the Jewish Council and senior Jupo had their homes. The road had once been paved, but a decade of tropical storms had reduced it to a patchwork of cobbles and puddles. No one knew who Boriziny was or why a street had been named after him.

Madeleine's mind was drifting, melancholic. She struggled to recollect what it was like to walk along here with the bulging weight of the twins. Had she made a mistake by returning? Her children seemed farther away now than they had the day before. She tried to cheer herself up, remembering the waddle she'd developed in the final weeks of her pregnancy. It would have made Burton smile.

"What number?" asked Abner.

Madeleine started. "Eleven thirty-eight."

"Everyone wants to live here, Leni. You should be prepared: your house will probably be taken."

"What about my things?" She thought of the suitcase she'd arrived with and the few items she had bought and bartered; she'd collected a stash of powdered milk.

"Gone."

She didn't care. At that moment all she wanted to do was lie down.

"You can live with me," said Jacoba. "It's nothing as good as this, just one of the tenements, but I'm sure my room will still be there."

Abner slapped a mosquito feasting on his arm. "I wouldn't bet on it."

Mist hung over the roofs. From somewhere came the voice of a soprano working through her scales. A few ragtag kids kicked around a ball, while women washed clothes or sat staring into space. Madeleine recalled the streets of Hampstead clearly, and the various houses where she had worked as a maid after arriving in London; the Vienna of her childhood remained vivid. But none of this was familiar.

The sound of the opera singer grew closer. She was one of Madeleine's neighbors: resentful that "an English" had been allocated a house along the street, more so because she was carrying a baby. With so few men in the city, and birth control encouraged by the SS, pregnancies were unusual. The singer was practicing on her porch but fell silent as they approached.

Abner climbed the front steps of number 1138 and knocked on the door. It was a cinder-block hut, weathered and brown, rust from the roof running down the walls. There was no reply. "Do you have the key?"

"I lost it."

Her brother examined the frame. "It's not that strong. I should be able to break it."

"No, wait," said Madeleine.

She joined him and removed the knife from under her trousers. It had rubbed against her thigh as they walked to Antzu till the skin was tender; every time it made her wince, she pictured Cranley. She eased the knife between the frame and the lock, twisting it until the latch gave. Inside, everything was how she had left it ten weeks earlier. Abner went to enter, but she barred him and turned to Jacoba.

"Will you come in? Rest?"

"I want to see my daughter first."

Since they'd met at the slurry lake, Madeleine had spent every day with Jacoba. Squeamish, snobby, accepting Jacoba; Jacoba, who had encouraged her through the previous night despite her own exhaustion, who'd let her cling to the hope of escaping the island even though she believed it impossible. The thought of being parted was more wrenching than Madeleine had imagined. She embraced the older woman. There was something so normal about the gesture—like two friends parting after lunch and a matinee or an afternoon's shopping, far from their sour clothes and the muddy streets of Antzu—that Madeleine felt tears rising. Jacoba gave her a final peck on the cheek and whispered, "I wish I could make it better." Then she slouched down Boriziny, taking one of the side streets in the direction of the river.

"I don't trust her," said Abner, entering the house.

"She looked after me."

"Do you ever think why? She's not family." Abner peered around the dingy interior. There was a small window with a fine mesh to keep out the mosquitoes, but only the houses of the Jewish Council had windows with panes; glass was a rare commodity. His eyes came to rest on the crate Madeleine had planned to use as a cradle.

"I'm going to the council," he said, "to pass on our news about the reservations. There's also a transmitter there—I need to speak to Ben-Ze'ev, tell him about the Ark."

"What about Mandritsara?"

"They burned our records, Madeleine. No one will care about your children now."

"You promised."

He offered a pathetic shrug.

"I'll go alone," she said, too tired to be persuasive.

Abner opened the door, letting in a waft of bread and sewage. "Then go. Back the way we came, left up the hill toward the governor's house, then on to the main road." He sounded more annoyed with each word. "From there it's forty kilometers, except a lone woman will raise suspicions, especially on Führertag. So you'd better go cross-country."

Madeleine hung her head and noticed that one of her laces was caught in a knot.

"You were slow from the train, Leni, white with hunger, and the terrain was easier than it will be between here and Mandritsara."

"Someone has to help me."

"Why? Thousands need help, millions—why are you so special?" He sighed, scratching a sore on his hairless head, and seemed to be calculating something. "Let me go to the council, speak to them on your behalf. But you have to promise to stay here."

"I want to come with you."

"This place is safest. Stay and get some rest."

He clomped down the steps, boots thick with mud, and walked off in the direction Jacoba had taken. Then stopped. "It's a nice house, Leni. Better than anything we had here, or how Mutti and Leah live now." He stared into the sky. "You should be grateful for what you've got."

Madeleine followed his gaze. She could see nothing through the mist but heard the approach of a helicopter. It clattered over the city and came in to land near the governor's house. When she looked back to the street, Abner was gone.

CHAPTER THIRTY-SEVEN

Antzu
20 April, 15:20

MORE FUCKING HORSES, thought Hochburg as Kepplar opened the helicopter door. Tufts of straw whirled around them.

The Flettner had landed in the stable block behind the governor's villa. A groom in a khaki shirt appeared and led Hochburg and Kepplar into the house, taking them first through a tack room, then into a vestibule adorned with vases and paintings and silver ornaments. There was a sickly scent of frangipani and ylang-ylang.

"To cover the stink of the city," explained the groom.

He passed them on to an adjutant, who escorted them up the stairs and knocked at a door. Hochburg pushed past him into a dining room: more tawdry opulence, more looted treasures, the air frosty. He had come across this before, Europeans who judged their status by the degree to which they could cool tropical air. Hochburg glanced at the lunch spread and felt nauseous. It was the new German way: excess, people stuffing their mouths till they couldn't breathe; a poor example from the upper ranks that was filtering down to the masses. Soon everyone would want this lifestyle.

The table was bowing, laid with the traditional Führertag meal of roast lamb with juniper sauce, ham wrapped in bread, potato salad, and red cabbage. There was a conurbation of wine bottles. For a decade, the authorities had encouraged citizens of the Reich to eat spicy nut loaf at this time of year, in keeping with Hitler's dietary preferences; it had never been popular. Jewish maids flitted around the room serving an obese woman with blond ringlets and five pudgy kids in uniform. The family were all draped in fox furs against the chill; jewelry flashed on their fingers, none of it costume. At the head of the table, his face as fat as a teapot, was a Brigadeführer: the sector's governor, Felix Quorp.

"Herr Oberstgruppenführer," said Quorp with lavish insincerity, "this is an honor. We have just drunk a toast to your forces in Kongo."

"I must speak with you in private," said Hochburg.

"Surely you can join us for a plate first?"

"Immediately."

Quorp let out a jowly sigh and indicated the French windows. They opened onto a veranda that circled the upstairs of the house. Hochburg was glad to feel the humidity against his cheeks again. Beyond the walls of the villa, half-sunk in the mist, was a bricolage of rooftops.

"Governor Globus phoned me earlier," said Quorp, shutting the door behind them. His tone was instantly aggressive. "He said you might show up. I'm to offer you no assistance. The city is jittery enough because of the Ark."

"I need a dozen of your men."

"Odilo and I are old pals, from our Carinthian days." He hid a belch behind his hand. "Loyalty means everything."

"This is a matter of the highest state security. Who do you take your orders from, Globus or the Reichsführer?"

"Both. And you are neither."

Hochburg turned back to the dining room. Kepplar was awkwardly rejecting Quorp's wife as she offered him a glass of champagne. Beneath the table, two red setters gorged on bowls of meat. "Your family, I presume." He looked forward to being reunited with Fenris.

"Of course."

"How old is your youngest?"

"Emilia is four now. She was born here, at Mandritsara; the facilities are excellent . . ." He caught Hochburg's single black eye.

Hochburg made no threat, simply allowed his voice to convey a gamut of possibilities. "Nice family," he said.

"You . . . you wouldn't dare," replied Quorp as if a bone were stuck in his throat.

Fifteen minutes later, Hochburg stood impatiently at the gate of the villa. The house, painted acid green, was surrounded by Bismarck palms and situated on top of the city's only significant hill. A simple barrier with two sentries led to a paved road—north to Diego, southwest to Mandritsara—and a third track headed down to the river and Antzu itself. It descended into thin, drifting mist. Hochburg smelled freshly baked bread. He twirled Burton's knife between his fingers.

"I'm eager to find Cole again," said Kepplar as they waited for their escort. "In Roscherhafen, I missed my chance to have a proper look at his skull. I predict a Category Four, possibly even a Five, wouldn't you say, Herr Oberst? Like a negroid."

Hochburg made no reply. He saw the mania in Kepplar's eyes. How little he understood of their mission in Africa. It came from too much indoctrination: his former deputy was dedicated but incapable of thinking for himself. Hochburg was growing weary of men like him. Of all men. He appreciated how his superweapon would free him from having to rely on drones.

The front of the villa was decorated with baskets spewing scarlet bougainvillea. A line came to Hochburg: *If I had a flower for every time I thought of you, I could walk in my garden forever.* Who had written that? A melancholy welled in him; he seized upon Feuerstein's predictions to chase it away. The scientist had spoken of an eye-shriveling flash as the device exploded.

"I will win back Africa for you, my love," he whispered to Eleanor.

America's interest in the bomb suddenly became clear to Hochburg. Nultz had been right: it was a form of insurance. Whatever pressure the American Jewish Committee was exerting on Taft, he had repeatedly vowed to remain neutral. The United States wanted the bomb not in order to attack but as a deterrent. Every time Globocnik crushed a township or sent more Jews to the reservations, America risked being drawn into conflict with the Reich. The threat of the bomb would curtail Globus, reduce him to a mere administrator. The AJC would be pacified, and Washington would have no need to embark on adventures abroad.

The clatter of boots roused Hochburg; four youths had arrived. They stood at attention clasping BK44s—all fresh and pink from Europe, heads shorn, excited to be carrying weapons. "Is that it?" said Kepplar. "Stable lads?"

"The lowest are often the keenest," replied Hochburg. Quorp had refused him any soldiers from the garrison.

"But can we rely on them? If the Jews—"

Hochburg silenced him, glancing at the villa. "Name me *any* man I can rely on. They wear the skull and palm tree; that is enough." Quorp was watching them from the dining room, his daughter at his knees. "He will have contacted Globocnik by now. We haven't much time."

Hochburg ordered the barrier lifted and marched toward the mist, slipping Burton's knife inside his uniform and removing Madeleine's file. He addressed the recruit next to him: the same groom who had met their helicopter when they first arrived.

"Do you know the city?"

"Yes, Oberstgruppenführer."

"Good. Take me to Boriziny Strasse."

CHAPTER THIRTY-EIGHT

THE ARGUMENT WITH Abner had robbed Madeleine of the last of her energy. She understood that he wanted to keep her safe, but she did not need his protection; it was bound to something selfish, a desire to prove himself. The only person who'd ever made her feel safe was Burton.

Madeleine closed the door, securing the lock as best she could. The air was saturated with an earthy, damp smell. For the first time in months, she was alone. In the abattoir she had craved moments of solitude; now it seemed deafening. Her house—the luxury that was Boriziny—consisted of a single room with a partition at the back that hid buckets and a hole to squat over; water came from a standpipe down the street. The walls, painted a coral pink by a previous occupant, were moldering, the floorboards rough and laid with banana leaf matting. The only furniture was a bed, the make-shift cradle, and a second crate she used as a table. A thought sneaked into her mind: that her brother had tricked her into returning to this place. Madeleine sat down on the bed, the frame creaking as if it would snap.

Perhaps her antagonism toward Abner was because he was right. There was no warrior spirit in her. If she wanted the twins, she should leave immediately and march straight for Mandritsara. She reached for the cradle, a sob filling her lungs.

"I'm too tired," she said aloud to ward off the silence. "I need to rest . . . just for a few minutes. You'll forgive me that."

She didn't know whether she was speaking to her babies, Burton, or herself. The sugar from the honey cake, so restorative a few moments earlier, coursed through her blood, making her heart palpitate. A sense of utter hopelessness was building inside her: finding the twins would be impossible; there was no escape from the island. Even if she did stand before Cranley again, he would bat her away like a bad smell. She wanted someone to blame: Burton for his recklessness, her husband for exiling her, Hochburg . . . If it wasn't for Hochburg, Burton would never have been drawn to Kongo. Madeleine thought of those weeks she'd spent waiting for him to return from Africa. More than once she'd been on the verge of taking Alice and leaving. Why had she been so foolish as to stay?

Behind her eyes it felt as if her face were crumbling. It was the exhaustion talking. *Never think when you're tired,* Burton used to tell her. *The world will seem black.* She needed to calm her mind, get some sleep. The flaking pink walls had guarded her children during her pregnancy; no harm would come to her here.

Madeleine yanked off her left boot, then turned to the knotted right one, trying to unpick it. Her fingernails were useless, blunt and soft with rain. She considered using her knife, but whole lengths of lace were too precious.

The second time she met Burton Cole she had been struggling with a knot. It was the autumn of 1949, a bright, breezy day on the coast. Later she reflected that all the important events of her life—fleeing Vienna, meeting Jared, the birth of Alice—happened as the year began to turn. Madeleine was walking along the beach, as she did most days when encamped in Suffolk. There were steep banks of shingle, the view empty in every directions except for a lone sail out to sea; inland were dunes and marshes. She wore the latest hiking fashions and a sturdy pair of Ayres & Lee boots. It was a relief to be free of the house and alone; the nanny was taking care of Alice, and Jared was in London till the end of the week. Time to fill her lungs and get her pulse hammering. The local countryside was too flat for proper hiking, the type she'd enjoyed as a girl; nevertheless, the exercise reminded her of her father. She wished he were there to confide in.

After she first arrived in London, wearing a hand-me-down uniform and scrubbing floors, she thought she would spend the rest of her life as a spinster maid, growing bonier by the year. Now she had a beautiful daughter, two beautiful houses, and a marriage that protected her from persecution (if not occasional snide remarks); Jared was sober, prosperous, and endlessly faithful. Life had never been so comfortable—and yet she was ashamed to admit how miserable she was.

Madeleine was no longer the woman Jared had offered a ring to. She had flourished in the rich soil he planted her in, growing in ways neither of them intended. When she let herself be clipped into shape, he only seemed more dissatisfied with the result. As much as she tried, as much as she loved him, she fell short of being grateful in the way he expected. The miracle of their first few years became oppressive: a storm swelling in the distance, forever darkening, never breaking. Like after Dunkirk, when the country held its breath for invasion. Sometimes she yearned for an argument, to shout and be shouted at, simply for the respite that would follow. Jared hadn't changed, though he wasn't quite the husband she had imagined. She sensed that he preferred the vulnerable, unwashed immigrant who first entered his office. It might have been more bearable if she had a confidante; however, few women wanted to be her friend, and those who did were kind but incapable of understanding the life she had led. In the meantime, she became more entrenched in luxury.

As Madeleine was striding along the shingle, her boot became loose. She bent down to retie the laces and found them caught in a knot. The more she tried to unravel it, the tighter it drew. When it wouldn't give, she slipped the boot off, raising it to her face to see better. The pebbles beneath her feet were spiky and sensuous. She wanted to feel them against her skin, so she tugged off her sock, burying her toes, arching her spine with pleasure. The knot was less pleasing: she plucked at it with her thumbnail, yet it refused to yield.

"*Verfluchter mist!*" she swore in German.

Madeleine continued to pry at the knot till her nail broke. She swore again, then again, speaking the forbidden language, her voice rising. The words came out in a flood. The beach was empty—what did she care? It felt good to roar. She cursed the lace and the boot and the muttering servants back home, working down through her register of insults till she reached the Nazis and Hitler, that kernel of pleasing, instinctive hate. Jared, ever the diplomat, tut-tutted whenever she spoke ill of the Führer in public.

The tension eased from her till she was giggling. When the knot still didn't budge, she hurled the boot through the air in frustration.

It bounced off the shingle and landed in front of a stranger.

Madeleine shrank with embarrassment, wondering how he had managed to get so close without making any noise. His face looked familiar, and she feared he might be one of Jared's friends. The thought of this incident getting back to her husband was too much to bear. The stranger was wearing a waxed jacket, his skin darkly tanned.

"Problem with your boot?" he asked in German.

His voice was soft, lethargic, exotic. She remembered him at once. "You're the nephew," she said, "the one in Africa."

"You know my aunt?"

"We met at one of her parties last year. I was playing Schubert, remember? Your name's Burton."

He gave a half-smile, flattered to be recognized. He looked as if he was recovering from a long illness. The stubble around his chin showed the first signs of gray. Madeleine had a good memory for names, a talent inherited from her father; he claimed that his success as a doctor relied as much on his familiarity with his patients as it did on his clinical skills. She remembered that night at his aunt's vividly, and the mistake she had made. After leaving him at the piano, she realized he was the first person she'd ever spoken to who might be able to answer her questions. She searched the house and gardens for him—but Burton had vanished.

He bent stiffly to retrieve her boot. "That's a bad knot."

Madeleine held out her hand for it, mortified that the innards might smell. That morning she had worn unlaundered socks—a silly, girlish act of rebellion. "Don't worry. I can undo it."

"By throwing it across the beach?"

She was unsure whether he was mocking her; his eyes gave away nothing. "Please, it's no trouble."

He returned it to her. She liked how he had not insisted, not proclaimed his superior skills. She fiddled with the laces for another thirty seconds before giving up. "I don't want to cut them," she said. The servants would tell.

He was looking at the ground. "Isn't your foot cold?"

She passed the boot back and rolled on her sock. He took the laces between his fingers, did something she couldn't see, and in an instant the knot was loose.

"How did you do that?" she asked, exasperated that it had been so simple.

"An old trick from the Legion."

"You were a soldier?"

He gave an evasive nod and offered her the boot. "Which way are you headed?"

"Toward Dunwich."

"Same as me. You want some company?"

Madeleine hesitated, unsure how to reply: not wanting to encourage him, not wanting to be rude. Knowing they might not meet again, and keen to question him.

They walked in silence except for the crunch of pebbles; Burton struggled to match her pace. She maintained at least a meter between them in case they chanced upon someone she knew. *A yard,* she heard her husband say. *You mustn't use these continental terms.*

"Are you back from Africa?" she asked. He gave another of his noncommittal nods. "I've always wanted to see Africa."

"There's nothing there. Just misery."

Madeleine eased her stride, building up to her real question. "What about Madagaskar—have you been?"

"Once."

"What's it like?"

He glanced at her, probably guessing that she had Jewish blood. She rarely admitted it, detesting the pity and poison that sneaked into people's faces. Burton's expression remained neutral.

"It was a long time ago," he replied. "Before they sent them south."

"I've never met anyone who's been."

He searched for something to say. "My last night, we were hiding in the hills above Majunga, waiting for a boat. The shelling had stopped, and it was quiet. Really quiet, just a chorus of insects." He offered a distant smile. "You could almost believe it was peaceful."

She continued to quiz him, surprised by how considerate his answers were; for some reason, she'd had him down as a brute. She knew there were no words of consolation; she no longer needed any. She simply wanted to make the beyond her family had passed into real, know the color of the earth and the smell of the sky from someone who had been there.

After ten minutes, he stopped abruptly.

"I can't go any farther." He gripped his thigh. "It hurts." He turned in the direction from which they had come. "Do you often walk here?"

"I like to."

"The doctor says I need exercise every day. To strengthen the muscle. Perhaps we'll meet another time."

"I'm not sure that's appropriate. I'm married."

He limped away, boots scrunching on the shingle, before he stopped again. "I remember the Schubert now," he said, "The Hungarian Melody. You were very good. But, I'm sorry, I can't remember your name."

"Mrs. Cranley."

"Your first name."

She wavered. "Madeleine."

"Like in the Bible." Burton smiled and switched to German: " 'Healer of wounds and evil spirits.' "

The next morning dawned warm and blue, ideal for walking. "The weather's been better since the Jews left" was a staple joke of the age. Madeleine stayed indoors, as she did the day after; then Jared visited till Sunday. As usual, he came with gifts and bonhomie, and that tightening of the atmosphere in the house. On Monday, it was pouring. Madeleine tied her hair in a bun and put on a mac, assuming she'd have the beach to herself, and found Burton patrolling the same stretch of shingle where they'd met before. They exchanged pleasantries as the rain lashed them, and he asked about her weekend. For reasons she never understood—the conspiracy of the weather, a need to unburden herself, instinct—she told him the truth. She said nothing bad about Jared but explained how suffocating she found the expectations of home, how with the servants always around there could be no lapse in her poise.

"You must think me awfully ungrateful," she said when she finished. *Awfully ungrateful:* she sounded like a bad parody of Celia Johnson.

"My aunt's a good woman; so is her maid," replied Burton. "They care for me like nurses. But sometimes I have to get out of that house or I'll scream."

Madeleine was soaked by the time she returned home. She ran a bath, and as she stood in her underclothes, steam billowing from the tap, she wondered whether Burton liked hot baths. *I could never marry a man who didn't like baths,* she used to vow to her friends when she was a teenager. Jared's new obsession was showers. *They're the future,* he told her. *Look at America.*

She went out the next day in quiet anticipation of meeting Burton. But when she saw him in the distance—a dark, limping figure against the gray shingle—she froze. What was she doing? They could never be friends. She should return to London with Alice straightaway. When he raised his hand in greeting, she hurried off in the opposite direction.

"*Ami!*" he cried after her. The sound bounced across the shingle into the boom of the waves. "*Ami!*"

Madeleine jerked awake now, convinced that she could hear Burton's voice echoing around her, as real as the pink walls and the pervasive damp.

Ami . . .

It was the call of a legionnaire as he approached a fort. She lurched to the door, her brain half-slopped, and looked up and down Boriziny Strasse. It was empty, the mist curling and shifting along its length. Nothing but the smell of baking. The woman opposite broke off from her breathing exercises to scowl.

Madeleine returned inside. She removed her other boot and concentrated on the knot, twisting the lace to either side as tight as she could while simultaneously pushing toward the center, the way Burton taught her. It took seconds. She tucked her boots away and massaged her feet. The soles were wrinkled and flaking, and she had a wart on her heel. She picked at the black dots in the crater, remembering how supple and beautiful her feet used to be and the way Burton squeezed them slightly too hard, the sensation delicious. She peeled off her shirt and her sopping trousers.

Behind the partition were a drain, a tub of ash, and several buckets of water, which had stood untouched for months. Madeleine took a handful of ash and, using it in place of soap, scoured herself till she was rosy, then emptied one of the pails over her head. Back in the room, she was aware of a stagnant odor rising from her skin. She retrieved her suitcase from under the bed and fished out the last remaining bottle of perfume Jared had packed. The rest she had sold in the market, amazed by the prices they had commanded and the vanity of some women among so many stinking bodies. She aimed the spray at her throat—but didn't depress the pump.

Madeleine had neither wanted nor planned an affair; only in retrospect did she understand how emotionally dormant her life had become. Jared could be attentive and affectionate, he doted on Alice, but he was capable only of giving love. He had no desire to receive it.

She continued to encounter Burton, and they walked farther as he grew stronger. He offered more recollections about Madagaskar, but soon she wanted to know about the rest of his life: Africa, the Legion, his childhood. It was like hearing a fellow voice in the gloom. She was touched by his moments of awkwardness, his doubts—so different from her husband's enameled certainty. For the first time, she spoke freely of her own past. Jared was from a blithe, successful family. His father was in good health, his mother had died peacefully at home. The bitterness of affliction was something he couldn't share.

As the mornings grew darker and the wind from the North Sea more biting, Madeleine let herself look forward to seeing Burton. He always kept an arm's length from her and never said anything suggestive—unlike some of Jared's friends, with their secret gazes, as if they wanted to test the Nazi propaganda about the Jew's lasciviousness. Once he met her with a crumb of breakfast stuck to his beard, and she brushed it off; it seemed the most natural thing in the world to do. She hoped his leg would take a long time to heal.

Eventually Jared questioned why she was spending so much time at their second home. "Alice will think she's a country girl," he said playfully but without smiling.

"Come and spend more time with us," she entreated, confident that he wouldn't. "You work too hard."

That weekend, they returned to London with him.

When Madeleine pictured Burton waiting for her, then walking the beach alone, she felt a draining in her chest. She wrote to apologize for her departure and signed it "Maddie" before adding a P.S., aware that a threshold had been crossed: she was committing them both to a secret. She asked him not to reply to her home address or mention their friendship to his aunt.

Madeleine found excuses to visit Suffolk, and Burton traveled often to London; for some reason, they always met on Thursdays. She wished it were summer so she could wear dresses, rather than being wrapped in wool and fur. They kissed for the first time at Christmas, after lunch at a Kardomah café, a tense, almost embarrassed pressing together of the lips that trilled with anticipation. She remembered carol singers and the cold of his face, the scent of roast chestnuts and petrol fumes. It was in Trafalgar Square, opposite the huge tree Hitler sent annually to Britain. A few years earlier she had wandered these streets like a beggar, blinking at the decorations and the restaurants crammed with diners, aware that she could never be a part of this world. Jared had allowed her access. The beard around Burton's mouth was soft. They kissed beneath garlands of light, her hands grasping his cheeks—and she didn't care if anyone saw her. She returned home to Hampstead elated and ill; for the next week, flu gripped her. After Christmas she told Burton that they must stop seeing each other. That same afternoon they made love for the first time. She had already imagined the moment; to her surprise, he had been less gentle than Jared.

Madeleine dropped the unused perfume bottle into the case and lay down, exhaustion tugging at her. The air was muggy, but her naked body felt exposed; she pulled the thin gray sheet to her chin.

She lay motionless, unthinking, her eyes open and gritty, and had a sense that she'd never sleep again. *Sleep is the only safe place in Madagaskar,* Jacoba once told her. In the abattoir, rumors had circulated of a machine the Nazis were developing to patrol their dreams, to make sure there was no respite, even in slumber. She glimpsed her knife resting on the cradle but was too weary to fetch it. She imagined her hand in Burton's.

The next thing Madeleine was aware of was the door opening. A silhouette blocked out the mist. Her eyelids fluttered before she rolled away from the light, back into sleep.

CHAPTER THIRTY-NINE

Antzu
20 April, 15:30

"DRAGONFLY, DO YOU receive? Dragonfly, come in."

Dragonfly: Cranley's call sign. He had chosen it with one of his empty laughs.

Salois spoke with his mouth close to the microphone, one hand gripping the stand, the other adjusting the radio dial to find the exact frequency. He was convinced that Cranley had made it ashore and was marching toward the radar station at Mazunka. Salois would continue to Diego Suarez until he learned otherwise; too many lives had been wasted to abandon the mission. He felt the weary throb of cheating death again, a sense of being somehow inferior to the men who had died on the beach. That, and what remained of his pride. He didn't want Rolland reporting that they had failed; the blame would inevitably fall on him, the Jew.

"Dragonfly? Cranley?"

Static whined in response.

Telecommunications were banned across the island for Jews. The radio room was hidden in a tiny cellar in the foundations of the synagogue, down three flights of stairs accessed through a trapdoor. There was no ventilation; a single candle shed its migraine light. He continued trawling the static until the door opened.

"Are you finished?" asked the rabbi. "Someone else is waiting."

Salois twirled the dial so the frequency couldn't be traced and picked up his rucksack. The previous night, he had gone back to the beach and salvaged everything he could. Half a dozen hand grenades, detonators, smoke flares (green to let the bombers know the air defenses had been destroyed, red to abort the raid). All the food was lost. He had devoured the two bowls of rice soup and yams the rabbi gave him but was still famished.

There were no explosives.

They climbed the steps, the rabbi's trousers swishing near Salois's face to reveal bony ankles. At the top, a man with glasses and a hairless, nut-brown head was waiting. The rabbi showed him below before he returned to escort Salois through a maze of gloomy corridors. Salois glimpsed empty schoolrooms and infrequent windows, the view blocked by banks of earth and rubbish. Some of the walls were piled high with sacks of rice marked JOINT DISTRIBUTION COMMITTEE; in places they had to squeeze themselves flat to pass.

"Is it true about the sacks?" asked Salois.

He knew the rabbi from before: he was famed for his charity and his love of dancing. He hadn't honored the Ha-Mered, the rebellion, but he hadn't shamed it, either. "There are too many rumors on this island" was the reply.

During the rebellion, the Nazis had impounded all food aid from America. There were tales that rice would be released, a sack at a time, for every ten Vanilla Jews the council handed over. The twenty-four members of the Judenrat, the Jewish Council, did not see themselves as collaborators. Subdued by years spent on the precipice, they accepted their lot in Madagaskar, believing it was wiser to obey the Nazis and build the best society they could than to engage in futile, unwinnable resistance. For Salois to come to Antzu and seek the council's help was a risk, but the Vanillas had no central command, and time was too short for him to wander the forest, hoping to encounter a band of fighters. He could think of no alternative. One of the councilmen, Zuckerman, whom Salois had known briefly from the work gangs of Diego, had a more militant streak and might be convinced to help.

The rabbi reached a heavy wooden door and offered Salois a kippah, a skullcap, as he had done when Salois first arrived. This time he was adamant: "If you wish to see the council, you must wear it." There were raised voices on the other side. Salois dropped the skullcap on his crown; it felt as unfamiliar as a Nazi helmet. The rabbi ushered him through the door, into a space that echoed like a warehouse. The air was a torment: hot, yeasty, and farinose.

Disquiet weighed upon Salois. The sanctuary was shadowy except for the Ner Tamid, the Eternal Light, casting a wan glow. Above, on the street level, was the gallery where women were permitted to sit and worship. It was only the second time he had set foot inside such a place. The previous occasion was in Antwerp, the day he'd fled the city, his hands still bloody. He realized that if he left, it would be more than his crime he was fleeing. He would be shedding his life, the ties of family and friends and everything that was familiar, even, it turned out, his name. There would be no way back. He had called upon God, vowing to remain and face his penalty if he was offered a sign. He sat in silence till nightfall.

The synagogue in Antzu was the only one on the island, a concession granted by Governor Bouhler with Heydrich's tacit authority. After the Nazis' clearance program in Europe, it became the only synagogue east of New York. Since building materials were restricted—the Nazis feared that iron and cement could be used for military defenses—it had been constructed from wood (apart from a brick chimney), like the synagogues of the shtetls. The "Malagasy" style, it was called. Workers from the Eastern Sector had temporarily been allowed into the city to erect it. Talmudic tradition dictated that the synagogue be the tallest structure in the city, something Bouhler refused until the council suggested a solution. SS engineers dynamited a great hole in the ground, and the synagogue was built at its base, making it the tallest building while the governor's villa was the highest.

The council was gathered around seven tables arranged in an octagon with the empty side as an opening. They were all elderly men, dressed in decade-old suits that were in good repair, well laundered and pressed. They wore shirts buttoned to the throat, no neckties, their sleeves rolled up so they could work. No numbers blackened their wrists; members of the council had been spared this indignity. In front of them: tubs of rice flour and salt, dough proving beneath cloths.

"What are they doing?" Salois whispered to the rabbi.

"It's forbidden for the council to meet on Führertag, so they're baking bread. If a patrol passes, they're simply preparing food for the needy."

"Will there be patrols?"

"It's the monsoon season; that doesn't mean it will rain today."

Salois scanned the elders for Zuckerman, but couldn't see him. In the shadows behind the tables, two bakers were working an oven. A pile of loaves was stacked nearby, the bread misshapen, fashioned by hands that belonged to amateurs.

"That's Wischblatt," said the rabbi, indicating a man at the top table. "He's been head of the council this past year." Wischblatt had the look of a provincial lawyer, his skin ricey, his head as smooth as a stone except for a band of starkly clipped hair above the ears. "You must wait till he calls you."

Heated exchanges were passing between council members, their ire directed not at each other or the Nazis but elsewhere. Some of their faces were stained with tears. They spoke in German, the official language of the

Judenrat. At first Salois struggled to pick up the thread of the discussion. Something had happened the previous night: the new rebellion was catching; it was the council's duty to dampen it and make clear to Globus that they condemned it. Salois was reminded of Rolland and Turneiro and Cranley. *Once again I stand before men who talk too much*, he thought. Then he realized what they were discussing and experienced a burst of grief and fury.

He shrugged off the rabbi's restraining arm and walked between the tables; it felt like entering a courtroom. "The Ark has been destroyed?"

"Burned down this very morning," replied one of the council. "Our records reduced to ashes."

Wischblatt silenced him. "Rabbi, who is this stranger you bring to us?"

"Major Reuben Salois. I fought with the Benelux and Vohemar Brigades during the Mered Ha-vanil. I've come to see Zuckerman." He dropped his rucksack at his feet—the clink of smoke grenades—and glanced round the tables for him.

"The Vohemar were sent to Steinbock when the rebellion was defeated, to work the mines." Wischblatt's voice was melodious, commanding, with a hint of vindictiveness he couldn't quite conceal. "We are better off without them. They wanted to drag us into the furnace."

"We never saw the mines. The Nazis made us dig our own graves, then executed every last man."

Wischblatt appraised him. "Then a ghost stands before us."

"Fate spared me, and I escaped to Africa. Now I'm looking for Zuckerman."

"Zuckerman? He has—what's your expression?—'gone to America.' "

Dead, thought Salois. Of course dead; everyone was dead. It was the release granted to all men except him. A fleeting hopelessness passed through him before his hatred flamed. The Nazis had destroyed their records, the island's last safeguard. It could mean only one thing: the population must follow. He had to continue now, with or without Cranley, without hope of success—so long as a blow was delivered, no matter how feeble. If the Ark was a symbol, so too was Diego.

Salois scanned the faces of the councilmen again; none of them looked as if he went to bed hungry. Surely at least one could be persuaded to help? It depressed him to depend on these men.

"It was not my plan to beg your—"

Wischblatt interrupted.

"This council advocates the detention of Vanilla Jews, of all the resistance groups, for your own sake as much as ours." He gestured across the table at a man with tangled black hair and a bullock's jaw. "Yaudin is chief of our police. It's time his wardens took you away."

Two Jupo men stepped forward.

Yaudin raised a hand to stop them. On his finger was a rarity among islanders: a wedding ring; most had long since been stolen or bartered. Yaudin appeared irritated by Wischblatt giving orders. "I was a friend of Zuckerman's," he said to Salois. "And Zuckerman would have said that it's a brave man who escapes and chooses to return. Any other day, I would have agreed with Herr Wischblatt; but the Ark is gone. Perhaps we should hear the major out." His accent was from the gutters of Berlin. "Why have you come back?"

"To destroy Diego Suarez."

There was a ripple of angry, incredulous mirth around the tables.

Salois outlined Cranley's plan, telling them only what they needed to know, hoping that his candor might sway them.

Wischblatt was shaken. "You're out of your mind," he said. "The reprisals . . ."

"It will bring America into the war."

"A boon for Britain and her flagging empire. Your masters will raise a glass as they look across the ocean and watch us burn."

"With the Americans in Africa, we have a chance."

"What chance? They will be the wrong side of the Mozambique Channel. You Vanillas will never defeat the SS."

"True. But there's a limit to how much blood Globus can shed before they'd have to intervene."

"Like they did during the first rebellion?"

"It is the only way."

There was a creak as the door opened. The man with glasses, the one who had been waiting to use the radio, entered.

"The only way is cooperation with our overlords," continued Wischblatt, full of reason and wheedling. "This council has proven that this is so. While you Vanillas have been hunted like dogs, we have built a community. But if you attack Diego they will not discriminate. You will be responsible for the death of every man, woman, and child on this island."

"They're dead already. By stealth or speed, the Nazis mean this place as our grave. The Ark should tell you that."

"Not in the Western Sector. Not in Antzu. Look what we've achieved." He gestured toward the dimness of the Eternal Light. "Here we live as we will; a Jew can walk the streets without fear."

"Your streets are empty."

"And where will you be," demanded Wischblatt, "while Globocnik takes his revenge? Palestine? America? The British would not abandon their soldiers or risk them being captured; they must have planned an escape."

"A boat will pick us up from Kap Ost, five days from now."

Kap Ost: the most easterly point of Madagaskar. It was within sight of the shipping lanes between Asia and South Africa.

"You see." Wischblatt was thrilled to be proved correct. He addressed the council: "He rouses the executioner, then leaves us to suffer the consequences."

"No." Despite Rolland's elaborate scheme to extract the squads, Salois had never intended to join them. "I will stay and fight."

"Then you'll die," retorted Wischblatt, before adding more, "but at least not a hypocrite." He spoke to the police chief: "Yaudin, we mustn't listen to another word of this."

Yaudin was staring intently at Salois, his eyes uncertain. "One thing I don't understand," he said. "Why risk coming here? Why tell us all this?"

Since fleeing Antwerp, Salois had harbored a suspicion of policemen, no matter what their uniform, but he could see a wavering in Yaudin's expression. "To try to convince you," he replied. "To entreat you. I need men and explosives."

"Then God smiles upon us," said Wischblatt. "There are no munitions in Antzu."

"You must have something."

An emphatic, satisfied shake of that smooth head. "You've had a wasted journey, Major Salois—"

"I know where to find explosives."

Salois and the councilmen turned to look at the man in glasses. Salois saw that his sleeves were rolled down past the wrist.

"Rabbi," asked Wischblatt, "who are these strays you bring before us today?"

"My name is Abner Weiss; I have spoken to the council before. Ben-Ze'ev sent me with news. It's more than just the Ark. The Nazis are shutting down the factories and farms; they're sending everyone to the reservations."

Wischblatt made a shushing noise. "Only those who have joined this new 'Pig Rebellion' of yours. Yaudin, I insist you arrest these men. There are more important matters to discuss."

The police chief's brow was gnarled with indecision.

Another of the elders pointed at Salois. "How do we know he's a Jew? This morning the Ark is destroyed; the same day a stranger arrives with promises of salvation if only we aid in his revolt. If it's true about the reservations, he could have been sent by Globus. An agent provocateur."

There was a murmur of assent.

"Can you prove who you are?" asked Yaudin.

"Do I have papers like you? No."

"So how can we trust your story?"

Salois met Yaudin's stare, then—one after the other—the eyes of every member of the council, lingering when he got to Wischblatt. He stepped into the center of the tables and loosened the cuffs of his caftan. It was patchy with salt stains and blood. He undid the buttons down his chest and tugged it over his head. The garment fell to the floor.

Salois raised his arms from his sides, palms upward, and slowly spun round, baring his torso for the whole room to see.

+ + +

The coals in the oven hummed. The two bakers had stopped their work and were gawping at him, mouths loose with horror. Wischblatt stared for as long as he could, then, like the rest of the councilmen, hid his eyes.

"Do you want to see my legs?" asked Salois. His voice was funereal, savage. "The soles of my feet?" He went to unbuckle his belt.

"That's enough," said Yaudin. "You have my apologies, Major, the whole council's. And our sorrow."

"All I want is your help."

The night of his execution, before casting himself into the Mozambique Channel, Salois had scrambled among the multitude of dead, reading forearms by moonlight, memorizing as many numbers as he was able to. The leaching of so many souls gave his mind a supernatural capacity. Later, as his body healed and fattened at the Inhambane monastery, he asked one of the Jesuits for a needle and a bowl of ink. He had spent days reciting every digit he could recall, tattooing his skin till every bare patch was indigo.

Abner picked up Salois's caftan and handed it to him. He looked cut through.

Salois covered his body once more. Whenever it was exposed, wretchedness weighed on him as if he were to blame for the history his skin told. "What type of explosives?" he asked, fastening the buttons.

"Mostly dynamite. The British smuggle in supplies for us."

"Where?"

"You mustn't," pleaded Wischblatt. "Do you think we like the Nazis? We hate them as much as you do."

"No," said Salois. "You want to cling to your perch here. You'd ignore your fellow men for a hut on Boriziny and an extra sack of rice."

Wischblatt's cheeks reddened. "We are wise to. With the Ark gone, we must be more cautious than ever."

"With the Ark gone, nothing will save you from Globus. Except the United States."

Salois despised the councilmen for their lack of courage, yet he understood how they wanted to preserve the fragility—the illusion—of the world they had created behind the walls of Antzu. A place where children could play without fear of being shot at and parents still died quietly in bed; where you could stroll with your spouse even if the air stank of open sewers. Perhaps that was why he was so resentful: they had families to protect.

"There's a pig farm," said Abner. "Nachtstadt. It's thirty kilometers to the east. We bury supplies among the pens."

"Will you help?" Salois stared into Abner's eyes and saw too much emotion to make sense of. Frustration and guilt. Hope, excitement, relief.

Abner shook his head. "I can tell you how to get there, where to find the explosives. But I have to stay in Antzu."

Salois tugged at the boy's sleeves, revealing a roll call of tattoos. "You're one of us."

"From the first days of the Ha-Mered."

"Then you have to join me."

"Twenty-four hours ago, I would have followed you the whole way. Things have changed. I found my sister, after years apart; I have to care for my family."

"Diego I can do alone if I must, but I need you to take me to the dynamite."

Abner's face was anguished. "I can send word to Ben-Ze'ev. He could bring you an army."

"How long?"

"Two or three days."

Salois brought the younger man close so the council wouldn't hear, hoping to gain his confidence and coax him to arms. "There's a train to take me into the heart of the base. No guards, no checks; the British set it up. I need to be on it *tonight*."

Abner stepped away. "Do you have a sister?" he asked. "A mother?"

"No."

"A wife?"

A clench of remorse, like an acid reflux. "Nobody."

"If you did, perhaps you'd understand."

Salois eased Abner to one side and addressed Yaudin: "Give me two of your wardens."

"I don't know," replied Yaudin. "My men protect this city. None of them wants to be a hero."

"Madagaskar doesn't make heroes." Salois faced the rabbi. "What about you?"

"I wield God's wisdom, not his sword."

Salois couldn't hide his disgust. "Will none of you help?" His voice swelled. "Not one fellow Jew?" Silence. He flicked a look to the heavens and breathed a small, contemptuous sigh. "Then you deserve your fate."

CHAPTER FORTY

16:00

HER HOUSE WAS empty.

Hochburg circled Madeleine's room, thinking what a foul way this was to live. It was cramped and dusky; each breath speckled his throat with mildew. She had been here recently; there was an indent in the mattress, wet footprints on the floor. His boots dwarfed her feet.

"Go outside," he told Kepplar. "Speak to the neighbors. See if anyone knows where she is."

Once alone, Hochburg continued his search, moving with speed. He felt a slither of exhilaration, more expectant than when he'd tracked down Feuerstein. Half-tucked beneath the bed was a suitcase. He lifted the lid, rummaged through the few garments, and found a bottle of perfume. Hochburg squirted two bursts in front of his face and inhaled. The scent was musky and expensive; he didn't like it. Judging from the fragrance and the clothing, Burton had given Madeleine a luxurious life. He opened her file and scrutinized it, hoping that some clue to her whereabouts might be hidden in its columns of facts and figures.

When Kepplar first handed it to him at Tana airport, he had been transfixed by the photograph. Madeleine's hair was black, her nose and brow heavier, her expression dismal for Interpol's lens—but there was something about the eyes, something about the inflection of her lips that struck him as belonging to Eleanor. So this was Burton's wife. Whatever path had led her to Madagaskar, she and Burton had shared the one thing denied to Hochburg. His envy at the airport had been ferocious and silent. He stared at the photograph again.

Walter Hochburg wanted to possess this woman.

The sensation rose from deep within his loins, as profound and powerful as his ambitions for Africa. He wanted to press his body on top of hers, taste the hot, salty decay of her mouth; wherever people were concentrated in poverty, their teeth rotted. He wanted her servility, for Madeleine to wrap her arms willingly around his back and drag him into her, to cradle and yearn for him.

Eleanor had been his second lover. Since her death, he had known only one other woman, a secretary in his office at Muspel. It had been a brief, miscalculated liaison triggered by a passing similarity: sand in the wound of his loss. Every time they lay together, he screwed his eyes shut and imagined that she was Eleanor; every time, she failed. When their affair ended, he wanted to bury her in the dunes; instead he transferred her to Windhuk and swore not to repeat his mistake. In the decades since, he had forsaken pleasures of the flesh and had known no stirring—until now. To cuckold Burton would be a revenge more unexpected than anything he had conceived before. Hochburg remembered the anguish of having to watch Eleanor retire to bed with her husband.

"Herr Oberst!" Kepplar called from outside.

The SS nickname for Antzu was Moskitostadt: the air hummed as if electrified. Kepplar and the grooms periodically slapped and scratched themselves. Not a single insect landed on Hochburg; they never had. *You must have acid for blood* was Himmler's peevish observation. The mist was beginning to thin.

"This Jewess saw her," said Kepplar. He indicated a woman in the house opposite; she had fine skin gone blotchy and wore an old silk shawl.

The grooms were milling about, their BK44s slung over their shoulders. When they first marched into Antzu, Jews scurrying away from them till the streets were empty, their faces had shone. Now they looked bored, youths tricked into believing there would be action: the disappointment of the untested.

The woman curtsied and spoke in the haughty tone of someone yet to accept that her world was irrevocably changed. "The English has been gone for months. No one wanted her house because it was hexed—"

"I've no time for superstition," replied Hochburg. "Where is she now?"

"What's it worth? Some rupees? A sack of rice?"

One of the grooms shoved her. "Watch your tongue, Jew. You're talking to an Oberstgruppenführer."

Hochburg held out a restraining hand. "I can find you some rice."

"We thought the English was dead. Then this morning, she turns up again. Her, an old woman, and a man. I never saw the other two before."

Kepplar's eyes sparkled. "It must be Cole."

"Where are they now?"

"The old woman left, then hurried back not ten minutes ago, all afluster." A mosquito landed at the base of her throat, and she picked it off. "The two of them went that way."

"What's in that direction?" Hochburg asked the grooms.

"The docks, Oberstgruppenführer, and the pit house."

"Pit house?"

He looked apologetic. "The synagogue. But we shouldn't go there. Governor Quorp warned us. It will cause problems."

The other grooms laughed. "Don't be such a louse."

"You have been most cooperative, Fräulein," said Hochburg, then addressed Kepplar: "Shoot her."

The woman paled. "But Herr Oberstgruppenführer . . . I'm trying to help."

"When will you people learn? So long as Jew sides against Jew, your extinction is guaranteed."

The sparkle had vanished from Kepplar's eye.

+ + +

Madeleine followed blindly, darting down alleyways that twisted left, right, then right again, the next turn always half-cloaked in mist. The smell of bread was getting stronger, but she no longer cared. Nausea and elation pumped through her. She dodged beneath the scaffolding, knocked over a paint pot. The ground ran yellow.

"Where are we going?"

They were running toward the river.

Only moments before, she had been wrenched awake by someone shaking her. Disorientation distilled into alarm . . . Then she realized it was Jacoba and shrugged her off.

"Wake up! I've found you a way off the island, girl."

At first Madeleine hadn't understood. "There's no way off . . ."

She glanced at the open door, expecting dusk or the impenetrable night, possibly the next day's dawn. Mist chugged by as it had only minutes before. She had been dreaming, the clarity of the images already nebulous. Something to do with the twins and Burton and Jared, an expression of disbelief on his face as she took a dagger and—

The significance of what Jacoba had said sharpened in her mind.

She sat up. Her eyes felt arid.

"You've got to come quickly," said Jacoba. "Before they arrest him."

Madeleine grabbed the first item she found in the case, a white dress polka-dotted with mold, tied her boots, and headed for the door. Then she stopped. It was as if she heard the knife calling after her, a trill of revenge. She retrieved the blade and left the house.

They stopped on Nabi Daniel Strasse, outside the synagogue. To either side of its nondescript frontage were warehouses that stored crops from the local farms—cotton, sisal, tobacco—before they were shipped downriver. Madeleine had been inside a few times when she first arrived in Antzu but soon stopped visiting. God's walls offered no comfort; they merely emphasized how alone she was. It had been the same during that early period in London. Years later, after Parliament passed the Evacuation Bill, she had watched with little emotion as Britain's synagogues were demolished or converted into hostels for down-and-outs.

"You came here?" she asked Jacoba.

A pair of stooped old men were painting the building opposite. They glanced up from their brushes.

"To see my daughter. I had to beg to be let in." She indicated a solitary Jupo guard by the entrance. "Then I heard them talking below. It's fate."

They hurried through the vestibule, the eyes of the dead staring down at them, and continued on to the balcony where women were allowed to worship. Below was a cluster of tables with the Judenrat gathered around them. She recognized the head of the council, Wischblatt, and also saw Abner, a skullcap on his fuzzy, blistered head; she'd never seen him wear one before. He was studying the toe of his boot in a way that reminded her of Cranley when she displeased him. The voice of the rabbi carried upstairs: "I wield God's wisdom, not his sword."

"Will none of you help?" came the reply.

The words were spoken by a man standing in the middle of the tables, dressed in a filthy burgundy caftan. There was something glowering about his presence, righteous.

"That's the one," said Jacoba, "Salois. He's full of stupid talk. Dangerous talk. But a boat is on its way to rescue him."

The two women went down the stairs, and Madeleine strode into the center of the tables. With the possibility of escape, there seemed hope for reaching Mandritsara. There was honey and fire in her veins. The council—the gray, bald men she used to see sashaying down Boriziny Strasse—scowled at her.

"Women are forbidden here," said the rabbi, bustling her back toward the stairs.

She broke away from him and marched to Salois. He had a gallows complexion. "You have a way off this island?"

He nodded. "Who are you?"

"Madeleine. I'll do anything for a place on your boat."

Salois appraised her. She felt his eyes absorbing her thin arms and straggly white dress. There was an intense, ethereal quality to them that made her think of empty spaces—like the desert vistas Burton used to describe or the endless span of the ocean. She couldn't name their color.

"None of these men will help me," he said. "Why will you?"

"Anything," said Madeleine fiercely.

"You don't know what I'm asking. You may not live to see the boat."

"Where's it going?"

"South Africa."

Abner stepped between them. "Y-you can't ask her. She's my sister, not a soldier. She barely had the strength to walk here."

Madeleine pushed him out of the way.

"She's the first person in this place willing to stand with me."

The words jittered in Abner's mouth: "She's not like you and me—she doesn't know what it is to kill. She doesn't care about America or your mission."

"I see the hate in her eyes," replied Salois. "That's enough."

Abner turned on Jacoba. "This is your fault. Why did you bring her here?"

Madeleine stilled her brother. "Did you ask the council?" she said. "About Mandritsara?"

"Of course not." Then, with a hint of embarrassment: "Not yet—there wasn't time."

"Ask them now." She used the same hectoring tone as their mother. "You said one of the elders might help us."

"I told you that to get you here. I know it was wrong, but it's for your own good. You're safe in Antzu."

She was more exasperated than shocked or angry. "I don't need saving. And I can't stay here. I'll never be able to live in that house, sleep in that bed without trying."

"Leni, please listen to me—"

There was a cry from the balcony. "A patrol is coming!"

Salois reached for the rucksack at his feet.

Jacoba shook her head at him. "The main doors are the only way out."

"They will not come here," said Wischblatt. "Not today. We let them pass, then end this nonsense once and for all."

They stood waiting; then the Jupo guard called again: "They're headed this way."

Salois turned to the rabbi. "Can you hide us?"

"There's no time."

Another yell from the balcony: "Six of them, with machine guns."

"For God's sake," said the rabbi, "make sure every last patch of your skin is covered."

There was a scraping sound as the door above them opened. A murmur of voices, then the ring of jackboots.

Madeleine clutched her knife. Salois saw the movement and told her no with his eyes. He was completely still, not only his body but the air around him. His poise made her think of her father when his mind was tackling a problem, or those mornings when he had to convey something to do with death. Salois moved quickly behind the tables. Madeleine followed, repeating that she would do whatever it took for a place on his boat.

He ignored her and scooped up a handful of dough. "Make bread," he hissed at the others. "Make bread."

+ + +

"What are these?" asked Hochburg.

The vestibule was sunk in a dirty gray light. There were thousands of photographs pinned to the walls, some with messages or desiccated flowers. Identity-paper pictures, informal snaps, even miniature paintings. Some were family portraits with the faces cut out, then reassembled like jigsaws with one individual missing. Along the floor were piles of small stones.

"Dead Jews," replied the groom who had accompanied Hochburg and Kepplar inside the synagogue. Two geriatric painters had seen the women enter the building and readily snitched. The rest of the grooms were outside, guarding the exit. "They post them as memorials, like our Totenburgs. It gives me the creeps."

Hochburg plucked a photograph from the wall but didn't look at it. The one picture he'd had of Eleanor had been a prized possession until a day came when he could no longer bear seeing it; he had incinerated it without regret. Hochburg screwed up the photo in his hand and tossed it away.

Kepplar had found the staircase. They descended into the sanctuary, where a group of men were preparing loaves.

A rabbi came forward, his shoulders bent low. *"Froher Führertag,* Oberst-gruppenführer. We are baking bread for the hungry, to honor this day."

"It's a long time since I read Exodus, but shouldn't it be unleavened? The bread of affliction."

Unsure how to reply, the rabbi offered a loaf.

Hochburg tore off a hunk. "It's good," he said, chewing. "Soft and salty." He handed the rest back and examined the bakers in front of him. The stench of yeast made him think of Globus's breath.

"My name is Walter Hochburg, governor-general of Kongo. I mean no harm to you. I am looking for a woman by the name of Madeleine Cole."

"Women are not allowed in this part of the building, Herr Oberstgrup-penführer," said the rabbi. "It is God's law."

Hochburg put a finger to his lips and scanned the tables.

He expected her to hide or run. Instead Madeleine stepped away from the group. The bespectacled man next to her put out a warning hand, but she shrugged past.

She was gaunt, anemic, her hair in clumps as if she had been exposed to a dose of radiation; Feuerstein had briefed him on the dangers of uranium. Hochburg preferred women to have complexions of honey and wheat, but there was a beauty to her darkness, even if it had been disfigured by hunger and exhaustion. Her eyes curtsied up and down, taking him in.

"You are Burton's wife?" he asked.

"I took his name"—her voice cracked, then tightened—"after you took Burton from me."

She doesn't know he's alive, thought Hochburg, his expectations dashed for a second time. He calculated whether this could be used to his advantage—and failed; all he could hear was the unslakable grief of her accusation. He understood the pain of surviving, he wanted to comfort her.

"Come closer," he ordered.

She crossed the floor till she stood in his shadow. Beneath her dress she wore boots like a laborer's; her calves were just shafts of bone. The black-and-white photograph in her file had robbed her eyes of their color. As she stood before him, he recognized their hue immediately. Burton must have known it, too: so we are condemned to chase the past.

Madeleine stared at him with defiance. Defiance, fear, loathing. And something else: a veiled dancing glimmer that was impossible.

When he'd first met Eleanor, she had nursed his grief with the tenderness of a mother, let him confess his sins. Later they japed and argued as though brother and sister. The closed world of the orphanage—four white faces among so many blacks—was like being in a family again. The summer after he arrived, he taught Eleanor to swim, till one day, at the end of a lesson, she reached the shore and happened to glance back at him. It wasn't that she held his gaze too long, it wasn't the water trickling through her matted hair; it was the indecipherable need in her eye—the same as in Madeleine's now.

That night he described the event in his journal, hoping for the catharsis that ink on paper often brought. As she'd waded out of the river, he had averted his eyes from her back and buttocks and concentrated on her ankles: that narrow band where the paleness of her heel met skin darkened by Africa. The only word he could summon to describe the color was *butterscotch*. It felt illicit: the course of his life changed by something as unportentous and mundane as an adjective. He became feverish, unable to meet her gaze, castigating himself. Eleanor's chaste, prohibited body spoiled his every waking thought; even sleep didn't shield him. At first he was wretched with the surety that she shared none of his feelings, later by the tragedy that she did.

Madeleine took another pace closer, her hands held primly behind her back. Hochburg stepped toward her, aware of Kepplar fidgeting close behind, till he could breathe in the scent of her. She was so emaciated, the weight of his body would crush her.

The Jews were staring at them; the groom guarding the stairs swayed his BK44 in disbelief. Hochburg didn't care.

He thought he heard her whisper Burton's name.

Then she was in his embrace. Madeleine stood on tiptoe and guided him toward her. Her delicate fingers reached around the cold thickness of his neck. She pressed her lips against his and opened her mouth.

CHAPTER FORTY-ONE

Boriziny Strasse, Antzu
20 April, 16:15

TÜNSCHER GAVE A harsh laugh and lit a Bayerweed. "Don't tell me—she's not in?" His face was sallow and sweaty, the rims of his eyes red. It had taken longer to march to Antzu than he'd promised: every hour he had to stop and rest.

Burton came down the steps from Maddie's house and joined him in the street. Mist wafted around them. If Burton hadn't been so agitated, he might have relished the irony: just like when he'd reached the farm, he had traveled halfway round the world to find an empty room. The only sign that anyone had been there was the indent of a head on the pillow—that and the stench. He had a lurching sensation similar to when he was first getting to know Madeleine, waiting on the beach, unsure whether he'd meet her or be left disappointed. If they walked together, her voice stayed with him for the rest of the day.

He opened Madeleine's file, the paper still soggy from the jump off the Ark, and double-checked the house number—but he knew this was the right place. He recognized the musky fragrance inside. It was the last thing he had expected; it made him feel sick.

The street was empty in both directions, the whole town seemingly deserted except for the jittery Jewish policemen they had encountered when they arrived. Tünscher had ordered them to open the gate, the bluff and pose of the actor in his voice again, and waltzed through. Who was going to question two SS majors emerging from the forest, caps low over their eyes, their sidearms on display? By then a bloodstain was also flowering across Tünscher's tunic; every time Burton asked him about it, the question was shrugged off.

Burton spied something in the periphery of his vision. Something dark and viscous, dripping from the shack opposite. He crossed the street and walked along the side of the building. There was a burst of crimson, like a child's painting, on the wall. Tünscher stubbed out his cigarette in it; the butt sizzled.

"It's recent."

They searched underneath the property, then around the other side. There was no body, no other sign of a struggle.

"Coincidence," said Tünscher. "Nothing to do with your girl."

His tone was so reassuring that Burton felt a stab of shame at his deception. They returned to Maddie's stoop. Tünscher feverishly checked his packet of Bayerweeds, then slipped it back into his pocket; he was running low. "So now what?"

In the Legion, if you were separated from your unit, you stayed where you were and let the search party find you, rather than you looking for it. Otherwise, you both ended up missing each other in the dust and wind.

Burton eased his cap back and peered up and down the street, hoping to see Madeleine returning with the bundle of their child. Not a soul.

"We wait."

They entered the house, and Burton's nostrils stung again. He held his stump against his nose to block the smell. Tünscher flopped onto the bed, wincing, while Burton examined the room for any indication of where Madeleine might be. His gaze lingered over the makeshift cradle, his heart twisting. How had she coped? How had millions coped, uprooted from the order and modernity of Europe's cities and dumped into this tropical ghetto? At least Burton had been born into humidity and the constant churr of insects, more comfortable with moonless nights than he was with electricity. In the years ahead, he would banish the memory of this place for her.

"Varavanga," said Tünscher suddenly.

"What?"

"I've been thinking it through. It's home to a fishery station—that's how we get you out."

Burton frowned. "But it's part of the SS."

"Department VIII. Codheads from the Baltic, all nets and sou'westers, not razor wire. As long as they don't think we're Jews, we should be able to strike a deal."

"With what?"

"One of your diamonds."

"You're getting the last of them."

"I'll forgo one to get you out."

Burton didn't bother hiding his sarcasm. "Very noble of you, Tünsch."

"I know. I also know I won't see a single pfennig if you're stuck here." He mulled over his plan. "It might work. We can pretend to be deserters. When they see there are no numbers on our wrists, they'll know we're not Jews."

"What about Madeleine? She'll have a tattoo."

Tünscher glanced at Burton's empty sleeve and flashed his yellow teeth. "Cut her arm off?"

"That's not funny."

He loved the slimness of Madeleine's wrists but had never considered that she would be tattooed. It horrified him, and yet there was something perversely reassuring about it, too: they were both scarred now.

Burton sat on the floor opposite Tünscher, who tossed him the remainders of the jerky they had taken from the hovercraft; it had sustained them through the trek to Antzu. Known locally as biltong, these strips of cured beef, laced with spices to preserve them, remained edible for months, even in Africa's climate. Burton broke off a piece as thick as chewing tobacco and ate in silence. Afterward he asked Tünscher to light another Bayerweed. "To get rid of the stink."

When he first knew Madeleine, she used to hide behind a miasma of expensive French perfume. After they parted he smelled of her for days, no matter how he scrubbed himself—not the natural scent of her body but fragrances bought by Cranley. Burton never said a word; he didn't want to sound possessive. As the months passed, Madeleine wore less and less perfume, till one day she stopped altogether. By then they were moving in and out of each other's thoughts with ease. Her true smell—honeysuckle skin and breezy sweat—was as close to home as he could imagine. Yet the house on Boriziny Strasse reeked of a time long past. Burton could make no sense of it.

Cranley's assertion that the baby was his forced its way into Burton's mind. It was a seed of wickedness, a doubt meant to torment Burton. He didn't believe it; the proof was in the journey he'd undertaken . . . but the thought remained, hidden in the recesses of his brain like a tumor.

Tünscher finished his cigarette with an elaborate exhalation. "Once I get my diamonds," he said, taking in the rot and the warped timbers, "I might get a pad like this myself."

"You never did say what you wanted them for."

"I told you: debts."

"What kind of debts?"

His friend went to reply, then changed his mind and sat up. A sharp intake of breath. He was looking paler.

"Are you hurt?"

Tünscher peeled back his uniform above the belt: his midriff was sticky with blood. He reached into the medical kit for some gauze and swabbed the skin. In the Legion he'd had training as a *martin-pêcheur:* a kingfisher, their name for a medic. "I got nicked when you hit that hovercraft."

"Is it bad?"

"What did Patrick used to tell us? *If it still hurts, it's not that bad.*" He grimaced. "It hurts plenty."

"Why didn't you say?"

Another of those shrugs that had accompanied them to Antzu. "What would you have done?" His earlier anger was gone, replaced by resignation. "Handed over my diamonds and waved me *auf Wiedersehen?*"

He stripped off his tunic to reveal a hairless torso and a locket hanging from his neck. Burton watched Tünscher clean and bind the wound; it was no bigger than a ha'penny but still seeping. *I should have left him in Roscherhafen,* Burton thought. A catch-up drink, a few Legion stories—and nothing more. Or at least told him the truth about the diamonds. He'd seen men slowly bleed to death from less serious injuries.

To ward off the guilt, Burton patrolled the floorboards, picturing the shock and relief on Maddie's face when she arrived home. He would see his child for the first time. A girl, like Madeleine had hoped for? It should have made him beam, but his thoughts kept drawing back to Patrick and the daughter he had failed to get home to.

The rhythmic creak of his boots was broken by a gunshot.

He went to the door and listened: the sound echoed over the corrugated roofs of Antzu. It had the unmistakable retort of a BK. He fiddled with the brim of his cap.

There was a second shot—then a barrage.

"It can't be anything to do with Madeleine," said Tünscher.

Burton was aware of the sloshing in his gut. "You're probably right."

He gripped his Beretta, descended the steps, and began walking in the direction of the gunfire. Soon he was at full sprint.

CHAPTER FORTY-TWO

AT THE COLONIAL Academy in Vienna, racial hygiene classes were mandatory. Because Kepplar had applied for Africa rather than Madagaskar (which technically remained under departments of the European SS), his instruction was in the dangers posed by the negroid. However, all recruits were given a basic introduction to Jewry. A famous Hauptsturmführer who had worked closely with Jews in the East warned about the spell a Jewess could cast. Kepplar was unconvinced: those who succumbed were looking to excuse their weakness or secretly craved pollution of their blood. Now he realized such witchcraft did indeed exist. That it was Hochburg, of all men, who had fallen victim caused him an ache of profound disappointment.

His skin felt dank, like he wanted to shed it.

Kepplar had watched Cole's wife from the moment she identified herself. He immediately sensed the threat and wanted to warn the Oberstgruppenführer. The Jewess was too fast; she put her scraggy arms around Hochburg and defiled his mouth. It was repellent to witness, yet Kepplar was unable to avert his eyes, like in Muspel when he'd seen the blacks rutting in their barracks at night and been magnetized by the horror of it.

He thought of the sailors who had been killed on the patrol boat and, before them, the body bags of loyal SS filled in Kongo: what would these men have thought if they stood here now?

Cole's wife revealed a dagger behind her back. Swung it at Hochburg.

Kepplar sprang forward, catching her wrist as the blade completed its arc. He wrestled her off, shoving her flimsy body to the ground; the knife clattered as it landed. Kepplar supported Hochburg as he emerged from the spell, and patted his superior's uniform beneath the armpit where the blade had been aimed. His fingers came away dry. Hochburg swatted Kepplar away, a glint of loathing in his unbandaged eye.

Cole's wife had reclaimed her blade. It had a serrated edge, Kepplar noted gratefully, and was meant for sawing, with no point to penetrate.

"Call the others," he yelled at the groom guarding the door.

Hochburg addressed the woman, his voice emollient: "Put down the knife, Madeleine." The only time Kepplar had heard that tone before was when he was speaking to Fenris. "I mean you no harm."

She retreated. There was sorcery in her eyes, inviting Hochburg closer so she could slit his throat.

From the balcony came the bang of the door being flung open. Panicky, raring-to-go faces stared down. Kepplar saw the groom who had shot the woman in Boriziny Strasse. When Hochburg had given him the order, Kepplar removed his Walther P38 and pressed it into the lad's hand, as if such a task were beneath his rank; he feared that his expression betrayed him. The groom dispatched the woman as efficiently as a vet administering a vaccine, pleased with the opportunity to show that he was more than just a stable hand. Now he aimed his BK44 at the scene beneath him and fired a warning shot. It smacked into one of the old Jews gathered round the tables. Kepplar heard a wail and indignant shouts. Then a second shot, followed by a stream of bullets as the rest of the stable staff joined in. Another of the Jews threw over a table, ducking low behind it as a shield, and reached inside his rucksack.

"Hold your fire!" shouted Hochburg, putting himself between the rifles and Madeleine.

There was a blinding pop and a fountain of sparks; Kepplar shielded his face. The synagogue began filling with billows of thick red smoke.

+ + +

Someone grabbed Madeleine's arm—cruelly, angrily—and dragged her into the smoke. She pried herself from Abner's grip, searching for Salois. Jacoba was huddled on the floor, arms covering her head, as the councilmen scattered and fell. Shots flashed in the scarlet murk despite Hochburg ordering his men to stop.

She yanked Jacoba to her feet and raced after Salois, calling him. He headed toward an exit at the rear, rucksack bouncing on his back, a bundle of loaves in each arm.

"The main entrance is the only way out," said Abner as he followed.

The firing stopped; boots thudded down the stairs.

Madeleine ran in the opposite direction, chasing Salois along a passageway till he reached some steps and stopped. He broke the bread he was carrying into pieces and stuffed it into his rucksack. Behind them the corridor was empty except for creeping fingers of ruby mist.

Abner clasped Madeleine and shook her. "What were you thinking?" he shouted in her face, his mouth so wide she glimpsed his rotten molars. "You could have been killed."

The moment Hochburg had announced his name, Madeleine had been possessed by what she must do, almost as though she heard Burton urging her to strike. As though the knife could lance her grief for him. If Abner was right, she'd never reach Mandritsara or find the twins; Cranley was thousands of miles away, protected from her hatred by locks and walls and his position in society. But she could finish this part of the story: it would be an act of devotion to the man she had lost. The night before Burton left, he'd showed her the silver dagger he planned to end Hochburg's life with. She had hidden her horror, at the same time remembering the abuse her father had endured and feeling a shiver of satisfaction. Now she understood the full lure of revenge.

When Burton had described Hochburg, she'd pictured a man forged from the shadows, with coarse curls of hair and the reek of the jungle. Instead, he was merely flesh. As she'd stepped toward him, the bandage covering his head made her think of Claude Rains. He loomed over her; if she lunged directly at his heart he had the strength to snap her arm. Then she read the expression on his face, was sickened by how tender his desire appeared, and understood his weakness. Her mind was numb as their lips touched, as if she were below the ocean kissing Burton's cold, dead mouth farewell.

There was a narrow, glassless window by the steps with a view of dirt: they were still below street level. Salois lobbed a smoke cannister in the direction they had come, and climbed the stairs, the others following.

They reached the next floor; halfway along was a door to a classroom. Inside there was another window. Salois opened the shutters onto banks of earth. He ran his fingers around the frame and seemed satisfied. From below Madeleine heard the baritone ring of Hochburg's voice calling her name, queasy with his familiarity. Salois threw another smoke grenade into the corridor and secured the door.

"We have to barricade it."

The classroom smelled of sap and damp, its walls made of rough timber.

Around the edge, piled to shoulder height, were sacks of rice. At the front was a blackboard chalked with words:

Mein Name ist _____
Ich bin ein Jude
Ich werde gehorsam und ehrlich sein

Education was banned on the island, with the exception of arithmetic to five hundred and German lessons—"an elementary kind of mimicry" as Hitler described it—so Jews could comprehend their masters.

The four of them worked to block the entrance with the rice bags. When they reached the top of the frame, they began a second layer.

"We're burying ourselves," said Abner.

Madeleine lugged a sack with Salois; she refused to let the strain of the weight show. "Will you let me on your boat?" she asked him.

"What about the Oberstgruppenführer?"

"He's nothing. I wish I'd killed him."

"You've got guts, more than the whole council—but if he's after you, that's bad for me."

"Then let's get as far from Antzu as possible." They dumped the sack; the barricade was already at waist height. On the other side of the door, she heard men coughing in the smoke and Hochburg issuing commands. "What do you need?"

"I'm going to Diego Suarez, to destroy the base." He said "Diego" as if it were a person he knew and hated. "I can do it alone but will have more chance with two"—he glanced at Abner—"or three. I also need explosives. Your brother knows where they are."

"She's not going with you," replied Abner. "Neither of us are."

There was a burst of gunfire from the corridor, the bullets thudding harmlessly into the sacks. Then the *bang-bang-bang* of rifle butts against the door.

Madeleine grasped her brother's hand. "You've got to help him."

"What about your babies? How are you going to get from Diego to Mandritsara, all in time to catch a boat? Assuming it's not torpedoed." He sounded choked with frustration. "If he blows Diego the sea will be teeming with patrols."

"It's the only hope I've got," she replied. "That or give up. What else can I do?"

"You can stay in Antzu: you're safe here."

The battering stopped, then started again with renewed ferocity. Something heavy was pounding the door.

"Safe?" She almost laughed.

Abner appealed to Salois: "It's too far to Nachtstadt. You don't have time—she'll slow you down."

"You could ride," said Jacoba. She was shaking with fear and had to force the words out. "Take some horses from the governor's stables."

"And new boots and breeches," snapped Abner. "A hamper for the journey."

"When I worked there, they weren't well guarded. Who would dare steal a horse?"

"You were going to stay with your daughter."

"I want to help Madeleine first."

Salois faced her brother. "It's your decision. Our fates are in your hands."

"You're just using her."

"The fate of the whole island."

Abner swore; he removed his skullcap and tossed it away.

They finished stacking the rice, Madeleine keeping close to Salois. Normally when she was next to an islander, she recoiled from the odor of their body or filthy clothes or whatever was churning in their stomach. Salois was scentless. He took a hand grenade from his rucksack and told them to build another wall of bags to shield them from the blast. Then he pulled the pin and lodged it beneath the window frame. Madeleine ducked behind the sacks, pressing her face into the burlap.

"He'll get you killed," whispered her brother. "Stay here, it's what Mutti wants. Papa too—you always listened to him."

"This is the only chance I may get."

"Not now. Please. It's too dangerous."

Madeleine covered her ears and heard her next words from inside her head: "If not now, when?"

The grenade exploded, punching a hole in the wall. The classroom was scattered with flames. Salois stood and bundled them outside.

Madeleine jumped, landing on the slope of the crater in which the synagogue sat. The climb was steep: scree and rubbish tumbled to either side of her, her hands digging into the mud till she was back on Nabi Daniel Strasse and the road that led to the docks. A column of smoke rose from the synagogue, its wooden walls sighing and cracking.

A soldier emerged from the hole in the classroom and aimed his rifle.

Another, dressed in the same black uniform as Hochburg, leapt into the crater after them.

"We can still hide," Abner said to her. "I know a place." He grasped her arm, tugging her away from Salois and Jacoba.

She broke free and ran with the others toward the heart of the city. Rising above the roofs, green through wisps of fog, was the governor's house.

"We can get in through the garden wall," said Jacoba.

Salois released a smoke canister to conceal their direction and they dashed through the narrows of the Spanish quarter, weaving beneath scaffolding and past the alleyways that led to Boriziny Strasse. Madeleine didn't think she'd ever see her house there again. If she died finding the twins, would her spirit haunt it? Or the house in Hampstead? Maybe eternity would grant her the farm. Was Burton waiting there? For an instant she thought she heard his voice, the cry so real it sent ice rippling down her back.

+ + +

Burton caught a fleeting glimpse of Madeleine. He stumbled: exhilarated, horrified. The mist around her was darkening, like wine poured into milk.

"That her?" asked Tünscher.

She was emaciated, her body nothing but hard angles, as if her bones had been recarved; her hair—her luxuriant, flowing black hair—was stubble. Worse than the physical decline, he sensed a newborn savagery in her. His image of Maddie, plump and radiant in cornflower blue, had propelled him across oceans and continents, even though he understood that it was a necessary illusion.

Its shattering was harder than any physical blow.

He recognized the dress she was wearing; it was an old favorite. The white material would cling to her thighs if they got caught in a shower on the farm; "my seduction frock," she used to call it, with a single-note laugh. It was smeared with muck. She had three companions: one with the familiar bearing of a soldier, an old woman dressed in a work uniform, and a third who was balding, the same age as Burton. He kept close to Madeleine, running protectively by her side in a way that made Burton want to pry them apart. There was no time to dwell on the absence of a baby.

In a blink she was gone.

"Madeleine!" he roared. His voice bounced off the alley walls, the mist deadening it. "Madeleine!"

He chased after her, Tünscher at his heels, into a maze of passageways thick with smoke. The sound of running clattered and echoed around him till it was impossible to tell what direction it was coming from or whether Madeleine was its origin. Burton stopped in a ramshackle square where numerous alleys met and spun round, not knowing which one to take. The air was scarlet and swirling. "Which way?" he demanded of Tünscher.

"I don't know."

Burton continued spinning, struggling to decipher the echoes and—

He stopped dead. Tottered backward into Tünscher.

A figure had emerged from the smoke, materializing like a djinn. He was dressed entirely in black, and half his skull was obscured by bandages. The faintest smile danced on his lips.

CHAPTER FORTY-THREE

EVERYTHING SEEMED DARKER. The alley walls crowded in, the smoke as thick and opaque as blood. Through it came the crackle of burning timbers, the sound reminding Burton of his childhood home as it was gutted. The breath lodged in his throat, and sank. This was the moment he had waited years for. He groped for the Beretta and wished he was reaching for the familiar handle of his Browning. The buzz of mosquitoes was unnaturally loud.

Hochburg.

Burton expected to see hatred in his single black eye. Instead: relief, a simmering, victorious pleasure. What had Madeleine called him all those months ago? A ghost. Don't resurrect him, she begged. If Burton had listened, he wouldn't be standing in this stinking muddy lane, his left sleeve would not be pinned at the wrist. Patrick would be alive, Tünscher not wounded and marooned on rhinestone promises. Burton, Madeleine, and their baby would be safe—if not surrounded by the Suffolk fields they dreamed of, then in some secret spot far beyond the reach of Cranley.

A second black figure joined Hochburg: the one-eared Nazi who'd hunted him in Roscherhafen. Then excited cub soldiers with shorn hair and machine guns.

"He must not be killed," said Hochburg. "Or harmed. That's my harp to play."

Burton's fingers contacted with the Beretta.

All he had to do was draw the weapon, aim at Hochburg's heart, and fire. But that ancient desire was gone . . . like the quince orchard: hacked down, exhausted by rage. That it had consumed him for so long made him feel dizzy and ashamed now; it was a kinship he should never have sought. Each step toward Hochburg was a step into the past, a step away from Madeleine. She was so close they were breathing the same air again. Burton heard his father from the pulpit, bellowing at orphans who sat quaking or indifferent: *To embrace him is death.*

Burton ran.

Tünscher kept close, his hand pressed against his flank. A volley of bullets sang over them. Burton heard Hochburg's voice—resonant, formidable—boom orders, and darted down a side passage, navigating through contorted backstreets till Tünscher guided him to a different alley. "This way."

"How do you know?" asked Burton as they were heading up an incline.

"If she's trying to escape, the main road out of town is at the top."

"And if she's not?"

"Then stay and check every fucking house. But not with me."

Ahead was a dead end. Tünscher ducked to the left, into an alley clad with scaffolding. It was so narrow that they kept bumping into the poles, the planks above wobbling. Another pocket of red fog swallowed them; Burton glimpsed a spent smoke canister in the mud. The clap of boots seemed everywhere, amplified and distorted—one second behind them, the next to either side, as if the soldiers were running along parallel streets. Above the boots Burton thought he heard Hochburg, but he couldn't be sure if it was in his head: a memory from the mission in Kongo, or further in the past.

Fee-fi-fo-fum, I smell the blood of an Englishman . . .

In front was another dead end, this time with no alternative route. "Back," said Tünscher.

Burton found the path blocked.

"Herr Oberst! I have him."

The one-eared Nazi was framed in scaffolding, a BK44 in his grip aimed low; it would shred their feet and shins.

"Oberstgruppenführer! Come quick." His voice was shrill and demented. "Hands behind your neck, Cole. Your friend, too."

Slowly, Burton raised his arms; Tünscher did nothing.

"Take off your hat," said the Nazi.

"What?"

"Do it! I want to see your head."

When Burton refused, the Nazi fired into the mud inches from Burton's toes. He tugged his cap free and let it drop. The Nazi scrutinized his skull before a look of disgruntlement filled his face.

Tünscher, whose hands remained at his sides, stepped forward till he was abreast with Burton. He was pallid and breathless, the skin above his lip beaded with sweat. The Nazi flicked the point of his machine gun at Tünscher's chest.

"The Oberstgruppenführer's orders were only not to harm Cole."

"We charge him," said Tünscher.

Burton checked the distance between them and the BK's muzzle. "I thought you didn't want to die today."

"He won't fire."

"Why not?"

"I can see it in his eyes, like when I signed up for Russia. You could tell who was going to spend the war behind a desk. Trust me."

"Silence." The Nazi called behind him: "Oberstgruppenführer! Anyone! Quick, while I have them."

Burton lowered his hand and stump.

The three of them stood staring at each other. Mosquitoes buzzed through the air.

"What do you think happened to his ear?" said Tünscher.

Humiliation and fury flashed across the Nazi's face as he raised a palm to cover his mutilated lobe. Tünscher hurled himself forward, knocking the Nazi into the bamboo struts holding up the scaffolding. The poles collapsed, flinging boards and paint in all directions.

+ + +

Jacoba avoided the front gate of the governor's house and sloped along the garden wall, leading them through thickets of spiny aloes. They were on the asphalt highway that led south, winding three hundred kilometers through onion-growing country to Mazunka. The wind had picked up, chasing away the mist. Across from the wall Madeleine could see empty meadows rolling down to the river. Jacoba kept looking up and diagonally to the roof of the house, searching for something.

"Here," she said at last. "Blind man's bend." It was a curve in the wall, dipping with the natural contour of the ground; the spot was hidden from the villa and its solitary guard tower. "Servants in the house would come here to sneak out food to their families. There used to be a basket. I'd smuggle out beetroot and peaches for my daughter."

Madeleine had forgotten about Jacoba's daughter. "Did you find her?" she asked.

"I saw her for a few moments. Then I heard Salois and had to fetch you."

"I'm grateful." She squeezed the older woman's bony hand. "Will you come with me?"

Fear and apology tussled in Jacoba's expression. "I'll help you with the horses . . . but after that I'll only slow you down."

"You can't stay here."

"I'm not going to Mandritsara." She extracted her hand from Madeleine's. "Antzu's not so bad. When all this has quietened down, I'll be happy enough. It's paradise compared to those pigs and Poles."

Jacoba offered a shaky smile, but Madeleine sensed her heartbreak. "If I can't make the boat," she replied, "I'll come back; we can live together in Boriziny."

"You're not coming back, girl."

Salois scaled the wall, using pockmarks in the mortar to climb. Madeleine doubted whether she or Jacoba would be strong enough to do the same. When he reached the top he asked Madeleine if she still had her knife. She passed it to him. He cut a gap in the barbed wire and pressed himself flat against the brickwork, his rucksack a hump over his shoulders. "I can see the stables," he said. "They're deserted."

"It's too high for us to climb," Madeleine called up.

"I'll find something," he replied and vanished over the other side. Madeleine heard the impact of his boots—*crunch*—then his footsteps rapidly fading.

From the city came the echo of gunshots. An alarm was ringing on the far side of the green house.

"That's the barracks," said Abner. "Your new friend better be fast or we'll be overrun."

They waited, crouched low by the wall, mosquitoes feasting on them. Madeleine rubbed at her calves: they were covered in scratches from the aloe thorns. Whenever she cut herself on the farm, Burton dabbed the wound with iodine, wincing along with her.

A coil of rose rope landed next to her, twisted with leaves and thorns. Abner picked them off and tugged it taut. "Jacoba, you go first."

"No," said Madeleine. "Me, Jacoba, then you." She worried that if they were left alone he would insist that she stay in Antzu, maybe cosh her into submission.

Before he could argue she grabbed the rope and climbed, the muscles that had carried her children straining. At the top she looked out over Antzu: a reddish haze hung over the streets they had run through, and the synagogue was on fire. She beckoned Jacoba to follow. Fruit trees had been espaliered against the other side of the wall; she used the branches to descend, landing on a gravel path. Jacoba joined her, then Abner. They stood with their mouths crumpled in disbelief.

"The Mered Ha-vanil began over a handful of rice," said Abner. "The Nazis told us there wasn't enough food." His shoulders slumped. "I've seen men—grown men, soldiers, killers—cry like children for a bowl of soup."

"This is just for the governor's house," said Jacoba.

They were in a kitchen garden. Madeleine had planned to grow one behind the farmhouse, but at a fraction of the size of the monstrosity in front of them. It expanded through a series of square sections, each dedicated to rows of vegetables and fruits of every imaginable kind. There were eggplants, pumpkins, sweet corn, bushes of red, orange, and gold chilies, melons, and pink pineapples. Not just tropical plants but European crops modified by Nazi agronomists to grow in the local climate: celery, turnips, cabbages. And coolhouses, temperature- and humidity-controlled glass structures for delicacies such as kale and berries.

"When I worked here," Jacoba continued, "the bins overflowed. Whole meals untouched and thrown out. The servants were so healthy because they ate the leftovers. Until Quorp forbade it."

A sob emerged from Abner like Madeleine hadn't heard since childhood when he was punished for some perceived injustice. He ran into the beds kicking and stamping on the crops, tearing up sweet potatoes. He broke off a supporting cane from some beans and stumbled forward, whipping zucchinis and cabbages till he reached a coolhouse spilling over with blueberries. He raised the cane to shatter the walls.

Salois caught his arm before it descended. "Cabbages are silent; glass isn't."

The gardens were empty and drizzly with mist. They passed a Jew tending some beds with a hoe. He glanced up, then fixed his eyes back on the earth. Gunshots continued to ring out from the city.

"We have to watch for the grooms," said Jacoba as they approached the stables—but the yard was empty except for a helicopter and its pilot. He scurried into the house as they approached. The rich smell of manure and bran mash hung over the cobbles.

It was too risky to go to the tack room. They found some bridles in the yard but only two saddles. Jacoba said the others should have them while she would ride bareback, and selected the horses, slapping their hindquarters to encourage them out of the stalls. She swung herself on top of a chestnut mare and in an instant was transformed: she sat confidently, with an elegance to her spine despite her lack of saddle.

"Can you ride?" she asked Salois as he levered himself up onto his own horse.

"I can ride a camel," he replied.

The only person Madeleine had known who could ride a camel was Burton. She fastened her saddle and mounted her horse. Riding lessons had been a gift—an expectation—from Jared.

"What about me?" said Abner from the ground. "I don't know how."

Madeleine offered her hand.

He didn't take it. "It's not too late to stay."

A black smudge appeared in the clouds. It approached rapidly, the thump of its rotors unsettling the horses.

"I never asked you to come with me," said Madeleine.

Abner climbed on behind her, his sleeves catching as he put his arms around her waist. She glanced down at the tattoos on his forearm. The three horses clip-clopped through the yard to the front entrance; the guards were missing.

"We need the southern road," Abner shouted at Jacoba, who was in the lead.

They wheeled left through the gate, and Madeleine thought she was going insane. It must be the exhaustion and lack of food, the sheer stress of the past days. Or maybe the taste of Hochburg, still cold and sweet in her mouth, poisoning her mind. For the second time she thought she heard Burton's voice—as real and clear as birdsong.

Madeleine!

She kicked hard against the horse, thundering past two SS soldiers who were spattered in a palette of colors. One of them was missing a hand; he signaled at her, rushing to block her path. On the wind she heard Burton's ghostly cry again.

Madeleine! Madeleine!

She glanced behind to see the soldier wave frantically, then turn and sprint in the direction of the stables. Above, the helicopter reached the city and followed the Mazunka road, roaring overhead.

"Now we're done for," cried Jacoba.

The helicopter came round and swooped low before patrolling the sky above Antzu. It circled the burning synagogue, then descended on the governor's villa.

The horses skirted the city walls. As they passed the southern gate the Jupo wardens they'd seen earlier rushed out, pelting them with rocks.

"Get ahead of the others," Abner said in her ear.

Madeleine bent into the wind with a sense of freedom she'd never felt before on a horse. As soon as she overtook Jacoba and Salois, Abner told her to leave the highway.

Their horse stumbled as it hit the soaked grass, then found its footing, hooves tossing up fragments of turf. They charged across a plain toward a ridge several miles away. The horizon was tinged mauve with the approaching sunset. They galloped till they reached the ridge; once they were riding down the other side, Madeleine slowed to a canter. Salois drew level.

"This is the way?" he asked. "To the explosives."

Abner nodded.

"You're sure?"

"Leni's thrown my lot in with you."

They crossed another hill, passing into a landscape of rolling, rocky peaks and grass so high it skimmed the horses' bellies. The animals were tiring. Another ridge, and then a wide, stony riverbed with only a trickle of a stream.

"Because of the Sofia Reservation," explained Abner. "It should be a torrent at this time of year, but they control the water supply."

When they reached the water's edge, they dismounted and let the horses drink. Night was beginning to gather. The muscles in Madeleine's thighs were stretched and sore. She associated the sensation with soaking in a tub and wondered if she'd ever have a hot bath again, or if she could: the thought of pampering herself, of any luxury, seemed immoral after what she'd witnessed. Far away there was a rumble of thunder.

Abner scooped up a handful of water and splashed his face and neck. "You should have stayed in Antzu; you'll regret it." He sighed, full of grudging magnanimity. "But I promise to help . . . not that you've given me much choice."

Madeleine wasn't listening.

She stepped away from him, searching the empty landscape behind. In the twilight Antzu was a distant sickle of fire. Her voice trembled. "Where's Jacoba?"

CHAPTER FORTY-FOUR

Antzu
20 April, 17:15

THERE WAS A swing to Hochburg's stride, a sense of renewal. He moved energetically through the villa, hoping to use the shortcut to beat Burton to the stables, but he felt a languid urgency. It was like chasing the boy round a concentration camp: where could he go? If he didn't apprehend him today, then tomorrow; his pursuit was drawing to an end. The chandeliers trembled and chimed from the helicopter coming in to land. From the dining room he heard Quorp's dogs barking and the cheering of children: *It's Uncle Globus! Uncle Globus!*

Hochburg reached the tack room to see Burton and his comrade galloping past on horses, toward the front gate. Globocnik's Walküre positioned itself above the stables, whipping the air. Hochburg closed the door on the noise and flicked his tongue over his lips. Madeleine's daring, her fealty to a man she believed dead, had stirred Hochburg. He wished Eleanor had possessed a little more of the same—and immediately regretted the thought. It let in the one thing he never wanted to admit: that her love for Burton had been stronger than for him.

From behind came a soupy squeak of boots: Kepplar, doused from head to toe in paint, the colors running into one another as if on an abstract canvas. A walking exhibit of the degenerate art so detested by the Führer.

"We can still catch Cole," he said. The fading clatter of hooves was audible over the helicopter.

"No, Globus will see us. He must not have my prize. For now, you must continue the pursuit alone."

"And you, Herr Oberst?"

"I shall smooth things over."

"Globocnik will be furious. I've heard tales of his temper."

"There's one less pip on his shoulder than mine. Let him foam at the mouth for all I care."

"He could report you to Germania."

"Your concern is touching, Derbus, but you needn't worry: the Reichsführer is a stickler for rank. Commandeer whatever means you can, track down Burton—and bring him to me."

"And the Jewess?"

Hochburg imagined Madeleine as his guest in the new Schädelplatz, saw himself spoon-feeding her rich stews and trifle till her cadaverous cheekbones were no more, while Burton suffered in the dungeons below, impotent to stop his wife from growing healthy.

"Burton is your priority; then his bride."

"She's a danger."

"If you find her, she is not to be harmed. Neither of them is."

Outside, Globus's helicopter touched down.

"Cole is a wanted terrorist," said Kepplar. "I don't understand why we can't tell Globocnik. It would make our task easier—"

"And then he would know my business," Hochburg replied irritably, "and shortly after, so would Himmler and Heydrich, and every last telephonist from here to the Baltic."

Kepplar's nose dripped yellow and blue. He wiped it with his sleeve. "Oil paint." He looked at what had once been black cloth. "It's ruined."

"We shall have another cut for you."

"But first I have to find Cole?"

A solemn nod. "We both understand what it means if you fail."

"And when I succeed?"

"Kongo again. Your rank and privileges restored. Now go, my friend."

Kepplar beamed . . . and then his smile faded. "The British defeated us at Elisabethstadt. What if they continue north? What if they take the whole colony?"

"I have the matter in hand."

Hochburg thought of his parting words to Feuerstein: *Muspel can be harsh; I trust the sun won't put any foolish ideas in your head.*

Jews are a desert people, the scientist had replied. *Leave us be, Oberstgruppenführer, and we will deliver.*

Kepplar bowed his head, stepping backward, and departed.

In the stable yard, the rotor blades were slowing. Hochburg stood meditatively, thinking of Madeleine once more; perhaps he could feed her till she burst. He filled his lungs with the tack room's smells of leather and steel and the rich aroma of wax.

The door was flung open. Globus. Still in his riding kit.

"I told you," he roared, "I fucking told you not to come here!"

He was shaking, the ruptured veins around his nose purple. Behind him came the mocha-skinned girl Hochburg had seen when he first arrived in Tana. She swirled a burning coconut shell, like a priest blessing the air with incense.

"Who's the nigger?"

"She's Malagasy, not one of your blacks. I can't stand the mosquitoes here. The smoke keeps them off."

Hochburg snorted. "Shamanism."

"You led a patrol into town. You torched the synagogue!" He could barely get the words out.

"You've wanted the same for years, except Heydrich wouldn't allow it. See it as a favor, from one governor to another. An early birthday present."

"Nightingale will have me by the balls."

"You didn't seem troubled by the Americans this morning."

Globus was frantically twisting his two wedding rings. He stalked across the room, spurs *ching*-ing like a cowboy's, till they were nose to nose.

"All this on Führertag! When word spreads what you've done, the whole island will erupt. Even with a thousand Walküres I wouldn't be able to stop them." His face and neck were in spasm; a hank of his hair came loose and swung across his forehead. "Everything I've worked for will be ruined."

"Calm yourself, Obergruppen—"

Globus punched him in the stomach, hard.

Hochburg dropped to his knees thinking he would never breathe again. A second blow, to the back of the neck, and he was on the floor.

Globus squatted on his haunches, and hissed: "You think you can come here and fistfuck me on my own island . . ." He bounced the Oberstgruppenführer's head and stood.

Next instant his boot contacted with Hochburg's bandaged eye. The darkness burned with stars—bright, intense supernovas—that slowly faded. The agony was nothing compared to losing Eleanor, or the decades he had endured since. Physical pain, for all its immediacy, was insipid. Hochburg became aware of more boots rushing in, men shuffling around him, Quorp and Globocnik conferring like two Carinthian gangsters, their voices dim, subaqueous . . . He was briefly searched, then his hands were yanked behind his back and he felt cold metal against his wrists. The click of cuffs.

Oberstgruppenführer Walter Hochburg was dragged away.

+ + +

Tünscher spotted the horse by chance. It was riderless, resting beneath the bowers of a solitary mango tree that was as broad as an oak. They had followed Madeleine's tracks off the road into the wilderness. Several times Burton caught sight of her party—a swiftly moving blotch of chestnut and piebald against the green hills—till the sky darkened and he lost them.

He dismounted, patted the animal's shoulder, and began to search around the tree, moving in wider circles till he caught sight of a body half-hidden in the undergrowth. He recognized the old woman he'd seen with Madeleine in Antzu. She emitted a desperate mewling as he approached but made no effort to escape.

Burton knelt. The grass around them was dotted with boulders. "Are you hurt?"

She said nothing. In the thickening purple light, her skull seemed luminous.

Tünscher checked her body. There was no blood, no sign of any wound. "She landed on a rock," he whispered. "I think her back's broken." He twisted the skin on her hand and spoke loudly: "Can you feel this?"

The woman remained silent, fearful.

"Forget the uniforms," said Burton. "I saw you with Madeleine. My name's Burton."

"Burton's dead."

"I survived. I came to find Maddie and take her home."

"How did you meet?"

"What?"

"Madeleine and I were the only civilized people in that awful place, the only people worth talking to. We shared our lives."

Burton understood: she wanted proof. "At my aunt's house. A party. She was playing Schubert." He thought back to that chance encounter, and their second random meeting on the beach. Then he recalled something Hochburg once told him: there are no coincidences of the heart. The wounded, the incomplete, seek each other out. Was it true? Was that how it had been with him and Maddie?

A smile warmed the woman's face, and she hummed a few bars. "The Hungarian Melody."

Tünscher pinched her again. He was looking feverish, his eyes dull.

"Nothing," she said. "The horse stumbled and I came off." She was full of self-rebuke. "I wasn't strong enough without a saddle."

Burton took her limp hand; the skin was cold. "What's your name?"

"Jacoba. It's fate you found me."

"I need to know where Madeleine's headed."

"Mandritsara. To the hospital."

"She's sick?"

"Mandritsara's not that kind of hospital," said Tünscher, dodging his eyes. "But this is the wrong way. Mandritsara is to the southwest."

Jacoba spoke again: "We were going to Nachtstadt first."

Tünscher tut-tutted, a sound that could have conveyed anything: disbelief, irritation, despair.

"Where is it?" asked Burton.

"I don't know. Abner was taking us—"

"You mean her brother?" Of course: the bald-headed man he'd seen with her earlier. He felt a foolish relief and looked across at Tünscher. "Any ideas how to get to this Nachtstadt?"

Tünscher reached in his pocket for his Bayerweeds. "Maybe." He didn't light one; he had to ration them.

Burton clasped Jacoba's hand for a few moments longer, then removed his paint-splattered tunic and went to cover her. His thanks were too immense to express. When she told him she didn't want the uniform on her, he rolled it into a pillow and eased it beneath her head. He took Tünscher to one side. The hills reverberated with approaching thunder.

"We can't leave like her this," he whispered.

"You should be more worried about Mandritsara. Your woman's crazy if she's going there."

"Meaning?"

"It's a bad place."

"We've seen plenty of those."

"Not like Mandritsara." In the fading light he appeared gangrenous. "They turn people inside out there. I mean literally. Experiments in flesh, like some kind of sick joke. You need to stop Madeleine from getting there."

"And Jacoba?"

"Same as the Viking."

"The Viking" was a soldier whose name was part of the Legion's mythos. His comrades had rescued him under fire but been unable to save him; all they could do was end his suffering.

"I haven't got the stomach for that shit anymore," said Burton.

"Why should you care? She's nothing to you. Shooting her would be kindest."

"She's Maddie's friend."

"Well, don't look at me, Major. Seven diamonds isn't enough." He stalked off toward the horses. "Seven diamonds isn't enough for any of this."

Burton felt a sudden urge to confess and wondered if during the years of their affair Madeleine had experienced something similar. Tünscher was looking rough. Burton swallowed his guilt and returned to Jacoba; she was struggling to say something.

"My pocket . . ."

He reached inside and found a photograph of a woman. Elegantly dressed, with a serious smile, she was the same age as Madeleine.

"My daughter," said Jacoba. "I went to the synagogue, to the wall of faces, to fetch her. I want her close."

"What happened to her?"

"My poor girl, she left me during the typhoid epidemic. At least she wasn't the only one; death is easier when you're surrounded by it." She was calm and resigned.

Burton placed the picture in the woman's hand, closed her fingers round it, and rested it on her chest. There was one other thing he wanted to know.

"Maddie was pregnant. What happened to the baby?"

"She had twins."

"Twins." He experienced a moment of elation that was gone in a heartbeat. His joy would be lifeless until his fingers were entwined between Maddie's again. "Boys, girls? What happened to them?"

"That's for Madeleine to tell."

She closed her eyes to avoid any more questions.

There was a gurgle of thunder, and one of the horses whinnied. Burton slipped out his Beretta.

Jacoba's eyes opened. "You will bury me," she said.

"I have to catch up with Madeleine."

"Please. I don't want to be carrion."

"I promise," Burton lied.

She closed her eyes and let herself drift, her breathing shallow but steady and refusing to dwindle. Burton leveled his Beretta at her temple, flicked off the safety, and averted his face. It would be instant, painless. The only bit of luck that matters, Patrick used to say.

He remained there for several moments, his finger the tiniest squeeze from firing. He was thinking about his children and the two half brothers he'd never known from his father's first marriage: they had been identical twins. As a boy he used to marvel at the photo of them in Father's study. Their symmetry was uncanny, miraculous; Burton demanded to know where his duplicate was. Something hereditary had passed this on to Madeleine. A knot deep inside him relaxed, one he hadn't been fully aware of. It was physical proof that Cranley had lied when he said the baby was his.

Burton released the trigger without firing.

Tünscher was under the mango tree, next to the horses, rattling his packet of Bayerweeds. His skin looked paler, his lips gray; shadows ringed his eyes.

"The shot will make too much noise," said Burton lamely. "It might bring someone."

Tünscher sighed. "You lousy bastard."

He snatched the Beretta from Burton's hand and stepped into the gloom. Moments later there was a single gunshot. He returned with a cigarette wedged miserably in his mouth.

Neither of them spoke. They watched the final mustard streaks of the day fade. The horses grazed behind them, swishing their tails. When Tünscher had finished his Bayerweed, he peered despondently into the packet. "Only two more left."

"And when they're gone?"

He sank into his uniform. "Things are going to be worse."

CHAPTER FORTY-FIVE

Nachtstadt
20 April, 20:15

A TOTENBURG STOOD on the hilltop above Nachtstadt. Designed by Wilhelm Kreis in 1942 as victory beckoned, memorials to the German dead like this one were scattered across the breadth of the Reich, honoring those who had fallen in the locality. Each one was identical, no matter whether it was driven into the permafrost or had to be swept clear of sand every day: four granite towers, thirty meters tall, chiseled with the names of the fallen, set in a square enclosing either a bronze obelisk or a pillar topped with a bowl of eternal fire. After the first rebellion, Globocnik insisted that every soldier who had sacrificed his life in Madagaskar be immortalized in stone.

Madeleine was woken by hushed arguing, like those low voices she occasionally heard in Hampstead and believed it was her duty not to eavesdrop on. She had been dozing beneath one of the towers. She sat up, her shoulder numb. There was a hint of barbecued meat in the air. From the valley below came accordion music and raucous, drunken laughter.

". . . it's that or nothing," said her brother. "I can't let her go alone." He meant to sound uncompromising, but she picked up on the desperation in his voice. Madeleine wondered if Salois heard it, too.

"We have to draw in the Americans," he replied. "Especially with what happened to the Ark, and now Antzu. Diego is the only way."

"I don't doubt it; I wish I'd had the idea myself. But I can't fight for the island if it means turning from my own."

"We both know what it means if she goes to Mandritsara."

"You try and stop her."

"Your sister's a brave woman," said Salois.

"She always got her own way, even as a girl."

Madeleine joined them. They were crouched by some rocks overlooking the farm. The sky continued to flare with lightning, though no rain fell.

"We're not going to Diego," said Abner.

She glanced from him to Salois. "I gave my word."

"We'll never cover the ground from Diego to Mandritsara in time. If you want your children, we have to leave tonight."

"And the boat? We need to escape after. That was the promise."

She had quizzed Salois about the boat before sleeping. It was a cargo vessel sailing from Singapore to Durban, South Africa. In five days it would approach Kap Ost, send out a distress signal, and make a rapid detour into German waters, coming right up to the Rings of Madagaskar before steaming away on its original course.

"Find me the explosives," said Salois, "and we're even. There'll be a place for you. Both of you."

Madeleine was flooded with inarticulate gratitude. She grasped his hand and squeezed; it felt like winter. To her surprise, he squeezed back. Something passed between them, she couldn't explain what. It wasn't charity or friendship or even pity, simply a moment of human connection.

"What's your first name?" she asked him.

"Reuben."

He let go, dragged over his rucksack, and shared out the bread he'd taken from the synagogue. Madeleine tore off a chunk and ate hungrily. It had a faint tang of canvas, but Hochburg had been right: it tasted good.

Salois chewed and surveyed Nachtstadt. Men were singing along with the accordion, their voices hoarse and out of tune. "Where are the explosives?"

"Down there," replied Abner around a mouthful. "Among the swine. It's one of the biggest herds on the island." He gulped down the bread. "Do you know what *Madagaskar* means?"

"The island of wild pigs," replied Madeleine. She had discovered it during her days scouring books and articles for details about her family's fate.

Abner flicked her an irritated, you're-such-a-know-it-all look.

At the base of the hill, contained by wire, were several hectares of mud and row upon row of pens, some with corrugated tin roofs, the majority thatched. Thousands of pigs snuffled around them, their hides ghostly against the dirt. Beyond the animals was another fence and the industrial sector of the farm: barracks for the workers, a veterinary hospital, barns and sheds and an assortment of other buildings, one topped with antennae. A lamp on the tallest aerial blinked red.

"Where do they slaughter them?" asked Madeleine. She didn't recognize any of the meat-processing facilities she was familiar with from the abattoir.

"It's not done on-site. They're transported to a factory in Tana. From there, I heard, the meat goes to Europe." Abner indicated a pair of water towers at the far end of the facility, where the camp merged into the darkness; beneath them were two parallel threads of steel. "It's a spur," he told Salois. "It leads to the main Tana–Diego line, so you can pick up your train."

"How far?"

"From here? Five kilometers."

Salois nodded, absorbing the layout below.

"What about the party?" said Abner.

"It'll help. I can't see many guards."

At the farthest point from the pigs, separated from the rest of Nachtstadt by a brick wall, was a cluster of houses and living quarters built around a cheerily lit square. Madeleine could make out red bunting, a spit roast, and trestle tables laden with bottles and steins of beer. Men were drinking and dancing.

While Salois continued to familiarize himself with the farm, Madeleine went to check on the horses. They were tethered behind one of the granite towers and more important than ever if she and Abner were going to ride to Mandritsara. She made sure the knots were secure, then peered into the darkness, half-expecting Jacoba to appear. When she had insisted they search for her, Abner's response was callous but true. Every minute spent looking for Jacoba was a minute she denied her children.

Madeleine hoped her friend had simply become separated from them and headed back to Antzu, all the while knowing that she must have fallen, maybe "gone to America." Like with so much she'd experienced on Madagaskar, the only way to cope with this was to deny her heart. The lack of security and sanitation wasn't the only way the Nazis had stripped millions of their humanity. She swore to tattoo Jacoba's number on her unmarked wrist.

Before she returned to the others, Madeleine squatted by one of the towers and urinated. There had been a time when she had been unable to go in the presence of other people, even Burton. The abattoir had changed that. Now she let out a steady stream, taking pleasure in pissing on the SS dead.

A crude flight of steps had been carved into the hillside, from the farm to the Totenburg. The three of them descended, skirting the perimeter fence, until Abner told them to stop. An infrequent searchlight roamed the darkness.

"It's been a while since I was here," he said. "I need to check things."

He bolted into the darkness while Madeleine and Salois pressed themselves against the dirt, their shoulders touching. Drunken roars drifted through the air. Madeleine was thinking about the names she had just defiled, unable to explain the shame creeping over her. Salois kept still, so still that Madeleine felt an irrational fright that he had stopped breathing.

"Why did you change your mind?" she whispered. "About needing my help." She wanted proof that he was alive as much as an answer.

"I had a child once."

"What happened?"

He looked at her with eerie eyes, as if it was the most obvious thing in the world. "Dead."

"I'm sorry."

"I never even held him. It's not right to know that emptiness. That's why you should go to Mandritsara."

She had the urge to reach out for him again but kept her fingers in the ground. "You're the first person not to warn me off."

Abner returned and guided them along the fence to a ditch choked with vegetation. He parted the foliage to reveal a drainage pipe barely wide enough to squeeze through.

"The workers are mostly convicts," he said, "or from the Eastern Sector. But over the years a few Vanillas have ended up here, too. One of them escaped and told us about this. We've been using it since."

"Why not somewhere easier?" asked Madeleine.

"The Jupo. They kept finding our stores and destroying them, to stop the rebellion. They'd never think of searching here."

Salois went first, driving his rucksack ahead of him, then Madeleine. A stream of water flowed through the pipe; Madeleine thought it might carry anything—snakes, rats. She took a deep breath, keeping her chin high and eyes fixed in front, and squirmed through the sludge. Her dress was black when she emerged on the other side.

"At least you're camouflaged," said Salois as he helped her up.

They were on the other side of the fence, among the pigpens, the air caustic with shit. Abner waded ankle-deep among the sties, checking for a sign the way he had on the approach to Antzu, until he ducked inside one.

Madeleine and Salois followed, stooping beneath the corrugated roof. A huge sow lay in the corner; she watched them with a glistening eye and looked so sad Madeleine wanted to stroke her.

Abner stamped on the ground, his boots squelching with every footfall until there was a hollow bang. He knelt, clearing straw and muck away. "Another reason why we use this *nachtstadt*"—his nose was screwed up against the smell—"no Nazi is going to root around in this."

He eased up a trapdoor to reveal a damp cavity that concealed four tea chests. Abner lifted the first lid—empty—then the second and found a case of dynamite. He broke it open, handing a bundle over to Salois. "Still dry," he said.

A strenuous satisfaction tightened Salois's face. He glanced down at the crate; it was stenciled in Gothic German letters. "You said the British supplied you."

"They do. But imagine what would happen if they were caught. That's why they use this Wehrmacht stuff."

Salois placed the dynamite in his rucksack while Madeleine helped her brother unload the rest. Her eyes watered; her chest was constricted. The stench and sounds of the pigs brought back the comatose grief of the abattoir and the fear that she would never escape. Abner asked if she was okay; she nodded unconvincingly.

"It's not enough," said Salois when they had transferred all the explosives.

Abner checked the other crates. In the third were some old rifles (no ammunition); the fourth was empty. "There are other stores," he said closing the trapdoor and covering it with straw.

They returned outside, Abner creeping forward, checking the sties till he found whatever informed him of the treasures within. He banged the hollow ground and lifted another trapdoor.

Salois remained outside, gazing toward the building with the aerials. "I need to use the radio. To contact my other team."

Abner tutted. "Too risky."

"It's a chance I have to take."

"What about the rest of the dynamite?"

"I need the same amount again. Then meet me by the railway."

"Take Leni." Her head was tilted to the clouds, counting the beats between the lightning flashes and thunder; she sucked in fresh air. "You'll need someone to keep an eye out."

The two of them bent low, using the pigs as cover, and made for the fence that divided the livestock from the rest of the farm. The stench was still intolerable, but Madeleine was relieved to be moving. There was a metal gate in the fence with a hut and a single guard pacing outside. As they approached, Salois pushed her to the ground and sneaked round the sentry box from behind.

A deep rumble of thunder rolled across the sky. Madeleine expected the first drops of rain to hit her face. Nothing. When she looked back, the guard was gone. Salois beckoned her with a bloody hand. They slipped through the gate—Salois careful to close it behind them—and onto a rutted track. On one side was a line of barns, on the other a razor-wire fence and the workers' barracks. They kept tight against the barns until Salois stopped unexpectedly.

He turned up his sleeve and raised his forearm. For the first time Madeleine saw that it was dense with tattoos.

"What are you doing?" she whispered.

He indicated the opposite side of the track, and she took a sharp breath. There was a single barred window in the barrack wall; three haggard faces peered through it. They stared at Salois's indigo skin; then one of them whispered into the shadows behind himself. A fourth man appeared and pressed his own arm against the bars. There were a dozen numbers on it.

"The guards told us the Ark is gone," he said.

"It's true," replied Salois. "And the synagogue."

This news was repeated. Madeleine sensed men waking and climbing down from bunks, an angry, wounded energy bristling through the hut.

Salois seized her hand, and they continued into the main farm complex. Most of the buildings were raised several meters off the ground to keep them free of the monsoon rains. Floodlights created spiky shadows. They flitted among the stilts, hiding once to let a pair of soldiers blunder by, till they were opposite the radio hut. Rising behind the masts and aerials were the two water towers that marked the start of the railway tracks. Salois told her to keep watch, then darted across the open ground and up the stairs. Shortly, he signaled her over. Inside was a bank of transmitters and blinking bulbs; clocks showed the time in various locations across the Reich. He was twisting dials to find reception. Static soared, then faded like waves crashing on a shingle beach. There had been only one radio operator on duty; Salois had left him slumped in the corner.

He thrust a rifle into her hands. "Guard the door."

There was a pot of pens on the desk in front of him. Madeleine grabbed one and a paper clip.

"What are you doing?" asked Salois.

"For Jacoba."

He regarded her pale arms. "I'll do it."

She took up a position at the top of the stairs, squatting below the baluster so she had a view of all approaches while no one would see her till they reached the first step.

The static had given way to whining. "Dragonfly, do you receive? Over," Salois said into the microphone.

Madeleine slipped the pen and paper clip into her pocket. She wondered about her babies: had the doctors at Mandritsara tattooed them? The idea of their unblemished skin pierced and soiled with ink brought a riot to her chest.

A group of men swayed into view. Madeleine's fingers tightened around the rifle till they passed by, arguing and belching.

"Dragonfly?" Salois cursed the radio and continued trawling the frequencies. "Dragonfly?"

A few splats of rain landed around Madeleine, then stopped. Another figure appeared below, his pace steady and sober, the single stripe of an Untersturmführer on his sleeve. He walked erectly toward the radio hut.

"Salois."

He glanced in her direction at the exact moment there was a burst of static and a voice came through, clear and confident: "Dragonfly receiving. Good to hear you, Major."

At first Madeleine did nothing; then she shot up as if an electric charge had exploded through her heels.

She watched Salois's lips move as he spoke into the microphone—but all she heard were the replies, filtered through crackling radio waves, penetrating her mind, the intonation crueler than she remembered.

The Untersturmführer reached the bottom of the stairs and stared up at her. "What are you doing, Jew? Get away from there."

When she ignored him, he unfastened his holster and began mounting the steps. Madeleine was too stunned by Cranley's voice to care.

CHAPTER FORTY-SIX

Nachtstadt
20 April, 20:45

"I HEARD A nasty rumor about this place," said Tünscher. Forming the words seemed to require an effort. He was lying down but kept twisting and rolling, as if no position was comfortable. His skin was sallow and damp, and the dark patches beneath his eyes were spreading like mold.

Music and carousing drifted up to them; in the distance, thunder.

"What rumor?" replied Burton distractedly.

They were on a hill across from the Totenburg. Burton had caught sight of Madeleine's horse grazing beneath the towers and was now scanning the valley below through Tünscher's telescope.

"I heard it belongs to Himmler."

Burton lowered the lens. "It doesn't look well guarded."

Tünscher shrugged. He had fished out the locket from round his neck and was nibbling the end to ward off his pain. "Some of my liquor must have ended up here. It's a Vit B post."

Vitamin B boys were the sons of party officials who got safe placements for their national service. No frontline duty; instead a year in some dull garrison before returning to their place in the bureaucracy.

Burton put the telescope back to his eye. Apart from the celebrations in the far corner of the camp, the place appeared deserted. He moved from the buildings to the sties; the herd must number in the thousands. Alice had wanted some pigs in Suffolk, or sheep or cows. *It's not a proper farm unless there are animals,* she had told him, crossing her arms. Burton glimpsed someone moving among the pens. He sharpened the focus: it was Madeleine's brother. Abner dragged a piece of equipment into the open, then held something up to the clouds as if taking a weather reading. Burton couldn't see properly.

"I'm going down there," he said.

Tünscher was passing his last Bayerweed beneath his nostrils, inhaling deeply. He had smoked the other an hour before and vowed to save this final one till they found Madeleine. He dropped it back into the packet. "I'm coming with you."

Burton helped his old friend to his feet. Tünscher grimaced as he got up, holding his side, and stood lopsided. The bandage round his midriff was soaked through, and now dark blotches were forming on his tunic.

Guilt tugged at Burton. He still carried the stain of Patrick's blood; he didn't need any more. "You should stay here."

"I'm good."

"You'll slow me down."

This was half-true. Riding through the night, Burton had hoped to catch Madeleine before she reached the glow of Nachtstadt, but Tünscher had to keep taking breaks, clutching his guts and folding so low his chin brushed his horse's mane.

"I said I'm good," replied Tünscher tetchily. "It doesn't help me if you get caught. I'm looking out for my investment—"

There was a burst of automatic gunfire, the noise careering indiscriminately around the hills. The music didn't skip a beat.

Burton squinted through the telescope again. He saw nothing but shadows and mud, pigs bumping into each other, agitated by the shots . . . then another muzzle flash outside a building crowned with radio masts; soldiers surrounded it. There was no sign of Madeleine.

"Wait here," said Burton, handing his friend the telescope.

"Forget it."

"You're in no state, Tünsch."

"This isn't the Legion, Major. You can't give me orders. Those diamonds don't leave my sight."

"There aren't any diamonds."

The words had come quickly, quietly, before Burton knew what he was saying.

"What?"

Burton's eyes swept to the ground. "I lied. To get your help." He braced himself. "There are no diamonds."

"But you gave me one." His friend let out a small laugh, trying to reassure himself. "I had it checked: five carats, from the Kassai mines."

"It's all I had."

Tünscher rubbed his blood-spotted flank and absorbed Burton's confession, shaking his head. He seemed to deflate.

Below, Burton saw a cloud of red smoke envelop the radio building. "I'm sorry, Otto."

"How could you do this?" All of a sudden his voice was molten. "I need those diamonds."

He reached for his Luger, prodding it against Burton's chest. The movement was weak, without conviction. Tünscher's eyes were tinged yellow, dull and exhausted. An expression of hatred spilled across his features, then desolation.

Burton brushed the pistol away. "I'm sorry," he said again. "Madeleine was everything. I had no choice."

"I know . . ." Tünscher replied. "I know."

His voice carried such understanding that Burton felt a deep plunge of regret. At the same time, he was aware that if Tünscher had betrayed him, his friend would have shrugged it off. How many times had he seen him flash his yellow teeth at some dupe and say, *You'll be wiser next time?*

Gunfire swirled around the hills once more.

"What will you do now?" asked Burton.

"Does it matter?" He slipped his locket beneath his tunic; his jaw was tense. "Get to Nosy Be. Or find a patrol: say I was ambushed by Jews, hand myself over—"

"They'll throw you in the brig. You know how much you hate bars."

"They can't connect me to any of this shit. I can be back in Roscherhafen by the end of the month, back to safari duties and smuggling till I'm rich." Once more, loathing and devastation swelled in him. "I needed that money, Burton. More than you can know."

"If I ever get it, Tünsch, I'll find you."

Tünscher emitted a bark of resentful laughter that caused him to flinch and press his wound. "Remember when it used to be you, me, and Patrick? He said you were the best of us. The only decent one." He shook his head. "Stupid Yankee bastard."

The clouds opened.

Rain beat through Burton's hair. He wanted to part as they had met: with a pumping handshake and mutual bravado—two men who had once belonged to something. The zoo seemed an age ago. Burton offered an ashamed half salute and began sliding down the hill.

Tünscher called after him: "If you find her, don't go to Mandritsara.

Make for those fishing boats at Varavanga. It's your only chance off the island."

"I'll try."

"*Bon courage*, Major."

Burton went to wish him the same—but Tünscher was already limping away, obscured by sheets of rain.

+ + +

Salois heard boots climb the stairs. He told Cranley to stand by and crossed to Madeleine. She was gawping at the radio, her eyes hazy, as if someone had struck her across the face. Halfway up the steps was an Untersturmführer. He froze when he saw Salois, staring at his rolled-up sleeve and indigo arm.

The Untersturmführer ran back down. Salois grabbed the rifle from Madeleine and aimed it between his shoulder blades. He thought of Steinbock, where the prisoners wore uniforms with X's painted on the backs to make it easier for the guards if they tried to escape. He lined up the shot—then relaxed the weapon, calculating that the report would bring others more rapidly than the Untersturmführer could rouse them.

Salois returned to the microphone. "Cranley?"

"What's going on? Over."

"Nothing."

"Are you in position?"

"Heading for train RV. I'll be at Diego by zero four hundred. Where are you?"

Madeleine joined him, bending close to the speaker to hear every word. She pestered Salois to say something, but he blocked her.

"Mazunka," replied Cranley. "Radar station in view. We're all set."

"How many are you?"

"Three, including Corporal Manny from your team."

So they had made it ashore. Exhilaration surged through Salois. "Do we proceed?"

"Have contacted Rolland: weather all clear for bombers. Mission is go. We'll do our bit; the rest is up to you. Copy?"

"Affirmative."

"Good luck, Major. Out."

As soon as Salois relaxed his grip on the microphone, Madeleine snatched it up: "Jared? Jared?" Only static replied. "Bring him back," she demanded Salois.

"He's gone."

"You're with him?" Her face was ashen. "He sent you to find me?"

Salois didn't understand. "I'm here to destroy Diego."

"But with Cranley . . . Where is he now?"

"Mazunka, on the west coast. You know him?"

"We were married." She looked at Salois in a daze of incomprehension. "He's a civil servant . . . swore to look after Alice . . ."

Salois was equally confused. "He can help find your children—"

She let out a shout of laughter, so vehement it stung.

An alarm began to ring.

Salois secured his rucksack and reached for Madeleine. She refused to be pulled away; she was gripping the microphone as if she expected Cranley's voice to come through it again.

Salois left her for the stairs. Soldiers were converging on the radio hut from every direction. They ran in crooked lines, stumbling and chortling, some wearing party hats. All were armed—but this was sport, not a serious security threat.

"Take the rifle," he shouted at Madeleine. "Open the hatch." In the ceiling was an access point so that engineers could maintain the aerials on the roof.

Salois had two smoke canisters left. He tossed the first down the stairs, shrouding the legs of the building in mist, then toppled over a filing cabinet to block the door. Madeleine levered down an aluminum ladder built into the hatch. She fastened it and climbed, Salois following her. He tore the pin out of the final smoke grenade, dropped it into the room below, and slammed the hatch shut. He still had green canisters in the pocket of the rucksack—but these were for Diego and as precious as the explosives.

They were on the roof, surrounded by radio masts that rattled and moaned in the wind. Red smoke wafted up on all sides. Salois saw the water towers clearly for the first time: one was new, made of steel that had yet to tarnish in Madagaskar's climate; the other was wooden, rotting, no longer in use. The railway line started at the base of the metal tower, curving its way out of the farm before vanishing into the darkness of the hills. On the far side of the tracks, camouflage netting concealed two helicopters.

"Is it Cranley's boat?" asked Madeleine. The light on top of the highest aerial flashed down on her, casting her face red—black—red—

"Yes."

In the alternating shadows, a hopelessness swept across her. He had seen that expression—the hanging of the mouth, the emptying of the eyes—many times before. In the hours that followed it, men often died: too lazy or despondent to care for their lives anymore. As much as he desired the same, his own features had never been marked by it.

Suddenly Madeleine's face was refreshed, as though she had swallowed something delicious and cold. "This is my chance, maybe my only chance. I'm going to wait for him at Kap Ost, and kill him."

Salois grunted; he'd been right about the hate in her eyes. The damaged and the damned could always recognize each other. "As long as he destroys the radar station first."

The soldiers were laughing below. One took a BK44 and fired at the windows. The sound of breaking panes. Salois and Madeleine ran to the edge of the roof: the next building was no more than a meter away. They leapt across.

More shots rang out, in the direction of the pigs this time. Over the rooftops Salois saw the workers breaking out of their barracks. They overwhelmed the few guards on duty and began to kick down the doors of the other huts. Some stormed the barbed-wire fence. The accordion continued its jaunty tune.

Salois and Madeleine reached the end of the building; the next roof was too far away. He swung over the side and clambered down, fingers clawing timber, and dropped the final meters. It began to rain, fat globs hitting his head and dissolving the smoke that had screened their escape. He caught Madeleine as she landed, and they ran.

A voice shouted after them.

They wove beneath the buildings, toward the railway track, the soldiers from the radio hut pursuing, roaring and joking. Bursts of fire flashed around them, the bullets erratic.

From the opposite direction came a squad of soldiers in breeches and suspenders, their shirts loose. One carried a bottle instead of a rifle. Salois skidded in the mud and rain, spinning around for any means of escape.

"The water tower," said Madeleine.

The wooden one was nearest. It was built on four legs, thick as tree trunks, with a ladder leading to a platform at the base of the tank. She scrambled up it, Salois behind her. He saw no alternative but already feared they had trapped themselves. The platform at the top ran the circumference of the tank; some of the slats beneath their feet were broken or missing altogether. The entire structure was warped and covered with patches of algae. Next door was the steel tower, but the gap between the two was too wide.

Ten meters below, the soldiers gathered around the base, a whiff of sweat and alcohol rising through the rain.

"The tower's dangerous," shouted one of them. "Come down before you break your necks." This was greeted with a round of laughter. "Join us for a drink," shouted another, followed by "A glass of wine for the lady." More howls.

They began to chant: *"Runter, runter, runter!"* Down, down, down!

Someone threw a bottle. It shattered above Madeleine's head, showering her in glass. Then a volley of bullets aimed high, like the wedding celebrations Salois had witnessed in the Sahara where Arabs blasted the sky.

A soldier stepped away from the group, toward the ladder. He was greeted with cheers and song as he climbed:

When Jewish blood splashes from the knife
Hang the Yids, put them against the wall.
Heads are rolling, Jews are hollering.

Salois remembered the lyrics from the work gangs at Diego. To relieve the monotony, the guards had arranged a soccer match: the Chosen Race against the tribes of Israel, they called it. Eleven Jews had taken to a makeshift pitch beyond where the runway was being constructed. They'd been exhausted, nothing but gristle, yet somehow they had beaten the Germans, pulling ahead till the spectators' songs were replaced by moody silence. Afterward, the victorious side was never seen again. The Nazis claimed to have been so impressed by their spirit, they sent them to Antzu as a reward; everyone pretended to believe the story.

The soldier was nearing the top of the ladder. Madeleine unslung her rifle and thrust it at Salois. He leaned over the side, rain pelting him, and took aim. The face of a boy looked up at him, startled and rosy with drink. Salois fired.

Click.

He squeezed the trigger again. *Click, click.* The weapon wasn't loaded.

The soldier continued his ascent.

Salois swung the rifle butt into the soldier's head. It cracked his skull, knocking him off the ladder. He landed on his back in an explosion of mud.

The singing stopped.

While several of the soldiers tended to their comrade, another raked the tower with a BK44. The Untersturmführer who'd first discovered them at the radio room stepped forward and stopped him.

"We want them alive for this," he said, loud enough for his voice to carry. The rain hissed around him. He issued an order, and the soldier sprinted away.

Salois searched for a way off. There was nowhere to jump to, nowhere to hide. A detachment settled on him like a silent fall of snow. At the same time he heard the ancient fisherman: *Death doesn't want you.*

Madeleine tugged at his rucksack. "Use the dynamite."

"I need every stick for Diego."

"You won't get to Diego."

"It's too powerful. It'll bring the tower down."

She looked at the men below, her eyes blazing and fearful. "We can't just wait for them." She was soaked to the skin.

There was splashing below, and the soldier returned carrying a bundle of sticks. He handed them out. Salois felt Madeleine clutch him in alarm. Not sticks: axes. The soldiers gathered around the legs of the water tower—and began to chop, resuming their song. *Heads are rolling, Jews are hollering . . .*

CHAPTER FORTY-SEVEN

Governor's Palace, Tana
20 April, 20:50

THE REICHSFÜHRER HUNG up without wishing him happy birthday or even saying good-bye. Globus held the receiver against his head for a few moments, brooding. His office was vast, with a cool stone floor and mahogany furniture; the desk alone was as wide as a stage. In the room beyond, his typing pool was silent. Usually there were a couple of secretaries at this time of night, gossiping or preening, but he had dismissed them. From outside the window came the noise of carpenters.

Globus rocked in his chair—imagining Himmler's sorrow if he toppled over and broke his neck—and stared ruefully at the telephone. It was half-hidden by presents: gifts from the sector governors and admirers in Europe; a magnum of vintage Pol Roger from President Vargas of Brazil. Globus had forbidden news of Antzu and the growing rebellion from being transmitted beyond the island, but he had little control over Nightingale's communications. The American had dispatched his diplomatic tittle-tattle across the Atlantic, from where it had found its way back to the Foreign Ministry in Germania and then SS headquarters. Himmler was contemptuous: *You can't contain the Jew any more than you can influenza. The only way to stop the contagion is to eradicate the virus. I thought you were the man for the job, Odilo; I staked my reputation on it.* He never used Globocnik's first name.

The phone rang.

Globus snatched it up, hoping it was the Reichsführer calling back with more sympathetic words. There was a time, during the afterglow of the first rebellion's defeat, when Himmler phoned with nothing but pleasantries and his schoolboy jokes, encouraging Globus to seek the governorship of Ostmark. Globus invited his secretaries to be present at the calls and lay on his back raising alternate legs, saying *"Ja"* every time he agreed with the chief of the SS. How they delighted at it.

Globocnik put the phone to his ear. It was Rear Admiral Dommes, the base commander at Diego Suarez. He was one of those quietly superior types with a neat, pointed beard and ice-floe eyes, respected in Germania and adored by his sailors; Globus found him grating. Dommes launched into a lecture about the security situation before the governor of Madagaskar interrupted, reminding him that the island came under the SS, not the navy.

"On the understanding that you maintain order," said the admiral. "This new rebellion is like wildfire."

Globus responded furiously. "Are there Jews outside your door? Is Diego ablaze?"

"Not at present. But should the situation worsen, I remind you I have the authority to take whatever measures to defend my base. And the island."

"That will never happen. I'll deal with the bandits."

"And if they do attack?"

"Then I burn them into the ground."

"By then it will be too late," said Dommes coldly. "You need to restore order now."

"The Kriegsmarine needn't worry; I'm tightening the noose. But can't you see that this is the Jews' plan: to set us against each other when we should be celebrating. What time shall I expect you and your officers later? You always enjoyed my birthday before."

An incredulous pause, then: "I've too much to do here."

The line went dead.

Globus leaned back in his chair again, teetering, daring it to give way. The walls of his office were covered with photographs of his many glories. At that moment, however, his focus was on a small picture of his father, hung in the space the door opened on to. His mother had given it to him when he became the gauleiter of Vienna; a reminder, she told him. At first he kept it out of sight, but after he was dismissed he started hanging it up wherever he was posted. His father had been a deserter during the Great War; Globus never wanted to shame the family like that again. Certainly not because of Jews.

There was a knock at the door, and Globus's physician entered. He had the manner of a man with no worries in this world. *This is how my subordinates live,* thought Globocnik, *thanks to the burden on my back.*

He offered his arm (he was still in the short sleeves of his riding kit) as the doctor opened a small case and removed a syringe and a vial. Globus had requested a double dose of his regular tonic, with additional testoster-one to boost the vitamins and amphetamine. His head was thumping like the hammers outside. He needed to stay fresh. His last proper night's sleep had been on the Friday when Hochburg arrived and roused him early from bed. Ruin had threatened since.

Globus looked away as the doctor administered the injection—he hated needles—his eyes returning to the walls. Pinned among the photos were the architectural plans for the governor's mansion he proposed to build in Ostmark. They were based on his own sketches, another of his neo-Mesopotamian designs. He intended to live out his final years there and afterward bequeath the building to the SS—assuming he got out of this shithole. He feared that as a punishment Himmler would make him the lifelong governor of Madagaskar instead of dismissing him. What a place for a man to die.

The doctor finished the injection, wished him a happy birthday, and left.

Globus was thinking of Hochburg again. In the space of forty-eight hours, he had tipped the island from challenging to a fucking calamity. What was his game? Why come searching for Jews? Perhaps Hochburg wanted to destabilize the island in order to bring it under his own control. On the phone to Himmler, he'd asked outright what Hochburg was up to. *He's in Kongo,* replied the Reichsführer, *winning the war. If only I could say the same for you.*

Globocnik stood, screeching his chair out from his desk, and flexed his arm. It was time to pay his prisoner a visit.

+ + +

Hochburg sat in darkness, hands cuffed behind him. Dull arcs of pain radiated from his dead eye, spreading across his skull like a map of shipping routes. The pain was aggravated by the noise outside: sawing, hammering, the cries of men at work. He took level breaths, each one flooding his nose with a fusty odor. The room he was being held in had the reek of a ward-robe stuffed with fur coats. It was too dark to see properly, but after he'd regained consciousness and his vision adjusted, he thought he could make out hundreds of eyes watching him. At his back he sensed a guard: a trunk of a man, trained in silence. Once Hochburg had spoken to him—but he made no reply.

From the corridor Hochburg heard bolts being snapped, then approach-ing boots and the ping of spurs. He was unconcerned: Globus had nothing to threaten him with; nor could he hold him prisoner indefinitely. Kepplar must be closing in on Burton, and once he captured the boy he would seek Hochburg. He cherished his release; his first act would be to court-martial Globocnik.

There were whispers outside the room, the door opened, and someone stood before him. He recognized Globus's yeasty breath.

"Why am I being held here?" Hochburg demanded. "On what charges? When Heinrich learns of this—"

"There are no charges, Oberstgruppenführer; otherwise you'd be in a prison cell. You're here for your own safety. You've had some kind of . . . nervous breakdown."

"What are you talking about?"

"There's no shame in it," said Globus. "I had one myself in forty-three. All those things they made me do. It's easy to give orders when you're in Germania, far from the ice and offal. We're decent men, but sooner or later these things take their toll. You must be under immense stress with Kongo."

"I haven't had a breakdown."

"How else can I excuse your behavior? I told you not to go to Antzu, or the Ark, yet both times you defied me. Now there's chaos. So you must be out of your mind . . . unless you have a better explanation."

Globus switched on the lights and moved to a liquor cabinet while Hochburg took in his surroundings. A guard was pointing a BK44 at his chest.

"Impressive, no?" said Globus, pouring himself a glass of schnapps. He knocked it down his throat. "We're deep in the palace; down here no one can hear us."

The room was an Aladdin's cave of taxidermy. A stuffed crocodile, tortoise, dozens of species of lemurs, some kind of bizarre big cat. Perched on the wall opposite, from floor to ceiling, were shelves of birds, their glass eyes reflecting the light.

"My private collection," said Globus. "I shot each one myself, not just in Madagaskar but before." He indicated behind Hochburg. "I had them brought with me from the East; they're like old friends."

Hochburg twisted in his seat, the cuffs digging into his wrists. Rearing up behind him, paws held out in attack, was a black bear, three meters tall. Globus served himself another schnapps and stretched out on a chaise longue. Dotted around the room were sofas and armchairs; in one corner was a gramophone. Not a single book, noted Hochburg.

Globus swilled his drink. "You've caused me untold trouble. The rebellion is spreading, like I said it would. If the Jews believe even Antzu isn't safe, what control is there? I've got farms rising up, plantations ablaze. Livestock slaughtered. That's revenue and profit lost. But it's no longer the Pig Rebellion. It's the Hochburg Rebellion: you're the spark." He leapt to his feet, screaming, "Is that why you're here? You want Madagaskar for yourself?"

In the silence that followed, the only sound was the construction outside and Globus puffing. He took something silver and sharp from his pocket and pressed it against Hochburg's remaining eye.

Hochburg didn't flinch. He'd sooner be blind, with Kepplar as his fool leading him around Africa, than divulge a word. Globus smiled and revealed a key in his hand. He undid the cuffs around Hochburg's wrists.

"You want this island," said Globus, "you're welcome to it. It's nothing but grief." He returned to the cabinet, his voice suddenly obliging. "Let's have a drink."

"Water."

"I forgot; you don't touch the booze." He was incredulous, as if talking to a man who didn't breathe or shit. Globus handed over an Apollinaris and paced the room. "Do you remember the first time we met, Walter? It was at Windhuk. I thought, *There's a man like me. A man I can do business with.*"

Hochburg was thirsty but sipped his water, reluctant to wash away the last taste of Madeleine. "We're nothing alike."

"We're both ambitious, do a dangerous job for a people who don't care, up to our necks in the racial sewer. When we succeed, no one notices; it's only when things fuck up that they're on our backs."

"You're just a thug," replied Hochburg, "who enjoys the power of killing."

Globus flushed but managed to curb his temper. "This from the master of Muspel. You've burned enough blacks to bury this island in ash."

"From which I took little pleasure. I'm a utopian, not a murderer."

Globus broke into a hearty crow of laughter, which lasted until he realized Hochburg wasn't joking. He paused next to a lemur and stroked its fur as though it were a cat. "Let me tell you about utopia, Oberstgruppenführer: 16 June 1992. The Führer and I speak of it often. A day that will live as long as men walk the earth. The date we calculate the *whole world* will be Jew-free."

"And how do you plan to achieve this 'miracle'?"

"You saw the reservation, the bulldozers at work. We're building a new phase for Argentina's Jews. President Perón has agreed to it with the Führer. It's secret; they start arriving in September." He rubbed his face. "Another reason I need to stamp out this rebellion. Brazil will follow. By the end of the decade, South America will be as rid of Jewry as Europe."

"You forget the United States."

"Eventually, they'll submit, too. Once the rest of the world is cured of the Jewish pathogen, it will stride forward with us, leaving America to lag behind. Decay. Eventually, the Yankees will realize their mistake; sometime in the seventies is our prediction. After that, they won't be able to ship them here fast enough. A generation of monsoon and malaria"—he made a triumphant click, like a neck being snapped—"and the Jew will be no more."

"You believe this fairy tale?"

"It breaks the Führer's heart to think he won't live to see it."

"The Jews have power in Washington. Influence."

"I discussed it with their previous envoy. After a bottle or two, he agreed that this was the future."

"But not Nightingale."

"Don't talk to me about him. He's been pissing in my ear since I got back from Antzu." Globus put on a surprisingly realistic American accent: "*I have reports that you destroyed the synagogue. That you're interning more of the population. The reservations are already at bursting. Now you're clearing Antzu. I insist that you stop.*"

Hochburg shifted on his seat; he wanted a breath that wasn't mangy with fur. "Is it true?"

"Your meddling left me no choice."

"Nightingale's right. Remember what he said at the dam: they want to send a warship. Since Taft was elected, things have shifted. You must see that."

Globus picked at his ear.

"It will hamper my efforts in Kongo," said Hochburg. "I'll need more of your troops. Your own position will suffer."

"Then I liquidate the Jews, and I won't need any men at all."

Hochburg's reply was severe: "Don't even think it. You'll drag the United States into the region, maybe the war in Africa."

"Americans draw their red lines . . . then do nothing."

"You'll never see Ostmark."

"Or maybe the Reichsführer will sit me on a golden throne. He's not intimidated by America, either. But I'm bored of this. I want to know why you're here. Last chance."

When Hochburg remained silent, Globus finished his schnapps. "Then I've something to show you."

They left the trophy room, Hochburg prodded at each step by the guard's BK44. He watched Globus's fat back and royal swagger as they climbed a staircase and emerged into the garden Hochburg had seen when he first arrived. He sucked in gulps of air tinged with damp vegetation and sleeping flowers. On the terrace, a gang of carpenters were at work beneath arc lights. They were building a gallows.

"For my birthday celebrations," said Globus. "A tradition I started in the East."

"Who's the drop for?" asked Hochburg, impressed by the size of the construction: there were places for at least twenty nooses.

"That depends on whether you talk."

Globus led him to another staircase. "This is the north side of the palace," he explained as they descended. "It's where my offices are, and, at the bottom, the dungeons. They were the only part of the original building I kept." They reached the lowest level, and he shot Hochburg a pointed look. "This is where the queen of Madagascar used to lock up traitors."

They passed through a series of locked doors that were heaved open by guards till they reached their destination. "Perhaps now you'll tell me."

Globus unbolted the door and thrust Hochburg inside, the ceiling forcing them both to stoop. The room was dingy and packed with stinking, shuffling prisoners. The stench of human excrement was thick as fog.

"I couldn't see the point of plumbing down here," said Globus, covering his mouth. "Lights!"

An electric lamp illuminated the cell.

At first Hochburg didn't understand what he was seeing. Then the anger surged through him and, for the first time, a tremor of fear.

From the corridor came the nick of boots on stone. An adjutant appeared at the door. "Obergruppenführer—"

"Not now." He was watching Hochburg's reaction intently.

"It's an emergency."

The adjutant spoke into his ear. Hochburg didn't catch the news—but the air crackled around Globus. "Radio back," he said. "Tell them to use maximum force. I'll be on my way soon."

Hochburg stared at the prisoners' terrified faces and kept his voice indifferent. "I've no idea why you've brought me here."

Globus waded among his captives. "You think I'd let you leave my island without first checking your cargo?"

Crammed inside the dungeon were the scientists Hochburg had gathered for his superweapon. He searched desperately for the most important.

As if reading his thoughts, Globus said, "I know one of them is Feuerstein; I learned that much on the Ark. But you've trained your monkeys well: none will talk, even when encouraged." On the floor lay several bodies with bullets through their skulls, one stripped naked.

Hochburg spoke in a whisper: "This is beyond anything you can understand. If you want Ostmark, you mustn't harm another of them."

"Does Heinrich know you're such a Yid lover?"

"It won't be just the ruin of your career, or mine; it will see the end of everything in Africa. Possibly the Reich itself."

"For a few stinking Jews?" Globus screwed up his face in disbelief. "You're lying. Talk—or I swear I'll shoot every last one until you do."

Hochburg said nothing.

He refused to allow his secret to fall into the hands of a man like Globocnik. He kept checking the prisoners and found Feuerstein hunched at the rear of the cell. Their eyes met for the briefest moment.

"Or I could shoot them for fun," suggested Globus with a leer. "Or just because they're yours."

He snatched one of the guard's pistols and waved it carelessly into the crowd. When Hochburg didn't react, he grinned, but there was frustration in his face.

"I must leave—important work for the Reichsführer. We'll talk more later." He turned to a guard. "Take him back to the trophy room."

As Hochburg was led away, he glanced at Feuerstein. He had discarded his suit and was in a tattered, soiled uniform, his face streaked with filth. The scientist didn't return his gaze; he retreated into the shadows, an animal again.

CHAPTER FORTY-EIGHT

Nachtstadt
20 April, 21:15

BURTON FOUGHT HIS way through the herd of hogs. The animals were restless, squealing, disturbed by the gunfire and thunder. A rippling lake of blond flesh and bristles. Between gunshots Burton heard another sound, one he couldn't identify. It stirred memories of chasing through the jungle as a boy and stumbling across loggers. Hochburg had warned him to avoid them: they were wicked men; felling trees killed the spirit of the forest.

Burton slapped pigs out of his way, working out where he had last seen Madeleine's brother. As he'd slipped down the hillside, sore with regret about Tünscher, he'd kept his gaze fixed on the spot, but now, among the pens, he was lost. He began checking every sty, poking his head inside. Blasts of ammonia stung his eyes.

Behind him he thought he heard a voice.

Burton doubled back, trying to locate the sound, and ducked beneath a corrugated roof that drummed with rain. Abner was on his knees, surrounded by open boxes, cradling a piece of equipment. He saw Burton's uniform and lunged for him.

They tumbled to the floor, crates breaking under them, rolling in shit and straw. Burton took a blow to the eye; another landed on his sternum, firing acid into his throat. He retaliated cautiously, wary of knocking Abner unconscious. He wedged the stump of his arm against Abner's throat and jabbed the Beretta into his kneecap.

"I'm not going to shoot," he said. "My name's Burton Cole, I'm Madeleine's—" He felt coy, unsure how to describe himself; *lover* seemed inappropriate. "I've come to find your sister."

He released the Beretta and held it wide. "Where is she?"

Abner rolled away, rubbing his neck, and flashed him a furious stare. There was a squeak to his voice from when Burton had pressed against his windpipe.

"You're supposed to be dead."

"So I've been told."

"She went with Salois. To the radio hut." He revealed the piece of equipment he'd been holding. "I found it in the boxes. They could have used it instead." It was a field phone and transmitter pack, the type used by the British Army.

"Why did you let her go? It's too dangerous."

"I tried to stop her, but she wouldn't listen."

"We've got to save her."

Abner squared his glasses and rubbed his throat again. He took the transmitter out of its canvas case and began filling the empty pack with dynamite.

Burton picked up a bundle, wondering if it could help; without a detonator it was useless as a brick. "I haven't got time for this."

"Salois needs the dynamite. He's going to attack Diego"—he grinned—"to bring the Americans."

As soon as Abner was finished, they went back into the rain. It was like wading into the currents of a swift river. The pigs had grown more agitated; they were scrambling around in the mud, knocking into one another, snarling, their fear contagious. Burton and Abner were bumped along as they headed for the gate, constantly driven off course. Beyond, the barracks had been set alight. The downpour was too heavy for a blaze to take hold; clouds of tarry smoke billowed upward. Not all the buildings had been torched. Workers stood on the remaining roofs, a few with rifles, and urged the rest to revolt. Remembering what happened on the Ark, Burton peeled off his tunic: it might prove helpful later but could get him killed now.

"Put this in your backpack," he said to Abner.

"No. Why?"

"Just do it."

Lightning bleached the sky for a second . . . then a cymbal crash of thunder that reverberated through the ground. The pigs' panic intensified. They charged blindly, propelling Burton and Abner toward the gate. Burton had a slipping, drowning sensation; his boots skimmed the ground.

He smashed into the fence, the mass of pale bodies crushing, then bouncing him against the mesh. A din of squealing and ricocheting metal. Abner's face was squashed into the wire. Through it, Burton saw the workers attack the railings around their compound and bring down a section. Farther into the farm, through the haze of rain and smoke, was the radio room, its windows throbbing red. The soldiers he'd spied earlier had abandoned it and were gathered around a water tower, crews swinging axes beneath its legs. The tower leaned over like an old man whose stick had been kicked away.

Clinging to the platform was Madeleine.

Burton climbed with a renewed determination. He grabbed Abner's collar and pulled him up; the material ripped. He reached again, clenching his fingers around the straps of the backpack, and heaved. Abner clambered up the fence and gave a nod of resentful thanks.

They reached the top and picked their way over the rolls of barbed wire. The pigs continued to rush helplessly, battering the fence. It began to lean, the mesh sagging.

Burton and Abner jumped down and ran between the barns and barracks. Behind them the fence burst outward.

Stampede.

+ + +

The accordion had finally stopped. The two alarms were ringing out of sync, one filling the other's silence, like the wail of babies demanding their mother, thought Madeleine.

At first she marveled at Salois's composure; then it unsettled her. He sat watching the soldiers below, while she flinched with every axe strike, struggling not to yell. Each time steel bit into wood, it sent sickening vibrations through the structure. The whole tower trembled.

"How can you be so calm?" she shrieked.

Through the broken slats at her feet, the soldiers seemed oblivious to the alarms and the burning barracks. They were too drunk to be accurate, the axeheads landing above or under the point they were chopping. One of the soldiers laughed so hard he had to give up. He staggered to a corner to vomit. The Untersturmführer stood apart from the others, his stare burning into her.

Salois replied as if he had been deep in thought and only just been roused by her voice. "Your husband—"

"He's not my husband."

"Cranley called me 'the invincible Jew.' I am death's orphan: it doesn't want me."

"Tonight you're wrong."

"I've tried harder than this to die." He offered her a wan smile. "I'm meant to live: it's my punishment."

A cracking sound; the tower began to dip forward.

"Punishment for what?"

There was a pause in the *chop-chop-chop* of axes, followed by a cheer. The groan and strain of timber; wood splitting. The crews fled their positions to watch the tower fall. It leaned over, plunging several meters—Madeleine screamed—then jolted to a stop. The gap between it and the steel water tower had narrowed but was still too risky.

Madeleine and Salois clung to the platform. He grasped her hand, encouraging her to crawl to the far side to counterbalance the weight. His manner was oddly careful and made her think of old couples, the way her father might have supported her mother's arm if their world hadn't been wrenched away.

The soldiers returned to the legs, seizing their axes.

Salois kept his voice low: "I did something . . ." He searched for a word as though he'd often thought about it and had too many to choose from. "Something wicked. Death would be too kind. Living is my penance."

"What could you have done"—Madeleine was surprised by her own anger—"with everything on this island, what could you have done to believe that?"

"I've seen too much loathing, Madeleine, to want yours."

"I haven't got any more to give."

His reply was so soft she had to lean closer to hear. "I killed my wife . . . or the woman who was going to be my wife." His voice was tender and tearless.

Madeleine remained close. "An accident? It can't be worse than here."

"A fit of rage." Something irreparable churned in his expression. "That's why I never held my child. She was pregnant."

The depth of his misery, of his self-disgust, was painful to hear—yet she didn't recoil. Madeleine didn't understand the catastrophe of his life but instinctively wanted to forgive him for it. She couldn't explain why. It was as if the God she didn't believe in had whispered in her ear. In a world that shunned atonement, Reuben Salois was determined to walk alone and be held to account.

A roar went up from underneath, something starved and berserk. The workers had broken free of their barracks and were running headlong into the soldiers, attacking with fists and wooden planks.

Salois slid to the ladder. "This is our chance." He began to descend, Madeleine following.

Amid the fighting, the Untersturmführer snatched up an axe and swung it in a frenzy. Madeleine sensed each blow through the rungs. The tower began to buckle and splinter, pitching again. It toppled over, accelerating—then crashed to a halt, its fall broken by the other tower. Madeleine dangled from the ladder, her legs loose inside her dress.

Salois dropped below. The Untersturmführer swiped his axe at him, the blade cutting through the rain. Salois leapt back and, as the Untersturmführer lost his balance, tackled him to the ground. He joined his fingers together and brought the club of his fists down onto the Nazi's face, fighting as if he truly believed in the conviction that he wouldn't die.

Madeleine let go of the ladder, landing hard. She felt spikes in her hips and rolled into the sluicing mud. A noise filled her ears, like from the abattoir when animals were taken to slaughter and one of them sensed what was about to happen.

She stood—and was knocked off her feet by a charge of pigs.

Hundreds swept past her. She was beaten and knocked around by a blur of hogs until she was dragged back into the air by Salois. In one hand he held a machine gun; with the other he encouraged her to run. For several moments she was too dazed and breathless to do anything but comply. Then she realized they were following railway tracks, heading into the darkness.

"What about Abner?" she said.

"He'll find us."

She ran, soaked to the skin and lit with energy. The night held the promise of finding the twins.

Madeleine . . . Madeleine!

The cry that had haunted her since Antzu echoed through the rain. She blocked her ears to it. Salois spun round and let off a short volley.

She heard the voice again: closer, more fraught, with nothing supernatural in its pleading.

"Maddie," it gasped, "stop."

Madeleine faltered, glancing over her shoulder, incredulity washing through her. An impossible, poisonous hope that had no place in reality.

A solitary figure was running toward them, a silhouette emerging from the lights of the farm, indistinct through the shimmer of the rain, pigs at his heels. His body was lean and weary; she couldn't make out his face. He ran between the tracks, the rails catching the light so they gleamed like beams of platinum.

Salois took another shot, the bullets sparking off the tracks near the feet of their pursuer, spitting flecks of stone at him.

Then another cry—resonant with a distant autumn morning; the call of a legionnaire as he approached a fort. She stopped dead, her heart cartwheeling. Salois lowered his weapon with a frown of expectation.

"*Ami! Ami!*"

+ + +

Burton's smile showed exhaustion but was crinkled with relief and a boyish exuberance. It faded almost at once.

Madeleine was bewildered.

Shocked.

She stepped back from him, her body tense—ready to bolt. Up close she was more wasted than the glimpses he'd had of her in Antzu, the light in her eyes dim; the corners of her mouth looked cracked and sore.

"Please," he said, "no more running."

She shook her head in violent disbelief. Pigs streamed to either side of them.

Every day as a boy Burton imagined the homecoming of his mother and the joy of seeing her again. He would skip and holler, grab her hand and drag her to the strawberry patch he'd cultivated, making her taste the fruit even if the berries were hard and white as pebbles. But if she had emerged from the jungle after years of absence, maybe his reaction would have been the same as Madeleine's.

A crushing weariness settled on Burton. He wanted to wrap himself in Maddie and sleep till they were old. Then he thought of Bel Abbès, the Legion fort that had been his home for so many years.

If you returned to it from the west, your first glimpse would be from the peak of Faîte du Pierre. It was most beautiful at dawn: the air cool, a saffron light creeping up the battlements. Burton always checked his fatigue at that point: between him and a bed, cooked food, and fresh water were still twenty miles of unforgiving desert.

Madeleine's eyes were busy, one moment resting on his face, the next falling on his ragged uniform. She reached out and touched him, tentative at first, tracing the shape of his skull as if she were blind. Her fingers brushed his brow and ran down to his jawbone. Then she was pinching his cheek, digging her nails into his flesh, convincing herself that he was real. Burton let her do it till it stung, then removed her fingers.

Tears ran down her cheeks. "Jared showed me your name. He swore you were dead."

"He lied."

A burst of laughter; Burton smelled the salt of her tears. Maddie held out her hands for his. He hesitated, offering only his right. He didn't want her to see his stump—not yet. Burton wanted to pretend that all of him had returned.

Footsteps rang out on the tracks. Abner caught up with them, splattered in mud, his backpack hanging heavily on one shoulder.

"They're launching helicopters," he panted before telling Madeleine, "I found him for you. In the pig shit." Burton detected a hint of satisfaction in his tone.

Salois joined them. "You get the rest of the explosives?"

Abner nodded.

"Then let's go."

The floodlights made Madeleine's skin look overexposed. Her eyes had shed their fear and were bright with wonder. Burton slipped his fingers between hers—they were bonier than before, the skin tough—and they fled: away from the light, back toward the darkness.

"I'm taking you home," said Burton.

"No." She looked possessed. "To Mandritsara."

PART IV

MANDRITSARA

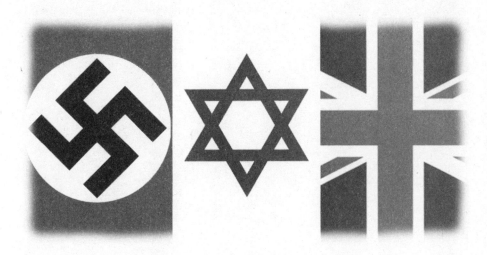

If you know what hurts yourself,
you know what hurts others.

Malagasy proverb

CHAPTER FORTY-NINE

Nachtstadt
20 April, 23:50

DEAD SWINE LITTERED the ground, the scene lit as starkly as a Nuremberg stadium. When the Jews had realized that they were defeated, they had begun killing the animals: stabbing, battering them with planks, cutting their throats. Many of the carcasses had Stars of David carved into their flanks.

"Fucking savages," Globus said.

He walked alone through Nachtstadt, inspecting the carnage. At first the farm commandant and his officers accompanied him, shaking their heads and groveling, their breath rich with alcohol. Globus soon tired of their presence and dismissed them. They were mostly Vitamin B boys; he often did favors for people in Germania, making sure their sons got soft postings. If he returned to Europe in shame, he hoped those same people would remember him. It had stopped raining, and there was a glistening hush to the farm. The puddles rippled occasionally as though sighing. From roofs came a *drip-drip-drip.*

He couldn't get that sound out of his head. It was his future—Ostmark and the mansion he dreamed of building—running away.

Wherever he went, Himmler's prized pigs lay slaughtered. Globus had seen enough animals at the end of a hunt to know that they often lay dead with open eyes and a curl to their lips—but every last pig seemed to be grinning as if it were in on some joke.

He was the butt of it.

The Reichsführer would be devastated, enraged, at the loss of Nachtstadt. Buildings had been burned, fences torn down, the veterinary hospital wrecked. It was a tiny but lucrative part of Himmler's private business empire, and he took a personal interest in its operation, experimenting with the latest livestock-raising techniques. Prize specimens were regularly shipped to his Wewelsburg castle for banquets. *I enjoy roasting Jew pigs*, he would tell guests, dabbing away the laughter. If Globus admitted what had happened here, he might as well admit to being no better than Bouhler, the first governor. Everyone remembered how his career ended.

Globocnik let out a sob. It was the same terrible sob that had erupted from him when his wife miscarried, their child growing deformed inside her; even the experts at Mandritsara had been unable to save the baby. Instinctively, he hadn't shared the news with Himmler when his wife first became pregnant.

He stopped in front of a pile of dead animals, all with Jewish stars sliced into their hides, and mulled over the graffiti painted on the Sofia Dam. If what happened in Nachtstadt was repeated in the reservations, he wouldn't have enough troops to cope. The only chance of controlling such an uprising would be to open the floodgates. But what had the Reichsführer repeatedly warned him? The gates could be disabled.

The thought buzzed in his head like a mosquito.

Globus picked his way through the carcasses to the main square. He was still wearing spurs, though they were clogged with mud and silent. The tables were covered with bowls of potato salad and purple cabbage swilling in rainwater. At least those pigs left alive would feast in the morning. Globus snatched up a bottle of wine, went to drink, then changed his mind. He threw it away, the shattering glass his first moment of pleasure since the dungeon in Tana. The itchy sensation that Hochburg was responsible for all his woes crawled over him again. Hochburg, who had deprived him of manpower; Hochburg, who'd wrought disaster for him at the Ark and Antzu; Hochburg, with his Jew secrets and fear of America. It had taken two hours to fly from his palace. Globus came in a Walküre, leading a formation of other gunships. The pilots were disappointed when they arrived and found that order had been restored. He should have caught up on some sleep during the flight, but his recent injection coursed through his bloodstream and the radio crackled ceaselessly in his ears with news of more outrages across the island.

Globus picked up another bottle and drained it, the coolness of the alcohol mixed with a hint of rainwater pulsing through him. The time had come to wrest back his career before the population ran amok or the Kriegsmarine intervened; losing control of Madagaskar to the navy would be equally humiliating. Heydrich's containment policy had proved a disaster. Who cared whether the Yids were gone in a generation if they were dragging the island toward catastrophe now? The Reichsführer had always been his sponsor.

Only he had clarity of vision when it came to the Jew.

It was also worth reminding himself about the persistent rumors of the Führer's ill health. In the days that followed his death, it would be Himmler who ascended the throne, not Heydrich

He smashed the second bottle, enjoying the tinkle of glass more this time, and strutted toward the radio room. He had defeated the Vanilla Rebellion, he would defeat this Pig Rebellion. On the way he met the farm commandant.

"Obergruppenführer, the ringleaders have been executed," he said. "The remainder are ready to be transported."

"I've changed my mind," replied Globus. "Shoot them."

"All of them?"

He thought of some advice Himmler once gave him: *If you're underresourced, my dear Globus, all you can use is brutality.* "Yes: all. We need to be more ruthless than we were during the first rebellion. That's been my mistake. Overwhelming force will win the day."

Globus climbed the steps to the radio hut. Inside, everything was dusted with a fine red powder. He was connected to Tana and reeled off commands: all leave was canceled; every man must report for immediate duty; every Walküre was to be fueled and armed.

He continued briskly: "Inform the regional governors that they must begin the mass transportation of their sectors to the reservations. No resistance to be tolerated."

"Tonight, Obergruppenführer?" said the operator.

"Tonight." He gripped the telephone. "I also want external communications from the U.S. envoy's residence shut down; not a squeak leaves him." Globus wasn't intimidated by Nightingale and his threats, but he didn't want him mouthing off to Washington either, not till order had been restored. "Then contact the Sofia Dam. Tell them to collect all the TNT they can find and prepare for my arrival. I'll need extra men, so have the garrison at Mandritsara sent to the dam."

While the operator confirmed the instructions, Globocnik glanced at the clocks above him. There were four: one told the local time, the second the time in Germania. The other two covered "the span of empire"—showing the hour in Dakar, Deutsch Westafrika, the Reich's westernmost city, and Ufa in the Ural Mountains, its farthest east.

In Madagaskar, it had turned midnight: officially, it was his birthday. He would allow himself one treat—a gift to his party guests from the absent host. Globus grinned and gave a final order:

"And hang Hochburg's Jews."

CHAPTER FIFTY

Nachtstadt
21 April, 00:40

WITH EACH PUNCH, Kepplar's hopes drained away. He pressed his good ear against the cell door, listening to the blows land. The grooms were vigorous, vicious—yet every thwack and squelch, every grunt of pain, was followed by silence. He needed to take over the interrogation personally. Hochburg had offered him everything he desired, if only he could find the will to grasp it. His master demanded a show of blood. Kepplar massaged his knuckles in preparation; they felt spongy.

The prisoner's belongings were piled on the floor. He rifled through them: a tropical uniform splattered in the same paint as his own, a standard-issue Luger from the East, a lighter, and a crumpled pack of Bayerweeds containing a solitary cigarette. One of the grooms had ripped a locket from the prisoner's neck. Kepplar undid the clasp; inside was a photo of a girl with plain, Slavic features.

Something slammed against the door, making Kepplar jump.

He decided to give the grooms a few minutes longer and moved to the next cell, locking himself inside, glad there was no one to see him. He was shivering with adrenaline, felt a desperate urge to shit. *I believe in our mission,* thought Kepplar, *I understand the value of physical punishment. What went wrong with me?*

At the academy in Vienna he was an enthusiastic participant in peer discipline. Every intake of cadets produced one *Versager* who let the rest down. After lights-out, the unfortunate recruit would be taught a lesson by the others. Kepplar was among the first to put his bar of soap inside a sock and administer a drubbing. If only he could retrieve that enthusiasm.

The cell was dark, barely large enough to contain a man, the walls stained brown—though whether with dried blood or excrement, it was impossible to tell. A wooden bunk was the only piece of furniture. Despite the recent downpour, the air was oppressive.

Kepplar felt feverish at what he must do next.

He stripped to the waist and lay down, concentrating on the noises from next door: the muffled percussion of fists and stamping boots, yelps and sharp intakes of breath. And mixed among them an occasional, contemptuous snort, as if the beating were nothing. That's what he feared the most.

His thoughts were interrupted by a firing squad outside: the workforce was being liquidated.

Kepplar had pursued Cole from Antzu, the grooms tracking hoofmarks through the twilight until they came across his companion, the one who'd dared to ask about his ear. He was wounded and gratefully gave himself in, until he realized they weren't a regular patrol. The grooms suggested Nachtstadt, with its punishment block, as the nearest place to interrogate him. They waited till Globus departed before riding in.

Kepplar needed something to calm his nerves and retrieved the Bayerweeds. His father had taught him to smoke as a teenager, though he abandoned the habit after the Führer spoke against it: "Smoking is the wrath of the Red Man against the White." Kepplar inhaled a lungful . . . then exploded in coughing and stubbed out the rest. His brain tingled. He sensed the extremities of his body and a nascent weariness, not from the past few days but the months prior. He had expended a deep store of energy for a single, insignificant man, not to mention the resources and lives of many others. The reasons were like this cell: spooled in shadow. Kepplar considered what might have been achieved if that resolve had been directed to winning the war in Kongo.

"I hope it's worth it," he said aloud, as though Hochburg were next to him on the bunk. He let his disillusionment fill the cell.

Kepplar could hold off no longer.

He stood and dressed, tugging all the loose creases of his uniform until they were sharp, methodically fastening every button and buckle, conscious that he was delaying. The paint on the front of his tunic had dried; it flexed and cracked with his movements. He resumed his position by the door. The prisoner was trying to say something: . . . am . . . an . . . SS officer. Every word was met with fresh blows. Kepplar had left the academy with the same fervor as these boys yet had lost it somewhere in Africa. As a young officer in Muspel, he'd been exposed to a mantra not found in lectures and text-books: nowadays you had to be a technician to be a killer.

He entered the cell. The air was glutinous with sweat and exertion. Gobs of blood spattered the concrete floor. Kepplar hoped the hammering in his Adam's apple wasn't visible.

"Enough," he said.

The grooms withdrew from the prisoner. He was naked, curled in the shape of a question mark, hands protecting his groin; his left ankle was manacled to the wall. When he realized the beating was at an end he heaved himself onto his knees, then his feet. Instead of weakening him, the beating had provoked a stubborn streak. He was shivering, but it didn't seem to be from fear or pain. Blood flowed out of his nose, his lip was split, and there were dozens of welts across his body that would turn black in the coming days, like the markings of a cheetah. Kepplar didn't have the stomach for anything so crude. He would target what Hochburg called "the morsels": fingers, toes, ears and eyes, the kidneys, the genitals.

"So you're the prick in charge," said the prisoner.

"Brave words from a man in your position. I am Brigadeführer Derbus Kepplar. And you?"

"Obersturmführer Tünscher, Section IX-c, Roscherhafen. Before that I served three years under Standartenführer Kanvinksy. You can check my record."

The grooms exchanged admiring glances, a respect they had never shown Kepplar.

Kanvinksy was infamous. A renegade colonel who had been one of Globocnik's deputies in Siberia, he was the only officer ever recalled by Germania because his methods were too extreme.

"Your record is irrelevant. I want to know where Burton Cole is."

Tünscher's expression soured—but he said nothing.

Kepplar unfastened his tunic, passed it to one of the grooms, and rolled up his sleeves in a manner he hoped suggested was his prelude to violence. He wished he were wearing gloves: a tight leather barrier between him and the prisoner. "You ruined my uniform," he said with menace. "In Antzu."

Tünscher regarded him more closely, noticed his missing ear, and for the first time seemed to recognize who he was. Was it Kepplar's imagination or did a smirk ripple across that bruised face? Kepplar curled his fingers into fists and searched for something to stoke his fury. He saw the Madeleine woman kissing Hochburg and felt again his dismay—his disgust—at the spectacle. The image was displaced by Hochburg's laughter in the Schädelplatz and the smell of sparks, as vivid as the day it happened. It should have caused him to erupt; instead he was consumed by humiliation. *The paperwork.* Was that really all that had spared his life?

Tünscher appraised him with the same expression he'd used in Antzu, as if he understood what was going through his mind.

"I've known Burton half my life. We trained together, fought together; we share the same *esprit*. I can't give him up to you . . . But there is another way."

"Another way?"

"A way that will be easier for you."

There was a shrapnel wound below Tünscher's ribs, gently weeping. If Hochburg had been there, he would have plunged his hand in and corkscrewed it around: a simple, effective method to get the Obersturmführer talking. All Kepplar had to do was insert his finger.

He understood his mistake. He should have started pummeling the prisoner's face as soon as he entered the cell. Now he was thinking too much, and his thoughts—no matter how angry or shameful or goading— had frozen him.

"Leave us," he said to the grooms.

They didn't move.

"Go! You've done well—it's time to rest." He realized his fists had gone flaccid and locked them behind his back. "I wish to speak to Obersturmführer Tünscher alone."

Kepplar waited for the footsteps to fade before circling his prisoner: he had shoulders almost as broad as Hochburg's and a Category 1 skull. He was unperturbed by his nakedness.

Tünscher sniffed him. "You got Bayerweeds?"

"I smoked your last one."

"Too bad."

From outside came another volley of shots.

"You were going to tell me about Cole," said Kepplar eventually. A fatigue was creeping up on him and the interrogation had yet to begin.

"We served in the Foreign Legion together. We're bound by a code." He made it sound contemptible. "Like there is between you and me."

"There's nothing between us."

"We've sworn the same oaths to the Führer."

"Go on."

"You can . . . you can buy my honor," said Tünscher.

"You know where Cole is?"

"I know where he's headed. Burton promised me a lot of money to get him to Madagaskar. Diamonds worth thousands of marks. He lied."

"You're willing to sell me the information?"

There was a queasy twist to Tünscher's mouth. He nodded. "I just want off this island."

"And if I find your suggestion demeaning?"

"Then it's going to be a long night."

A flood of intolerable emotion tumbled through Kepplar: gratitude toward Tünscher that he might be able to find Cole without bloodying his hands; shame that he felt so grateful; anger that Hochburg had left him in this position. "Let's say I buy this information—how do I know it's true?"

"How can you be sure if you beat it out of me? In the East, during interrogations, I saw partisans say anything for a breather. The time we wasted on bullshit confessions."

There was logic to Tünscher's words, but Kepplar resisted, aware of how keen he was to acquiesce. Yet they could torture him for days before he gave up Cole . . . or Kepplar could learn his quarry's whereabouts at once. He remembered the previous year, in Kongo, when they captured one of Cole's fellow assassins and beat him till his teeth sprinkled the floor—he hadn't revealed a thing. Kepplar had lost valuable time; if he'd got him to talk faster, he might have caught Cole and not failed Hochburg.

Kepplar's mind turned to the embalmed parrot he had confiscated from the dhow and its breast of golden coins; he had left it for safekeeping at Lava Bucht. There were helicopters stationed outside.

"The lousy bastard cheated me," said Tünscher. "I need that money more than anything."

"For what?"

"Debts."

"What kind of debts?"

Despite the chain round his ankle and his bruised body, the reply was impudent: "That's my business."

"If you expect me to pay, you need to convince me."

Tünscher lowered his head. Blood was still dripping from his nose. He spoke quickly, in a whisper. Kepplar's stomach bulged with contempt. The explanation was like one of those tawdry novels his wife enjoyed, stories of life on the Eastern frontier, so nauseating, so sentimental it could only be true.

Tünscher sensed his scorn. "It's a big island," he said, toughening his voice. "You'll never find Burton without me. This might be your only chance."

"I'll think about it," replied Kepplar, and left the cell.

CHAPTER FIFTY-ONE

Governor's Palace, Tana
21 April, 00:45

A BREEZE VENTED the must of the trophy room, blowing in through the window and broken shutters. Hochburg had kicked them open in an attempt to escape. Below was a sheer wall and a drop that would break any climber that fell. Schubert was playing on the gramophone.

He gazed out at Tana. For the past hour he had watched Walküre gunships, laden with missiles, clatter over the city into the darkness; they returned spent. The mournful call of train whistles echoed from far away. The carriages must be chock-full with Jews being shipped to the Sofia Reservation. The night felt unbridled; Hochburg sensed violence, escalation. He had searched for Nightingale's residence, locating it in a cluster of buildings from the French colonial period. Every window was illuminated. Had the envoy spent the evening dispatching reports to Washington about Globus's crackdown? Could an American warship already be en route to Africa?

There was a loud snap from the garden terrace above, followed by the hum of filaments, and the night was illuminated.

He moved to the door. "What's happening?" he asked the guard on the other side.

"Governor's orders. They're hanging your Jews."

Hochburg experienced a sensation as vertiginous as dangling headfirst from the window. He pictured Feuerstein jerking at the end of a rope, his secrets lost forever.

"They are mine," bellowed Hochburg. "I demand to see them." Nothing. "You will open this door!"

He pounded his fists against the wood; each blow was met with silence.

Hochburg stepped back into the room. Earlier he had ransacked it for a means to break out, searching among the stuffed birds, digging through drawers. In his frustration, he toppled the bear. A locked trunk offered a momentary hope, until he smashed it open and found it full of vinyl records, mostly Austrian folk pap but also some classical music, including Keilberth's recording of *The Ring*. Hitler had sent it as a gift to senior members of the SS for Christmas 1950. Hochburg's had burned in the Schädelplatz; Globus's was still wrapped in cellophane. There was also an unopened copy of Schubert's Impromptus. They were always Eleanor's favorites.

He had put on the record to soothe himself, righted the fallen bear, and continued his search, finding nothing more than a stocking caught among the cushions of the chaise longue. He sat, folding his arms in contemplation, and felt a hard lump against his chest. Hochburg reached inside his tunic to find Burton's silver knife. He had quite forgotten about it and was thankful that the body search after his arrest had been cursory.

Now he took the blade and strode to the window, leaning his whole body out. A blast of wind hit him. Ten meters above was a balcony with a wrought iron balustrade—but the climb was suicidal. The walls of the palace were made from huge, smooth blocks of stone. Hochburg ran his fingers along the mortar between the blocks—there was scant purchase—then tried the knife, digging it into the cement and testing it. It might be enough to take his weight. He remembered the knife from Eleanor's dinner service, the one she used only for the best occasions. Burton had fashioned the metal into a lethal dagger.

From the terrace came men shouting orders and the burble of excited, drunken chatter. Numerous times during his incarceration, the noise of a party had seeped through the walls of the trophy room. Globus may have been absent, but his guests were enjoying the Führertag celebrations.

Hochburg cursed Kepplar.

Hours had passed. He should have found Burton by now and brought him back; he should have released Hochburg. Once more his former deputy had shown he could not be relied upon. It was further proof of the necessity of Feuerstein's superweapon. If even the most devoted failed Hochburg, he needed the means to fight without having to depend on mere men. Perhaps Kepplar had reached the end of his usefulness.

A new sound came from above: the somber beat of the executioner's drum.

Typical Globus theatrics! Doubtless he would have also insisted on long ropes. There would be no short drop and break of the neck for the Jews; they would kick and fight and choke for several minutes: a spectacle for the audience. And with their final breaths Hochburg's ambitions for Africa would expire.

He retreated from the window and hammered on the door. The eyes of hundreds of dead animals watched blankly.

There was an exultant crescendo from the gramophone, then the scratch and pop between tracks before the next piece began. Hochburg recognized it at once: the Hungarian Melody. It was a slower, more solemn interpretation than he was used to. He remembered how Eleanor played it after nightfall to the murmur of kerosene lamps. At first it was enchanting; later he became a restive audience. After they fled together, they never listened to it again.

Impelled by the music, Hochburg returned to the window and stepped onto the ledge. He was buffeted by the wind. The bandage around his eye felt as if it would be snatched away. He drove Burton's knife into the mortar, using it like an ice pick, and began scaling the palace exterior.

Hochburg climbed slowly, precisely. His body wasn't built for this. He wished he had the narrow fingers of a monkey to wedge into the crevices, or that he had taken off his boots: bare toes would give a better purchase. He kept focused on the balcony just meters out of his reach. He couldn't hear the Schubert now or the drum, only the wind. It screamed around him in gusts, one moment slamming him into the stone, the next keen to rip him from the wall.

Hochburg wedged the knife between the blocks and hauled himself up. The blade loosened.

He felt a weightlessness . . . then a plunging sensation.

Hochburg clawed his other hand into stone, swinging free, as he tried to bury the knife back into the wall. He saw the rocks below and their sharp peaks.

He slipped, his grip weakening, and in that long second he didn't think of Eleanor or of saving Feuerstein; his thoughts were with Burton and the vengeance he had been denied. How unsatisfying life had proved. He plunged the blade into the wall with a new strength, finding a weak spot in the concrete. The knife disappeared to the hilt.

Hochburg hugged the stone, then willed his body upward till his hand grasped the ironwork of the balcony. He heaved himself up to a French window that opened into a suite of rooms. The interior was still and warm, charged with silk. There was a dressing table groaning with perfume and trinkets, dozens of pairs of high heels left carelessly on the floor.

Out of the wind, the drum beckoned.

The door to the room was locked; Hochburg drove all his weight against it. It took several blows before he crashed through, into one of the palace's stone corridors. He ran up the central staircase, the beat growing louder with every floor, and reached the garden. There was a rapid roll of the drum . . . then abruptly it stopped.

On the terrace below, the gallows were silhouetted against powerful arc lights. The Jews stood lined up, their backs to him, facing the city. Nooses around their necks. Beneath their feet were brightly colored boxes, gaudy as presents for a children's party. Guards stood watch.

In the silence, Hochburg thought he heard the last notes of the Hungarian Melody drifting up from the lower levels of the palace. He clutched Burton's dagger.

The hangman nodded to the Hauptsturmführer overseeing events—then walked down the line of Jews, kicking the boxes away.

+ + +

In the artificial light, the garden, with its cascades of roses and bougainvillea, looked anemic. The gravestone patio had a pewter sheen.

A section of the terrace had been cordoned off for guests and given over to plush chairs beneath an awning. The delicate fragrance of flowers mixed with the smell of hot bodies, fruit, and champagne. There were officers in disheveled dress uniforms and lots of young women. Globus's typing pool had an insatiable hunger for new flesh; Hochburg never allowed any of his female staff to apply for Madagaskar.

He tore down the steps to the gallows and pushed through the convulsing legs to see the Jews' faces. The brittle sound of ropes creaking. Feuerstein was puce, eyes bulging, his tongue flicking around his lips. Like the others, he had his hands tied behind his back, but his feet were unbound and jerking (another Globus detail for a better show). Hochburg used the knife to cut the rope around the scientist's wrists, then placed the blade in his palm.

"You'll have to free yourself," said Hochburg.

He ducked beneath the scientist, secured the struggling man's bare feet on his shoulders, and supported his weight. Feuerstein sawed at the slack noose around his neck.

One of the female spectators stood up. She was loaded with pearls, had coils of silver hair and the same heavy features as her son. "You're ruining it!" she shrieked, needles in her lilting accent.

The Hauptsturmführer strode undecidedly toward Hochburg.

Feuerstein tumbled to the ground. Coughing, gagging. He got to his feet and helped to support the next man. Hochburg cut his wrists loose. Along the gallows, eyes full of ravenous hope implored him, but there were too many to free them all before they choked. Each scientist might be as essential to the Muspel project as the individual components of the bomb; he didn't want to risk losing a single one. Some were already bucking on the ropes, their faces ballooning and purple.

As soon as Hochburg sliced through the cord, he handed the knife over and addressed the assembled guards. They were startled, unsure how to react. The Hauptsturmführer had taken out his Luger but held it low. Hochburg deepened his voice, making it resonant with the authority of his rank and the territories he ruled.

"These Jews are worth more than all the wealth of this island. You will help me save them." Nobody moved. One of the party girls hissed. "You will help me or you will spend the rest of your lives digging the mines of Kongo."

Still none of the guards moved. Hochburg grabbed the nearest and shoved him beneath a scientist. The Hauptsturmführer came forward.

"You next," said Hochburg.

"No Jew is going to stand on me." He raised his pistol. "I'm warning you—"

Hochburg dealt with him as he had done the Americans at the Shinkolobwe mine. He grabbed the Hauptsturmführer by the scruff and propelled him across the terrace. There was an updraft as they reached the edge. Tana lay twinkling below them. Hochburg hurled him over the side. Unlike the American soldiers, he didn't scream.

That was something, he thought, a momentary hope flitting through his gut; the SS in Africa would prevail yet.

Not all the guards obeyed, but enough came forward, grasping the Jews' scrawny ankles and lifting them up. Filthy bare feet stood on shoulder lapels bearing the sacred runes. A few of the more drunk guests brayed with laughter at the spectacle. The remainder were either shaking their heads or leaving in disgust. Frau Globus stormed past, talking loudly: "He'll be strung up with the rest of them tomorrow, you'll see."

More knives were found and a guard sent up to the beam of the gallows. Under Hochburg's supervision, the rest of the Jews were cut down. He wasn't fast enough to save them all. Several dropped to the ground asphyxiated.

"Baranovich's wife," said Feuerstein, closing the eyelids of a woman. His voice was like a rag that had been wrung out.

"You said you didn't want to be the only widower," replied Hochburg. "Life will be easier in Muspel."

"I didn't mean it. I wished I'd . . ."

The rest of his response was drowned out as the next squadron of Walküres roared over, on their way to quell the rebellion.

"Where are the others?" asked Hochburg when the helicopters had passed. No more than twenty had been brought to the gallows.

"Still below, in the cells." Feuerstein looked at Hochburg, full of gratitude and revulsion with himself for meaning it. He massaged his bruised neck. "Twice we owe our lives."

"All I want is my weapon."

The other Jews crowded around him, coughing and spluttering, their eyes misty. They reached for his sleeves as though he were an idol, fingered his uniform, an unearthly wail rising from them. Hochburg brushed them away and stood at the edge of the terrace, looking down on the city. Among the banners and swastika flags he found the single Stars and Stripes.

CHAPTER FIFTY-TWO

Tana–Diego Railway
21 April, 00:55

SALOIS HAD HEARD many terrible sounds: the wailing that hung over the beaches of Dunkirk; men drowning in cement during the construction of Diego; the childlike screams of lemurs when the Nazis torched the forest to flush out rebels.

But no sound disturbed him as much as a man and a woman arguing.

Madeleine and Burton fought in whispers, their quarrel more desperate for their efforts to keep it discreet. Salois had slipped away from them—to where the cover of the tamarind trees gave way to open grass—yet he could hear every word. The leaves shook and dripped above, whipped by the wind. There was no sign of the train Cranley had promised. Suddenly Madeleine called to him; he was startled to hear his name.

"What do you think, Reuben?" she asked.

Salois glanced from her to Burton. He hadn't met a fellow legionnaire during his whole time in Madagaskar. Here was a man who had endured the same brutal training, tramped the same desert, eaten the same filthy food (though now a bowl of camel meat and dates would be a feast). The Legion was based in two forts: Saida, where Salois had been billeted, and Bel Abbès; the two camps were fierce rivals, linked by friendship and hatred. As they fled Nachtstadt, following the spur to the main railway line, Salois and Burton exchanged names, seeking a common bond, and found none till Burton mentioned a familiar one. *Ah, l'Américain!* Salois had replied. *Un vieux camarade.*

Madeleine pressed her question, eyes imploring. Salois felt uncomfortable; he was intruding on grief, on fear, that wasn't his.

"Burton's right," he replied. "There's no hope—you mustn't go to

Mandritsara. But . . ." A deep loneliness stirred in him. "But if I had the chance to hold my child, if only for a moment, I'd risk everything."

The branches above shook, scattering them with raindrops, as Abner slid down the trunk. "The train," he said breathlessly.

Salois picked up his BK44 and one of the rucksacks, slinging it over his shoulder, it was heavy with dynamite and detonators. Abner took the other; he wasn't traveling to Diego but had offered to help Salois get aboard.

"After everything I told you," said Burton, "you're still going?" He had explained what had happened to him in Kongo and Cranley's involvement.

"Destroying Diego is the only chance this island has."

Burton's jaw was tight. "You can't trust him."

"The train's here, like he promised. It will be different this time."

"How can you be sure?"

Salois gave them both an apologetic smile. "I'm not having an affair with his wife." He fastened the rucksack. "He's not the only one running the show. There's Rolland and the Mozambicans. The agreement with America. Even if Cranley is what you say he is, I can depend on the others. We want the same thing."

A whistle blast.

Salois had nothing else to add. He offered his hand to his fellow legionnaire, then took Madeleine's.

"Can I keep your knife?" he asked.

She nodded and pressed her cheek against his. "It doesn't seem right to say good-bye."

"After Mandritsara, you've got four days to get to Kap Ost and the boat. They won't wait."

"We'll be there."

Salois sensed that she wanted to say more—but there was another blast of the whistle. "Look after her," he told Burton, then left the cover of trees, Abner at his side carrying the second rucksack.

They raced across the grass—waist deep and wet as a paddy field—until they reached the raised bank of earth along which the railway ran. There was a set of points: the line divided here for several kilometers so trains could pass each other as they headed in opposite directions. The single yellow eye of the locomotive trundled toward them. Cranley had arranged for the train to slow at this spot so the team could clamber aboard. It was reducing its speed.

"Good luck with Diego," said Abner. "I wish I were coming. The Americans are long overdue."

Madeleine joined them. "Do this for me?" she said, placing something in Salois's hand. "In case I don't make it from the hospital." He glanced down: it was the pen and paper clip she had taken from the radio room. "For Jacoba."

He nodded.

She hugged him fiercely. He put an arm around her shoulders, the other keeping hold of the BK44. "Perhaps it's not a punishment," she whispered in his ear, her words mixing with the sluicing-steel sound of approaching wheels. "Perhaps you've been spared, Reuben. Spared for some great deed. They call this railway the 'Line of Fates.'"

"Find your children," he whispered in reply. "And never come back."

The track was vibrating. Salois let the carriages chug past, counting them till the tail of the train was in sight. The second from last, Cranley had told them during his briefings. Salois started to run, Abner following.

"We'll watch for the skies," Madeleine cried after him.

There was a narrow platform at the end of the carriage; Salois reached for it, half-leaping, half-dragging himself onto the train. Below, Abner was sprinting to keep up. He reached out with the second rucksack, holding it above his head like an offering. Salois caught the straps and hauled it on board.

Instantly, Abner and his sister began to recede into the moonless night. Salois saw Madeleine wave good-bye and raised his own hand in farewell.

He was alone again.

Salois opened the door to the carriage and shoved in the equipment. He was expecting a cattle truck; instead he found upholstery, an empty buffet table, a stainless steel urn, and stacks of crockery that rattled with the sway of the train. The air smelled of tobacco, bananas, and coffee dregs. Cranley had chosen the guards' carriage for the team, not him; he imagined their complaints about traveling like Jews. There were kerosene lamps set in the walls. Salois made sure the blinds were closed, lit a single wick, and began preparing the explosives. He removed the dynamite from the rucksacks and spread it out on the table; next to it he made a pile of detonators.

For the raid on Mazunka, Cranley had equipped his team with radio-controlled detonators, the latest technology. He'd offered the same to Salois, but Salois preferred the type he'd been using for two decades. His detonators were mechanical, connected to a timer with a clock face and a counter that could be set from ten seconds to fifty-four minutes.

The train was picking up speed. Gold tassels shook on the furniture.

Salois tested each detonator in turn, a tiny spark flaring between his fingers. Satisfied, he pulled off his caftan and cut the sleeves into ribbons. He used them to bind together the individual sticks of dynamite—four to each bundle—then pressed the detonator into the dynamite and secured it with another strip of material. When the counter reached zero, it would spark, triggering a blast. He worked till all the dynamite had been prepared, then divided it between the two rucksacks. He selected a cup from the stack of crockery and sat down. Since it would be another two hours before they reached Diego, he should rest—but first a promise to keep.

He poured the ink from the pen Madeleine had given him into the cup and took the paper clip between his fingers. Apart from his face and hands, there were only a few patches of his body that weren't indigo; they looked incomplete, as though ravaged by a disease that bleached the skin. Even the soles of his feet were crisscrossed with numbers; the Jesuits had helped tattoo his back. He sharpened one point of the paper clip, then dipped into the ink and lanced a spot below his left ankle, meticulously adding Jacoba's number. He had done it so many times he was numb to the sensation.

As more of his skin vanished, he thought of Madeleine and wished he'd laid down his weapon to hold her with both arms before he left. She wasn't the first person he had confessed to. There had been previous times when it seemed death had finally come for him and he wanted to unburden himself. Those who shared his secret never lived long. If death wasn't hungry for him, it was voracious for his companions. Had he abandoned her to the same fate? An unsettling sense of responsibility crept up on him—but, no, she had her brother to protect her, and now Burton, too; only the barest details had passed his lips.

He rarely thought back to the day of his crime—it had obsessed him for too long to have any meaning or the power to move him. It was breakfast time. His memory had painted the kitchen scarlet: the floor, the ceiling, the furniture, everything. He knew this wasn't true—the table was stripped pine, and it had been the bluest of mornings outside—but he could recall these events only in red.

Frieda was barefoot, the bulge of their child hanging low around her belly. When she'd started showing—unmarried, barely in her twenties—her family disowned her. She didn't care as long as she was with him. They were arguing. He lashed out (his usual response), his fist catching one tooth, breaking the skin between his knuckles. It was one of those sliver cuts that bleed profusely. Blood pattered onto the kitchen floor. Frieda offered him a look of such forgiveness, such pity, that all he could do was hit her again. He couldn't bear those ache-filled eyes. The second time he didn't punch her; he struck her open handed across the face with enough ferocity to swipe her off her feet. The unfamiliar weight of the baby caused her to lose her balance and keel over. He heard the crack of her neck against the kitchen table as she fell. The sound stayed in him; he knew at once he'd killed her. He cut some bread. Toasted it, buttered it, savored it. Then he bent down to Frieda and told her to stop pretending. When he checked her pulse, her skin was already cooling . . . yet he sensed some tiny vibration in her that said all hope was not lost. He lifted her nightdress and, in the years and nightmares that followed, was convinced he had seen tiny fists beating against her abdomen, the final throes of their drowning baby.

Salois's throat was gnarled and dry. He finished Jacoba's number, blotting the drops of blood with the remains of his caftan. He had shared barely a dozen words with Jacoba, none at all with the many corpses whose tattoos he had memorized on the beach—yet they continued to exist on his body. For Frieda and their unnamed child, there was nothing, only the arrest warrant Cranley had produced and Salois's memories: disconsolate, seldom acknowledged, washed in red. He considered Madeleine's parting words. In kinder moments he'd also wondered whether he was being saved for some greater good; it was a comforting explanation for his survival.

But the world was not kind. Whether he succeeded or failed at Diego he was resigned to the certainty that he would endure. If years of hardship had let him forgive himself for striking Frieda, the source of their argument, its pettiness—its irony in this new world order—remained. There was to be no release for Reuben Salois.

+ + +

Salois napped, his head jerking every time he began to slide into deep sleep. When he judged an hour had passed, he got up and peeked through the blinds. Looming out of the darkness was Die Teekiste, a vertical-sided, flat-topped mountain that had been fortified by the French during the colonial period and saw their final stand against the Nazi invasion. Waffen-SS paratroopers eventually seized it, descending on the fortifications with nerve gas. The railway skirted the mountain; on the far side was Diego Suarez.

Salois stretched, his upper body knotted, and checked his watch: 03:45. Cranley would hit the radar station in fifteen minutes. The bombers were already high above the Mozambique Channel. He pictured Colonel Turneiro at their base, pacing the runway, and Rolland hidden inside his control center, waiting for the radio to bring news, a glass of whiskey cooling his nerves.

There were a few stale lumps of bread left in the pockets of the rucksack. Salois wolfed them down, drank some cold, muddy coffee from the urn, then searched the carriage until he found a duffel bag stuffed with Kriegsmarine uniforms—exactly as Cranley promised it would be. Whatever his motive, he wanted the base destroyed as much as Salois did.

"Do you know why the first rebellion failed?" Cranley had asked the night they left Mombasa. His tone was uncharacteristically chummy, conspiratorial.

"We had rocks and knives, they had gunships. The world stood aside."

Cranley shook his head. "You Jews are brave; you hate—but you don't fear."

Salois emitted a bark of scornful laughter.

"Not like the Nazis," continued Cranley. "They're terrified of you and everything you are. A deep primordial fear—like the fear of death itself. Only when you learn to fear them more than they fear you will the tide turn."

Despite Burton's warning, he had no doubts about the man.

Salois stripped and put on the Kriegsmarine uniform. If he weren't so tense, he might have laughed: white trousers, white jacket, belt with a shiny buckle. Perfect for moving through the shadows. The only concession to the hour was a striped midnight-blue neckerchief. There were three other uniforms in the bag; Salois laid them aside with a pang of regret.

He extinguished the lamp and crouched by the window. Outside, scrubby fields gave way to a shantytown. This was where the Jews who serviced Diego lived: the men who stoked the coal bunkers and swept the streets; the gangs of stevedores; the maids who tended the officers' villas. It remained separate from Globus's domain. Jews were considered menial but essential to the running of the base and were treated as such. There had been no rebellion here. Next came an industrial area of factories and workshops, the skyline obscured by chimney stacks. Then a brief interlude of barracks. Few sailors were quartered on the base itself, most living in an area to the east called Französinnenbucht.

There was a burst of noise and color. Salois ducked beneath the window as the train passed into the center of town. The beerhouses were still rowdy with sailors celebrating Führertag. If any of Turneiro's bombers dropped their payloads early, these streets would be obliterated.

Good, thought Salois.

The carousing was left behind. The locomotive slowed as it entered the vast marshaling yard around the docks. Salois glimpsed warehouses and the long necks of cranes. Diego was home to a substantial merchant navy as well as the East Africa Fleet. Vanilla, cocoa, and ships laden with pig carcasses began their journey to the Reich from here. The train was at walking pace now, the wheels and couplings clanking. The whole carriage shunted forward as it hit the buffers, shook, then came to a halt. There was a final, weary exhalation of steam . . . then silence.

Minutes later the drivers walked past, chatting. Their voices faded.

Salois opened the carriage door. Under the mercury lights of the yard the landscape was bluish green, empty. He dropped to the ground and fastened the rucksacks to himself, one on his back, the other on his front. "You'll be the fattest Jew on the island," Abner had joked.

The air smelled of propulsion, of coal, diesel, and greased steel, and on the breeze the tang of the ocean. Several hundred meters away, the yard ended in a wire fence and a short cliff that led to sea level. Salois darted between trains and wagons, the weight of the rucksacks making his movements cumbersome.

He thought he heard a noise and stopped, pressing himself against a cattle truck. In front was a stack of concrete pipes tall enough for a man to walk through. He squinted into the darkness. The yard was deserted.

Salois was preparing to move when he heard the noise again. This time it carried clearly. Someone was calling his name.

CHAPTER FIFTY-THREE

Western Sector (North)
21 April, 02:30

THE HELICOPTER PILOT shook Kepplar awake and indicated his headphones: "Emergency broadcast."

Kepplar sat up, disoriented by the blackness below; he hadn't meant to fall asleep. In his lap was the coin-stuffed bird he'd fetched from Lava Bucht. He put on his own set of headphones and heard Hochburg's voice.

> *. . . taking control of Madagaskar with the full agreement and author-ity of the RSHA and Reichsführer-SS; Diego Suarez will continue to remain under Kriegsmarine command.*

The pilot sharpened the frequency.

> *Governor Globocnik has been temporarily relieved of his command. Any orders you have received in the past forty-eight hours are rescinded. The security situation is critical. All Jews are to be held where they are. Those in transit must be delivered to the reservations or, if feasible, returned whence they came. Extreme measures against the Jewish population, their settlements, and their property are expressly forbidden unless the lives of you or your comrades are under immediate threat. Gunships must return to base. Any man, of whatever rank, found disobeying these orders will face court-martial. I repeat: the security situation is critical; Jews are not to be harmed. Reinforcements will arrive shortly. Heil Hitler!*

"Where are we?" Kepplar asked the pilot. He had no idea how long ago they had left Lava Bucht. His brain felt slurred.

"We're almost there."

Hochburg's message repeated itself:

> *This is Oberstgruppenführer Walter Hochburg broadcasting from the Governor's Palace in Tana. As of zero one hundred hours on 21 April I am taking control of Madagaskar with the full agreement and authority of . . .*

Kepplar listened to the words loop again and again. His ear with the missing half was uncomfortable and hot inside the headphones. For the first time he was exhausted by the futility of his task, forever closing in on Cole but never apprehending him. All he wanted was to return to Kongo and the familiarity of his problems there. He had chosen Africa to purify it—in his grander moments, he strove to bring in the age of German civilization—not to chase a fellow white man, whatever his crime. How Burton Cole's capture furthered that purpose remained obscure.

Unexpectedly, he felt a spark of resentment toward Hochburg for not trusting him enough to share the secret. The Oberstgruppenführer's orders droned on in his ears. Resentment settled into despondency. He closed his eyes and tried to doze, but sleep had deserted him. He became aware of numerous physical discomforts: he was hungry, the muscles beneath his shoulder blades ached, there was stubble on his chin (he hated not shaving).

Nachtstadt emerged from the darkness like the cone of a volcano, a glowing circle that billowed vents of smoke. Kepplar shook his head, scolding himself. He was closer to discovering Cole than ever.

The helicopter landed.

"Refuel," he told the pilot. "We leave in fifteen minutes."

"What course?"

"I'm about to learn."

The farm commandant waited by the landing pad, still fighting to sober up; his breath reeked of coffee and menthol. He had dithered when Kepplar demanded the use of a helicopter until Kepplar said he would have to answer to Globocnik if not. Now the commandant was unsettled by the orders coming over the wires.

"I didn't know what to do," he said. "We'd already shot them. I thought it best to hide the evidence."

The air was savory with the smell and pattering ash that reminded

Kepplar of Muspel. He shrugged off the commandant and strode toward the punishment block, passing between huge flaming pyres.

The cell had been hosed down and a mattress found for Tünscher's bunk. He was lying on it in a pair of trousers and nothing more, as carefree as the border guards at Rovuma Brücke. He had received the medical attention Kepplar requested. His flank was bandaged; the cuts on his face had been cleaned and stitched. A Bayerweed dangled from his mouth.

"Where do I find Cole?" said Kepplar.

"Straight down to business," came the reply. "Good."

"I want off this island as much as you do."

Tünscher swung his feet over the edge of the bed and sat. "Thanks for these," he said, through a mouthful of smoke. "You get the money?"

Kepplar threw him the parrot. It landed in Tünscher's lap.

"Is this a joke?"

His tone was so slovenly that something hot flared in Kepplar's throat, as if he might beat the answer out of him after all. "Open it."

Tünscher tried twisting the bird, then tugged at the head till it came apart in his hands. Gold coins scattered everywhere, tinkling and rolling around the concrete floor. Tünscher scooped up a handful and examined the hallmarks.

"Tell me where," said Kepplar.

Uncertainty clouded Tünscher's face as he voiced his thoughts: "Burton lied about those diamonds; it should be easy, but . . ."

"Cole had you here on false pretenses. Loyalty is not a hard bond to break."

"What will happen to him?"

"That's not for me to decide."

"Will he die?"

"No," lied Kepplar. He assumed—he hoped—that Hochburg would be true to his word and burn Cole alive, as he was determined to during the Kongo pursuit. Kepplar would relish the spectacle, lean close to his master and share a joke about paperwork. "I paid you, Obersturmführer; now tell me where to find Cole."

The words emerged stickily from Tünscher's broken lips: "The hospital." He rolled a coin between his fingers; swallowed; then made up his mind. "At Mandritsara."

Kepplar was familiar with its reputation. "Why on earth would he go there?"

"Ask him yourself when you catch him."

Mandritsara was twenty minutes by helicopter. Should he inform Hochburg first or head directly there? Jubilation prickled through his chest, though not as noisily as it once would have done.

"Will his woman be with him?" asked Kepplar. He saw her again in the synagogue: the mucky knees and rancid hair.

"Maddie? You're after her, too?"

"Yes."

Tünscher was suddenly squeamish, unsure. "When you find them, don't say it was me." He crushed the cigarette he was smoking and knelt to gather the coins on the floor, his mood low. He glanced up at Kepplar watching him. "What did happen to your ear?"

Kepplar went to cover it, remembering the mess and shame of that day, then let his hand drop. "A nigger bit it off," he replied, and laughed. "She was only young—twelve or thirteen—vicious little bitch."

Tünscher joined his laughter. "Perhaps she was hungry. What did you do?"

"You mean to her?" The merriment was spreading through Kepplar. He couldn't remember the last time he had laughed so much. "My superior knows the Old Testament. An eye for an eye, he always tells me, a tooth for a tooth. It's official policy in Kongo." He wiped away a tear with the back of his hand. "I let her live—but she never heard again."

This provoked Tünscher more; soon they were both howling.

Kepplar laughed till it had all spilled out of him and there was nothing more than spasms of his lungs. He felt empty and sordid, and turned to leave. He couldn't be sure, but it was around the time of the girl that his estrangement from violence began.

"What about me?" said Tünscher, the last of his own laughter dying.

"You've got your money."

"You can't leave me here."

"It's unwise to trust a man who would betray his friend."

Kepplar rapped on the door and was let out by one of the grooms. Once it had closed behind him, he spoke with Tünscher through the grille. "Assuming I find Cole in Mandritsara, I'll come back for you. A guarantee of your honesty."

"And if you don't?"

"You'll have to trust me," said Kepplar, enjoying the moment. "I'll make sure nobody mistakes you for a Jew." He was about to leave when he stopped and fished out Tünscher's locket. He handed it through the bars. "She's not worth it—they never are."

"This one is."

Kepplar wasn't listening. He needed to radio ahead, to the hospital, and prepare them for Cole.

CHAPTER FIFTY-FOUR

Diego Suarez
21 April, 04:15

"MAJOR SALOIS!"

Salois recognized the voice. He watched two figures emerge from their hiding place inside the pipes. They were dressed in black, their faces smeared in oil. The mercury lights above cast them in an unearthly hue. For a crazy moment he thought it was Grace and Sergeant Denny, that they had survived the beach to join him.

"We didn't know if you'd make it," said Yaudin, chief of the Jewish Police. He was wearing soft boots and a black beret; an antique rifle was slung over his shoulder. Behind him came one of his wardens carrying a scythe.

Salois couldn't remember the last time he smiled so warmly. After the horrors he'd witnessed, even the most fleeting joy felt like a betrayal to the dead.

Another warden appeared from the pipe and joined them. These men might lack military experience, but together the team was back to its original strength. Salois loosened the straps on the front rucksack. "You made the right decision," he said.

Yaudin removed his beret. His thick black hair was shorn to the scalp. "We're here to stop you, Major."

"What?"

They spoke in violent whispers.

"After you burned the synagogue, the Nazis cleared a whole block of the city as a warning," he said in his gruff, guttural voice. "They marched old women and kids to the Sofia reservation. People who thought they were safe in Antzu, who want no part in your rebellion. Since then Globocnik has tightened the noose. We saw towns ablaze on our way here; the air was thick with gunships."

"All the more reason to fight."

"Think what Globus will do if you hit Diego."

"You're too late," said Salois. "The bombers are on their way. I can't stop them."

"Give it up now and they won't get through."

Salois's reply was hot-blooded, exhausted. He was sick of having to explain the obvious to men who had deluded themselves that they alone would be spared; or maybe a tiny part of him doubted it, too. "The United States is the only hope we have."

"If you do this, Major, all the Americans will find is bones."

Salois leveled his BK44 at them.

"Do it: shoot." Sweat ran down Yaudin's huge jaw. "You'll raise every sentry in the yard. If we can't stop you, they will."

"Then you'll die with me."

"Probably. But my family will have a chance."

When Salois didn't reply, Yaudin appealed to him: "I've two boys and a girl. A wife and mother. Aunts, uncles, neighbors." He gestured at his two wardens. "We all have. They don't deserve to die."

"You saw my skin. None of them deserved it."

Salois charged Yaudin, the weight of the rucksacks driving them both over. The Jupo chief clawed at one of the wardens as he fell. They all tumbled down, Yaudin grunting as the wind was knocked from him. Salois struggled to regain his feet. An arm locked around his throat as the other warden dragged him off. Salois sank his teeth into the man's arm and kicked back with all of his force. They crashed to the ground, the warden's leg catching on the rail track. Salois leapt up, the rucksacks threatening to topple him, and stamped on his knee.

The quiet of the yard was broken by screams.

Salois smashed the warden's head with his rifle, knocking him unconscious, and ran, stumbling over tracks and cross ties, heading for the perimeter fence. He checked behind: Yaudin was on his feet, aiming a pistol.

At first Salois thought the bullet had missed . . . then he realized it was a flare gun, the shot traveling high above and exploding. A tiny orange sun hovered over the marshaling yard, washing everything in shades of tangerine and copper. The light was excruciating; it would summon every guard on the base.

Salois pressed himself against a cattle truck, his Kriegsmarine whites glowing. Somewhere a dog barked.

The flare began its slow descent, elongating the shadows as it fell. Salois saw the shape of his body on the earth, the explosives strapped to his front protruding like the belly of a pregnant woman. He ducked underneath the car, then sprinted across open ground to the cover of the next wagon and waited for darkness to return. Searchlights had come on and were skimming the yard. He heard brisk footsteps and Yaudin encouraging his warden to find him. Salois let them pass before emerging. He darted between gaps in the trains and found himself behind the police chief: he was creeping ahead, holding his rifle out like a game hunter. Salois silently caught up and cracked his skull with the butt of his BK44. Yaudin slumped.

Salois rolled him over and raised the weapon again. "Do it," he heard Cranley say. "He's jeopardizing the mission." The police chief's eyelids fluttered as if trying to stir himself from a bad dream. *History is a nightmare Jews can't wake from,* Frieda had once said. Salois felt the same about his own life. He wished she could have seen the man he became.

He lowered his rifle. He hadn't come to Madagaskar to kill Jews.

Salois dragged Yaudin's body beneath a cattle truck and hid him behind the wheels; he was moaning softly. In the Legion, when they captured an Arab who had escaped the cells, they cut his Achilles tendon to prevent further breakouts. He considered doing the same to Yaudin—but it would cripple him for life. Diego would soon be ablaze, and in the months ahead every man would be needed for the struggle. As the rebellion spread and took hold, the Jupo would have no choice but to fight.

There was no sign of the other warden. Salois crossed the rest of the marshaling yard to the perimeter fence. He poked his fingers through the links, the wire brittle from the salt air, and was dazzled by the light.

Below him was the naval base of Diego Suarez.

The first time he had seen it was in 1943 as a pioneer, one of thousands of men arriving on the island who believed they would be building a future: houses, hospitals, schools. He spent two years slaving on fortifications. By the time Salois left, Diego was a polygon of concrete and iron. It was divided naturally into individual coves, each several kilometers wide, like compartments in a tool box. Across the water was Donnerbucht and the submarine pens of the Monsoon Group; to the northwest Weissfelsenbucht, the largest and deepest of the bays, could accommodate aircraft carriers and H-class battleships. More than a dozen vessels were at anchor. It seemed as if every single light in Diego was illuminated, the base glittering.

Salois took out Madeleine's knife and began sawing through the fence. Each link pinged open. On the other side of the wire a slope led to a second fence, then the quayside and the air defenses he had come to destroy: four missile batteries that protected the base's southern approach. For the moment, he ignored them, his eyes fixed on the scrubby peninsula of Kap Diégo and its runway.

There was a line of Me-362 fighters on the apron, their wings catching the glare of the lights; more were hidden in hangars, only their nose cones visible. Every single aircraft stood silent and unmanned.

The other team's raid on Mazunka had been a success. The radar station was out.

Salois gave a grunt of satisfaction and squeezed through the hole in the fence. *We'll do our bit,* Cranley had said on the radio. *The rest is up to you.* His hour had almost come.

CHAPTER FIFTY-FIVE

Mandritsara
21 April, 03:20

"WE DON'T HAVE to do this."

Madeleine's face was hard in reply.

"We can just go. Get out while we can."

"How can you say that?"

He wanted to squeeze her hand again. "They can't have survived, Maddie. There's nothing we can do."

"They're your children."

"None of this is your fault."

"Is that what you think? That I'm doing this out of guilt?" Her voice was emphatic: "They're alive."

Burton gave a sad shake of his head. "It's not possible."

"Did you think I was alive?"

"Yes."

"But you didn't know. Anything could have happened to me. So why did you come here?"

"I . . . I just believed."

"The same with me. It's more than hope—I know they're down there, Burton. Waiting for us—"

Abner intervened: "Let me go."

They were crouched in the undergrowth on the lee of a hill. Around them was the forest that encircled the hospital. New eucalyptuses had been added to the trees; most were already tall and leafy, but there were also younger saplings attached to stakes. Burton had planned to do the same on the farm, thickening the wood at the edge of the south meadow to give the house more privacy. The air was breezeless and bloated with a wet heat, their faces dewed with sweat. Chinks of light from the hospital glinted through the trunks.

"They're our babies," said Madeleine. "It's not your risk to take."

"There's less chance of being caught if it's only one of us," replied Abner. He scratched the sodden, leafy earth, avoiding his sister's gaze. "I want to make up for before, Leni."

Burton also sensed that he wanted to give them some time alone. For that he was grateful. Since being reunited, they had spent every moment within earshot of others; there had been no chance to pour out everything that needed to be said. The feverish bliss of the first few hours was giving way to confusion and reproach. He reappraised Madeleine's brother.

"If I'm caught, get out of here," Abner said.

Burton offered his Beretta. "Take it."

Abner refused. "I'll see if there's a way in. Then come back." He risked a glance at Madeleine. "Burton's right: you should leave while you can. We all should."

He was gone before she could reply.

They watched him slide down the slope, submerging into the trees, silencing the insects as he went. Gradually the clicks and whirrs returned, enclosing them in an incessant chatter; some creature made a strange whooping noise. Farther along the valley Burton sensed a building pressure of movement and unseen forces—like in Dunkirk as they waited for Guderian's tanks. According to Abner, it was coming from the direction of the Sofia Reservation. In the distance: helicopters and the occasional plaintive whistle of a train. Madeleine stared at the hospital through the trees, her eyes as bright as if she had a fever. More than anything he wanted to touch her, to hug her body against his, feel the heat of her breath.

Finally, he spoke: "I never imagined it like this."

"Neither did I."

"What did you imagine?"

"I thought you were dead, Burton. I grieved for you, I emptied myself of you. It was the only way to survive."

Silence between them again.

"You understand why I didn't want to come here," said Burton. He was as gentle as possible. "I want to save them, too. But they're gone."

"I've heard stories. They keep people alive in this place . . ."

"So they're alive. So Abner finds a way in. They won't let us steal them away. If we step inside that hospital, it's over." He stretched out his hand as though she were a stranger. "All I want is for us to get away and live safely. We can have other children." He was aware what a stupid thing it was to say.

"Remember our last night on the farm, when you told me about Hochburg? We both knew you shouldn't have gone to Kongo. You told me the only way to secure the future was to lock up the past. That's why I'm here."

"I was wrong."

"Then let me be wrong, too."

Once more they lapsed into silence, until Madeleine said, "I saw him—Hochburg—in Antzu. He was balder than I thought." They shared an uneasy smile. "I tried to settle your score with him."

Pride and shame jostled in Burton. And then a heat rising through his chest to his gullet, burning like vomit. "Can life ever be the same?" He was stunned by the sheer depth of his regret.

For a long time Madeleine didn't respond. She shivered, despite the mugginess of the night. "There was a time when I thought I'd never be happy again. Then we met, found the farm, made all our plans."

"We can never go back there."

"I want to live in the mountains, or the desert. Somewhere dry. I'm sick of all this . . . lushness, this humidity. My bones feel sodden."

Burton remembered the description of Patrick's house in Las Cruces, New Mexico: the baking sun and distant peaks. "Let's go to America—"

"That's a Vanilla phrase. It means something different here."

"—I know a place where no one will find us."

"Exile?"

"A place to start over. A new home."

Burton's mind became dislodged, random memories beckoning him. He thought of those early days on the beach when he was desperate for Madeleine to slide her arm through his and feel her bumping against him. It wasn't desire, not then; it was loneliness, the urge to share the blandest intimacy with her. He recognized that they were the same: people who had been broken and glued themselves back together but were never going to be quite so strong again. They both needed someone to tend their weak points, the invisible fissures that made them.

Madeleine was shivering more violently now, as if she couldn't control it, though whether because of cold or fear of what lay ahead, he didn't know. Burton shifted closer, till their thighs were touching. Another memory assaulted him.

"Do you remember the pretzels in the Tiergarten?" he asked. He could almost smell them. "And the cotton candy? And those almonds baked in honey?"

"Don't, I'm starving."

They had been strolling in the Tiergarten, Germania's largest park, sandwiched between the Great Hall and the Führer's Palace, browsing the phalanx of stalls selling snacks, watching acrobats and fat, red-faced men playing tubas. Nerves had been chasing Burton all afternoon. They had promised to discuss the future—the lover's eternal question of *What next?*—yet neither of them seemed willing to broach the subject. Burton was certain it was more than just an affair but didn't know whether Madeleine would leave her husband.

Resting in the undergrowth of Mandritsara, he felt a similar sense of uncertainty hold him back. He put his arm around her shoulders, hesitated, then inched her closer. She no longer smelled the way he remembered her, and her body was all bones, as if he were clutching a sack with her remains in it. He felt a rumble of tears that didn't come, remembering the full, taut, arousing flesh of her body. She eased out of his embrace and took hold of his severed arm, tracing her fingers over his brand.

"Show me your tattoo," he said, wanting to see her scars.

"I don't have one."

"Why not?"

"They processed me in a rush when I arrived. I guess nobody cared." She examined the flaps of skin where his wrist ended. "Will you tell me what happened one day?"

He tried to withdraw his stump. "Alice said you wouldn't like it."

"It's a miracle to have the rest of you." She nuzzled the tip of the bone; he had never felt so disfigured. "How is Elli?"

"Missing you. I promised to bring you back."

"How will we ever get her away from *him*?"

Once more he wanted to tell her it was impossible—saving the twins, snatching Alice—but he didn't have the strength. "I don't know."

"Salois's boat," she breathed.

"There are other ways off the island."

"Cranley will be there. We wait for him, kill him."

"Revenge is vanity," replied Burton, recalling his aunt's words. "Look where it led me."

"It's the only way back. I can't bear the thought of him in Britain, home and thriving. Somehow we have to win."

She had lost all reason—but when he stared at her, he realized she was quite rational. As rational as he'd been when he decided to go to Kongo to assassinate Hochburg. There was a coppery gleam to her skin. He noticed tiny etchings around her eyes, a downward twist to her lips that hadn't been there before. Burton had admitted more of his life to her than to anybody else, but there were still experiences he hadn't told her about. There was no need to repeat all the cruelty he'd witnessed. Now he understood that Madeleine had seen things that she would never share. They were more equal than ever.

"What are you smiling at?" she asked.

He removed his stump from her grip and slipped it behind her waist, holding her tight. "The future."

+ + +

Madeleine's breathing shallowed, her face relaxed. She dropped into a deep sleep as if she had stepped off a cliff. Burton traced her eyebrows; they were dark and dense, so unlike the delicate, plucked lines he remembered. From her brow he ran his fingers through the tufts of her scalp. "You've got a soldier's haircut now," he whispered. The individual strands of hair were weak and wasted. Yet no matter what damage his own body suffered, it always revived once he was free of Africa. The air of the continent was noxious, poisoning any who inhaled it, as though the ills of the world were gathered in its breath.

He let Madeleine sleep until an uneasiness began to build in him. That bounce of courage he'd felt on meeting Salois, a fellow legionnaire, had passed. The sky was showing the first muted signs of dawn. Tenderly, he roused Madeleine. She woke with a start, kicking away from him, then clutched his face to convince herself that his return hadn't been a dream, and kissed him. A gust blew through the trees and set the branches whispering.

"Abner's been gone too long," he said.

"Perhaps he was caught."

"We'd have heard."

"What do we do?"

There was no point in telling her to stay put. "Let's take a look."

They descended through the forest, through intimately knotted branches, following Abner's path to the tree line. There was an asphalt road and a perimeter fence separating them from the grounds of the hospital. On the crest of the farthest hill was a Totenburg, its four massive columns standing guard over the valley.

"He can't have come this way," said Burton.

"How do you know?"

"Listen." There was a steady hum. "The fence is electrified."

They retreated into the trees and crept along the road till they reached the main entrance: a locked iron gate with machine-gun posts on either side and a guardhouse, all well illuminated.

"Where are the sentries?" whispered Madeleine.

The entrance was deserted.

They watched for several minutes in case someone appeared: nothing. The faint smell of burning drifted from the direction of the Sofia Reservation. The earlier drone of helicopters was reduced to intermittent fly-bys.

Burton took out his Beretta. "Stay here," he said and darted across the road, expecting a spotlight to hit him at any second. As he approached the gate he slowed, stood tall, and walked with Tünscher's swagger. There was no sign of anyone. In the guardhouse was a telephone he assumed must be connected to the main building. He lifted the receiver; it rang endlessly. He thought of what Patrick used to say in similar situations: *This is damn peculiar.*

Madeleine appeared at the door. "Anything?"

He shook his head.

"Perhaps they evacuated the place, because of the rebellion."

"They would have left some security."

The road continued for several hundred yards to the front of the hospital. Halfway along the drive was an unmanned barrier; guard towers with searchlights dotted the perimeter fence. All empty. Next to the telephone were some enamel mugs. Burton took two, leaned out of the window, and hurled them into the air.

They landed with a noisy clatter. The searchlights remained dark.

Madeleine left the guardhouse and strode toward the hospital. Burton raced after her.

"The twins could be in there." She was edgy with excitement. "We can get them and be gone before anyone knows."

"Then where's Abner?"

Instead of replying, she quickened her pace. Her steps rang out.

Burton moved in front of Madeleine. It was a pointless gesture: an attack could come from anywhere.

The hospital was built from blocks of russet-colored stone that had been quarried locally. There was a central building of two stories with a pagoda-

style roof supported by brick columns. Beyond it were dozens of other buildings connected by enclosed passageways, as if the complex had been
constructed over a number of years without any formal design. The tops of
palms peeked over some of the roofs, suggesting courtyards. He figured the
place must be considerably larger than it appeared from this angle. To the
rear of the compound were a radio tower and two tall, fat chimneys.

"You remember any of this?" he asked Madeleine.

"No. They flew me in; when I left I didn't care."

Parked outside the entrance stood a driverless Mercedes Geländewagen.
Burton peeked inside. It had room for six passengers, and in the rear was
an empty cradle.

The lights were the only sign that the building wasn't derelict. They
reached the main door. Burton flicked off the Beretta's safety catch. He
wished he had the familiar grip of his Browning: it was his juju as much as
a weapon. Silently he opened the door with his boot. They were in a vestibule, a space that operated like an air lock to keep the chilled environment
of the interior from the outside. There was an office where staff members
and visitors signed in—unmanned—and the obligatory portrait of Himmler. In front was a pair of double doors.

Madeleine pushed against them. They parted a few inches, then
jammed. She tried again but didn't have the strength. Burton shouldered
the wood, heaving harder, till the doors opened wide enough for him to slip
through.

"What can you see?" asked Madeleine.

He was in a long white corridor, the ventilation system hammering. His
breath condensed. Blocking the entrance was a harvest of dead bodies.
Doctors, nurses, and guards—splayed and folded over each other, all clawing their throats.

CHAPTER FIFTY-SIX

THE COLD ANTISEPTIC air, so familiar from her previous stay, bored into her nostrils. Madeleine felt thick with dread and an eviscerating sense of loss. She hugged her belly. The lights pulsed as though the power was being diverted elsewhere.

Burton knelt by the bodies. "They've been dead awhile," he said, lifting a doctor's arm; it juddered in his grip.

"They were gassed," she replied.

"How do you know?"

Madeleine pointed behind him. On the floor lay two gas masks, like severed heads. She picked them up.

"One each," said Burton, "as if we're expected." He dropped the doctor's arm; it remained rigid, a half salute to the Führer. "We should go, while there's still a chance."

"We've come too far."

"This place is a tomb."

She refused to submit to her fear. "They were tiny bundles of skin, Burton, pink and perfect. Gulping for life. They're you and me."

"Where were they taken?"

"I don't know. I never saw them again."

They moved down the corridor, checking every room they passed, their boots squeaking on the linoleum floor. On this level it was mostly offices or cupboards stacked with filing cabinets; one door opened on a dispensary. They came across more bodies: nurses, medics, orderlies who had dropped where they stood, their faces contorted and spumed with saliva. Madeleine and Burton carried their masks at their sides. Apart from one moment when Burton thought he smelled a waft of chlorine, they didn't put them on. The air had a synthetic aftertaste. They searched the rest of the ground floor, a memory coming to Madeleine of when she worked as a maid in London. One weekend her employers had been away, and she had sneaked through the house, a mausoleum of a place, gliding from room to room, looking for something she couldn't name. Years later, she attended a party there with her husband. If the family remembered her, they made no show of it.

On the walls were signs and arrows indicating various parts of the complex, but everything was written in numbers and acronyms. Madeleine had little sense of the layout of the hospital from before: she had either been confined to bed or drugged and wheeled about the endless corridors, conscious of nothing more than the ceiling lights repeating above her.

They reached the central staircase and paused. The building was completely silent, apart from the air conditioners. Madeleine's dress hadn't dried out from the rain, and a chill penetrated her.

"Gas sinks," said Burton. "We go up first."

More corridors, more rooms, arranged in a quadrangle, and the first indication that they were in a hospital. They discovered rows of empty beds and an operating theater. Madeleine didn't find the ward where she had given birth or the yellow-walled room where she was imprisoned afterward while the doctor with the scorpion smile ran endless tests. There was no pediatrics wing or any sign where the twins might have been taken. No trace of Abner, either. The place felt mothballed.

"Perhaps . . . perhaps I got it wrong," she said when they had completed their circuit of the floor. Her voice reverberated loudly, making Burton gesture at her to be quiet. His fingers were white around his pistol.

"I was sick with grief," she continued in a whisper. "Didn't know what was going on . . . what if it was another hospital?"

Burton stepped to the window and looked over the compound. In the distance were the sparsely scattered lights of the Sofia Reservation. "There's a lot more of the place yet."

They returned to the ground floor. Burton paused on the steps, put on his gas mask, then followed them down. Madeleine tugged on hers; her breathing became fuggy and labored. They descended two flights before they reached the basement. The lights were more feeble down here, the corridor gloomy as a bunker. The passageway ran for several hundred feet, with doors on either side at regular intervals. Halfway along it, another body lay twisted on the floor.

"It must lead to one of the outbuildings," said Burton, his voice muffled through the mask.

They each took a side of the corridor, checking the doors. They were all fastened shut. The *click-click* of twisted door knobs echoed along the passage.

Madeleine convinced herself that they wouldn't have shut her babies away; this had to be a storage area, the doors hiding nothing more than stacks of paperwork. Burton moved faster than she did. She wanted to tell him to slow down, to be certain each door couldn't be opened. She pushed against the wood after she found it locked, then placed her ear to it, listening for the cry of children. All she heard was deep silence. The eyeholes of her gas mask were steaming up.

She became aware that Burton had frozen.

He was standing by an open door; she watched him go inside. Moments later he stepped back warily as if he'd disturbed a dangerous animal. A greenish light spilled from the room, patterning the corridor.

Madeleine ran over, her breath dense and moist through her respirator. "What have you found?" The lock on the door was broken.

He spoke slowly, his tongue thick, barring her with his stump. "Don't go in there."

She hesitated, then brushed past him.

+ + +

There were no windows, no natural light, only the throb of electricity, more muted and nauseating than ever. A jade green tinged with something bilious rippled across the ceiling. Madeleine couldn't determine its source. Then she saw two specimen tanks full of cloudy liquid catching the overhead lights. She was in a small ward that held no more than twenty beds, gathered in pairs. The significance of the detail hit her at once. Half the beds were occupied.

She heard the mechanical wheeze of Burton's breath through his gas mask, close behind. "You don't need to see this," he said. "Go outside and I'll check."

Madeleine crept deeper into the ward, glancing at the beds and ignoring them at the same time, until she stopped short. On the mattress below her were two girls—identical twins—about the same age as Alice. They were naked, clutching each other, their limbs entwined. Golden hair splayed over the sheets. She grazed her fingers against the nearest foot: the skin was icy.

"Poor babies," she said.

Burton's hand was on her shoulder. "The gas would have been instant."

For the first time, Madeleine saw that the ward was longer than she'd realized and divided by a pair of green curtains. They were closed, but at some point someone had rushed through them, leaving the join twisted and hanging loose. She slipped between them into a space that held six cribs. The slatted wooden sides of the cribs were too high to see into; she would have to peer into them, like staring down a well, to discover the contents. The green light continued to ripple above.

Madeleine's heart banged up toward her throat, thumping in her ears. Her insides were meltwater.

She checked the cribs one at a time.

They were all empty.

She felt such relief that a shout of air, almost a laugh, erupted from her respirator. Relief became uncertainty. Madeleine had a sensation of vertigo that threatened to make her black out. Hanging from each of the cribs was a set of medical notes: two columns of figures and observations comparing Specimen A with B. Above them was a date. One had caught her eye.

Madeleine stepped closer to read it properly, and tore off her gas mask.

Born: 7 February 1953

The day she had been flown from Antzu to Mandritsara.
She snatched up the paper and read her own details:

Mother: Austro-German/British, aged 37 yrs
Health category: B
Blood group . . .

She plunged her hand into the crib. There was the tiniest double dip in the mattress. As soon as her fingers made contact with it, the shape wrinkled and vanished.

"Where are they?" she demanded. Tears drummed behind her eyes, plopping onto the mattress. "Where did they take them?" *They, them:* her babies still didn't have names.

Burton reached out for her. She shoved him away.

"What did they do to them?"

She was screaming, screaming like she had done that night in the maternity ward.

Burton fought to hold her, to calm her. His face was hidden behind his mask: black, alien, threatening. She wouldn't be silenced by him. She roared louder, the accumulation of shock and exhaustion and everything she had endured in the past months breaking out. Chunks of her heart were missing.

"Please, Maddie . . ." begged Burton.

He covered her mouth and she bit hard, enjoying the hot, salty squirt of blood on her tongue. She snarled and beat him—a vixen—and only when it was too late did she become aware of the sound.

+ + +

Burton ripped off his gas mask, gulping in sterile air. The hysteria that had overcome Madeleine faltered as she realized she'd given them away. She stared and blinked as if she'd been shaken awake.

From the corridor came the rush of boots.

Burton flung the curtains wide and aimed his Beretta at the entrance, blood trickling down his wrist where he'd been bitten. Nausea and failure rampaged through him. He was dismal in the certainty that the children he would never see or hold had already passed through the hospital's crematorium.

Now one thought dominated: they needed to get out of this place; he'd drag Madeleine if he had to.

The door opened.

"I've been looking for you." Abner stumbled into the room, cheeks glowing. "I found them."

Madeleine flew past Burton. "My babies?"

"I think so." He glanced around the ward with revulsion. "Twins; tiny young things."

"Are they alive?"

He hurried from the room, Madeleine at his side. Burton chased after them.

They sprinted to the end of the corridor, through a set of swing doors, and into an identical passage. Halfway along was a staircase. Abner raced up to ground level, leading them to another door. It was ajar, yellow light pouring from the interior.

"They're in here," he said eagerly.

Madeleine pushed past him, Burton following. The air was warm, sharp with tartaric acid. He just had time to register gas masks scattered across a table, a pile of spent canisters.

Something hard cracked Burton's skull.

He staggered, vision wheeling, and felt a metal ring press against his temple. The pistol was cocked. Half-conscious, Burton recognized the distinctive click at once, as familiar as the greeting of an old friend. It was the sound of the pistol he knew best.

CHAPTER FIFTY-SEVEN

Governor's Palace, Tana
21 April, 02:20

"THANK YOU FOR coming at such a late hour."

Nightingale's eyes darted around the room. His hair was matted, his previously smooth chin blue. A cloud of fresh aftershave and day-old sweat hung around him. "Where's Governor Globocnik?" he asked.

Hochburg had taken over Globus's study and was sitting in his chair. His desk was hidden beneath a welter of dispatches that Hochburg had been signing for the past hour. Beneath his signature he added, *per pro der Reichsführer-SS*. The room outside was lively with ringing phones and voices, the sustained rattle of typewriters. Hochburg had vetted every man for his loyalty to the SS, not Globus. Sitting in the corner behind him was Feuerstein, a plate of cake crumbs in his lap. He was transfixed by the photographs on the wall: Globocnik and the Führer; Globocnik and Himmler; Globocnik and Heydrich; Globocnik and a myriad of other party faces. The scenes were a mixture of the official and informal: dinners, shooting parties, the Winter Olympics in Garmisch-Partenkirchen. "A gallery of lions," Hochburg had called it, "the complacent and crooks."

He invited Nightingale to sit. "Globus has fled to the Sofia Dam. I am going there presently—to arrest him. First I wanted to speak to you." He poured them both coffee from a freshly brewed pot; the air was pungent with it. "Would you like some cake, too?" Earlier he'd gone to the kitchens and found a gâteau speared with birthday candles in the shape of Ostmark. He cut the envoy a slice.

Nightingale ignored it. "I heard your broadcast, Oberstgruppenführer, but it's too late."

"Meaning?"

"I did caution you about further outrages. My duty is to keep Washington informed. They know about the synagogue being burned, and the mass transportations. I've seen the trains from my own window."

He listed other grievances until Hochburg held up his palm. "I'm wresting back the situation."

"My government has already decided. President Taft was coming under too much pressure from the American Jewish Committee. He's dispatching the USS *Yorktown*."

"*Yorktown?*"

"An aircraft carrier, sixty wings. Plus support vessels."

Hochburg absorbed this information. The American carrier would be a minnow against the fleet at Diego, he thought. The danger arose from their proximity. Mistakes could be made—an aircraft accidentally shot down, a torpedo fired without orders—and with mistakes events could escalate beyond reason.

"Contact your government," he urged Nightingale. "Tell them I've taken control—"

"My communications were cut, shortly after the *Yorktown* news."

"You'll find they have been restored. We both believe in your country's neutrality. Tell Washington there's no need for intervention."

The envoy shook his head.

"Only you can stop things now, Oberstgruppenführer." He took a sip of coffee. "Restore order to the island; shut down the reservations. End the killings. And there'll be no need for any warships. They can sail home."

"There's still a rebellion. I can't command every man in the field."

"So long as there are no major atrocities."

Hochburg hid a smile: the eternal expediency of diplomacy. "The Jews have my protection," he said with feeling.

"Can I trust you?"

"You said it yourself, Herr Nightingale, at the dam. My troops in Kongo will not thank me if America intercedes. To safeguard my army is to protect the unfortunate inhabitants of this island."

"This is official policy?"

Hochburg had severed all lines to Germania. "I have the Führer's wholehearted blessing. He understands the importance of peace in Africa."

"Pax Germanica."

"There is no other."

Nightingale drained his coffee and stood. "I pray you're right. I don't want to fail my country, Oberstgruppenführer."

"Neither of us does."

They shook hands, Nightingale promising to relay Hochburg's guarantees to his superiors. He paused at the door.

"Once this is over, you need to turn the island back five years. That will keep the Jews at home quiet. The original plan for Madagaskar was something we could all live with."

After the envoy had left, Hochburg passed his untouched gâteau to Feuerstein; the physicist accepted hungrily. His face remained streaked with filth, despite Hochburg's offer of a basin and washcloth.

"In the days of the Ha-Mered," he said between mouthfuls, "we were convinced the United States would save us."

"It was an American who led me to your weapon. They want it as insurance against this island."

"To defend us or themselves?"

"That's very cynical, Doctor. Could they build one?"

"Nightingale is your answer," replied Feuerstein.

Hochburg took Burton's knife and cut himself some cake. That was another reason to temper the situation in Madagaskar: to reset the clock, as Nightingale suggested. If the island was stable, the United States would have less reason to develop its own weapon. He reclined in his seat and chewed: nourishment for the long night ahead. When he was done he wiped the blade clean and returned it to its place inside his tunic.

An adjutant appeared. "Your Walküres are fueled and armed, Oberstgruppenführer."

Hochburg stood, indicating that Feuerstein should do the same. "We leave immediately."

The adjutant clicked his heels and exited, passing Kepplar on the way out. The Brigadeführer's face was gray in contrast to the riot of his uniform, the paint dry and cracked.

Hochburg sighed. "Empty-handed. As usual."

His deputy dipped his eyes in shame, but there was something else, something never seen before: a flash of resentment. Hochburg would not tolerate that.

"I know where Cole and the woman are," said Kepplar.

"Then why not bring them to me?"

"After all this time, Herr Oberst, I thought the pleasure should be yours." He faltered, then slumped like a runner at the end of a long race. "I was twenty minutes from them; I planned to go myself. But the stakes are too high. If I failed again . . ."

Hochburg regarded him pitifully. "It means that much to you?"

"I can't be sent back to Roscherhafen, or Germania. All I want to do is serve."

"Where are they?"

"The hospital, Mandritsara."

Kepplar's bland devotion was touching, in the same way that Fenris's was, yet difficult years lay ahead. Sentiment was a luxury for future generations. Nevertheless, Kepplar had delivered Burton's location, if not his beating heart. Perhaps his skills would be better deployed in Muspel, overseeing Feuerstein.

"Mandritsara: you're sure?"

"I stake my life on it, Walter."

An icicle smile curled Hochburg's lips. "And we remember from the pyre in the Schädelplatz how much you value it." He reached below the desk and threw Kepplar a bundle. "It may need alteration, but it will do for now."

Kepplar unfastened it to reveal a black uniform. His eyes glittered. "May I wear it?"

Hochburg had found a pair of handcuffs. He beckoned Feuerstein to his side and clamped their wrists together. "You don't leave my sight."

"What about my colleagues?"

"They are safe."

After his excursion to the kitchen, Hochburg had come across Globus's private screening room. It had forty easy chairs and canisters of films: Japanese pornography, some Heinz Rühmann comedies, Disney cartoons. He had left the other scientists with buckets of food watching *Dumbo*; the guards were ordered not to molest them.

Hochburg turned to Kepplar. "When I have Burton, you will be a Gruppenführer again. I shall go to the hospital; you to the Sofia Dam."

"Let me be with you," replied his deputy, unbuttoning his tunic and sprinkling the floor with flecks of congealed color.

"Your task is too important to trust to anyone else. Go to the dam and detain Globus. Redeem yourself."

Kepplar bowed his head and slipped on the pristine black cloth.

+ + +

The air was thunder, wind, aviation fuel. Red and white lights flashed on the tarmac. Two Walküres stood waiting for the order to take to the sky, next to them another two helicopters: troop carriers full of soldiers.

Hochburg marched toward the nearest gunship, Feuerstein scurrying to keep up. Behind them, Kepplar's new buttons strained against his chest;

the seat of his trousers sagged. He pretended not to care, but Hochburg caught him hitching up the waist when he thought no one was looking.

"The other Walküre is yours," said Hochburg. "A troopship will follow. Do your best to take Globocnik alive, then bring him here. Before you leave the dam—and this is important, Derbus—make sure the sluice gates cannot be opened or tampered with. If Globus tries to flood the reservation, my assurances to the Americans will be undone."

"What about you, Herr Oberst?"

He hesitated, wondering whether he should arrest Globus himself—but he couldn't lose Burton again. He had a banquet of reprisals to choose from now. "I will return with young Burtchen. Then home to Kongo."

Kepplar's gunship lifted off first. Hochburg watched its lights shrink into the darkness. Banks of clouds, charcoal against the night, were massing; the wind was freshening up. Moments later Hochburg felt a lurch as his own helicopter ascended. Feuerstein was squashed into the same seat as him; he gazed down through the glass bubble of the cockpit at the receding palace.

"A plane in the morning, Herr Doctor, a helicopter for the evening. A day to remember for a man who's never flown."

The physicist cupped his mouth as though he was about to vomit.

CHAPTER FIFTY-EIGHT

Mandritsara Hospital
21 April, 04:45

"IT'S IMPORTANT THAT you see this," said Cranley.

He spoke in a cool, careless way, but his eyes shone with malice. He was dressed in dark combat fatigues oily with the jungle, in his grip a pistol whose handle was carved from ivory. Madeleine recognized it as Burton's gun, and remembered the times she'd scolded him for not hiding it when Alice visited the farm.

Burton was on his knees before her husband, neck limp from the blow he'd taken, the back of his head bloody and matted. A soldier stood behind him; another held Madeleine. Her wrists were bound in front of her, the cord so secure that her fingertips were numb. The soldiers had attempted to tie Burton but had given up when they saw his missing hand.

"Are you watching?" asked Cranley. His voice was intricate with emotions: forced composure, rage, a need to brag. Madeleine noticed how carefully tended his hair was. He swung the pistol against Burton's face.

The blow felled him. He hit the floor, mumbling threats, a bright spatter where his face landed. The soldier dragged him back to a kneeling position. A gash had opened across Burton's cheek. Madeleine had seen him nick his thumb on a piece of farm machinery, she had laid her tongue upon his scars, but she had never seen him bleed like this. A coldness drained through her stomach.

Cranley wedged the pistol into his belt, then cracked a fist into Burton's nose. And again. His knuckles came away trailing blood.

Madeleine fought to free herself from the soldier's hold, snapping and hissing and stamping at his feet. Meat-hook hands held her fast. Abner stood to one side, silent and sheepish, his eyes darting around the room, never meeting Madeleine's.

Cranley prowled in front of Burton. "Second button down," he said.

Burton had fastened his tunic against the chill of the hospital; the second button lay at the base of his throat. Cranley's punch landed with utter precision, the middle knuckle driving the button into his gullet. Burton dropped, cawing and choking.

Madeleine couldn't bear any more; she screwed her eyes shut.

"I told you to watch."

She didn't have enough hair for the soldier to grasp, so he grabbed her ears and forced her head up. Fingertips pinched her eyelashes and raised the lids. Cranley filled her vision, overwhelming her intimate space. He wore a concentrated, almost pleading expression that she associated with the bedroom in the first months of their marriage.

For the first time she registered that his skin was leathery with burns; it suited him, seemed to complete his face.

"Keep watching," he said. "There's not much more to go."

He slipped away from her and delivered a final fist into Burton's sternum. Madeleine let out a shout of horror. Burton crumpled, groaning as if an organ had ruptured. This time the soldier left him where he was.

Cranley leaned over him and administered an injection.

Madeleine struggled in the soldier's grip. "What are you doing?"

"It's a new type of epinephrine the Germans have developed. While I was waiting for you, I found some in the dispensary. They have the most extraordinary selection of drugs I've ever seen. It's used in interrogations to give the prisoner a boost, so you can prolong the questioning. There's no honor in beating an unconscious man." He withdrew the syringe. "He'll be as sparky as a sandboy in a few minutes."

All the furniture in the room had been cleared except for a large table in the middle. Cranley perched on it in a pose she'd seen many times over the years. Against the walls were microscope stations, a refrigeration unit full of vials, gleaming centrifuges. There were piles of clamps and calipers that looked like twisted black bones; drums of chemicals. In one corner stood a full-sized skeleton that someone had turned inward, as though they didn't want its hollow eye sockets to witness the events about to unfold.

Madeleine faced her brother, heat blooming in her cheeks as if he'd slapped her. "You did this?" Her voice was piercing. "You brought us to him?"

Cranley answered on his behalf: "My agents have been supplying the Vanillas for years. It took a while, but we tracked him down in the end."

"Your husband's here to help, Leni."

"You idiot boy," she replied.

"He's the only chance we'll ever get."

"Stupid fucking idiot boy."

"He already saved Mutti and Leah."

That brought her up short. "You said they were in Zimety."

"I couldn't tell you the truth. They're in South Africa, waiting for us. Colonel Cranley arranged it."

Madeleine was suddenly dizzy: Colonel Cranley, his "agents," South Africa . . . Who was this man she'd been married to? She tried to organize her thoughts. "He's lying."

"I saw them off."

"But you didn't see them arrive. You can't just take people off this island."

"Actually, you can," said Cranley. "We've been doing it since the island was first settled. So has most of the CONE; America, too. The SS has a secret hostage exchange program."

"Why?"

"Scoop up the dirt and there will always be a few gems. Jews who didn't believe they'd be shipped out or thought they could make new lives for themselves. A cache of treasures arrived with them. Do you remember the Renoir we saw?"

A trip to the National Gallery. Alice had been excited, then bored, Jared uncharacteristically animated. She had wondered about it at the time: neither of them had much interest in art. They stood in line to glimpse the new exhibit, its provenance a mystery. Afterward they took tea at Fortnum's. Madeleine had worn her happiness all afternoon, until her smile ached. She longed for the day she and Burton could go out as a family.

Cranley continued, boastfulness clinging to his words: "We acquired it for the country and bought its previous owners passage abroad. They're safely in Brazil now. I did the same with your mother and sister." His smile was chilling. "Governor Globocnik is well recompensed; it also means a few fewer Jews for him to worry about."

She switched her attention to Abner. "You don't understand what you've done."

"Mutti's ill," he replied, anxious to persuade. "Leah can't cope with much more. Papa and Samuel have gone to America—"

"Don't use your stupid slang."

"I did the best I could."

"For who?" demanded Madeleine.

"The family."

"What about Burton?"

He was beginning to stir at their feet.

"He's not my concern," said Abner, shifting awkwardly.

"After everything I told you."

"I don't know him."

"He's the man I love. Look what they've done to him. They're going to kill him."

"Colonel Cranley never mentioned anything to do with him. He's not supposed to be here."

"And what about me?" said Madeleine. "Where do I fit into everything?"

"You're going to Britain"—a hint of envy—"back to your old life."

She spat out a laugh, but Cranley nodded in confirmation. "I'm taking you home, Madeleine."

Another laugh, a mixture of incredulity and scorn . . . then a breathlessness as she understood that he was quite sincere.

Cranley gestured to the soldier behind Burton. "The epinephrine should be taking effect by now. Get him up."

The soldier hauled Burton to his knees and shook him. His eyes flickered, then stayed open, the pupils artificially wide and alert. A loop of glistening, bloody saliva hung from his chin. Madeleine wanted to shield him from Cranley, to wipe his face clean, but the soldier behind her held tight.

Burton stared at Cranley, his jaw wobbling, and spoke as if he'd bitten his tongue. "I'm going . . . to kill you . . . this time."

"Very amusing. Before you do, it's important you know I'm taking Madeleine back to London. It was my intention all along. Like I told you during our last parley: I don't believe in swift retribution. And what was the one thing worse than Madagaskar? The luxury of home; having to spend the rest of her days as my dutiful wife. Appreciative and pliant."

"You're lying," said Madeleine. She felt sick. "You wouldn't be able to bear it."

"I managed six months without you suspecting a thing."

"That's why there's no"—Burton coughed red spittle—"no tattoo."

"Correct," replied Cranley to Madeleine. "I made sure you weren't numbered. I couldn't have you back in society with a Jew tag for a bracelet. I also arranged for the house on Boriziny Strasse. It cost a fortune in bribes."

"You want me to be grateful?"

"Next time I'll abandon you to the slums."

Madeleine rubbed her bare wrists, the rope chafing around them. They felt sullied. She wished they were as purple as Salois's.

"My original plan was to leave you for a year, maybe two," continued Cranley. "That's why I chose Boriziny—so I could keep track of you. By the end, you'd be begging to come home. Anything to get off this island. That appealed to me: you desperate for your own punishment. It's only your lover who brought me here early."

"I'll never come back." She thought of Salois and his daily torment. "I'd rather die."

"Than see Alice? Than live like a human being?"

"I'll never come back," she said, as if repeating the words would convince him.

"Which is why I moved your family. They're settling into a handsome little homestead in the Natal hills." He gave a tight, indulgent smile. "If you refuse me, I send them back to Madagaskar. Your mother is doing poorly, Madeleine; I doubt she'll survive the return. Nothing breaks the spirit more than dashed hope."

"You've got to go with him," said Abner. There was a demented, evangelical blaze to his expression, a yearning for her to agree. "It's no hardship, Leni, not like this place. You can be with your daughter again."

"You've lost all sense."

"Think of us for once. You don't know how hard it's been. There was enough upset when you left; we're not going to suffer anymore. You have to do the right thing this time."

She heard the fervor in his voice, the regret and resentment that had been simmering since she fled Vienna and he stayed, like the borscht their mother used to make, left on the stove till it was boiling over. His desire to save the family—to save himself—had convinced him of his righteousness. She hated him but couldn't entirely condemn him, either. Perhaps Abner believed he was doing the best by her.

Madeleine's voice ached. "How can you have done this?"

"If you'd been here ten grueling years, if you knew the rebellion was doomed and there wasn't a spark of hope left in you—if Samuel had died in your arms—you'd have done the same."

"You could have warned me."

"I know you too well, Leni: you'd have vanished—and you made it hard enough as it was. First you wouldn't go back to Antzu; then you chased after

Salois. If you'd stayed in Boriziny a couple of hours longer, we'd already be away."

"Sounds like you had a perfect plan."

"No thanks to you. It's only luck I found a radio in the pig pens; otherwise I couldn't have told your husband where we were headed."

"He's not my husband."

"A huge effort has gone into finding you," said Cranley. "I could have sent any of my agents, Madeleine, but I chose to do it myself. You're coming home."

There was a tremor in his voice that she didn't recognize, a vainglory that hid something. She rubbed her unmarked wrists. "What about Salois?"

"Your brother wasn't aware of him."

"He thinks you're in Mazunka."

Cranley straightened himself. "If my presence convinced him of the mission, all the better."

"He believed in you."

"A necessary deception. It's essential that he reaches Diego, for all our sakes."

"To bring America into the war," said Abner, as though these wider ambitions proved her husband's benevolence.

"No," replied Cranley. "To keep it out."

+ + +

Abner spoke cautiously, confessionally. A man who had made an unwitting blunder that might cost him his passage to freedom, thought Madeleine. "But I helped Salois find new explosives." He continued, justification blurring into apology. "I . . . that is, the Vanillas thought we'd never win without American involvement."

"For which I'm grateful," replied Cranley.

"He'll be able to attack Diego."

"I want him to. I just don't want him to succeed."

Burton coughed up a glob of blood. "Sounds like Kongo again," he said, and spat it at Cranley's feet.

"It's the second phase of the same operation, yes; a wider scheme to ensure stability for us all. Globocnik is no different than Hochburg; they're both marauders. Detached from any sense of realpolitik. Before President Taft it mattered less, but it took Jewish money to win the White House, and now his financiers are watching Madagaskar. It's only a matter of time till Globus provokes them." He addressed Madeleine. "I sent Salois to stop him."

At home, Jared was discreet in his ministerial dealings, the visits to foreign capitals and meetings at Downing Street. Now names and details flew like cracks of a whip. She suddenly understood why and felt revulsion for the man.

He wants to impress me, she thought. That's why he had come to Madagaskar, why he was dressed in fatigues, handling a pistol. Beneath his bumptious confidence he was scared, or at least baffled. She had chosen a soldier—a man emerged from dust and privation, a man who couldn't even provide her with a decent bathroom—over him. It made no sense to his beliefs. He wanted to prove his power to her, over not only Burton but the currents of the world itself. If he controlled them, she would have no choice but to submit to his will.

He fixed his eyes on hers. "Salois attacks the base at Diego Suarez. In the midst of a new rebellion, it proves that Globus has finally lost control. He's Himmler's man, and Himmler hates the slightest whiff of failure. So either Globus shoots himself in humiliation or he is recalled to Germania. Whatever happens, the threat of him is removed. Washington is pacified."

Madeleine regarded him with disdain. "As simple as that?"

"Governor Bouhler was dismissed for less."

"And in Globus's place they send someone worse."

"There are others who want to see the end of Globocnik, not only in London. My counterparts in Germania have let it be known that should anything happen to the governor, the navy will temporarily take charge and quell the rebellion, as sailors, not butchers of the Schutzstaffel. Afterward, the island will remain part of Heydrich's office. He has a successor in waiting, Herr Bischof. An accountant. One trusts the auditors to placate any situation."

"But the bombers," said Abner.

"There are no bombers! There never were. Salois destroys the air defenses—but that's all. The damage will be minimal, the East Africa Fleet remains untouched. And at the center: a Jew, unequivocally a Jew with his inky blue body. As far as anyone knows, it's an internal security matter. Further proof of how ineffective Globus is."

"You're sacrificing Reuben?"

"On an altar that's overflowing."

"He's a good man," said Madeleine.

"Who murdered his pregnant wife. I bet he didn't tell you that." When she made no comment, he added, "There are plenty of good men in this world. What difference does it make?"

"So he never had a chance."

"None of you did."

CHAPTER FIFTY-NINE

Diego Suarez
21 April, 04:40

THE FIRST OF the charges was set, the tiny cogs inside the detonators inexorably ticking toward their end.

On the dhow, sailing to Madagaskar, Salois had taken one apart to check the workings and been reassured to see FABRIQUÉ EN BELGIQUE stamped on the metal. At 04:55 the dynamite would bring the missile batteries down in a flash of intense orange fire. Minutes later Turneiro's bombers would swoop over the base. If the rest of the population heeded the signal and joined the rebellion, there would be no slave gangs to rebuild. By the time Diego was operational again, the U.S. Navy would be patrolling the Indian Ocean.

The bad luck that had dogged the mission since the island first appeared on the horizon was gone. Yaudin's flare had drawn most of the sentries away from the quays, to the search railyard. The guard at the inner gate chose the exact moment Salois approached to step into a corner to relieve himself; he was still pissing when he hit the ground. Even the Kriegsmarine whites Cranley had supplied, the most useless camouflage Salois had ever worn, vanished in the fierce glow of the lights. Salois flitted around the base as though he were translucent.

He reached the second battery, concealing himself at the foot of the girders, and attached a bundle of dynamite. It was like standing beneath a prehistoric monster. Salois adjusted the timer and moved to the next leg.

In the closing months of the war against Russia, the Soviet Air Force had launched a final, desperate raid on Berlin. Although it failed, it spurred German scientists to develop new air defenses so the Reich would never be vulnerable again. The first was the Taifun, a rocket-based unit that launched lethal but indiscriminate salvos. In the decade that followed came radio- and infrared-guided prototypes: Projects Enzian and Rheintochter (an off-shoot of the latter produced missiles capable of striking Washington). Despite successful testing, they were not yet ready for deployment. Diego was protected by an intermediate system known as Loge that used manually aimed rockets.

The base's central defense system consisted of four Loge batteries. Three of them were stationed on the quayside, each mounted on a crane topped with a rotating platform that housed the launcher and operator's cradle. Each crane was painted honey yellow, its four legs on rail tracks so that the whole structure could be moved along the waterfront. The fourth Loge sat on a strip of concrete that jutted out from the quay at a right angle, situated to pick off any targets that evaded the main battery. Flak guns watched the high ground. There were also searchlights and gigantic angled mirrors. Hitler had personally insisted that these be installed at military bases. "Blinded by the reflection," he told his commanders, "enemy pilots will not be able to see a thing."

Salois set the third detonator. Cranley was adamant that they plant explosives under all four legs, but experience had taught Salois that three would suffice. Every moment in the open increased the chances of being spotted and the mission failing. As he worked he kept glancing at the runway on Kap Diégo, expecting an alarm and jets to be scrambled. It remained silent.

A two-lane road ran the length of the quay along the batteries; on the other side was a maze of offices, workshops, and armories. Salois hurried across to them; it would be easier to move undetected with the buildings as cover. They were all jagged angles and hard lines, the roofs checkered with corrosion. He ducked behind some bins, unhooking the empty rucksack on his front and burying it among the rubbish. From this angle he could see the two missile operators in their glass cabin high on the platform: one in the firing seat, eye pressed into the sight scanning the bay, the other checking the radio dish and antennae. Salois paused to watch them; they were so oblivious to the approach of death.

Below, the ring of boots.

A patrol came into view, one of the guards leading a Doberman. The dog stopped, snout twitching, and pulled in Salois's direction. If he ran, they'd see him; the bins weren't large enough to hide behind. Then the voice of luck:

"Hey, over there. Could you give us a hand with this?"

In the wall opposite was a steel door with a sign above that read

DANGER! KEEP LOCKED AT ALL TIMES. A young sailor was struggling to shift some crates. Salois darted across to him.

"Trolley's kaput," he said. "And the others are skiving somewhere."

Inside was a second steel door painted with diagonal scarlet and white stripes. The sailor put a key in the lock, and it swung open on oiled hinges. Salois helped him carry in the first of the crates and let a shiver of wonder chase up his spine.

This was more than luck.

The Doberman patrol padded past outside. One of the guards glanced in and, satisfied, continued on his way.

"Not seen you before," said the sailor. He reached for the next crate. "What's your name?"

"Nobody," replied Salois, gripping his knife.

Afterward, he dragged the sailor's body through the second door and surveyed the room. It had a dull brass glow. He was in the arsenal, surrounded by rack after rack of munitions and antiaircraft shells the size of watermelons. Salois took a bundle of dynamite and set it for two minutes after the main charges. The firestorm from the detonation would make it look as if a much larger force was attacking. He closed the inner door, bent the key in the lock, and slipped back into the night, heading toward the last of the missile placements on the quayside.

He was halfway there when a geyser shot into the sky. There was a hiss of spray, followed by silence. The Doberman barked.

Seconds later: another tower of water.

Salois stared in the direction of the explosions, shielding his eyes from the lights. On top of the first battery, the two operators were on their feet, peering below. A third eruption spattered the cabin window.

At the base of the crane, his head bound in a makeshift bandage, was Yaudin. He had acquired a BK44 and looked around expectantly, urging alarms to ring.

There was another boom and spray, this time from the second battery. The other Jupo warden was beneath it, already removing the next bundle of dynamite. He tossed it into the water, where it exploded.

Salois watched, helpless and desolate—then sprinted in the opposite direction. Two sentries raced toward him, tightening the straps of their helmets beneath their chins. They lowered their rifles when they saw his uniform.

"Jews!" shouted Salois. "They're attacking. You've got to stop them. I've been ordered to guard the other defenses."

He hurried past until he was under the pylon of the third battery. He grabbed two bundles of dynamite and set both timers to twenty seconds. Then he was running again, toward the final Loge.

Behind him came gunfire. The two sentries shot the warden. He staggered backward, cradling the last of the dynamite. Another volley: he dropped. More guards appeared, converging on the far end of the quay.

The third battery exploded.

Salois felt the blast like a hot spade between the shoulders. He was hurled forward, the air ripped from his mouth and ears, but kept running. As his hearing returned, he heard metal twist and wrench, a *tdschhh* of sparks. There was no time to check how effective the dynamite had been.

The final Loge was situated on an artificial peninsula that had been engineered into a mesa. Every year the monsoons battered the concrete; plants had grown in the cracks, giving it a scattering of scrub and pink flowers. A flight of steps had been cut into the rock. Salois mounted them two at a time. High above, on the missile platform, one of the operators assessed the damage below. He caught sight of something behind Salois and mouthed a warning.

Salois looked back only when he reached the top. The battery was lopsided, veiled in smoke—but the explosives hadn't brought it down. A fire crew reeled out hoses; the quayside was packed with sailors bearing arms. But his Diego luck hadn't deserted him yet. The crane had buckled in the explosion, precariously tilting the firing platform. Even if the missile system remained operable, it could only launch into the sea.

At the bottom of the steps Yaudin chased after him.

The yellow pylon legs clanged and reverberated: a missile operator was climbing down from above. Salois aimed his BK at the bottom rungs of the ladder. Boots appeared, a belt buckle, a face. Salois fired twice, hitting him in the chest. The operator dropped off the ladder and rolled out of sight, into the bushes. Salois rested his weapon against the pylon and delved inside his rucksack for the last of the dynamite. He would plant a bundle beneath each of the legs this time to make sure the battery was destroyed.

A klaxon rang out, echoing over the bay. Another joined it, then another, like wolves taking up each other's call.

Salois glanced at the runway—still quiet—then his watch, the face pale against his indigo skin. The bombers must have crossed Mount Amber now and would be starting their descent from the southwest; they could reach Diego before any fighters took to the sky.

He was setting the final charge when Yaudin reached the top of the stairs. The Jupo chief raised his rifle; he was breathing heavily and struggled to speak.

"Stop this madness . . . put it down, Major."

Salois glanced at the BK he'd left propped against the side and began edging toward it, clutching the last bundle.

Yaudin fired a warning shot.

A voice whispered inside Salois's head: cold, determined, provident. Giving the bombers every chance mattered more than his survival. He set the detonator to ten seconds and clasped it to his chest.

Salois had never thought of ending his life. After he fled Antwerp, neither his self-pity nor his self-loathing tipped far enough. Later, in Madagaskar, the very notion was abhorrent. Amid so much death, it would be an insult to life and the piles of bodies. There was also a tiny, locked-away part of him that dreaded the fisherman's words: *Death doesn't want you.* What if it was true? What if he attempted to kill himself and failed? The realization that he would be granted no relief was a punishment too hard to bear. He watched the dial count down to zero.

Yaudin raked his legs with gunfire.

For a heartbeat Salois was so incredulous he almost erupted in laughter.

Then he felt the bullets pass through him, tearing sinew, shattering bone. He tumbled backward, landing heavily; the dynamite rolled from his grasp.

Yaudin leapt forward and hurled it over the edge. The explosion showered them in fragments of concrete. He moved swiftly to defuse the other charges.

Salois crawled after him, begging him to stop, but his body was sapless. Blood from the bullet holes bloomed across his trousers until the white material was engulfed by a brilliant red stain. A wave of pain and numbness welled up through his hips, making him want to retch.

He was unbuckling his belt to use as a tourniquet when he saw the other missile operator sliding down the ladder, Luger in hand. He glanced at Salois's uniform, raised a finger to his lips, and crept toward the police chief.

"Yaudin!" shouted Salois. His mouth was metallic and bubbly with spit.

Yaudin spun round and fired.

The German dropped next to Salois, pistol still in his hand. Salois didn't bother taking it: with both missile operators dead, the tower was no longer a threat. Yaudin gave a nod of thanks, unaware of what he had done, and returned to the last of the charges.

While he was occupied, Salois slid over to his rucksack. He removed the smoke grenades and lobbed them in the direction of the steps, one after the other. They plunked and chimed as they fell. A wraith of luminous green smoke snaked upward.

"What are you doing?" asked Yaudin. His shaved, blackened face had an emerald sheen.

Salois tightened the tourniquet around his thigh, then reached to the dead German and undid his belt to use on the other leg.

Two missile batteries out, he thought. *It should do.*

The first of the bombers would probably be shot down; they could deplete the batteries for the aircraft that followed. An ocean of Jewish blood had been spilt; let the Mozambicans sacrifice a drop for Turneiro's "famous victory." If the pilots were sufficiently skilled and brave, they could aim at the aircraft carriers as they plummeted from the sky. Or the submarine pens. Or the white fuel silos beyond. Diego abounded with targets.

A searchlight burst into life, a solid wand stretching into the heavens. Others joined it, hitting the reflecting mirrors. The sky dazzled.

Salois edged himself to the farthest corner of the tower for the best view of the base. The air around him was shrouded in a halo of green smoke. Yaudin stood by the steps, agitated, unsure what to do.

There was a tremendous, throaty *whoosh* that shook the ground.

A fireball rocketed into the sky from the arsenal. It was followed by a myriad of smaller explosions as the munitions ignited: bolts of red, white, gold, and aquamarine, as if the base were under attack from an armada in the Indian Ocean. The BK44 dropped from Yaudin's grip. He hung his head in his hands.

Salois gave a blissful grimace. *It's the most wonderful thing,* he used to tell Frieda as the bump of their child grew: a balm for the night before. The flames over Diego Suarez were as miraculous. He turned his body to the southwest, dragging his legs, and watched the horizon—waiting for the drone of bombers.

CHAPTER SIXTY

Mandritsara Hospital
21 April, 04:55

HE LOOKED QUEASY to Madeleine, unsure of himself. Abner was standing by the window, a floor-to-ceiling pane of frosted glass that looked out onto a courtyard. He tried to control his stutter, which made it worse. "But w-why keep America away?"

"What do you care?" she replied. "You've bought your ticket out of here."

"America can make a difference. Salois believed it. All us Vanillas did."

Cranley spoke: "The Americans will bring havoc to the world."

"Your world," said Madeleine.

"Which you enjoyed for many years; which our daughter will grow up in. I've dedicated an entire career to preserving the country, to buttressing its future. Only a fool would give it up for this festering island."

"But if the two of you came together," said Abner.

"Do you know what Hitler calls the United States? 'The principal competitor of the British Empire.' The Colonial Office agrees. So do Halifax and Eden—"

"Not Churchill," said Madeleine, recalling his speeches after the invasion of Rhodesia and his appeals across the Atlantic.

"Whose mother was American. Churchill never accepted his failure at Dunkirk; belligerence is his compensation. Worse, he has a clear grasp of our shortcomings." Cranley puckered his mouth as though he'd swallowed a dose of vinegar. "Britain is weaker than we dare admit: economically, militarily. Kongo was supposed to be a snap war, over by Christmas. Instead, our victory in Elisabethstadt only proved the limit of our reach. If America sallies forth, it will be the end of us. The colonies will start peeling away. Either the United States will fill our footsteps, or calls for independence will ring loud. The empire will face years of decline."

His tone became anguished, aggressive. "And who benefits?"

"Together you could defeat the Germans," retorted her brother. "Free Madagaskar."

Cranley shot him the look he reserved for disciplining the servants. "Taft swore to preserve America's isolationism. Neither he nor his nation wishes to intervene, despite the pleas of the American Jewish Committee. Our duty is to ensure that position." He contemplated this. "The world is like a marriage: add a third party and what worked well for so long collapses."

Abner was insistent. "But what if America—"

Cranley rounded on him. "Do you really want to have this argument?" Madeleine's brother fell silent. "Washington's great gift is its neutrality. There is nothing more to say."

"What about the troops from the Far East? Salois told us you were going to bring thousands to fight in Kongo. He saw your forward station."

"Another necessary deception, to convince him of our sincerity. So long as America is not drawn in, Africa will remain in a deadlock between us and the Germans. From deadlocks come negotiations, settlements. Stability. The world balanced between two pillars; that's all I want. We will return Elisabethstadt in exchange for a guarantee of . . ."

While he continued to hold forth, Madeleine glanced at Burton. The worst of the bleeding had stopped; his split cheek was cherry red and puffing up. He appeared vigilant, absorbing the details of the room for anything that might help their escape, despite the rifle in his back. He gave her a furtive, reassuring nod, but there was little doubt about what would happen next. She felt hot whips of panic. No matter how she was threatened, she would refuse to watch.

Cranley caught the exchange between them.

"She never loved you," he said sharply. "Not in the way she loved me. She used you as a diversion, a means of escape, but she never loved you. Tell him," he commanded. "I want to hear you say it."

"It's not true," she replied.

"Tell him."

"The three of us know it."

"One word from me, and your mother and sister will be on a plane to Tana."

Was that going to be the rest of her life? A plane fueled and ready every time she disagreed or demurred? Or didn't show enough enthusiasm for her imprisonment? Or glanced murderously at a knife while eating dinner? How trivial could her misdemeanors become: If she wore the wrong earrings or shade of lipstick? Heels that were too high, or too low, or too anything?

"They're only words, Leni," said Abner without conviction.

She thought of the twins. From those brief seconds when she'd held them she could recall every crease of their faces, the coral-and-quince gleam of their skin, the crinkles that were their mouths. When she recalled her mother or Leah, all she pictured were shadows and a hazy spin of guilt. "I lost them a long time ago. You can't threaten me with them."

"Then why spend so many years searching for them?"

"Burton's my family." She spoke steadily. "You can take me back to London, but you'll never make me say it."

The words bit Cranley. He aimed his pistol at Abner. "You harangued the clerks at the Colonial Office for the slightest detail about them," he reminded Madeleine. "Anything to confirm that the Weisses were alive. You won't sacrifice them now."

She said nothing.

"Perhaps you think I'm bluffing."

"Leni!" entreated her brother. "Don't be so stubborn."

The report of the gun was deafening. The bullet slammed Abner against the window, leaving a messy butterfly on the glass as he slid down it. He landed on his front, elbows at awkward angles.

Madeleine broke free of the soldier's grip and rushed to her brother. She rolled him over: his glasses were twisted across his forehead, his grubby white shirt already wet. Her tied hands scrambled across his chest, trying to find the wound to stanch it; blood seemed to be pumping between every rib.

He tried to say something. Scarlet ran between the gaps of his teeth. She leaned close to hear; the decay of his molars was rank and coppery. All that emerged from him was an incoherent choking. Then he was limp, his pulse a memory.

Abner had gone to America.

Cranley cocked the pistol. After the blast, the click had an oddly intimate quality. He was pointing it at Burton's heart.

"I never loved him," she said mechanically.

"To him, not me."

Burton was a blur. "I never loved you."

Cranley gave an unsatisfied humph. He eased the hammer back on the pistol, twirled it, and slipped it into his waistband. He addressed the soldier who had been holding her: "Go to the Mercedes. Make sure the cargo is secure and prepare us to leave." He spoke to Madeleine: "We're flying out of here."

She wasn't listening. She straightened Abner's glasses. His expression was rigid with shock and—was she imagining this?—shame. "Idiot boy," she whispered and stroked his hairless scalp.

"I could tell you your sister is pregnant," said Cranley, his breath in her ear. "That I can get her husband to South Africa if I choose. But I doubt it will have much effect. You're harder than I imagined, Madeleine." He put his arms around her from behind, enveloping her body. "What does he have? He's a common soldier who'd have to kill to afford a ring on your finger. Or use one of the diamonds I paid him with."

"If you let him go free, I'll come back with you."

A bark of mirthless laughter. "This is not a negotiation. Only one deed will put it right—"

Lumps of acid spouted in Madeleine's throat.

"—and you have to do it."

He forced her to stand and walked her across the room till they were in front of Burton.

"Dear God, you're thin—even thinner than when we first met. We'll have to feed you up when you get home." There was affection in his tone and a hint of disgust.

She squirmed in Cranley's grip, but he was too strong, clamped around her like she was the soft innards of a crab, he the shell and pincers. Burton stared up at her, still on his knees, wearing the fatalistic calm she'd seen in so many other faces on the island.

Cranley put the pistol in her bound hands and fastened his fingers over hers, raising the gun so it quivered inches from Burton's forehead. The soldier guarding him watched uncomfortably.

"Where did it begin?" asked Cranley. "I know everything else: the hotel trysts, your promises to each other in Germania, fucking in the quince orchards. Just not the start."

"On the beach," replied Madeleine. "The Suffolk house." Tears rolled down her cheeks.

"Did you ever weep for me?"

"She did," said Burton. "Betraying you was the hardest thing she ever did."

Madeleine heard something trip in Cranley's breath. Then he pushed her finger against the safety catch, flicking it off. "One shot and it will all be wiped away. I'll forgive everything. Alice will be so happy to have you home."

She fought against him. "I'll never look at you without wanting to cut your throat."

His voice dropped, became maniacal. "Your lover is not leaving here. What happens to him is the one concession I'll grant you. So do it—or I shoot him in the gut and he'll bleed to death for hours. It will be agony. His life will still be trickling out of him long after our plane is in the sky."

"Please, Jared . . ."

He cocked the weapon with his thumb. There was a black crescent of mud along the nail. She had never seen his hands dirty before; even when he tended his prized alpine bed in the garden he always wore gloves. He inserted her finger into the trigger guard before slipping his own on top of hers. He put no pressure on her: he wanted her to do it herself. The warm steel of the trigger hummed millimeters from her skin.

Burton remained composed, his expression tremorless.

Madeleine sagged against her husband, her arms kept rigid in his grip. "I won't . . . I can't."

"You should have accepted my offer, all those months ago, to stay. It wouldn't have ended like this. It's your own fault. There was no need for you to suffer. You or the twins."

"You know about the twins?"

"Squeeze the trigger," he coaxed. "Squeeze it, and three days from now you'll wake up in your own bed. Think about that: your own bed."

"My bed's on the farm." It was old and musty and sometimes gave her a backache; it was the only place she wanted to wake.

From far away came a deep boom that she felt in her heels. It was followed by another sound, like a long cry of pain drawn out until it vanished beyond the range of her hearing.

Madeleine focused on Burton, but the image of him distorted as tears brimmed in her eyes. He fractured and melted, the fragments of him catching the light, as she became aware of Cranley's finger exerting a delicate pressure. Then she heard Burton's voice from far away: *It's okay, Maddie, it's not your fault.*

It was the same soothing voice her father used the last time she saw him. She was on a platform at the Westbahnhof, awaiting a train bound for Zürich. She had left a letter at home, not expecting anyone to read it until she was across the border. Papa had appeared through the smoke moments before she departed. He was out of breath; Jews were no longer allowed to ride the trams. Neither of them shed any tears, and he didn't kiss her good-bye or embrace her. He simply laid his hand on hers—that creased, neat hand, parched from a lifetime of being scrubbed between visits with patients—and said, *A parent gives their child two gifts: Roots. And wings.* Und jetzt geh, meine Kleine . . .

There was a rumble beyond the window; it intensified, becoming a roar, like thunder below the ground.

With all her effort, Madeleine sent the gun in her hands toward the ceiling.

Cranley was too fast and too strong. Even as she lifted her arms he forced them down, aiming the pistol at Burton's chest. She released her muscles, and in an instant Cranley's exertion drove the pistol toward the floor. Madeleine squeezed the trigger, the bullet flaring on the tiles, and then their hands were fighting for control of the weapon.

She tried to aim at his foot. Another blast, sending out a burst of sparks. The muzzle rose again toward the center of Burton's body, Cranley over-powering her limbs. In the narrow space between trigger and guard, his finger curled around hers.

Madeleine used the last of her strength to twist her arms—not up or down but the last place he expected. She buried the pistol into her belly, a spot where once her babies had kicked and bounced to be let out into the world, and crushed the trigger.

CHAPTER SIXTY-ONE

Sofia Dam
21 April, 04:45

"I WANT MORE," said Globus. "Every last stick you've got."

The sapper swallowed, as though he had mumps. "It's not necessary, Obergruppenführer."

They were inside the Sofia Dam, two levels from the top. A relentless dull pounding, like the headache above Globus's eyes, filled the air. The floor was painted in bottle-green gloss.

"The detonation is a triangle," explained the sapper. "The base explodes first; gravity and the force of the water do the rest. You need less ordnance on the higher levels."

Globus remained unconvinced. He tried to picture what the sapper had said, but he was struggling to focus; the injection he'd been given in Tana had worn off. He squatted, checking the cables that ran from the TNT, along the passageway, and out of sight to the control room, though he had no idea what he was looking for. He swayed as he stood.

"I don't trust gravity. Double the charges here and on the level below. Then get your men out."

He strode to the metal staircase that led to the surface. His boots had been cleaned on arrival, and his spurs were singing again. He adored that sound: it made him think he was a cavalry officer.

"This is a precaution, isn't it, Obergruppenführer?" said the sapper. "You're not really going to detonate."

"That's up to the Jews." He pulled on his suspenders. "We're carrying out the Reichsführer's orders. I should have done this months ago."

He mounted the stairs and emerged on the road that ran along the top of the dam. The night was deafening, thick and cool with spray. Globus dredged his sinuses and spat over the side.

Beneath him, the sluice gates were open.

Great chutes of water thundered from the dam. "Globusfalls" he'd called it in the control room; the technicians had laughed unconvincingly. He had ordered them to calculate the volume of discharge necessary to give the Yids a fright. His plan wasn't to wash the reservation away (at least not tonight), merely to wet their ankles. To remind them who controlled their fate.

It should have cheered him, and yet, watching the water gush out, Globus was left uncertain, dejected.

He thought about his birthday last year, when the governorship of Ostmark wasn't a dream but a reality in waiting. Just this morning, on this very spot, while Hochburg and Nightingale conspired against him, he'd remained confident about his future. He remembered birthdays as a boy: it was impossible to imagine being fifty-three, but even then he was sure he would become one of the emperors of his age.

In the valley below, some of the barracks were ablaze; he could make out Jews with torches on either side of the new river. They must be the same bandits who defaced the dam the previous night. The Mandritsara garrison had failed him. After they helped mine the dam, he'd sent them into the reservation to maintain order, but unless he supervised every last man, weakness prevailed—while the blame rested on him. It was so unjust. At first light he would fly a squadron of Walküres low over the valley floor.

He would earn back Himmler's favor.

+ + +

The control center for the dam was a large, subdued space. There was a bank of what looked like kitchen cabinets with dials the size of plates and, behind them, desks set with levers and buttons where technicians were at work. Because of the silting and the defunct turbines, most of the equipment was redundant and used only to alter the water flow or for communications. A map of the island's northern electricity grid was behind a dust sheet. Two huge viewing windows, at opposite ends of the room, showed the valley and reservoir. Despite millions of liters cascading through the sluice gates every minute, the level of the reservoir had not perceptibly dropped.

A sapper met Globus as he entered and presented him with the detonator. It was the size of a cigarette lighter, with a fat red button on the top. "Press and hold for three seconds," he said. "That creates the circuit. Same again to disarm. Once it's live, two rapid clicks will set off the charges."

Globus's worn-out brain absorbed the instructions: *one long . . . two quick.* He tugged the cord to make sure it was connected.

Five radio operators sat monitoring the airwaves; Globus had assembled them so he could communicate with the rest of his island. The situation was not good: the rebellion was spreading wider and farther than ever before. One of the operators had a swollen lip and the beginnings of a black eye. Earlier, he had shared the news of Hochburg's broadcast.

Globus stood behind him, hands resting on his chair. "When will the others be here?"

He had summoned the regional commanders to the dam. It would play well with Germania: while Hochburg was grandstanding in Tana, he was in the thick of the Jewish threat, battling to restore order. Word had also been sent to Diego Suarez, informing the Kriegsmarine command that he, and he alone, remained in charge of Madagaskar.

"Governor Quorp is en route," replied the operator. "We've yet to contact the rest."

"It's chaos out there. They must be out in the sectors, crushing the Jews."

In truth, they had all been invited to his party. If Hochburg had taken over the palace, they must have been detained. Perhaps Hochburg had exchanged them in the dungeons for Feuerstein and his pestilent crew.

Globus prowled the control room, his chest crammed with frustration, theatrically clicking the detonator on and off.

Arm/disarm.

The dam technicians and radio operators kept their heads down, working in silence or whispering into headsets. An unappreciative audience. He should have brought a couple of his secretaries with him; he chose them for having a good sense of humor as well as their typing skills.

One of the technicians had a box of sandwiches by his work station. Globus helped himself, white bread and pork, and ate by the window, looking out on the valley. A pair of blinking lights appeared from where the river curved out of sight toward Mandritsara and its hospital. They skimmed above the reservation like fireflies. It must be Quorp: fat, loyal Quorp. There had been several fits of unrest in Antzu during the night; he had quashed them all. Globus felt a shift of guilt for the time he invited Frau Quorp to see his trophy room. He liked her flirtatious manner and girlish ringlets, but afterward her immense girth left him revolted.

The lights became a gunship and troop carrier. The helicopters landed and men disembarked, one of them standing at the edge of the landing pad to observe the open sluice gates.

The radio operator with the busted lip cautiously raised his hand. "Diego Suarez is on the line, Obergruppenführer. They're under attack. From Jews."

"More likely drunken sailors, setting off fireworks for Führertag."

"I . . . I think you should speak to them."

He made a dismissive gesture and waited for Quorp and his men.

A dozen troops entered, forming a perimeter around the room. They were equipped for a showdown: helmets and BK44s, grenades clinking on their belts. Globus recognized some of them; they stared through him, their faces steely. An officer followed, dressed in the black uniform of Kongo, half an ear missing. He glanced at Globus, then asked who was in charge of the dam.

After a pause, one of the technicians stepped forward. "I am the chief engineer."

"Shut the floodgates."

"Leave them," said Globocnik. "My island, my dam. I built the thing."

The one-eared officer repeated his command, and when the technician remained undecided he moved to a radio operator and conferred in whispers. A switch was flicked, and Hochburg's voice filled the room:

> . . . I am taking control of Madagaskar with the full agreement and
> authority of the RSHA and Reichsführer-SS . . . Governor Globocnik
> has been temporarily relieved of his command . . .

Globus looked forward to stuffing Hochburg's mouth full of Feuerstein's ashes. He killed the recording.

The technician began issuing commands to shut the gates.

"You must be one of Hochburg's girl Fridays," said Globus. "Who are you?"

"Brigadeführer Derbus Kepplar. I am placing you under arrest."

Globus detected a slight distaste in his tone, and forced a chuckle. "On whose authority?"

"You heard the recording. This island is under the emergency control of the Reichsführer. I have the paperwork here."

"Where's Hochburg?"

"Mandritsara."

Globus stared out the window into the inky darkness and raised the detonator. "Call off your men." He addressed the technician. "And I want the sluice gates left open."

No one moved.

Globus held down the red button to the count of three. "The dam is rigged, Brigadeführer. A couple of clicks—and the whole thing goes."

"Don't be so rash. Think what the United States will do."

"The Yankees can go fuck themselves."

Kepplar made a signal, and the soldiers raised their weapons; a ring of muzzles was pointed at Globus's head. He felt no alarm, only bubbling rage. Kepplar's holster remained fastened. He demanded the detonator.

Across the room the radio operator raised his hand. "It's Diego again."

Globus ignored him.

A second operator raised his arm, then the one next to him and the one after—till they all had their hands in the air, like a line of schoolchildren. Every one of them had Diego.

The first operator cleared his throat. "It's Admiral Dommes. He needs to speak to you urgently."

Without taking his eyes off Kepplar, Globus stepped back, picked up the phone, and was assaulted by a barrage of accusations.

"You guaranteed the Jews wouldn't attack," said Dommes. "That you were restoring the situation."

"So now the navy can't deal with a few bandits."

"The whole sky is ablaze."

"Don't be so dramatic."

"Listen," replied Dommes coldly and held the receiver away. Down the telephone line Globus heard a rapid series of bangs like the firecrackers his men used to toss at Jews in Vienna. Crumps and booms.

"We're being attacked by an army," said the admiral. "The air defenses are out. The southern quay is a fireball. Is this your promise of order?"

His voice remained as level as a calm sea, the same way Globus's father's used to before he horsewhipped him as a boy. It wasn't the beating he hated the most or being punished by a deserter; it was the man's lack of passion.

Dommes continued in his monotone: "If you can no longer control the island, Governor Globocnik, the Kriegsmarine will."

The phone dropped from Globus's ear. He let it settle against his chest, wondering whether Dommes could hear the furious thud of his heart. There was a din inside his head, a sense that his brain was being squeezed. First Hochburg wanted his island, now the navy; neither would get the better of him. He would prove to Germania who was the bloodiest of all. A speech came to mind that he'd given during his final days in the East. "We ought to bronze tablets," he had told his listeners, "on which it is inscribed that it was we—*we*—who had the courage to complete this gigantic task."

He buried his thumb into the detonator.

Once.

Twice.

Kepplar sprung forward as he depressed it. "Herr Oberst is down there—"

Globus shoved him away and listened. There was a faint tremor through the floor that reminded him of the war, when panzers rumbled past on their way to smash the Soviets. He peered through the window, expecting the dam to vanish at any moment.

Nothing.

Then the sound of rain whipping the opposite window, the one that overlooked the reservoir.

Globus and Kepplar spun round to see huge spouts firing into the sky. A wave rolled across the body of water, away from the dam.

"Fucking sappers!" bellowed Globus. He should never have trusted them; they'd set the charges on the wrong side.

Kepplar was ashen. "That's just the detonation."

They both turned to the view the front again. The ground was shaking now. Red lamps flashed on the control consoles. The overhead lights flickered and died. Parts of the ceiling dropped.

The dam was cast in a weak silver glow. From this distance Globocnik could make out the remainders of the graffiti the Jews had painted, a ghostly Star of David that his men had scrubbed off. Cracks were appearing, widening, splitting, coughing out streams of water. A great section fell away in the shape of a heart.

Then the entire structure collapsed, unleashing a mountain of black water.

CHAPTER SIXTY-TWO

Mandritsara Hospital
21 April, 05:00

THE BROWNING SLIPPED from Madeleine's hands and clattered to the floor. The blast of the gunshot filled the room and took a long time to fade, as though it were a gas dispersing. Only when the last reverberation had ceased did Burton become aware of the rumble outside.

He stared into Madeleine's face. Every muscle was straining, the light in her eyes frozen. Then her expression relaxed, her jaw loosening and her tongue sneaking between her lips. She offered him a brief, watchful smile like when they used to return to London by train. As they approached the city they sat apart, in case they were spotted, and she would flash him crafty grins from the other side of the carriage. Burton experienced an infinitesimal moment of hope that hidden beneath her dress was a steel plate that had protected her from the bullet.

Madeleine remained in Cranley's grasp. He was blank with shock. He let go, and she dropped away from him, landing on her side. There was no exit wound; Cranley patted his torso in disbelief.

Burton watched a spot of burgundy expand around Madeleine's stomach. She had shot herself in the same place that Patrick had taken shrapnel at Dunkirk. His friend had cursed and bellowed, lost pints of blood—but Burton had managed to sew him up in the basement of a bombed-out building. He had survived. Madeleine was lying in a hospital; they were surrounded by rooms of cotton batting and bandages and drugs.

The rumble outside was deepening.

Burton looked at his Browning: it was trembling across the floor toward him. He snatched it up before Cranley could.

The walls started to shudder.

There was a cracking, buckling sound from the fabric of the building.

The skeleton in the corner toppled over. Microscopes and centrifuges crashed to the floor. The soldier who'd been guarding Burton looked round in bewilderment. Behind him, through the frosted glass, Burton saw the trees in the courtyard bow and vanish. A black wall surged upward, filling the window. Filling his entire view.

The glass exploded inward.

All the breath was punched out of Burton. He was underwater, pinned against the far wall by a bone-flattening force. Bubbles detonated around his face. There was nothing but deafening noise in his ears. Next instant his mouth was in the air again. He sucked in choking gulps of oxygen.

The whole hospital shook. Fissures ran up the walls as the torrent churned through the room. The air was thick with the roar of water and stinking, stinging brine. Burton was whirled around. He refused to let go of his Browning and buried it under his belt. The soldier crashed into him, then vanished. Seconds later he saw Madeleine, semiconscious, jerking like a broken doll. Somehow he caught her, looping his arm through her bound wrists.

A section of wall disintegrated. The water level dropped several feet, sucking them out of the room, into the corridor beyond. Burton felt as if he were running; then his feet hit the ground and he was splashing forward, the water frothing at his waist. His arm was still caught around Madeleine. There was no time to check her. He heaved her onto his shoulder and staggered forward.

They were in a windowless passage, the water surging as it pumped from the room they had just been washed out of. A terrible sound—stone-screeching, disemboweling—rocked the air. So far the lights were unaffected; Burton feared trying to escape in pitch blackness. He waded to the end of the passage, the level rising the whole time, and turned into another corridor where the water was lower. There were doors on one side, a bank of windows on the other. At the far end, a sign indicated an emergency exit.

Burton carried Madeleine toward it as another ominous rumbling began to build.

He was halfway there when the windows darkened and burst inward. They went one after the other, as though detonated in sequence. Burton had a flash of memory: Tünscher idiotically drunk in Marseille; he'd gone to an aquarium and fired at a tank.

He was swept off his feet, clutching Madeleine, positioning her body so she was knitted into him. They rolled and banged down the corridor, streaking past the emergency exit, one moment submerged, the next inches from the ceiling.

Submerged—ceiling—submerged again—

A plunging sensation . . . and they were dumped onto the floor. They bounced to a halt. Another corridor, the water inexplicably at knee height.

Burton lifted Madeleine up. She was limp, her eyes closed. He pressed his fingers beneath her jaw and detected a weak pulse. He crushed his mouth against hers, blowing all the energy from his lungs. Her chest expanded; water flared from her nostrils. He breathed into her again: another lungful of life.

A new roar rebounded through the corridor—elemental, unstoppable.

The ground shook as if from an earthquake. Burton secured his Browning, hugged Madeleine tight into his arms. Braced himself.

The wave broke over him as it had done on board the Ark. He cartwheeled, his nose and mouth charged with bubbles. There was no memory of Germania this time, no sweet ice cream breath or Maddie clambering on top of him. No whispered talk of the life they were going to share.

Burton sensed that they were accelerating. Objects bobbed and battered around them; he tried to protect his head as best he could. He felt cuts along the length of his body. Every time he broke the surface, he could make out nothing except lights and rushing walls and the sheer force of the water. He heaved Madeleine into him in an effort to pump her chest and keep her airways open. She was as heavy as a corpse. They disappeared below the water.

Burton became aware of black clouds and humidity. They were fluming through trees.

He caught hold of one, his fingers digging into the bark. The trunk was bending against the flood. He struggled to get a better grip. If it had just been him, if he had two hands to anchor himself, he might have held on.

He saw the hospital behind them. Water surged and foamed around the building, blasting wide every opening, crumbling the structure, snatching up trees like they were matchsticks. The waves carried a cargo of flotsam. Burton glimpsed movement on one of the pagoda roofs. He thought it was Cranley: a huge black gecko, skittering over the tiles to the main building. With its deep foundations and solid walls it stood steadfast. Beyond, the night was black: every light in the Sofia Reservation had been extinguished.

Burton's grip weakened . . . and broke.

The current dragged them away. All he could do was hold Madeleine as they were spun and whirled and ducked.

Gradually the ferocity of the water began to subside, and they drifted through a steep-sided valley. Debris bobbed around them: timber, pieces of torn corrugated roofing, the broken spines of trees.

And bodies.

Hundreds of bodies: floating facedown, some with their clothes ripped free of their skin. The naked flesh was grotesquely white in the darkness.

Burton grabbed hold of a wooden joist and used it to keep them buoyant. Madeleine spluttered and moaned. He used his good arm to beat against the waves, in the direction of the shore. Ahead, on top of a hill, was the Totenburg he'd spied earlier. A powerful searchlight illuminated it from behind, turning the granite towers into silhouettes.

He aimed toward them, landing on a muddy bank. Burton heaved himself out of the water, then Madeleine. He leaned close, a grateful laugh exploding from him when he felt the tickle of her breath.

He placed his hand on her forehead. "Maddie . . . ? Maddie, we got out."

She opened her eyes; they were drained of color. "I'm cold."

He lifted her dress and examined the wound. It was a perfect circle, washed clean but pouring blood again. He pressed around it to feel how deeply the bullet had entered. Madeleine had fired at such close range that it hadn't gained velocity: the shell was lodged close to the surface.

Tears of relief speckled his eyes. He should be able to pry it out.

It would be an excruciating procedure, but so long as he stanched the bleeding he could save her. More scars for them to compare one day. He bolstered himself with a glimpse into the future. They were in bed—goose down and warm, dry cotton—caressing each other's war wounds, Burton insistent that a bullet to the belly was worse than losing your hand. And a lot more reckless.

The water continued to rise. Madeleine's calves were submerged.

Burton glanced above at the Totenburg; the light gleaming from it had a serene, celestial quality. It would be a good place to shelter her. Then he would find a guard tower, an outpost, anything that had medical supplies, patch her up and get her back to Antzu. When he and Tünscher had first arrived at the city, they passed a primitive hospital. Burton wished his old friend were with him now, and not only for his medical training. He hoped he'd gotten away safely. Perhaps he was already in Nosy Be, being fussed over by nurses, smoking a Bayerweed.

"I'm going to have to move you, Maddie. I'm going to carry you up top."

She nodded weakly.

He scooped her into his arms and trudged upward through the mud, struggling not to slip. The water chased him the whole way, lapping at his boots. Once he stumbled, and Madeleine let out a shriek of pain. He fought his way on. There was a rushing in his ears like the great rivers of Africa he had known: the Niger and Limpopo, the cataracts of Congo.

Each step he took caused Madeleine to wince. He kept murmuring apologies until she placed her finger over his lips. Her hands were still bound.

Burton managed another twenty feet before he had to stop. The slope was too steep now, slippery with mud and grass. His strength was deserting him. He laid her down and settled next to her, panting for breath.

"You're going to have to climb on me," he said. The crest of the hill was a sickle of light.

"Piggyback? Like with Elli on the farm?"

"Like with Elli."

"Promise me you'll take care of her."

"We can make it, Madeleine. You'll have to fight for every hour, but we can make it."

Her voice was bleak. "Jacoba was right. There's no way off this island."

"We use the fishing fleet at Varavanga."

She was silent for several moments, her face buried in the mud, then asked, "What about the hospital?"

He shook his head.

"Do you think the twins were—"

"Nothing can happen to them anymore."

"I wish you'd seen them, that I could have passed them from my arms to yours. Just once."

"We'll mourn them when we're far away." He lay flat. "Climb on, we're nearly there."

At first he thought she was refusing or had given up and wanted to wait and die; then he realized she was building herself up to it. She rolled on top of him, crying out before she settled, her hands gripping his shoulders.

Burton continued upward, half-crawling on his hands and knees. They had left the waterline, but their clothes were soaked and heavy. Every time his stump disappeared into the earth, a shard stabbed through him. The ascent was agonizingly slow, the mud as sludgy as fresh cement.

Suddenly Madeleine's weight was gone.

He watched her flailing legs disappear over the brow of the hill, into the light, as she was lifted up and away. Burton struggled after her—before a huge, brutal hand was thrust into his face.

"Take it," said a familiar voice.

Burton was too exhausted to fight. He let out a sigh that emptied his throat, then grasped hold. There was something almost reassuring about its strength and solidity. He looked up: a single black eye bored into him, as black as the devil's hangman.

CHAPTER SIXTY-THREE

Diego Suarez
21 April, 05:10

SALOIS HAD FAILED.

The heavens were full of planes—but they were Me-362s, their tail fins spotted with swastikas. He watched them take off from the runway at Kap Diégo in silver pairs, then circle low over the base. A cauldron of jet engine roars, repeating over and over, with moments of quiet before the next fighters screamed past. Their vapor trails were gray threads against the lustrous sky.

Rolland would not be able to sail thousands of fresh troops to Africa; the war on the continent would slaughter itself to a stalemate. America, the distant hope of every Jew, would remain a bystander to their extinction.

The last wisps of green smoke for the bombers were fading. Salois tightened the tourniquets that were keeping his life trapped inside his legs. He felt no anger. Or injustice or blazing disappointment.

Yet he was aware that something had been extinguished inside him. Should he have heeded Madeleine and Burton? In preparation for Diego, Cranley had commissioned an intricate model of the base for Salois and his team to study. At the end of one briefing, Cranley rested his hand on it.

"When it's over, I'll have this installed at home, to remind us of our achievement." He offered a smile to Salois, and for once it was full of humor. "Much better than a medal."

Why come all this way on a pretense? During their last radio contact, Cranley said he was in position near Mazunka. His raid could have failed; he could have been captured or killed. A storm front might have swept across the Mozambique Channel, forcing the bombers back to the base. Or maybe they had run into a random Messerschmitt patrol. Salois thought how often he and his fellow guerrillas had stumbled across Nazis in Kongo and the intense gun battles that followed. Battles that left the jungle littered with bodies, while he remained untouched.

Salois searched himself and knew that Cranley hadn't betrayed him.

Across the water in Weissfelsenbucht, the aircraft carriers had slipped their moorings and were reversing out of port, heading toward the darkness and security of the ocean. The arsenal on the quayside below had spent most of its munitions; it sounded like a wet log dumped on a fire now: thrumming with heat, popping and cracking occasionally. Its beauty was no longer spellbinding—but cruel. A reminder of how close he'd come to success. Teams of firefighters doused the blaze. Yaudin watched the scene without triumph.

"You should go," Salois said to him, "while there's a chance."

"Where to?" replied the Jupo chief. "I'll never escape. As soon as you didn't surrender, Major, I knew it was up for me."

"You could have stayed in Antzu."

"Just because we don't want to fight the Nazis doesn't make us cowards."

Salois wondered who Yaudin had been in his previous life. His rough accent could encompass anything: builder, tram inspector, hoodlum.

"What will happen to your family?"

"The same as Antzu." He was choked with anguish. "As the whole of Madagaskar. It's a disaster—"

Salois cast his eye over the intact base. "Doesn't look like it to me."

"We both failed, Major. There are terrible days ahead; Globocnik will ship us to the reservations for this. Or worse."

"That could still bring the Americans."

A bitter snort. "Is that the best you Vanillas can wish for? To soak this island in blood and hope that a distant land might save us? We'll never defeat the Nazis; we can only try to live with them."

"A dupe's promise."

"Before I left Antzu, I gave my wife two pots: one of poison, one of honey." His voice was plaintive now. "Honey is so rare, I'd been saving it for a special occasion. If the worst happens, I told her, mix it with the poison . . . for her and the family to feast. I don't want them to suffer or starve; I don't want my children to see murder. Let them go quietly."

"That's the best you can wish for? To go quietly?"

"All I wanted was to preserve the thin slice of life we have. To keep death at bay."

"The hardest punishment of all," replied Salois.

He reached for the tourniquets around his legs, unbuckled the first belt—but didn't loosen it.

"I don't want you to see me die," he said.

Yaudin moved away, to the edge of the steps: a shadow against the fulgent light of the bay and the dying flames. Jet fighters continued to patrol overhead, flying so low that the missile battery trembled with each pass.

At least mine won't be a quiet death, thought Salois. He undid the belt around his left thigh, then the right. Immediately he felt heat soaking through his trousers, spreading across the ground, as if he were an old, incontinent man. A mortal man. And behind it the first hint of a deep, pitiless cold. So this was the hand of death.

He had been dazed by the speed with which Frieda's body lost its heat. It leached out of her, out of the whole room, till the air numbed him. Of all the deaths he would come to witness, hers was the most pointless. The most meaningless. He had killed Frieda over what to call the child growing inside her.

He had been named after his father and his father's father, a choice that veiled the family background; it was a tradition he expected to continue. Frieda was too free a spirit for such conventions; she was proud of her heritage. She had something else in mind.

—*So now you don't like my name,* he'd said. His temper was slipping, flaring. He enjoyed the power it gave him.

—*Of course I do! That's why I want us to marry, so I can take it.*

—*But not my first name.*

—*I want to call the baby Reuben.*

—*What if it's a girl?*

—*He's a boy.* Frieda patted her belly. *He's a Reuben.* She smiled, but he saw that she was nervous. *Listen close and you'll hear him say it.*

He wouldn't be contradicted. *No son of mine will ever be called that. He'll sound like a Jew.*

—*We are Jews.*

—*The world doesn't need to know.*

She looked so crestfallen; it enraged him further.

—*We're not calling him Reuben,* he had yelled, the devil rising in his heart.

They were the last words Frieda Salois, the woman who was going to be his wife, heard.

Troops with machine guns had gathered at the base of the steps leading to the missile battery. They began to climb.

A band of intense orange dawn was breaking over the ocean. There was a whiff of ylang-ylang in the air.

Salois took out Madeleine's knife. She'd wondered if he'd been spared for some great deed; she was wrong. There was no redemption. His death would be as meaningless as the millions before his, and the millions after. At least she and Burton and Abner had Kap Ost and the boat to freedom. He cut open his trousers, then peeled off his jacket and hurled it away. He was naked except for his boots. Blood continued to gush from his legs. When the Nazis found him, he wanted them to see the color of his skin. Somewhere on his forearm, lost among thousands of other digits, was his own number. He had gladly let it be obscured: it was a number that belonged to a man who never existed.

When he had arrived in Algeria to begin his service—the "ride on the tiger" they called it—all recruits were instructed to adopt new identities; it was the Legion way. That suited him well; the life he'd once lived was over. No one—his family, his few friends, the authorities—would be able to trace him. He stood in line, the sun hammering down on him, waiting for the clerk *d'engagements* to fill in his papers. It was hotter than he had ever known, hot as hell. A fitting location for his penance.

When he reached the clerk, it was obvious what name to assume. He would give life to the dead. "Reuben Salois!" he declared.

The clerk copied it down. "Fucking Jews," he muttered under his breath.

Yaudin cocked his head. "They're coming, Major."

Shouts and the thump of boots were rising from the steps. Yaudin threw down his rifle and lifted his hands in surrender.

"Turn around!" ordered a voice.

Yaudin did as he was told, repeating his family's names to himself. He avoided Salois's stare.

There was a burst of automatic gunfire. A guard dragged Yaudin's body out of the way and put a final shot through his skull.

The rest surrounded Salois: a semicircle of men roused from sleep or celebrating Führertag. They aimed their weapons at him but kept their distance, not wanting to step into the glossy dark pool creeping from his body.

Salois watched his blood with immense gratitude; it was a relief to meet this moment. A stillness settled on him. There were worse things than death.

That had been his last thought as he stood on the beach before his execution during the Mered Ha-vanil. He closed his eyes and remembered the firing squad and his miraculous escape from Madagaskar. The mass of numbers he'd recited as he drifted across the waves to Africa.

It was time to leave the spell of this bare island again. Salois spread his arms and offered his indigo chest.

CHAPTER SIXTY-FOUR

Mandritsara
21 April, 05:20

HOCHBURG LIFTED MADELEINE and carried her across the mud, into the refuge of the Totenburg. Once her eyelids flickered and she stared at him with dull pupils—but she was too spent to fight and retreated into semi-consciousness. Feuerstein jangled on his wrist, still cuffed to him; Burton followed close behind.

There's a dying woman in my arms, thought Hochburg, *a Jew wizard and a vengeful son on my tail.* He figured there must be a parable in it, a lesson he could take back to Africa, or maybe some tragic, convoluted joke.

Kepplar's Walküre flew over the granite pillars and came in to land. Hochburg glimpsed him in the bubble cockpit, anxiously peering below. Hochburg's own gunship was parked close by, its searchlight switched to full power, illuminating everything in an eerie glow.

He laid Madeleine down inside the Totenburg, next to the bronze obelisk. Dawn approached, its rays kindling the bronze; the reflection caught Madeleine's face, giving her an orangey hue, full of mocking vitality. Soldiers stood in pairs at the bases of the towers; they had automatically positioned themselves, as though guarding the names of the fallen. The air smelled autumnal, of earthy vegetation and skin pressed against metal.

Hochburg removed his jacket, warm from his chest, and draped it over her body. "What happened?"

"She's been shot," replied Burton. His face was marked with vicious cuts, swabbed clean from the flood. The soldiers had disarmed him and given Hochburg his pistol. "A stomach wound. I can save her if I get medical help."

"There's nothing around here."

"I need to stop the bleeding."

"But there is the hospital at Lava Bucht."

"It's too far, it'll take hours—"

"Not if I fly her. She can be in surgery in thirty minutes."

Burton let out a crushing, hopeless breath of air. He hid his face, and nodded.

"It's an SS hospital," said Hochburg. "She'll receive the best care."

He raised her up, legs dangling over his elbow. Madeleine gave a little cry and arched her chest to reveal a thin, pale throat.

"Careful!" hissed Burton.

Kepplar's helicopter had landed, its rotors buffeting the air. Hochburg strode through the wind and noise, beneath the towers of the dead . . . and was transported to a different time, a different setting, far to the west of Madagaskar. He heard Eleanor's closing breaths, shallow and broken, as if he were clasping her again. Was overwhelmed by his incapacity to save her . . .

A silence descended within him.

He looked at Madeleine. Then Burton, their eyes reaching into each other's.

The boy understood at once, in a way that only a fellow traveler on the same hard road could.

Burton's mouth shriveled in panic. "No. Please, no."

Hochburg knelt, laying Madeleine gently back on the ground, Feuerstein bending with him like a supplicant. He folded his tunic around her to keep her comfortable. Here was the vengeance he had been seeking since he ordered the *Ibis* torpedoed. Since he lost Eleanor.

A vengeance more complete than death, more agonizing than torture or taking Madeleine as his own.

He stroked her face. She was peaceful, her cropped head giving her a vulnerable appearance while at the same time hardening the contours of her cheeks. He mapped the shape of her skull.

Burton leapt across her body and grabbed Hochburg. "You save her!" he roared.

The soldiers restrained him, forcing the boy to his knees.

Hochburg signaled that Burton was not to be harmed. He spoke in a low, beguiling voice: "It is time you learned the true meaning of what it is to suffer, as I have suffered these past twenty years."

Burton crawled toward him. "Please, Walter. I beg you. You can save her."

"You must share my daily torment. Know what it is to have the light inside you gutter."

There was a click of heels as Kepplar joined them. He bustled past Hochburg, stood behind Burton, and with juvenile triumph clamped hold of his shoulders. Burton barely noticed; he was squeezing Madeleine's hand, cooing that he'd save her, the same futile way Hochburg had once done.

"I feared the worst," said Kepplar. "I thought you were down in the valley."

Hochburg looked through the towers at the writhing water below. It had lost its destructive force and was now no more turbulent than a river during the rainy season. In the dawning light it was the color of coffee and seemed infested with crocodiles. No, not crocodiles: bodies. Thousands of them, the reservation flushed away, as Globocnik had threatened.

"I should never have trusted you with the dam," he said to Kepplar. "Once more you fail me."

"I tried to stop him," replied his former deputy. "It was too late."

"Where is Globus now?"

"Cuffed and under arrest. I left him at the dam."

Hochburg sighed heavily, impressed again by the limitations of those beneath him. He adjusted the bandage around his eye. The need for his superweapon was more urgent than ever. "Did he have anything to say?"

"He was delirious. He wanted cognac to toast his mansion in Ostmark."

"Ostmark! Globocnik is finished; he'll be court-martialed for this. I'll make sure he's found guilty."

More corpses flowed by, as if their source were an endless font of bodies.

"It's time for us to leave, Derbus."

Hochburg stooped and pried Madeleine's hand from Burton's. It was cold, as cold as Eleanor's the last time he held it. "She's beautiful," he said, pressing her skin to his lips. "Too beautiful for this godforsaken place. Beauty that must die."

He gave Burton a curt nod, snapped his fingers at Kepplar, and walked away.

+ + +

"You're just leaving him?" Kepplar experienced a rush of incredulity.

"Yes," replied Hochburg. His voice was staid, certain, with no hint of jest.

There was a pitting in Kepplar's stomach. He glanced at the soldiers, hoping they had been briefed before he arrived and that their expressions might convey what was happening. His hands were welded to Cole's shoulders; he was glad he had the other man to keep him steady.

"But . . ." Kepplar could find no more words.

"Let him go," said Hochburg impatiently. "We've a long journey ahead." He made a spinning gesture with his finger to the pilot of his Walküre. The engine began to burn and whine.

Kepplar stared at the back of Cole's head, where the medulla oblongata joined the neck, and thought how he wanted to strike him; you could kill a man with a single punch there. A dullness was creeping behind his eyes, a pressure building in his sinuses as if he'd gulped down a glass of ice water. He shunned cold drinks, despite the heat: Hochburg viewed them as a sign of weakness.

"I've barely slept since Roscherhafen. Haven't eaten, haven't shaved." His voice yo-yoed.

"That is the price of your position, *Gruppen*führer. Why you are dressed in black."

At last he was a Gruppenführer again. Kepplar felt cheated. "But all those men who died. On my patrol boat—and before that, in Kongo." It took an effort to speak. ". . . And now you're letting him go?"

"Yes," repeated Hochburg.

"Why?"

"If I have to explain, you'll never understand."

"He deserves a pyre, like you promised last year." He drummed his chest. "Like you were going to do with me. That was Cole's sentence."

Hochburg replied with a lilt of satisfaction: "His punishment must be more severe."

"You promised."

"There will be no burning."

Hochburg stepped over to him and freed his hands from Cole's shoulders; Kepplar hadn't realized how tight his grip was. "This morning we fly to Muspel. I have a secret task for you there: you will help build me a wonder weapon. A weapon to deliver us the final victory against the British."

"I don't want to go to Muspel."

Kepplar remembered the pure blue skies and furnace winds, his lips either perpetually cracked or congealed with petroleum jelly.

"To serve is to obey, Derbus. Given your failure at the dam, I'm being generous."

"You blame me for Globocnik?"

"I'm making what I can of your limitations."

His tone was paternal and mildly derisive. He would never speak to Globus in that manner, thought Kepplar, or to other thugs lower down the ranks. The pimply grooms in Antzu had been afforded a modicum of respect. Hochburg was contemptuous of these men, yet their shared easiness with killing made them equals of a sort, an approval denied Kepplar even though he was the one who had delivered Burton Cole.

The sheer irrelevance of his doggedness was clear. There was only one way to be worthy of a man who paved his home in skulls.

"Our work here is done," said Hochburg, putting his arm around Kepplar's shoulders to lead him away. Kepplar recalled those months in Roscherhafen when he'd longed for the Oberstgruppenführer's touch. The rest of his life would be defined by his shortcomings unless he acted now.

Something broke in Kepplar, like the dam burst he'd just witnessed.

He shrugged off Hochburg's arm, implacable with rage. If he didn't understand the hold Cole had over his master, he understood how to destroy it. Kepplar unfastened his Walther P38 pistol: he would shoot Burton through the head, then put the woman out of her misery. Two shots to free himself of his humiliation in the Schädelplatz. Two shots to prove himself to Hochburg.

He flicked off the safety catch and felt a sense of release.

"Put it down!" he heard the Oberstgruppenführer say.

He remembered the first service weapon he received in Africa and his anticipation of thrusting it in a black face.

Kepplar didn't feel the blast. The sound bounced around the towers, like the toll of a bell, distorted and unnatural, as if it would never end. A pfennig-sized hole appeared in the breast of his uniform. The material around it thickened, sopping wet and terrifyingly hot. It was too black to show the blood. The uncocked P38 slipped from his hand.

Hochburg lowered his smoking pistol and caught Kepplar. There was no remorse in his expression.

"I couldn't let you kill him," he said. "Not when I finally have him like this."

The breath was withering in Kepplar; he went to reply—and found it impossible to inflate his lungs.

He grasped feebly at Hochburg. "But the paperwork . . ."

+ + +

Burton watched Hochburg lay the one-eared officer on the floor, then order the guards to clear away his body. He handled the Browning.

"A fine weapon. I shall keep it, as a memento of this time."

Madeleine stirred and called out for Burton. She kept having snatches of lucidity, separated by silence; the gap between them was getting longer. Her breathing was steady but flimsy. Burton tucked Hochburg's tunic around her to keep her warm. He was convinced that he could still save her. Madeleine had survived too much for it to end here; she had earned her right to life. Then he heard Patrick, tapping out his pipe and whispering: *Hope is the last thing to go.*

"You don't have to do this," said Burton.

Hochburg drew himself up to his full height. "Man's cry to the heavens since the beginning of time."

"Double your revenge on me—but spare her."

A sad, cruel shake of his head.

"I beg you."

Hochburg stared through the pillars at the churning, reborn river. The thousands of bodies. He spoke pensively:

"After today, no amount of threats or diplomacy will assuage the United States. They will send their navy; the American Jewish Committee will be unmuzzled. War is coming, the likes of which we cannot imagine." There was a miserable-looking Jew chained to his wrist. Hochburg raised him to his feet. "I know you'll search for me, Burton; I'll be waiting. Back in our homeland. In Africa."

He retreated to the edge of the Totenburg, surrounded by soldiers, then paused on the threshold and removed one of the troops' helmets. He tossed it at Burton.

"To dig with." He indicated the black uniform covering Madeleine. "You'll find everything else you need inside."

Hochburg bent into the wind of the helicopter. Moments later his Walküre roared overhead, bearing south till the sound of it faded. Water trickled down the massive stone towers and dripped noisily into hidden culverts; from the valley came the rushing of the river.

The life was vanishing from Madeleine's skin. She was awake again, blinking at him. Burton eased back Hochburg's tunic and examined the wound. Her arms were still bound where Cranley had tied them. Her dress was soaked red. He found the bullet buried a fingernail's depth beneath her skin and tried to think of it as nothing worse than a splinter. Like the splinters he'd removed from her on the farm: soaking a finger in hot water till it was plump, carefully easing out the sliver of wood with tweezers.

As if overhearing his thoughts, she shook her head. "My papa used to say that the worst place to go was on the operating table."

"I've got to try—"

She shook her head again, and gazed at the roiling currents below. "The island will rise up now. It's what Salois wanted . . . Abner too."

"I don't care."

Silence except for the river. Then:

"Not in here, Burton."

He had to look away, his eyes resting on the pillars. Only one of them bore names of the fallen, the others smooth; the names were in oversized letters, as though engraved by children. Not enough Germans had died during the first rebellion to fill the memorial.

"I want sky," she breathed. "Sun and grass, not stone."

He scooped her up, Hochburg's tunic as tight around her as a shroud. She mewled as she was lifted, her body sagging in the middle. Burton brought her from the shadow of the Totenburg into the dawn. The sky was broken with dark clouds; there was a sprinkle of fading stars and a strip of light on the horizon.

"There," she said.

Farther along the ridge stood several trees, their trunks sheltered by low palm fronds. He carried her to the spot; it reminded him of the copse where he'd hidden with Alice all those months ago in Hampstead. The ground smelled mushroomy and damp. After he laid her down, he broke off some fronds, arranging them under her as a mat, removed his jacket, and propped it behind her head. She murmured, "Thank you." The first of the birds had started to call and sing; it was agonizing to hear. Burton raged, raged against the quickening of the light. Pink and yellow were seeping into the clouds.

"It's a Battenberg sky," he said. "Remember when you came up with that?" His voice broke. "How we used to watch them on the farm?"

Her eyes were closed; the rise and fall of her chest was becoming weaker.

Burton curled his fingers into hers and sat cross-legged, gradually sinking lower and lower to catch the wisps of her breath until his ear hovered over her heart. He was overpowered by the riot in his head, mute with the things he wanted to say. Everything seemed at once too portentous and too trivial.

He wanted to slide on top of Maddie and bind himself to her—but feared causing her more pain. He wanted to die. Most of all, he wanted to see her as an old lady: skin loosening around her neck, hair in a gray bun, her face wise, wrinkled, and beautiful, smiling at him.

A shaft of watery sunlight broke through the branches. Suddenly she lurched awake and grabbed his severed arm where the bone ended. Her voice was ferocious.

"Find him," she said. "Kill him."

+ + +

Burton wasn't aware of her final breath; it was too delicate. Not even enough to blow out a candle. All he knew was that there came a moment when he looked at Madeleine and everything they had together—everything they built and planned and dreamed of—was gone.

CHAPTER SIXTY-FIVE

THE GREAT HALL of the Reich rose over Germania like a snow-covered mountain.

It had been inaugurated on 30 January 1950, twenty-five years after a convict in Landsberg prison sketched his first designs for it. The hall reached a quarter of a kilometer into the sky, was fronted with a colonnade of bloodred pillars, and could accommodate 180,000 people beneath its cupola. On top of the dome stood the Nazi eagle, its talons clutching the globe. Symbolism for the simplest of minds.

Burton and Madeleine sat outside a café on the Kurfürstendamm, the hall glimpsed through the trees, looming over every other building. It was visible from every part of the city. You couldn't help but be awed by it: its sheer scale, the ambition of a mind that could conceive of such a structure. Even Madeleine was grudgingly impressed.

It was a mild, sunny afternoon. An accordion was playing close by; waiters in starched jackets flitted around them. On the table was a coffee-pot and slices of poppy seed cake. Madeleine had an elaborate sundae of cherry and pistachio ice cream drizzled with chocolate sauce that she was scooping up with a long silver spoon. Like an anteater, Burton joked—which only made her laugh like a sea lion, till they both had to stop eating to control themselves. Burton felt slightly dehydrated, lazy, and relaxed. It should have been a perfect afternoon, and yet neither of them had steered the conversation to the subject of their future.

"Why did your husband bring you here?" asked Burton suddenly.

It had been troubling him since he arrived. Cranley often shuttled between European cities and took Madeleine with him to spend long days alone. Bringing her to the heart of the Reich, however, was unnecessary. Her passport listed no ethnicity other than British, and with her dark looks she could have been from Rome or Madrid, but Burton was aware of her constant tension, her anxiety whenever someone shouted nearby or footsteps approached quickly from behind.

"He thought I should see the capital of the world."

The streets thronged with uniforms and sightseers from every continent. The Reich Tourism Association offered subsidized flights to Americans, Japanese, citizens of the CONE, and white subjects of the British Empire so they could marvel at Germania, then return home to spread the word.

Maddie continued eating her ice cream. Then laid down the spoon, coming to a decision. "Do you want the real reason?"

Burton was embarrassed; he had probed unnecessarily. "It doesn't matter."

"He wants to remind me how lucky I am. How I owe him everything." She had never been so critical of her husband. "Maybe he wants to scare me a little, so I don't take any of it for granted."

"I'd never do that to you," he replied.

She tapped him with her spoon. "I know." Her expression became serious. "I don't want to live like that anymore."

Burton felt emboldened, reckless. There had been a lack of permanence in his life; being with Madeleine had changed that. He wanted to build something. Here, now—in Germania, of all places!—seemed the right moment to begin. The words he'd been edging round the whole day were ready to spill out.

"I want you to leave him."

The accordion player reached the end of his tune. There was a ripple of applause.

"I've never said this to any woman, but I want us to live together. To grow old together."

Madeleine had simply replied yes, her face aglow as if she were holding a giant buttercup to it.

After they finished the ice cream, sharing dollops from the same spoon, they strolled to Burton's hotel. Hand in hand. As he walked, a contentment radiated through him that he had not known before. He had kept it locked out since childhood, not through fear or because of how fleeting it could be, but because he had no interest in being content. Happiness was for other people.

Now its warmth engulfed him.

He glanced at Madeleine and knew her heart was beating the same way.

+ + +

Burton remembered that moment as he dug her grave, a nugget of time that he wanted to last forever.

He had carried her body from the trees where she died to the next ridge: a lower, more secluded spot overlooking the river in one direction and rolling hills that eventually led to mangroves and the blue of the ocean in the other. He scraped off the top layers of earth with his hand, then used the helmet Hochburg had given him to dig, like he was bailing out water. The soil was soft and wet, easy to excavate.

The sun continued to dawn: the color of a ripe golden quince, the light diffuse. The wind was picking up.

He stripped to the waist and kept digging, deeper than was necessary, as if what had happened would become real only when he stopped. He tried to replay the rest of the afternoon in Germania—returning to the hotel, the fierceness of their lovemaking as though they were fighting over the bed, the breeze cooling them through the open window afterward—but the images kept deserting him. All he could muster were the first few paces away from the café, repeating over and again, with the Great Hall dominating the skyline.

Burton clambered out of the ground, removed Hochburg's tunic from Madeleine's body, and searched for a sharp piece of stone to cut the rope around her wrists. Once they were free he laid them across her chest, wondering how Cranley had managed to prevent her forearm from being tattooed. Then he licked his fingertips and used them to clean her face and smooth down her hair. He tidied her torn and filthy dress.

Finally, he lowered her into the hole.

It wasn't long enough. He had to pull her knees to her chest to make her fit. It gave her the look of a sleeping child, like on the farm when they checked Alice before retiring to bed.

Not once did he shed any tears. He was a husk.

The hardest part was throwing the first handful of dirt on top of her. Burton had to keep his eyes closed. When he opened them again, most of her body was covered, only an elbow and heel poking out of the soil. He replaced the rest of the earth, found some rocks, and piled the grave with them. There was nothing to make a headstone with.

What did it matter? He would never return to this spot. Or to Madagaskar. He would head to Varavanga and Tünscher's fishing boats.

By the time he had finished, the sun had risen fully and was beating on his back. He was immune to the light. Burton stood over the grave till the sweat dried on him, then slipped on his shirt. He heard the clatter of approaching rotor blades and watched a Bell helicopter follow the path of the river. On its tail fin was the American flag. It circled the valley twice; the man in the passenger seat was surveying the carnage through binoculars, taking photographs.

In the sunlight the river was a foaming millrace, orange-brown and bloated with bodies. Burton became aware of movement below. At first it was individuals, then groups of two or three, then tens and hundreds. Jews who had survived the flood were climbing the hills to higher ground and safety. Men, women, children; lone survivors and families. They raised their faces to the sun, basking in its rays.

The helicopter completed its second pass and headed back in the direction of Tana.

The next bank of rain clouds was gathering darkly to the west. Burton hurled the earth-smeared helmet over the side of the hill and knelt by the grave. He reached out, placing his single hand on the stones; the sun had begun to warm them. His throat was tight. He felt as though he had been knocked unconscious and was starting to come round, unable to piece together what had happened.

Burton went to say good-bye—but the words wouldn't come. He was incapable of speech.

He turned and walked away, picking up Hochburg's tunic; something solid knocked against him. In the left pocket he found a piece of sacking. He dumped the jacket and unwound the cloth: inside was the knife he had saved from his mother, the steel jagged from the years he'd spent whetting it. This was the weapon he had taken to Kongo to avenge himself against Hochburg. He tested its weight.

Find him. Kill him.

Who had Madeleine meant? Hochburg? Or Cranley?

Burton twisted the knife in his hand, the blade catching the morning light. It was sharp enough for both.

AUTHOR'S NOTE

The Madagaskar Plan is a work of fiction with a basis in historical fact. This history, and its interpretation, remains contentious and pivots on whether the Nazis were always determined to exterminate the Jews or if merely expelling them from Europe would have sufficed. It is beyond the scope of this note to examine all the controversies and contradictions raised by the "Madagaskar-Projekt." Nevertheless, I want to show that it was discussed at the highest levels, that multiple branches of government took the possibility seriously, and that given certain deviations from history it could have come to pass.

Although the Nazis' plans for the Jews were never benign, they may not always have been genocidal. In the early stages of the war, a policy of expulsion and ghettoization was pursued. The Lublin Reservation was established in October 1939 on the eastern fringes of the Reich, in conquered Poland. It was hoped that the entire Jewish population would eventually be deported there; transports began at once. Those who arrived found harsh conditions but no systematic killing. Lublin was run by an ambitious police chief and protégé of Himmler's: Odilo Globocnik. However, a lack of planning combined with a typhus epidemic and squabbling between different elements of the SS caused the project to collapse. There were also fears that Lublin was not a remote enough location in which to "quarantine" the Jews.

On 25 May 1940, Himmler formally suggested a more ambitious scheme (as the first epigraph of this novel shows): to deport the Jews to an African colony. Given previous statements he had made, he can only have meant Madagascar. The date is also significant: the eve of Dunkirk and less than a month before the French surrendered. The defeat of France would put its colony of Madagascar at Germany's disposal.

Hitler responded by stating that Himmler's idea was *"sehr gut und richtig"*— very good and correct—and that he should put it into action at once.[*]

The concept of exiling the Jews to Madagascar dates to the eighteenth

---

[*]Peter Witte, ed., *Der Dienstkalender Heinrich Himmlers, 1941/42* (Hamburg: Christians, 1999).

century, though the first treatise on the subject wasn't written until 1883 by Paul de Lagarde, professor of philology at Göttingen University. De Lagarde's work was later taken up by the Britons, an organization dedicated to spreading anti-Semitic propaganda throughout Europe. It was headed by Henry Hamilton Beamish, who met Hitler in 1923 to discuss the Madagascar Plan (the first occasion we know for certain when Hitler became aware of it). As the notion of banishing the Jews to the Indian Ocean became more widely known, various governments—including the British and French—considered it as a panacea for their Jewish populations. The plan found its most enthusiastic reception in Poland, which twice debated it (in 1926 and 1938) and which on the second occasion sent a delegation to Madagascar to draw up a feasibility study. The Lepecki Commission (two members of which were Jewish) reported challenging living conditions for whites and endemic malaria and concluded that a maximum of seven thousand families could be sent there. SS officials used this material when they began drawing up their own plans.

Why Madagascar? Over the decades, other remote possibilities were suggested, from British Guiana (Prime Minister Chamberlain's preference) to Ethiopia (President Roosevelt's), as well as Brazil and Angola. It was to Madagascar, however, that anti-Semites' imagination continually returned. The island's insular location obviously appealed, but much was also made of biblically inspired theories that Madagascar had been settled by Jews centuries before and that its inhabitants, the Malagasy, were their descendants. Spurious evidence included the Malagasy people's widespread circumcision and their observance of the Sabbath.*

After Hitler approved Himmler's plan, in May 1940, he discussed the subject with Mussolini, remarking that "an Israelite reserve could be created on Madagascar" (18 June), and he reviewed the logistical feasibility with the head of the German navy, Admiral Erich Raeder (20 June).

Feverish planning to create a *Grossgetto* (superghetto) in Madagascar gripped the Nazis in the summer of 1940. An initial proposal was completed on 3 July by Franz Rademacher of the Foreign Office, its purpose made explicit in the first paragraph: "all Jews out of Europe." It should be noted that this was not the first time the plan appeared in official Nazi documents. The first-ever mention is as early as 24 May 1934, in a memorandum to Reinhard Heydrich. Six years later, Heydrich insisted that the SS play a leading role in Rademacher's scheme and assigned Adolf Eichmann and Theo Dannecker to the task. All the discussion was of a "*territorial* final solution" (my italics). The finished

---

*For a detailed explanation of "why Madagascar?" see Eric T. Jennings's essay "Writing Madagascar Back into the Madagascar Plan," *Holocaust and Genocide Studies* 21, no. 2 (Fall 2007): 187–217.

text of the "Madagaskar-Projekt" was delivered on 15 August 1940 and circulated by Heydrich at the ministerial level. This is the most detailed account we have of how the Nazis intended to run the island, its stated aim

> to relocate approximately 4,000,000 Jews to Madagascar. In order to avoid lasting contact between the Jews and other peoples, an overseas solution of an insular nature is to be preferred to any other alternative.

To transport this number of people, a fleet of 120 ships would have to be procured, each ship with a capacity of 1,500 "units," two ships to leave daily. With a return journey time of sixty days, the document notes, "this would equate to a total of around one million Jews per year." This exodus was expected to take four years. Jews were to be sent in waves, with the first transports consisting of "farmers, construction experts and craftsmen." It would be financed by the compulsory acquisition and sale of all Jewish property and assets.

The island itself would be divided into sectors by country of origin. Jews would be put to work on a "large scale program to expand the transport network," building new roads and railways; rivers would be redirected. The WVHA, the SS economic department, wanted to take over existing French businesses using Jewish labor, especially the cash crops of "coffee, tea, cloves, vanilla, perfume and medicinal plants."* Madagascar was (and still is) the largest producer of vanilla in the world, something the SS expected to continue profiting from. The plan also mentions the establishment of a meat export industry.

A council of Jewish elders would help run the regional sectors, a system Heydrich had used in occupied Europe; the council would be subservient to the SS. Jews would also be allowed their own internal postal, health, and police services. As Madagascar would be a German mandate, and because Jews were barred from German citizenship, they would hold no nationality. Categorically, Madagascar would never be allowed to become a state. The island would be placed under the direct control of an SS police governor. Although it is not mentioned in the 15 August plan, documents elsewhere name Philipp Bouhler (head of the chancellery in Hitler's personal office and an old comrade of the Führer's) as the first candidate for the job.

Two further points are worth noting from Rademacher's initial proposal: (1) "Diego Suarez, . . . which [is] strategically important, will become a German

---

*The plan has little to say about the 24,000 French colonists living on the island, other than they would be "resettled and compensated," and nothing about the 3.6 million native Malagasy.

naval base"; (2) "the Jews will remain in German hands as a pledge for the future good behavior of the members of their race in America."

Was any of this credible? The issue divides historians. Some—Philip Friedman and Magnus Brechtken, for example—are dismissive of the plan, believing it to be a fantasy, a smoke screen to mask the true intentions of the Nazis. Others, such as Hans Jensen and Christopher Browning, insist that it must be taken seriously. There is plenty of evidence to suggest that many people at the time accepted the plan as a viable proposition.[*]

Aside from the involvement of Hitler, Himmler, and Heydrich, as well as Göring and other key figures not mentioned in this note, a huge amount of bureaucratic energy was expended on the plan in the summer of 1940. As early as July, Hans Frank, governor of the General Government (the Nazis' name for occupied Poland), was informed about Madagascar. He was sufficiently convinced by the sincerity of the plan to halt the construction of the ghetto in Kraków, deeming it no longer necessary because the Jews were going to be sent to Africa. A similar decision was reached in Warsaw. The same month, the Polish Jews themselves were informed that shortly "they would all leave for Madagascar."[†] In October, French Jews were readied for their journey below the equator. For those who question the sheer logistical difficulties of shipping four million people to Madagascar, it should be noted, as historian Mark Mazower does, that the years 1939–45 saw the largest experiment in socioethnic engineering in history, with millions of Jews, Poles, and ethnic Germans moved around Europe like pieces on a chessboard.[‡] Given this massive upheaval and the fanaticism of the SS, it is not impossible to imagine something similar happening—but by boat rather than rail.

The American Jewish Committee also considered the plan in earnest, issuing a detailed report in August 1941 stating that it would be a catastrophe: "no pogrom in history would equal . . . the indiscriminate dumping of millions of helpless people into a primitive, hostile environment."[§] This is perhaps the clinching piece of evidence for the plan's credibility. Even though the Nazis were still pursuing an expulsion policy in the summer of 1940, they had no interest in the Jews' long-term survival. The unfortunates arriving in Madagascar

---

[*]Hans Jensen's *Der Madagaskar Plan* (Munich: Herbig, 1997) is a comprehensive, book-length study of the plan and was indispensable in the writing of this novel. Unfortunately, it is not available in English. Christopher R. Browning's *The Origins of the Final Solution* (London: Heinemann, 2004) was another helpful text. Browning is especially interesting on how the Nazis evolved from a policy of expelling Jews to mass murder during the years 1939–42.

[†]From a diary entry by Adam Czerniaków, head of the Jewish Council in Warsaw, 1 July 1940.

[‡]See Mazower's *Hitler's Empire* (London: Allen Lane, 2008).

[§]Eugene Hevesi, "Hitler's Plan for Madagascar," *Contemporary Jewish Record* 4, no. 4 (August 1941).

would be exposed to an unforgiving tropical wilderness, disease, and starvation. Many would perish—but through a passive process. This would have suited the Nazis, with their doublethink mentality: they could deny direct responsibility. Indeed, Rademacher went further, saying that "use can be made for propaganda purposes of the generosity shown by Germany in permitting [Madagascar] to the Jews."

History, however, tells that the Madagascar Plan was never implemented. It relied on a turn of events that didn't happen: a settlement with the British. To move such huge numbers of Jews, the Nazis would need the shipping lanes of the Mediterranean, Red Sea, and Indian Ocean opened to German vessels. After the fall of France, it was assumed that either Britain would be defeated or peace with the island nation would be negotiated. This was a prerequisite for shipping the Jews from Europe to Africa.

I have written elsewhere of how an accommodation between the British Empire and the Third Reich could have come about. Assuming it did, what fate would have awaited the Jews of Britain? Eichmann identified 330,000 for transportation. We can never know what might have occurred, but anti-Semitism was widespread in all sections of society, and there were some ominous signs at the governmental level. The possibility of deporting the country's Jews to Madagascar was raised in Parliament in April 1938. A month later, Lord Halifax, the foreign secretary, addressed the issue with his French counterpart, who was at the time engaged with his own version of the plan. In November, Chamberlain and Hitler conferred on the subject through a South African intermediary. Elsewhere Britain's record was unpromising. When Jews were fleeing persecution in Germany in the 1930s, Britain refused 90 percent of these refugees.* The other alternative—sending them to Palestine—had little support, for fear of stoking Arab nationalism and destabilizing the empire. Anthony Eden (Churchill's foreign secretary from 1940 to 1945 and later prime minister) was described as being "immovable on the subject of Palestine—he loves Arabs and hates Jews."† It should be remembered that both the Balfour Declaration and the Peel Commission came to nothing. The Vatican was also opposed to sending Jews to Palestine.

In Berlin, in the autumn of 1940, an SS unit consisting of "suitably qualified technical experts" was made ready to travel to Madagascar to ascertain, among other things, landing sites, the scope for camp construction, and the "total absorption capacity" of the island. It never left. When peace with the

---

*The 10 percent that were permitted mostly filled gaps in the economy. There was an acute shortage of domestic staff during the period, and women willing to go into service were allowed entry—hence why Madeleine works as a maid.
†As quoted from the diary of his private secretary Oliver Harvey, 25 April 1943.

British didn't come, the plan stalled. In the months after, minds in Berlin were diverted by the looming invasion of Russia.

This corresponds with the conclusion Hans Jensen draws in his study of the subject: If Hitler won the war, it would mean exile to Madagascar for the Jews. If he lost, extermination.* In the parlance of alternative history, this is a "point of divergence." To state my own view, I suspect that if the Nazis had succeeded in conquering western Europe in 1940, including a settlement (of whatever kind) with Britain, a serious and determined attempt to ship the continent's Jews en masse to the Indian Ocean would have been undertaken, even if the project was never fully realized.

Intermittent discussion of the Madagascar Plan continued through 1940 and 1941. It was officially abandoned on 10 February 1942, when Rademacher received the order ending the program from Hitler. Several weeks earlier, at the Wannsee Conference, Heydrich had put in motion a more murderous fate for the Jews.

+ + +

Many other elements in this novel are also based on fact.

Hitler intended to rebuild Berlin on an imperial scale after the war and to name his capital "Germania." The first phase of construction, including the Great Hall, was due for completion by January 1950.

The Nazis had extensive plans for Africa, wanting to reacquire the colonies they lost after the Versailles Treaty and to conquer a swath of new territory stretching from the Sahara to the Indian Ocean. For a fuller discussion of this subject, see my "Author's Note" in *The Afrika Reich* (Henry Holt, 2013).

Germany led the world in atomic research during the 1920s and '30s. However, the purging of Jewish scientists from German universities, combined with Hitler's suspicion of what he described as "Jewish physics," curtailed the Nazi program to develop a weapon. The uranium for the bombs dropped on Japan at the end of World War II came from the Shinkolobwe mine in the Congo that Hochburg visits.

Kraft durch Freude (KdF), the Nazis' leisure organization, became the largest tour operator in the world.† By 1937 it was organizing vacations for 1.4 million people; its cruise liners took Germans to destinations as varied as the Norwegian fjords and the oases of Libya. In Prora, on Germany's Baltic coast,

---

*Compare Goebbels's diary entry for 18 August 1941, after he'd discussed Madagascar with Hitler: "Since the '30s there have only been two possibilities for the Führer: in the case of victory, banishment for the Jews; if he fails in his goal and loses the war, sweeping revenge and their destruction."

†For a detailed account of the KdF, see *Strength Through Joy: Consumerism and Mass Tourism in the Third Reich*, by Shelley Baranowski (Cambridge: Cambridge University Press, 2004).

the KdF built the biggest hotel in the world: a prototype for things to come. Its ruins are well worth a visit and are as gargantuan as this novel suggests; it takes a good hour to walk from one end to the other. After the war, the KdF intended to expand its network of hotels to the Crimea ("our Riviera," as Hitler described it), Sweden, Argentina, and Africa.

If Germany had defeated the Soviet Union, it is likely that a protracted guerrilla conflict would have continued east of the Ural Mountains. Hitler was "delighted by the prospect," believing that it would be the proving ground for a generation of Nazi youths. The discussion of the Madagascar Plan above refers only to the Jews of western Europe. The Nazis differentiated between them and the *"Ostjuden"*—eastern and Soviet Jews—whom they deemed inferior and more dangerous. The plan was to force the *Ostjuden* on death marches across Siberia, to exile in Birobidzhan, in the far east of Russia. Birobidzhan had been created by Stalin in the 1930s as a Jewish enclave; Hitler planned to make it his eastern dumping ground. It is difficult to imagine the extremes of Birobidzhan: monsoons in the summer, thirty degrees below zero in the winter. A community of four thousand Jews lives there today.

The Nazis' repugnant medical experiments on Jews are documented elsewhere. Of relevance to this book is their obsession with twins. Between 1943 and 1944, for example, fifteen hundred pairs, including young children, were experimented on in Auschwitz, mostly with fatal results.

Globocnik was involved with building projects on a scale comparable to the ones I've imagined in Madagaskar. In 1940, he oversaw the construction of a "Jew ditch" at Belzec, Poland. Intended as a defense against Soviet attack, it was to be 54 yards wide and 325 miles long (though only 8 miles were ever completed). He wanted 2.5 million Jews to work on it, moving the earth by hand, though in a memo Heydrich limited him to "a couple of hundred thousand."

In 1948, a team from Électricité de France went to Madagascar to survey the island's waterways for hydroelectric development. One of the key rivers they identified was the Sofia near Mandritsara, though concerns were raised about silting. To date, no dam has been built.

ACKNOWLEDGMENTS

I was lucky to visit Madagascar during the research for this novel and would like to thank the many people I met and who shared a little of their lives with me, in particular:

Helen Cox of Reef and Rainforest for helping to organize the trip; in Antananarivo (Tana), Oliver at Soci-Mad; in Antsohihy (Antzu), everyone at Hôtel Anaïs for their hospitality; in Mandritsara, Dr. David Mann, Dr. Adrien Ralaimiarison, and Robert and Christine Blondeel; at Diego Suarez naval base, base captain Commander Randrianarisoa Marosoa Nonenana and his executive officer, Commander Vaohavy Andriambelonarivo Andasy. Most important, for their comradeship, insight, and humor over the many miles we traveled together, my driver Radimbiniaina Harison Zoé, and my guide and translator, Ramarolahy Tafita Mamy. *Misaotra betsaka!*

For answering my questions on pregnancy and childbirth, I thank: Jo Cole, JD Smith, and Cally Taylor. For their help with research and translation: Sebastian Breit, Stella Deleuze, Jennifer Domingo, Elizabeth Ferretti, Oliver Gascoigne, John Smith of the French Foreign Legion, and Tim Vale. For the U.S. edition: everyone at Henry Holt, especially Molly Bloom, Meryl Levavi, Jason Liebman, Molly Lindley, Brooke Parsons, Richard Pracher, Courtney Reed, Stella Tan, and Bonnie Thompson.

Also: William Boyd, Richard Burnip, Linda Christmas, Andrew Dance, Carlie Lee, Laura Macdougall, Sarah-Jane Page, Rodney Paull, Lorrie and Robin Porter, and Aaron Schlechter. Special mention to Ana and Chris Biles for the generous use of their mountain house in Slovenia where an early draft of Part II was written.

Finally, heartfelt thanks to my UK agent, Jonathan Pegg, and my editor at Hodder, Nick Sayers; and in the U.S.: my agent, Farley Chase, for his advice and levelheadedness; and my editor, Michael Signorelli, for his enthusiasm, feedback on the manuscript, and for always finding me a little extra time as each new deadline loomed.

ABOUT THE AUTHOR

GUY SAVILLE is the author of *The Afrika Reich*, an international bestseller. Born in 1973, Saville studied literature at London University. He has lived in South America and North Africa, and is currently based in the UK.